Guy Walters was a journalist on *The Times* for eight years, where he travelled around the world and reported on a wide variety of subjects. He is married with one son, and lives in Wiltshire. His first novel, *The Traitor*, is also available from Headline.

Also by Guy Walters

The Traitor

The Leader

Guy Walters

headline

First published in 2003
by HEADLINE BOOK PUBLISHING

First published in paperback in 2004
by HEADLINE BOOK PUBLISHING

2

ISBN 0 7553 0058 0

Typeset in Goudy by Avon DataSet Ltd,
Bidford-on-Avon, Warwickshire

Printed and bound in Great Britain by
Mackays of Chatham plc, Chatham, Kent

Papers and cover board used by Headline are natural, recyclable
products made from wood grown in sustainable forests.
The manufacturing processes conform to the environmental
regulations of the country of origin.

HEADLINE BOOK PUBLISHING
A division of Hodder Headline
338 Euston Road
London NW1 3BH

www.headline.co.uk
www.hodderheadline.com

This book is for
WILLIAM

Acknowledgements

I AM EXTREMELY grateful to several people for helping me breathe life into *The Leader*.

On the Isle of Man, I was shown around Peel by William Bolton and Eddie Leece, the founder of the excellent Leece Museum. Its curator, Roy Baker, took the trouble to supply me with various documents concerning the internment camps during the Second World War. I am also thankful to Sandra Bolton for allowing me to rummage through her vast collection of Manx books.

In Galloway, I was well looked after by Mr and Mrs Collins at Damnaglaur House near Drummore. Visitors to the Rhinns could do no better than to stay with them.

I am indebted to the following for helping me with my research: John Lee for his encyclopedic political knowledge; Vanessa Andreae for allowing me once again to pick her medical brain; my father Martin Walters for his knowledge of steam engines; my mother Angela Walters for supplying a vast amount of pertinent books and newspaper cuttings; Adrian Weale for explosives manufacture; Meryl Keeling at Buckingham Palace for matters of royal protocol. Members of staff at the Wiener Library were kind in allowing me to view Captain Ramsay's 'Red Book'. Long may the library flourish.

Once again, my editor, Marion Donaldson, has been immeasurably helpful in ensuring that what follows is up to scratch. I have an enormous respect for her abilities, not least because she is eerily capable of zeroing in on any shortcomings and not letting me get away with them. My agent, Tif Loehnis, has provided support on an intravenous basis, and her advice is always spot on. I am lucky to have the backing of two such capable professionals. Their respective assistants, Sherise Hobbs and Carl Parsons, have also tolerated my demands with good grace.

Finally, I am indebted to my wife Annabel Venning, and her parents Richard and Venetia Venning, for enduring my authorial moans and complaints. Now that Annabel is an author herself, I hope that I will be capable of providing as comprehensive a support service for her as she has afforded to me. However, this book is not dedicated to Annabel, but to a joint project whose gestation period exactly coincided with the writing of these pages.

Prologue

A Day to Remember

June 1937

HE HAD AT least a hundred flags to put up – eighty down The Mall, and another twenty or so in front of Buckingham Palace. Neatly folded and piled up in the back of his van, half of them had only arrived last night. He had wanted to make a start a few days ago, but was told he had to wait until *all* the flags had arrived. But couldn't he just put up what he had and wait for the rest? No, absolutely not, he most certainly could *not* do that. That would give out the wrong message, they said, that would not do at all. But didn't they know how long it took to put up a hundred flags? They didn't care, and furthermore, if he didn't do as he was ordered, he would lose more than his job.

So Albert started work at five that morning, the day before the state visit. He had young Eric to help him, and together they started to unload the flags in a companionable silence. It was a good time of day, thought Albert, the early morning air clear and golden. He loved London like this, quiet, majestic, the centre of the world.

It was Eric who broke the silence.

'Hang on, what's this?'

'What?' said Albert.

'This one,' said Eric. 'This don't look like a Union Jack.'

Eric was spreading a vast flag out on the pavement under the plane trees. Together they looked down at it. It was blood red, a white circle in its centre, a circle that bore a black swastika.

'When did that happen?' asked Eric. 'When was we supposed to put up *German* flags?'

Albert took off his cap, scratched the top of his scalp, and then put his cap back on.

'No idea,' he said. 'P'raps there's been a mistake. Must have been slipped in the van accidentally. A mistake, it has to be a mistake.'

Albert repeated the word 'mistake' a few more times, as if by the repetition he would ensure that he was right. He walked round to the back of the van and climbed in. In the gloom he could make out the neat piles, and as his eyes got used to the darkness he could discern the patterns on the folded edges of the flags. Around half of them showed a mixture of red, white and blue, but the remainder showed only red. In a near panic, he lifted a couple of Union Jacks up to reveal what he had already suspected – another German flag underneath them.

'So?' said Eric.

Albert looked back.

'I don't understand it,' he replied. 'At least half of them are bleedin' Nazi flags.'

'You sure?'

'Course I'm sure! This can't be a mistake, they've got to be for the visit.'

'I don't like it,' said Eric, 'not one bit.'

'Ssh! People might hear!'

And indeed there were a few people around, tradesmen on horse-drawn carts, the odd early-bird on his way to work, and, several yards away, a couple of policemen.

'But *Nazi* flags, Albert . . .' Eric started.

'I don't care!' Albert snapped. 'Let's just get on with it! It's not our business if they change the flags, is it?'

Eric did as he was told. He was getting used to doing so these days. He wondered how many would turn up tomorrow, how many really wanted to see the German leader. He knew *he* wouldn't, that was for sure, but he'd heard that people were being forced to come. Some neighbours in Eric's street in Peckham had been sent tickets, tickets stating that they had been picked out of a hat to attend the German leader's visit, and that therefore they were very lucky indeed. But Eric had heard that there was a catch – apparently the tickets said you *had* to go, and if your ticket was not used then you could expect an investigation into your 'patriotism'. Eric had tried telling Albert about that, but once again Albert had told him to keep quiet, to keep his opinions to himself. It was for the best, he said, these days it was for the best.

Later, much later, when they had finished, even Eric had to admit that The Mall looked magnificent. The Nazi flags and the Union Jacks were splendidly triumphant in the evening light, their colours marvellously bright in amongst the lush green of the plane trees. And as they had worked, they had received a lot of attention. Passers-by had pointed at the flags, some with smiles on their faces, but most with frowns, frowns accompanied by grim shakes of the head, before walking briskly away.

They saluted with little enthusiasm, if any at all. They knew that in their midst there were those who would report them if they didn't, and so they saluted as bored children might, sarcastically slowly, limply. Brass bands lining The Mall drowned out an absence of cheers, an absence that would have been especially felt when the open-top cars went past.

In the first car, the crowds could glimpse King Edward VIII and Adolf Hitler saluting back at them. The two heads of state were smiling, talking easily to each other. In the second were a beaming Queen Wallis and the Leader, Sir Oswald Mosley, his chin thrust proudly upwards; in the third, the German ambassador Joachim von Ribbentrop and the Leader's beautiful wife, Diana.

The Treaty of London had been signed that morning, and the future had been sealed. Today was a good day for Britain, the Leader said, a good day for Germany, a good day for Europe, fascist Europe. The Germans are our friends now, he said, good National Socialists, fellow travellers. We have lots of work to do, and much to achieve. Herr Hitler has brought miracles to his country, and I shall do the same to ours. But for now, enjoy this day, a day which means we can work together in peace.

There was a loud cheer when the six stepped out on to the balcony of Buckingham Palace. Stalwart Party men and diehards had been placed there, been given special tickets to ensure enthusiasm up at the front. In picture palaces all over the country, the newsreels showed the delight on the faces of those on the balcony, while a breathless State Broadcasting Corporation newsreader commented on the fact that the King was wearing his fascist uniform for the first time, and that both the Queen and Lady Mosley were sporting very elegant Party armbands, which featured a black circle with a silver lightning flash through it. A great day indeed, said the newsreader, a day to remember in our hearts.

*

At Peckham police station late that evening, one of the regulars at the Black Lion found himself filling in a form, reporting some anti-patriotic remarks he'd heard earlier at the bar. Today of all days, said the duty sergeant, not a good day to be making jokes about the Leader. Your friend Eric had better mind his tongue.

Hampstead, March 1937

Otto regrets wearing his overcoat as soon as he has walked a hundred yards down the road. He thinks about going back to the flat, but a glance at his gold Omega tells him that he doesn't have the time. Instead, he takes it off and drapes it over his left arm, cursing its unexpected weight in Russian. This little slip – and it is only little, because no one could have heard him – causes him to curse further, but this time in English.

'Shit,' he says.

Otto doesn't normally make mistakes like that. Even though he is only thirty-two, Otto is very experienced, one of the best Moscow has ever employed. His Austrian passport says that he is a 'university lecturer', and indeed he could be, because he has a PhD – with distinction – in chemistry from Vienna University. But Otto rarely frequents universities, and spends much of his time engaged in meetings similar to the one he is about to have.

The walk up to Belsize Park underground station takes little more than five minutes. Predictably, the station's lift is out of order, and soon he is walking down the damp and winding stairwell that leads to the platforms. Although he can neither see nor hear anybody following him, Otto knows that does not necessarily mean he is not being followed.

Otto walks to the southbound platform, and sits on a bench shined by countless weary backsides. He looks casually up and down the platform, taking in his fellow passengers. A couple of young women seemingly engaged in some revelatory gossip, a slightly shabby man whom Otto fancies to be a schoolteacher, a bowler-hatted businessman reading *The Times*, even a vicar carrying a suitcase – a typical smattering of mid-morning passengers all on their way into London.

Which one is it? Otto wonders. Certainly not the vicar, because he is too noticeable, and besides, he is hampered by his suitcase. The businessman? No, and not the schoolteacher either. He suspects one of the young women, the one who occasionally looks up from her conversation, as if to check for the arrival of a train. Otto allows himself a brief smile, because he knows the woman is looking at him. How can he be sure? He just is, and even if he is wrong, there is no harm in it, for you can never be too cautious.

Otto feels a cool waft of stale air stroke his face. The train will be here in a few seconds, and he watches the other passengers move towards the edge of the platform, as if pulled by some invisible force. The young women continue to talk, letting out loud peals of laughter that struggle to compete in volume with the arrival of the train, the train that he knows he is not going to take.

He stands up, deliberately leaving his overcoat on the bench, and walks towards the decelerating carriages. Their interiors are largely empty, a contrast to how they would have been a couple of hours ago. He waits for them to stop, and after the doors have opened he gestures the vicar on to the train before him. He would have done the same for anybody, because Otto thinks of himself as a gentleman. However, he has little time for priests, because he is a *mosaisch*, an observant Jew, and he takes his religion almost as seriously as he does his love for the Communist Party.

Otto takes a seat and sits back, seemingly waiting for the doors to close. He has seen the young women get into the same carriage, which has confirmed his suspicions, as they were standing nearly two carriage lengths further down the platform. He waits for five seconds, and then stands up abruptly.

'My coat!' he says to no one in particular, in the sudden outburst of the eccentric, and then jumps off the train, just as the doors close behind him.

He walks to the bench and picks up what has become a useful prop. He turns to see the train start to move away, and can draw no conclusion from the fact that the two women are just as engrossed in their conversation as they were before. The businessman flashes a look over the edge of his newspaper and then he is gone, along with the train and its temporary cast of characters.

Otto smiles once more, and then crosses over to the northbound platform. He will eventually end up going south, but he needs to make sure. He looks at his watch – there is enough time to go to Golders Green and from there to take a number 13 bus down to Baker Street. It seems preposterous, a real waste of time, but it is a delay he has allowed for.

It takes Otto an hour and a half to complete a journey that should have taken just over a third of that time. When he arrives at the café near Clapham Common station, he is only five minutes late, which he knows will cause his contact no concern. They have met many times before, and have no need to explain why delays are all too common.

The café goes by the name of Gordon & Eve's OK Café, and Otto sees Gordon and Eve themselves behind the counter. Gordon waves a hairy arm at him through the smoky air, a gesture that is met with a distracted but perfectly polite nod, for Otto is looking for his contact amongst the gaggle of clerks and labourers.

It does not take long for Otto to find his man, because his man is tall, and even when he is sitting down he towers above his fellow diners. Otto walks over to the chipped table and sits down.

'Hello, Tony,' says Otto.

Tony is not the man's real name. Otto knows his real name, but never uses it, not even when they meet in private. For his part, Tony refers to Otto as 'Stefan', but unlike Otto, he does not know his contact's real name. There is no need to know, and neither does Tony wish to know. All Tony knows is that Stefan works for Moscow and, like him, is a loyal Party member. He does not even know that Stefan is an officer of the Narodnyi Kommissariat Vnutrennikh Del – the People's Commissariat for Internal Affairs, or NKVD. The NKVD has many agents in Britain like Tony, but few are as well placed as him.

'Stefan,' says Tony, tilting his head in a slight bow.

They make small talk for a few minutes, throughout the prosaic business of ordering and receiving two plates of ham, eggs and toast.

'So is it going to happen?' Otto asks eventually.

'It looks like it,' comes the reply. 'I expect we will come to power in a week, maybe two.'

'And Mosley's still promising you the job?'

Tony nods.

'You will have a lot of power, Tony, a lot of power indeed. You must use it carefully!'

Tony has never seen Otto look so intense.

'I will use it as you and the Party see fit,' says Tony.

'Good,' says Otto quietly, spooning sugar into a scummy mug of tea.

The two men sit in silence for half a minute, a silence that is broken by Tony as he reaches under the table for a parcel.

'What's this?' asks Otto.

'A birthday present,' says Tony.

Otto looks startled, or an approximation of it, because it is very hard to surprise Otto. He shakes the box as if he was a child, putting his ear close to the wrapping paper.

'A board game!' says Otto.

'Well done.'

Otto unpicks the wrapping carefully, methodically, stretching out the anticipation.

'Monopoly?' he finally asks. 'What is Monopoly?'

'It's proof,' says Tony quietly. 'Proof that capitalism has got so decadent that they've turned it into a game even children can play.'

Otto studies the back of the box.

'*Not* something we'll end up seeing in Moscow,' he says.

Tony takes a sip of tea before speaking.

'Or here for much longer,' he says, which makes Otto laugh, wryly.

Chapter One

The Party

April–June 1937

'WE ARE NOW in a dictatorship,' said Armstrong.

'James, you're drunk,' said his hostess.

The table, which consisted of many old friends and colleagues, had gone quiet. Armstrong pointed at his wine glass, which was still half full.

'I assure you, Patricia, I am not drunk. I'm perfectly sober, *depressingly* sober in fact.'

Patricia glowered at him. She did not like conversation at her dinner parties to steer too close to the rocky shores of politics. The Season, the South of France, sailing – these were Mrs Fallowell's favoured havens of chitchat. Never mind that there were three MPs at the table, in addition to Ted Frost, the editor of the *Daily Sketch*, and John Iremonger, the owner of a firm whose mustard could be found in every kitchen cupboard in the land.

'I'll say it again,' said Armstrong. 'We are now in a dictatorship. And it's thanks to people like you, Harry,

11

the people who voted for him on Saturday.'

The man whom Armstrong was addressing, the man who was now looking back at him with an open mouth, was his host, Harry Fallowell. Harry had entered Parliament with Armstrong in the 'khaki election' of 1918, and the two men had developed a strong friendship as they had jostled their way down to the front benches. Both men had returned from the trenches with a deep belief that society owed the younger generation a massive debt, and that it was their job to ensure that the older generation – the generation that had sent them to die – paid up.

'You take that back,' said Harry.

'I'm sorry, Harry, I won't. We didn't *all* vote for "the Leader", did we?'

Armstrong looked over at Duncan Ratcliffe, another Conservative MP. To his frustration, Ratcliffe stayed silent. Typical, thought Armstrong, Ratcliffe had always been a man to sit on the fence. It had come as no surprise to anybody that he was an abstainer on that Saturday.

'I disobeyed your whip,' said Harry, 'because I thought – and still do think – that voting against the Emergency Powers Bill would have been an act of gross disservice to this country. Goddammit, James! Can't you see that Mosley's what we need?'

'I dispute that,' said Armstrong.

'Hear, hear,' said Ted Frost.

'Thanks, Ted,' said Armstrong. 'In fact, I wonder how much longer your paper will stay in print? I wonder how much longer any of them will . . .'

'Oh, come off it, James!' said Patricia, almost giggling.

'I'm being serious, Patricia. Men like your husband passed a bill that allows Mosley – amongst other things – to have the

12

press subsumed into the civil service. I give the *Sketch* another week, maybe two.'

'He's right, you know,' said Frost. 'We've already had a visit from the Ministry for Information. They've installed a couple of men on the editorial floor whose job it is to read every news report and opinion piece.'

'And they're just going to be *reading* them, are they?' asked Armstrong.

'Thin end of the wedge,' said Frost. 'They've already objected to our running a piece that told our readers that the *Sketch* was now being censored.'

'How did you get that past them?'

Frost knocked back the rest of his drink.

'Arts pages. First time they've been read in months!'

A gentle laugh broke some of the tension.

'Do you see, Harry?' said Armstrong. 'That's dictatorship. That's got Hitler and Mussolini written all over it.'

'*Balls*,' said Harry. 'Complete balls. This country has been going to the dogs ever since the King refused to abdicate. I don't need to tell you what happened after *that*.'

'It's not balls, Harry,' said Armstrong. 'Otherwise why would we all be staying here tonight? Let's not forget the curfew!'

'These are small prices to pay,' said Harry. 'You only have to walk down any street in any town in Britain to see the scars of chaos. Shop windows smashed, graffiti everywhere, soup kitchens . . . anarchy! In times like these, a firm hand's what's needed. Don't forget, James, it is only temporary.'

'I doubt that,' said Armstrong. 'Come on, Harry, you've seen them for yourself. The Blackshirts aren't about stability and order, they're a bunch of thugs who happen to have found the right leader. How would you feel if you were Jewish?'

13

Harry shrugged and lit a cigar.

'Refu-jews,' he said nonchalantly, the first wreaths of smoke starting to envelop his head.

'What was that?' Armstrong asked.

'*Refu-jews*,' Harry repeated. 'Someone came up with it at the club. Rather good, I thought, considering that most of them are bloody immigrants. Anyway, if my name was Goldberg, I'd probably feel a lot safer now that there's firm government in charge.'

Up to this point John Iremonger had stayed silent. However, Harry's attitude had clearly struck a nerve.

'For God's sake, Harry!' he exclaimed. 'You know as well as everyone else round this table that they're in for a rough ride! Last week my general manager received a form asking us to state how many Jews work in our factories, what their names and addresses are, et cetera, et cetera. What the hell's all that about?'

Harry drew on his cigar.

'I'm sure it's for their own protection,' he said.

Armstrong shut his eyes before speaking.

'Did you fill in the form, John?' he asked.

Iremonger looked around the table. Eyes gazed down at half-finished salmon steaks.

'Well then,' said Armstrong, 'did you or didn't you?'

Patricia cleared her throat.

'James,' she said, placing a heavily jewelled hand on his wrist, 'John doesn't have to answer that question, does he? Does he, darling?'

The last part of that was addressed to her husband, who continued smoking.

'Actually, Patricia,' said Armstrong, 'I think he does.'

Iremonger held a shaking glass of burgundy to his mouth and drained half of it.

'Come on, John!' Armstrong urged. 'None of us are informers, are we? We're old friends. Whatever you say goes no further, isn't that right?'

'Of course,' said Ted, accompanied by murmurs of agreement from the men's wives and Ratcliffe. Armstrong noticed that their host continued smoking.

'Harry?' asked Armstrong.

'My loyalty has always been to the Crown,' said Harry, 'and therefore to His Majesty's Government.'

A gasp. There really was a gasp, Armstrong noted.

'Including the all-new His Majesty's Secret State Police?' he asked.

Another draw on the cigar.

'If necessary,' said Harry.

It was Armstrong's turn to take a slug of burgundy. This was *Harry*, he told himself – good old 'Fare Thee Well' Fallowell – what in God's name was happening to him?

'You *are* joking,' said Armstrong. 'Aren't you, Harry?'

An impassive expression partially obscured by a defiant cloud of cigar smoke told Armstrong the worst. He shook his head.

'Christ, Harry – what's happened to you?'

'What's happened to *you*?' came the cold reply.

Iremonger threw his napkin forcefully on to his plate.

'You want to know what I did with that form, Fallowell?' he asked.

'What?'

'I threw it in the fucking bin, that's what. What are you going to do now, eh? Ring the police? Or rather, the secret police? I expect you've already got their number.'

Harry looked over at Ted.

'None of this goes in the *Sketch*!' he barked.

'None of it would be allowed in,' said Ted, staring witheringly at his host.

Touché, thought Armstrong. He had always liked Ted, had always found him good company. Over the years, they had enjoyed many lunches, and Ted was the only journalist with whom he had allowed himself to be indiscreet.

'So, Harry, are you going to inform on him?' asked Armstrong, folding his napkin carefully.

Harry started laughing, a slightly forced attempt.

'Come on, you two! Stop taking all this so seriously! Of course I wouldn't inform on John here – that would be absurd. Come on! Let's eat up and talk of more merry things!'

Armstrong stood up, smoothed down his waistcoat, took one more sip of wine and then looked at his watch. Ten o'clock. The curfew had started two hours ago. He wasn't allowed to leave, but he desperately wanted to. With no taxis or buses, he would have to walk home. He might get caught, but then so what? What could they do to him? The penalty for breaking the curfew was a £100 fine or three months' imprisonment. He would refuse to pay a fine, so let them lock him up. What would people say then? It would expose the new law for the absurdity it was.

'Where are you off to?' said Harry.

'Home,' said Armstrong.

'But the curfew . . .' Patricia began.

'In Harry's words, *balls*,' said Armstrong.

Iremonger stood up as well.

'I'll give you a lift,' he said. 'My driver's here tonight. Fallowell – tell your man to go and get him.'

'The *curfew*,' Patricia bleated once more.

'I'd rather be locked up than stay here a minute longer,' said Iremonger. 'You coming, James?'

Armstrong nodded.

'I'm sorry, Patricia,' he said. 'I appear to have ruined what should have been a lovely evening. Nevertheless, I'm sure you'll be able to find plenty of other things to talk about. Sorry to have been such a bore!'

He bent down and kissed her on both cheeks. She smelt of Chanel and a trembling unease. It was only then that it finally sank in. The posters, the Blackshirt marches, the Emergency Powers Act – these were merely the signs, thought Armstrong. What had gone was trust. Mosley had abolished it, and with its abolition, freedom had been crushed.

It was just a ruined dinner party, but in its small way, thought Armstrong, it was a social breakdown.

Armstrong and Iremonger sat in the back of the Rolls-Royce in silence. Both were preoccupied with the conversation they had just left, as well as the risk they were taking in breaking the curfew. Iremonger had promised his driver £50 if he took them, which the man readily accepted, telling him that he'd have done it for free, but seeing as Sir John had offered him all that money, well, who was he to refuse the missus a few baubles? All three men had laughed at that, and Armstrong expressed a secret gratitude that the bulldog spirit was still in evidence.

'Do you think that bastard Fallowell will really shop me?' asked Iremonger, offering Armstrong a cigarette.

'I wish I knew,' Armstrong replied, shaking his head at the cigarette. 'Two, three weeks ago I would have said that Harry was the last man to do such a thing.'

'But it's *monstrous!*'

Armstrong nodded and looked out of the window. A huge fascist banner billowed gently under the newly built

Constitution Arch at Hyde Park Corner. It was illuminated from below, its redness strikingly bold against the whiteness of the arch and the blackness of the night. Lit up for whom? As there was a curfew, no one could see it. Empty pomp, thought Armstrong. Even when you couldn't see them they wanted you to know that they were still there.

'Yes, it is monstrous,' he said. 'I really didn't think this was going to happen. I was naïve, I'm ashamed to admit it.'

'Come off it, James! We all were. No one could have anticipated all this. I've got half a mind to go and tear down that fucking flag back there. You on for it?'

Armstrong smiled.

'We need to tear down a lot more than flags.'

'Huh?'

'We need to destroy the whole bloody thing. It's not just flags and drums and black shirts. We've been invaded, that's the word, *invaded*.'

'You're not wrong.'

'And it's going to get worse,' said Armstrong, watching the high wall surrounding the gardens of Buckingham Palace speed by. 'We're going to hop into bed with Hitler and Mussolini soon, you mark my words. And then where will Europe be? France will fall to fascism – Spain will doubtless do so as well. Soon America will be the only democracy left.'

'Well, that's where I'm going.'

'What?'

'I'm going to push off to Virginia, got some land there.'

'No!' Armstrong snapped. 'No! John, you must *not* go, you must *not* leave. We need men like you around. Otherwise we'll be left with people like Harry and wet blankets like Ratcliffe. You've got to do your bit and stay!'

Iremonger exhaled a long jet of smoke.

'Well?' asked Armstrong.

'You're a persistent bugger, aren't you?'

'Yes.'

'All right, perhaps I'll stay, stick around, "do my bit", whatever that means. In fact, what *does* it mean?'

'It means that I'm going to form an opposition,' said Armstrong.

'How? Parliament's been closed.'

'No, not that sort of opposition—'

Armstrong was cut off by the sound of a loud ringing approaching rapidly from behind. They turned to see a police car speeding towards them, its blue light flashing frantically.

'Oh shit,' said Iremonger, his tone resigned. 'What should we do?'

'I think we should do what rich men do in every country such as this.'

'What do you mean? Bribe them?'

'Exactly. Offer them twenty quid per head and we'll be on our way to bed.'

'In a cell. We'll never get away with it.'

Ten minutes later, Armstrong and Iremonger were indeed on their way to bed.

'I don't know whether I'm more troubled by the curfew,' said Iremonger, 'or the fact that the good old British bobby is now corruptible. You owe me thirty quid, by the way.'

Something else had changed, thought Armstrong, reaching for his wallet, something about the policemen's uniforms. They were wearing Party armbands. That was new. How much longer would bribery last?

* * *

It was continuity that kept the Blackshirts in place. That was Armstrong's opinion, and he was proved right. People still went to work, people still fell in and out of love, the buses were still red, people still ate ham – things were, after all, still *British*. If anything, the situation was getting a little better, because how indeed could it have got worse? Since Mosley had entered Downing Street, where were the riots? Where were the shortages? Queues had all but disappeared from the high street. If you ignored some of the more excessive elements of the new regime, dismissed them as necessary to ensure stability, then life, some people said, wasn't so bad.

Some people. For most, and Armstrong was certainly one of these, the air was poisoned. Neither did he shy away from saying so. Anybody who asked him his opinion, and even those who hadn't – *especially* those who hadn't – would get the full force of Armstrong's argument. After all, he was still an MP and the chief whip of the Conservative Party, Parliament or no Parliament. What were they going to do? he would ask. Lock him up? If they did that, they would have to lock up nearly every MP who wasn't a fascist, every trade unionist, every 'suspect' journalist – the list would be very long. It would be like Germany, he said, and Germany had happened because people had not spoken out, had retreated into a satisfied world of continuity. The Germans had absorbed themselves in those things that reminded them of better times – mostly the countryside – and it was this absorption that made them feel that not much had changed.

But much had changed, in Germany and in England too. One incident Armstrong would use to highlight the dangers took place in his own constituency in the West Country. It was an everyday event, he said, an event that was becoming all too common. The victims were a Mrs Jones and her seventeen-year-old son Richard, who were out shopping together one Thursday morning.

'Rick and me was walking down Princes Street,' she told Armstrong one Saturday in March, 'when we hears this tremendous crashing and banging. Pipes and drums and all that. I ain't really heard anything like it before, Captain Armstrong. Anyway, around the corner comes this large group of Blackshirts, waving their flags and singing something about hanging the Yids. There must have been two – no, three hundred of 'em, and they were marching down the street sending everyone scattering for cover.

'Well, you may not know this, Captain Armstrong, but my son Rick – well, he's a little slow, you see? Not the brightest of buttons. Gets into trouble a bit, but he's a good sort really, never means no harm to no one. Anyway, so there we were, all these Blackshirts walking past, and one of them turns to us and says, "Why aren't you saluting?" '

'Saluting?' Armstrong asked.

'That's right, saluting. "Why aren't you saluting?" And he's got this expression – well, I don't know how to describe it – fierce, real fierce, nasty. So I just stares back at him, 'cos to be honest I don't really twig at first. And then he asks me again, "Why aren't you saluting?" By this time the march has stopped and I can feel all these eyes on me . . .'

Mrs Jones started to sob. Armstrong got up from behind his desk and walked round to hand her his handkerchief. Perching on the front of the desk, he assured her that everything was all right now, and that she should continue her story.

'Well, Captain Armstrong, I'm not so sure that it is all right, because . . .'

And she started sobbing again, Armstrong would say later, but this time at such a volume and at such length that he was minded to call a doctor.

'No, that's kind of you, sir, but it's my son who needs doctors, not me.'

'Mrs Jones – *please* – you must tell me what happened.'

Interrupted by frequent tears, Mrs Jones continued her story.

' "Why aren't you saluting?" this man says, and then I realise that he wants me to give one of them fascist salutes, you know, with your right arm in the air. Well, I was scared you see, and so, well, I had no choice, did I? My husband Peter always said them Blackshirts were no good and that me and Rick was never to pay them any attention, and that it was good men like you, Captain Armstrong, who would get this country out of the crisis.'

'Where is your husband now?'

'He's in the navy, sir. Most of the time it's just me and Rick, just the two of us.'

'Do carry on, Mrs Jones.'

'So I salute, don't I? I'm not proud of that, not proud at all, but you have to, don't you, when you've got hundreds of 'em threatening you like that.'

'And what about Rick?'

'Well, I told you that Rick was a good sort really, and that he has good manners most of the time, but Rick goes and *spits*, spits at this Blackshirt who was making us salute. Now I can't abide spitting, Captain Armstrong, but Rick just goes and spits and tells them that they're a bunch of so-and-sos.'

More tears followed, many more tears.

'Well, you can imagine what happens next,' said Mrs Jones after she had calmed down a little. 'They give 'im a beating, don't they? Some of 'em grab me and hold me against a door, while I have to watch my poor little boy being kicked and punched and all the time he's screaming for me. "Help me, Mum!" he's crying, but I can't and I see that he's getting hurt real bad. It goes on for ages until Rick stops crying. Then they stop, you see, and have a laugh, a *laugh* at poor Rick all bleeding on the ground. And then one of the Blackshirts comes up to me, and tells me that the next time they'll do me in as well and Rick is lucky to get away with such a light beating. But do you know what the worst thing was, Captain Armstrong?'

'What?'

'That Blackshirt, the one who told me that Rick was lucky, he was one of Rick's friends from school, boy called Norman Lovell, used to come round for tea. He was always so . . . so *nice*, please and thank you, wiped his feet. I don't understand it, Captain Armstrong, what's . . . what's going on.'

'You're a very brave woman, Mrs Jones,' said Armstrong. 'Please tell me about Rick, how is he?'

'Not so good, Captain Armstrong. The doc says nothing's broken, but last night he started to cough up blood and so I went round to the Black Horse and called for an ambulance. He's in a bad way, they say that his insides might be damaged. Oh God! My poor Rick!'

'And the police, Mrs Jones, what have they said?'

'They told me that they would "look into it".'

'Is that all? Just "look into it"?'

Mrs Jones nodded.

'And have they?'

'I don't know,' said Mrs Jones. 'I don't think they want to, though. They don't . . . don't seem to care, Captain Armstrong.'

When Armstrong told people Mrs Jones's story, he would finish it by relating how, when *he* had contacted the police, they had fobbed him off with the same vague promise of action. And as there was no local newspaper any more, nobody heard about poor Rick except by word of mouth. By the time he visited the town the following Saturday, Armstrong noticed that the atmosphere had changed; people were sullen, quiet, even though the weather was fine. His Saturday morning meeting with constituents was packed, crammed with those who had suffered either physically or financially at the hands of the Blackshirts. He felt powerless, unable to help them. There was no point making representations to the new Government, because it was the Government itself which was waging war on its own people.

However, Mrs Jones's story touched a nerve in Armstrong that he would only admit to in private. He could have told his constituent that he had a son of his own, a six-year-old boy called Philip, but he wanted Mrs Jones and others like her to be able to talk to him about themselves, and simply to regard him as someone who could help. Armstrong knew that might be construed as being somewhat worthy, but that was the way he preferred it. Philip was a part of his life that was outside – and indeed far beyond – Westminster and his constituency.

When Armstrong returned to the flat after Fallowell's dinner party, he crept past his housekeeper's room and into the nursery. He sat on the edge of Philip's bed, something he did every night, no matter how late it was. Although the light from the corridor did not wake Philip, it allowed Armstrong to study the boy's face, and to watch the blankets gently rise and fall with each little breath. As usual, Philip was clutching his favourite bear, a bear that had been given to him by his grandmother a few days after his birth.

Armstrong leaned further over the bed and stroked his son's dark hair. Philip shifted slightly, mouthed something incomprehensible, and then fell silent. So peaceful, Armstrong thought, so fragile in his innocence. Armstrong felt his eyes tightening, readying themselves to stifle a small tear, a tear brought on by the knowledge that Philip would have to leave. There was no way his son could stay here – it would be too dangerous for him. Armstrong was ready to risk his own life, but not Philip's. There was no cause that was greater than Philip, no matter how irrational that felt. The days were darkening, and Armstrong knew that they would get blacker still. He couldn't let Philip become a victim of his father's forthcoming actions, no matter how right he knew them to be.

* * *

The clouds had started to gather the previous year, when Edward VIII had declared that he would give up neither his throne nor Mrs Simpson. He was entitled to both, and nobody could tell him otherwise. *I am my own man, and I will not be pushed around.* There were many who thought that rich. He followed Mrs Simpson around like a child who refused to be parted from his mother, lighting cigarettes for her, fetching her drinks, fawning over her.

By the end of November, the situation had become intolerable. The prime minister, Stanley Baldwin, had secured promises from the leaders of the Labour and Liberal parties, Clement Attlee and Archibald Sinclair, that they would support Baldwin's National Government in the event of the King insisting on marrying Mrs Simpson. If such a marriage took place, Baldwin said, he would resign, and Attlee and Sinclair assured him they would not attempt to form administrations if he did so. It was the perfect threat to hold up against the King – marry, sir, and your country, with no one willing to form a government, shall go to the dogs.

For the next ten days, it looked as though the King would go. The press, inspired by a sermon by the Bishop of Bradford, in which the cleric denounced the monarch's lack of interest in Christianity, went on the attack. Some newspapers supported the King, but maintained that it was clearly time for Mrs Simpson to leave the country. On the evening of Thursday 3 December, she sailed for France. The King missed his mistress dreadfully – some said that her absence had made him feel ill. One visitor noted that he was chain-smoking and constantly held a handkerchief to his head 'as if to ease some hidden pressure or pain'.

However, Baldwin had reckoned without Winston Churchill. There had been much talk of the creation of a 'King's Party'. The idea, which was enthusiastically backed by the press magnate Max Beaverbrook, was for Churchill to form a government loyal to the King if Attlee and Sinclair stuck to their agreement with Baldwin. The plan, though, had been dismissed as too fantastical, too divisive. The King, many said, would never allow it to happen.

Had those doubters been at Fort Belvedere, the King's retreat in Windsor Great Park, on the night of Sunday 6 December, they would have thought differently, and the country might have been spared fascism. It was not the intention of the conspirators that night to elevate Oswald Mosley to the premiership, but as a result of their actions, they inadvertently did so.

Sitting at the King's table were Churchill, Beaverbrook, the First Lord of the Admiralty Sir Samuel Hoare, and the Secretary for War Duff Cooper, who had not arrived until around one in the morning. He had been stuck at an 'interminable' dinner party at the Eaton Square home of Chips Channon, the Tory MP and socialite. There, he reported, he found the mood very pro-King, and had been told by one of his fellow guests, none other than James Armstrong, the Conservative chief whip, that many members of the Conservative Party might well break away from the National Government in support of the King. However, Armstrong had warned, there were doubtless other dinner parties that night in London at which far more 'Roundhead' sentiments were being expressed.

How many might break away? the King had asked. Cooper told him that Armstrong's estimate was around forty, but that number could swell massively if the public's support for the King continued to grow. Beaverbrook had said that he and his newspapers – one of which was the *Daily Express* – would do their best, but only if he was certain that the people present in the room were *really* ready to form a new party. It was not the type of occasion at which there was a show of hands – more a collection of nods accompanied by long draws on cigars and brandy balloons.

So the emboldened King did not abdicate. Chaos ensued as the crisis reached fever pitch in the run-up to Christmas. Share prices, which were low enough already, tumbled. As the economy slumped, many found themselves laid off, and soon the miseries of the dole queue and the soup kitchen were a commonplace fixture on the streets.

The leading pro-monarchy group was Mosley's British Union of Fascists, which had recently been renamed the British Union, although to the public they were simply known as the

'Blackshirts'. Operating from the self-styled 'Black House', a former teacher-training college on the King's Road – 'On the King's Road and For the King's Way' – Mosley finally saw his chance to make vast political capital. The Blackshirts claimed a membership of around 150,000, people who were beginning to see fascism as the way not only of saving their King, but of rescuing the country from its state of misery, a state that many even outside the party were beginning to blame on the Jews. Hadn't Hitler done a good job in dealing with them? some asked quite openly. Look at Germany now, they said. Now that the Jewish influence was removed from the banks, the newspapers, the law courts, the country was *thriving* again. It was time to close the doors on all these damn immigrants, and it was essential to ensure that those who were already here were fully integrated into society, and not allowed to live in their ghettos.

Although the Blackshirts had no MPs, Mosley told meetings up and down the country, as Christmas approached, that this was the hour for fascism, that the British public should follow the lead of Germany and Italy, and embrace a new doctrine that would result in a greater Britain, and a stronger Empire. No longer should the British people suffer the perils of Bolshevism and international finance – a euphemism for the Jews – but they should embrace the Third Way, a way that led to a synthesis that would guarantee a glorious future.

To the private delight of the secret King's Party, Stanley Baldwin resigned on Monday 4 January 1937. The King was obliged to summon both Attlee and Sinclair to Buckingham Palace, but neither would accept the Seals of Office, telling Edward that he would have to abdicate first. That night, the country, without any clear leadership, suffered appalling riots in every town and city centre. It was estimated that nearly seventy people were killed, and the nation feared a descent into anarchy. Shops were looted, many of them, although it was not noted in the press at the time, owned by Jews. Fascists fought street battles with Communists, despite Mosley's apparent attempt to control his Blackshirt hordes. 'How can I be held responsible for the excessive zeal of my subordinates?' Mosley asked, in a statement that was to be echoed by his fellow fascist leader in Germany some years later.

At nine o'clock the following morning, Winston Churchill was asked to the Palace, and, assuring the King that he had enough support in Parliament to form a government, accepted those twice-refused Seals. For a few weeks the country attempted to return to a state of normality, but behind closed doors, in committee rooms and in smoking rooms alike, Churchill found it impossible to govern. Despite the best efforts of the Beaverbrook press, the public, as well as many in Parliament, were not convinced by this new ministry. Attempting to seize what little initiative remained, Churchill called for an election, nearly setting the date for 15 March, until his wife Clementine pointed out to him, when he was in the bath, that holding an election on the Ides of March – the date of Julius Caesar's assassination – was hardly propitious. The date was changed to the eighteenth, a Thursday.

By the Friday afternoon, it appeared that the result was inconclusive. Churchill's King's Party, nominally called the 'Independent Conservatives', had won around 100 seats, the Conservatives themselves, under Baldwin, just under 150. Attlee's Labour Party became the largest single parliamentary party, with 220 seats, but the biggest shock of the poll saw the return of Oswald Mosley to Parliament, accompanied by fifty other British Union MPs. The remainder of the House was filled with Liberals, Ulster Unionists and Labour and Liberal Nationalists.

That evening, the King sent once more for Attlee, to form a minority Labour administration, but Attlee, a man of high principle, rejected the offer, again telling the King that he had to abdicate. Baldwin let it be known that he had no intention of going anywhere near the Palace. And so once more the King called for Churchill, who said he would do his best.

There followed the most extraordinary week in British politics, a week that was to see, by its end, Oswald Mosley as prime minister. Churchill was unable to form a new government, as Attlee and Baldwin rejected his advances to join a coalition, both insisting that the King should abdicate, and for the sake of the country, as soon as possible. On the morning of Thursday 25th, Churchill returned to the Palace, and told his King, with tears in his eyes, that he had failed. Perhaps, sir, we have tried too hard, he told the monarch, perhaps the country is not ready for men like ourselves. But the King knew of a man who could help him, a man whom he and his beloved had always admired, a man whose political views were similar to their own.

It was well known in court circles that the King admired the European fascist dictators. In a conversation he had in July 1933 when he was still the Prince of Wales, Edward was reported to have been 'quite pro-Hitler, said it was no business of ours to interfere in Germany's internal affairs either re the Jews or re anything else, and added that Dictators were very popular these days and we might want one in England before long'.

In a phone call made from France that Thursday evening to the King, Mrs Simpson was overheard telling her lover, 'This is our best chance, a chance to be together, and for you to stay where you are. The people will love you for it – you will have *saved* the country, you must see that, David. He's our only solution. Don't forget what you can do. Remember, they made Macdonald prime minister when he only had two more seats than Mosley.'

Sir Oswald Mosley accepted the Seals of Office at 11.35 on the morning of Friday 26 March. A fascist was now at 10 Downing Street. Everyone, especially Members of Parliament, was taken by surprise. Britain was divided. Some of the more populist newspapers believed that Mosley was the beleaguered country's only chance, although the heavyweights, such as *The Times* and the *Manchester Guardian*, were appalled.

For the next fortnight, civil war loomed. People were either with the Blackshirts or against them, and the effect of that polarisation was felt in the savage violence on the streets. The police were hopelessly overstretched, and Mosley called in the army to maintain law and order. Keen to appear accountable, he convened an Extraordinary Session of Parliament on Saturday 10 April. There, he put before the House an Emergency Powers Bill that would enable him to govern temporarily with an emergency cabinet of just five men. The Bill was enacted that afternoon, with substantial numbers of MPs from both Conservative parties supporting the fascists, despite the efforts of whips such as Armstrong. There were many, including Armstrong, who believed that Parliament had just voted itself out of existence.

Mosley's measures were enforced almost immediately. He announced a nationwide curfew; the end of the right of assembly; the formation of a new secret police force – His Majesty's Secret State Police, HMSSP – to combat 'anti-patriotic' activities and to take over the work of MI5, which was secretly made defunct; greater powers for the armed forces; the introduction of identity papers; and a ban on firearms. The press was to be taken over by the state, and absorbed into the civil service. All these measures, Mosley said to the nation in his broadcast on Sunday morning, were only temporary, 'for the good of us all'.

During the next week, the posters started to appear, giant portraits of Mosley in his Blackshirt uniform that read, 'The Leader – For the Good of Us All'. It was these posters, Armstrong claimed, that were the first manifestations of dictatorship, a parading of the cult of personality rather than policy.

* * *

Armstrong lunged forward, the point of his sabre thrusting straight towards his opponent's heart. But the other man was too quick and brushed Armstrong's blade upwards, almost knocking it out of his hand. Armstrong stepped back, ready for his opponent's reply, watching the other man closely, trying to second-guess his next move. The sound of his own breathing was magnified by the mask, reminding him briefly of the sensation of wearing a gas mask.

The other man was devastatingly fast, and before Armstrong could flinch out of the way, he felt the sharp thud of steel against his solar plexus.

'Hit!' cried a voice.

Damn, thought Armstrong, damn. He knew he would never win, but he fancied that he might have taken at least more than his usual one bout off his opponent. The two men removed their masks simultaneously.

'You're improving!' said the other man, panting slightly.

'Oh I don't know about that,' Armstrong replied. 'I'm getting a little slow.'

'We all are – all the fun of hitting one's forties!'

Armstrong could never have wished for a better friend than Alec Scott. Like Armstrong, he had been a captain in the 8th Gurkha Rifles, and had served with distinction during the war, winning a Military Cross, an award that Armstrong himself held in addition to his Distinguished Service Order. Pleasantly burdened by a useful inheritance, Alec now spent much of his time fencing, his love for which Armstrong believed was stronger than that for his wife Anne, or even for Antony and Nigel, his twin sons. Alec's skill with the sabre had earned him a place in the Olympic team that had visited Berlin last year, and Alec had narrowly missed out on a bronze medal.

Although Armstrong was by no means as proficient a swordsman, he did not disgrace himself in his monthly duels with his old friend. His aim on each occasion was to win at least one bout, which normally kept Alec on his guard. Although Armstrong had expressed some dissatisfaction with his performance that day, secretly he was glad that he was maintaining his level against a far superior opponent, especially as his mind was as far from the piste as it could have been.

'Steam room?' Armstrong suggested.

'Why not,' said Alec. 'And then lunch on me?'

'Where?'

'Somewhere without too many Blackshirts. The Mirabelle?'

'In that case it's definitely on you.'

Armstrong was glad to find the steam room empty. The two men sat next to each other on a bench, letting the hot water vapour seep into their pores.

'You know, Mosley's not a bad fencer,' said Alec.

'I'd heard,' said Armstrong.

'He was runner-up with the épée in the British champion-ships a while back. I'd love to have a crack at him!'

'Listen, Alec, I've got something important I need to talk to you about.'

'Good heavens, James,' said Alec. 'You're not getting all ginger beer on me, are you?'

Armstrong laughed gently.

'No – let me assure you that if I was like that, you'd be the last person I'd pick.'

Alec narrowed his eyes.

'I can't work out if that's an insult.'

'Don't worry, it is.'

Alec leaned forward.

'So, what *do* you want to talk about?'

Armstrong took a deep breath.

'I need your help, Alec, need you to help me do something vitally important.'

'Good God, man – anything. You name it.'

'I want to get rid of Mosley.'

'What?'

Armstrong looked round the room before repeating, 'I want to get rid of Mosley.'

'We all want that, old chap, but how? The man's there perfectly legally.'

'So is Hitler, Alec, so is Mussolini. That's part of the problem. That's why what I have in mind is somewhat *extra-legal*, if you will.'

'Go on.'

'I'm intending to form a movement,' said Armstrong, his voice low, 'a *resistance* movement, if you like, dedicated to removing the fascists. I'm not going to sit by and watch this country go the way of Italy and Germany. What's happening now is just the beginning, I'm sure of it. We've *got* to stop it, Alec, before Mosley sinks his teeth deeper into the very fabric of society.'

'But think of what you're up against! The army, the police, the secret police – the whole bloody lot!'

'I know there are elements in the army who think that Mosley's one of them,' said Armstrong, 'and he's bribed them with vast new budgets, but there are many who are not convinced, Alec, good men who can help us.'

'Who?'

'Well, I have several names in mind, but I was rather hoping you would be able to rustle up a few more.'

'What?'

'That's right, I need you to help me draw up a list. You've kept up a lot of your contacts in the army, and Anne's family are all navy, so I'm also expecting you to know a few reliable sailors.'

'Even if we did have a list of names, what then? What would you have them do? Run around blowing up bridges, that sort of thing?'

'Nothing quite so *amateur*, Alec,' Armstrong replied. 'These men will go into action when Mosley is removed, seizing radio stations, train stations, even members of the secret police.'

'But how are you going to actually *remove* Mosley?'

Armstrong looked straight at Alec.

'Jesus, man,' said Alec, 'you're not serious.'

'I am,' said Armstrong. 'And I'll do it myself if necessary. But we can't do it until we are sure that we can replace the Blackshirts–'

Armstrong broke off with the arrival of another man in the steam room. It was none other than Harry Fallowell.

'Hello there, Harry,' said Armstrong. 'Pleasant surprise.'

But Harry didn't reply, and sat down at the other end of the room, his stomach folding over the top of his towel. Had he heard what they were saying? Unlikely – the noise of the steam was too loud, and besides, they had been speaking quietly. After an uneasy minute, Armstrong and Alec got up and walked past him.

'Hang on!' said Harry.

'What?' said Armstrong, his tone mildly exasperated.

'I think you should know, Armstrong, that as of yesterday I've joined the Blackshirts. And that you'd better watch your step. I only tell you this as a courtesy.'

Armstrong calmly wiped some sweat off his face. This was certainly not a surprise.

'So you weren't joking at dinner the other night, were you?'

Harry slowly shook his head.

'Well, I'll tell you this as a courtesy,' said Armstrong. 'You can stick your black shirt up your arse. Goodbye, Harry.'

For the next forty-eight hours, Armstrong and Alec worked steadily in Armstrong's flat. As they drew up lists of potential members and targets, it never ceased to amaze them that what they were doing was nothing less than planning a coup. It seemed, said Alec, a little *continental*, but nevertheless, there they were assigning their old friend Colonel Bob Simmons the task of seizing Crewe Junction. Brigadier Michael Kintore was to use his Highlanders to storm the Blackshirt headquarters in Edinburgh, as well as to take the offices of the State Broadcasting Corporation. Lieutenant-Colonel Martin Cavendish would take his battalion of the King's Own Yorkshire Light

Infantry into York and intern every Blackshirt under the stands of the racecourse.

Two scalps they desperately needed were those of Major-General Charles Clifford, the head of the Signals Corps, who would be able to transmit any orders over the army's radio network to the fellow conspirators, and General Sir Edward Galwey, the chief of all the armed forces in London and the south-east of England, whom Armstrong wished to recruit as caretaker leader of an interim martial government before the restoration of democracy. Galwey could also be relied upon to seize control in the capital in the event of a successful assassination. Armstrong knew both men well, and was certain that they would be more than willing to help oust Mosley. It was like a game, he thought, a hypothetical situation cooked up for the amusement of friends, but as the plan took shape, it developed an air of serious reality.

After two nights they had a detailed outline, along with a cipher and a list of code-words that they would issue to those on the list. However, the plan lacked two important elements. It needed a trigger, said Armstrong, an event that would set it into action. Secondly, they needed to contact those who were to be involved. Without them, it was, after all, still only a hypothesis. The transition from a plan on paper to something that actually existed was the beginning of risk, the beginning of a process that Armstrong knew could lead them to the gallows. They took the decision quickly, but they did not take it lightly. There was no other way to deal with Mosley, a man who saw suppression and violence as legitimate tools of government. There were too many stories now similar to that told by Mrs Jones. It would not be long before public noticeboards announced the names of those who were about to be executed – that was happening in Germany, and if Mosley remained, then it would surely happen here.

Armstrong did not know whether his telephone was tapped, but he assumed it was. However, he did know that his post was being opened, because he had sent himself a letter from a fictitious relative, into which he had placed a hair from his own head, a hair that was no longer there when he opened the letter two days later. At first he was worried that they were already on to him, that perhaps Fallowell had told the HMSSP that his parliamentary colleague was in some way suspect. It was only when he asked another MP to try the same trick that he realised they were censoring the post of all MPs, as well as, no doubt, that of trade unionists and journalists.

Armstrong and Alec would have to make contact the hard way, by actually visiting those on the list. Alec suggested calling them from phone boxes, but Armstrong said they had no way of knowing whether the phones at the other end were tapped. Visiting would be time-consuming, but it would be safer. Besides, a trip around the country would enable Armstrong to establish the tightness of Mosley's grip, and whether the air was as poisonous in Manchester or Liverpool as it was in London and in his own constituency.

* * *

Armstrong first suspected he was being followed as he was waiting for a train at Bristol Temple Meads station a week later. Having finished in the West Country, he was now heading towards Cardiff and Swansea. He had met five former comrades, all of whom were still serving in the army, and were more than willing to help. 'Just give us the word,' they had said, and Armstrong had promised he would keep them informed with a series of coded letters and postcards. Crucially, both Galwey and Clifford had agreed to help, and were already drawing up plans that would dovetail with those made by Armstrong and Alec. Meanwhile, Alec himself was working his way through the Midlands and the east of the country.

He spotted them as he was buying a newspaper at a kiosk. There were two of them, both wearing ill-fitting suits and snap-brim hats and loitering next to a pillar over to his left. They looked away as soon as he noticed them, their heads darting back into their newspapers with a rapidity that suggested something more than a mere polite reluctance to hold a stranger's gaze.

'I'm sorry, squire, there ain't no *Times* today.'

'What?' asked Armstrong. 'You can't have sold out already.'

The newsagent took a drag on a filthy squib that passed for a hand-rolled cigarette.

'Not sold out, never got it.'

'Well then, how about the *Daily Sketch*?'

Another drag, and then a slow shake of the head.

'No *Times*, no *Sketch*, no *Post*, no *Chronicle*, no *Telegraph*,' he said. 'But what I can offer you is either *Action*, or *The Blackshirt*. They say it's *distribution* problems.'

'I'll bet. All right, I'll take both.'

Armstrong dug into his pocket for some change, keeping his anger in check for the benefit of the two loiterers. *Action* and *The Blackshirt* were the Party's newspapers, now elevated to the only newspapers in the land. His prediction at dinner a few weeks earlier had been spot-on.

He decided to confirm his suspicions about the two men by going for a walk. He looked at his watch – his train was not due for another fifteen minutes. He strode purposefully towards the ticket hall. As he approached its wooden and glass doors, he could see the reflections of the pair as they followed him. So he was right, a fact that sent his heart racing. Why were they shadowing him? What could they know? Surely none of his old comrades could be one of *them*, that was impossible. The image of Fallowell and his cigar kept running through his brain. If Fallowell could turn fascist, then anybody could. Perhaps they were following him as a matter of routine, spying on everybody they regarded as 'the enemy', even if their opposition had not been manifested. That thought gave Armstrong a little more hope, an ironic hope.

How long had they been following him? Since Plymouth? Since Truro? Armstrong walked through the ticket hall and left the station completely. There was no way he was going to allow them to follow him to Cardiff. He would have to get a later train, or find some other way of getting there. *Jesus Christ*, he thought, this couldn't be happening. He was on the run in his own country, on the run because he wanted to live somewhere where you didn't have to run from anyone.

Outside the station he was presented with a throbbing line of taxis, their engines ticking over lazily. There was a short queue – should he join it, or just keep moving? His stalkers were bound to have a car, or at least the ability to commandeer one. No, keep walking, lead them a merry dance while he worked out how to lose them.

The streets were crowded, bustling with people on their way to work. As Armstrong weaved through them, he often caught sight of a Party armband or a lightning-flash pin speared through a lapel – presumably the more 'gentlemanly' way to display one's fascist colours. There were many Blackshirts too, walking in twos and threes, their chins thrust out in imitation of their beloved Leader. Armstrong noticed that passers-by gave way for them, some meekly offering fascist salutes as they passed. However, in the eyes of many he could see only hatred, derision and fear. It was for those people that he was fighting, Armstrong thought, for the majority of the British people, who wanted to rid themselves of this cruelty within their ranks that had taken them over and set them against each other.

Armstrong looked round. The snap-brim hats were a good thirty feet behind, enough for him to start running as soon as he turned a corner. He ran as fast as the crowds allowed, which wasn't fast enough, because after a minute he looked round to see the same hats the same distance behind. Shit, he thought, *shit*. He was trapped.

The pleasing smell of coffee caused Armstrong to turn his head to the right. Queen Charlotte's Tea Rooms – perfect. He would sit in there, read the papers, take stock. If they'd wanted to arrest him they would have done so already. There was no hurry – let them wait. There might even be a back entrance or a lavatory, out of which he could slip. He peered through the small windowpanes, their thick glass revealing a distorted picture of Bristolian matrons sipping tea and eating cakes and pastries.

As Armstrong gently pushed open the door, he saw that a printed notice had been hung above the Open sign: *No Jews – By Order of the Management*. With no prospect of taking his custom elsewhere, Armstrong stepped into a warm fug of bitter coffee and sweet perfume. The place was packed, and he quickly noticed that he was the only man there. He walked up to the counter and enquired whether there was room for 'just one'.

'Oh dear,' replied a woman whom Armstrong took to be the proprietress. 'We are a little full, sir.'

'I don't mind sharing a table.'

'Well . . .'

'I'll happily pay the other person's bill,' said Armstrong. 'I'm desperate for a cup of coffee – been on the go since five this morning.'

The proprietress, who Armstrong couldn't help noticing had the most enormous bosom, spoke over his head into the room. As she did so, Armstrong allowed himself to ponder what had made this woman believe that Jews were so undesirable that they should not even be allowed to enjoy a cup of Earl Grey.

'Would any of you girls mind sharing a table with this nice young gentleman? He says that he's willing to pay the bill of whoever it is he shares with.'

At least ten hands shot up immediately. Young, thought Armstrong. He hadn't been called that in a while.

'Well, it would appear that you have a choice,' said the proprietress approvingly.

Armstrong sat with the nearest of those who had put their hand up.

'It's very kind of you,' he said. 'As I said, I'm desperate for a cup of coffee. Would you like something else, madam? On me, of course.'

The woman, who was in her late sixties, perhaps older, smiled gently.

'I'd love another pot of tea,' she said, 'as well as a couple of slices of Mrs Shipway's *luxurious* shortbread. She makes it herself, you know. And perhaps I'll have a couple of Bath buns to take home . . .'

Just as it occurred to Armstrong that he was being fleeced, his two pursuers walked into the room, opening the door so violently that it bashed into the wall.

'Do you mind?' barked the proprietress.

'Sorry, madam,' said one of the men. 'Don't know me own strength!'

London, the voice was London, thought Armstrong. Had they been following him for the past week? No. He surely would have noticed them before.

'Well that's not good enough,' said the proprietress. 'That's no way to come in here! Anyway, we're full.'

'But . . .'

Armstrong had to resist the temptation to smile. This dragon of a teashop owner was doing his work for him.

'I'm not having your sort in here,' she snapped. 'Come on! Out!'

Missing only a broom with which to hit them over the head, Mrs Shipway dispatched Armstrong's pursuers out of the shop.

'And don't come back!'

She slammed the door on them, using more force on it than they had done. Armstrong saw the men standing outside, talking to each other. That was one of the disadvantages of being a secret policeman, he thought, not being able to say who you were. However, despite the levity of the moment, Armstrong did not allow himself to relax. They would doubtless wait for him outside, all day if necessary. He needed to get moving, before one of them went round the back. He had to assume they weren't fools.

The one problem was his small suitcase. If he took that to the lavatory, it would look suspicious. He would just have to abandon it – there was nothing in it that would identify him, besides an ivory hairbrush bearing his initials that had been given to him by his father. Too bad. Everything he needed was in his briefcase – he would have to take that with him, even if it did look odd. He turned to his new companion.

'Do you know if there is a lavatory here?'

'Yes – at the back of the room.'

'Thank you,' said Armstrong. 'In the meantime, do please order whatever you like, won't you?'

The woman nodded, her face suggesting that Armstrong should be in no doubt that she would do so. As he walked to the lavatory, hoping that it had a window, he imagined the argument that would follow when they found that he had bolted. He expected Mrs Shipway would make the poor woman pay up. That would teach her, he thought, teach her to be so greedy.

He opened the door to the lavatory, thanking God when he immediately spotted daylight coming through a frosted window just to the right of the lavatory itself and above the basin. Great – it looked big enough. He locked the door and put his briefcase on the floor, then leaned over the basin and pushed up the lower sash, already wondering whether he should go back to the station or perhaps catch a coach.

The window stopped moving after a mere five inches. Armstrong briefly shut his eyes. It must have some sort of stopper or wedge. In heaven's name, he thought, how many old women had attempted to escape coughing up for a pot of tea? He looked up and down the runners, but could see no obstacle. Perhaps it was just stiff. Another heave, but still it wouldn't budge.

Hit it, that was what you had to do, hit the frame. That normally loosened it. But that would make a racket. Once again, too bad – by the time they had opened the door to investigate, he would be long gone. He bashed the window frame with the side of his fist, wincing at the ensuing din.

Another heave – still it wouldn't move. He tried pulling down on the upper sash, but that was even more reluctant. Perhaps he should flush his papers down the lavatory and then confront his pursuers. No – too foolhardy. He could get this bloody window open.

He hit it again, harder this time. They *must* have heard that. Another heave and then up it shot, so rapidly that it hit the top of the frame. Armstrong took a deep breath. Through the window he could see a small yard, at the end of which was a door set in a high brick wall. It had better not be locked.

He climbed over the basin and then through the window, taking his briefcase with him. He looked up and around, praying for the absence of faces in overlooking windows. There were none, or at least none he had seen. Keep moving, keep moving.

Like the window, the door was reluctant but not locked. Armstrong stepped into a cobbled alleyway that ran between the backs of houses and shops. To his right he could see a busier road, and started to head towards it. He'd go to the bus station, but he wouldn't take a bus to Cardiff. He needed to go somewhere else. He needed to see Philip to make sure that his son was safe, and stayed safe.

* * *

Mary had died in April 1931 giving birth to Philip. She had suffered a heart attack during the delivery, and was dead before Philip had uttered his first scream. Armstrong had known something was wrong as soon as he saw the consultant's face, but had naturally assumed it was about the baby.

'Captain Armstrong?'

'Yes?'

'Would you like to sit down?'

'Why?'

The consultant didn't labour the point, recognising that this was clearly a man who made up his own mind.

'Your wife, sir, I'm sorry . . . I'm afraid we lost her. She died just as your son was being born.'

He didn't ask how it had happened because it didn't seem to matter. The consultant carried on speaking, but Armstrong didn't hear. It occurred to him, even then, that he had found out the sex of his baby in the same sentence that revealed that Mary had died. So he had a boy, and if it was a boy he was going to be called Philip, after Mary's late father. A boy called Philip. And a dead wife called Mary. It was he, Armstrong, who should have died; he was the one who had killed in the past, who had seen death close at hand, day in, day out. He was ready for it, he had nearly been there so many times, and it was she who had stopped him, had given him his life back, had given him a son, had now paid the highest price, just for him. It was wrong. Why did *she* have to be taken away when she was capable of giving so much?

It was Mary who had nursed him after he had suffered his breakdown in the winter of 1923. The shellshock had hit him just outside Fortnum & Mason on Piccadilly. It was Bonfire Night, and someone had thrown a firecracker that had happened to explode a few feet away. He couldn't remember a thing after that, but the doctors told him that he'd collapsed in the street and had had some sort of fit. He was probably overdoing it, they said, an MP's life was a busy one. Take it easy for a bit – you'll see.

He didn't take it easy, because he knew that the attacks could come at any moment, and the best way to stop them was to keep going. He medicated himself with whisky, the best part of a bottle a day, but deep down he knew that he was losing, that some day he would have to give up, that it would beat him.

And beat him it did, just before Christmas, at a dinner in his constituency to celebrate his return to Parliament in that month's general election. He'd been feeling particularly shaky that day, and the chairman's wife, who was sitting next to him, noticed that he couldn't keep his knife and fork still enough to cut his beef. As he stank of whisky, she thought him drunk.

He collapsed just before he was to give his speech. Perhaps it was the racket of the brass band, perhaps it was the whisky, perhaps it was purely the stress, but he crumpled all the same, hit the floor of the marquee and screamed, in a way that told the veterans present all they needed to know. All the chairman's wife could do was to ask the band to play a little louder, in fact a lot louder if you please.

A week later, heavily sedated, he woke up and looked into the face of the woman who was to become his wife in less than twelve months. He found it impossible, no matter how hard he tried to maintain a professional relationship, not to fall in love with this person who was doing so much for him, caring for him, spending all this time with him. They chatted easily, and they could make each other laugh. He felt young again; he trusted her, because she knew everything about him, and he didn't feel ashamed of his illness.

He surprised himself when he kissed her. It happened during his physiotherapy, when he was learning to walk again. He had been making good progress and could walk well – if a little unsteadily – without a cane. However, on the day in question he made as if to fall, and she held him. He could see the slight shock in her brown eyes at the firmness of his grip, a shock that was increased by his pulling her round to face him.

As soon as he had kissed her, he felt a fool. He was just another lecherous soldier, making a pathetic pass at a pretty nurse. It must have happened to her hundreds of times. She would beat him off, get herself transferred to another ward, and then he would lose her.

Armstrong looked out of the window as the coach climbed up into the Malvern Hills. She had kissed him back, of course, and in a way that kiss had killed her. Seven years later he had to bury her, throw a sod on top of her coffin, wondering all the time whether she'd heard Philip's first cry, whether she had known, even for a few seconds, that she was a mother.

Ten minutes after getting off the coach, he found himself knocking on the door of a substantial townhouse.

'James!'

'Hello, Elizabeth.'

'You should have phoned! How lovely to see you, though. Come in, come in! What are you doing here?'

Armstrong took off his hat and kissed his mother-in-law on the cheek.

'I'll tell you in a second – is Philip here?'

'He's upstairs with a friend,' she replied. 'Shall I go and get him?'

'No, it's all right, I'll go up on my own.'

Armstrong crept up the stairs as quietly as he could, stopping when he reached Philip's door. From inside he could hear the distinctive sounds of two young boys playing soldiers – the simulated explosions and machine-gun fire, the drone of an aeroplane accompanied by the whistle of a bomb falling.

He gently eased open the door before jumping into the room and uttering a loud 'Boo!'

The Leader

It took Philip a second or two to recover from the shock.

'Daddy!' he shouted, getting up. 'Daddy!'

Armstrong bent down and picked his son up.

'You're getting heavy!'

'Not *that* heavy! Not as heavy as you!'

'Not long now.'

Armstrong put Philip down and held him by his shoulders.

'Now then, young man, would you like to go to France?'

'France, Daddy?'

'That's right, France, with Grandma.'

'Are you coming as well?'

Armstrong shook his head.

'Not straight away, but I shall catch you up. I promise.'

Chapter Two

Rule Britannia

June 1937

THE LEADER WALKED with a pronounced limp, something he did his best to hide. He had badly broken one of his ankles in May 1915, when he had crash-landed his Morris Farman Longhorn aircraft in front of his mother at Shoreham-on-Sea. He had only just gained his pilot's certificate, and had to leave the Royal Flying Corps and return to his old regiment – the 16th Lancers – before his leg had fully healed. The trenches were no place for an injured leg, and its worsening condition meant that he was sent back to England in March 1916. Two operations saved the limb, which had been given a fifty-fifty chance of being amputated. Thereafter, the man who was to become the Leader walked with one leg an inch and a half shorter than the other.

Although the presence of the limp surprised many, it had no such effect on the four men who stood up as the Leader entered the Cabinet Room in Downing Street that morning. They were his oldest colleagues, men who had been especially

51

loyal to the movement, men who were now Members of Parliament and, more importantly, members of the five-strong Emergency Cabinet. All four were wearing the full 'Action Press' uniform, which consisted of black army officer's tunic, black shirt and tie, black breeches and riding boots. The tunic was held together by a thick black belt fastened with a large silver buckle. Around the upper left arm of each man was the Party's armband, bearing the symbol of the black circle with silver lightning flash through it. Critics back in the early days had called it the 'flash in the pan' – not a remark that would be made today. On the table in front of them, alongside their papers and red ministerial boxes, lay the four men's headgear – black peaked hats, also bearing the Party symbol.

'Good morning, gentlemen!' the Leader boomed, his white teeth flashing underneath his neatly trimmed moustache.

'Good morning, Leader,' replied the men in unison, along with the most erect fascist salutes they could muster.

Mosley returned the salute and sat down.

'Sit, sit,' he commanded. 'Now then – God, it's hot today, pour me a glass of water, would you? Thank you . . . I'd like to talk about a problem that affects us all – a problem that we know to be the root cause of our present troubles. I'm speaking of course about immigrants.'

The four men smiled and the Leader smiled back at them. They all knew that 'immigrants' meant 'Jews'.

'You know that my solution,' Mosley continued, 'is to create some sort of national homeland for them. It is my firm belief that this would put an end to all the friction between us and them. This friction has changed the Jew into . . . into a gangster, and I fear that it has brought about a certain, shall we say, *brutality* in our own people. Let's not forget those riots earlier this year and who was responsible for them. All this is bad for the immigrants and bad for us. We need to deal with it immediately, get things moving.'

One of the four caught the Leader's eye.

'Major-General?'

The man who spoke was Major-General John Fuller, nicknamed 'Bony' because of his remarkable thinness. He had been chief of staff of the British Tank Corps in the Great War, and had masterminded the Cambrai offensive in 1917. Since the war, he had written extensively on tank warfare, arguing that tanks should be used in lightning concentrated thrusts. That call had been rejected by the British army, but it had gained a lot more currency in the newly formed Panzer Corps in Germany, especially with a young Panzer leader called Heinz Guderian. Fuller had joined the British Union in 1934, and had been a prolific lecturer and writer for the movement. It was only natural, then, for the Leader to place such a man in charge of the armed forces. Fuller was an excellent man, Mosley thought, truly first-rate, and what was essential was that the forces were loyal to him, saw him as one of their own.

'There is of course a practical issue here,' said Fuller, his voice much deeper than his slight frame would suggest. 'There must be tens – hundreds – of thousands of Jewish immigrants in Britain. Transporting them overseas would use up an immense amount of resources, resources that we need to get the country back on its feet.'

'Then why don't we get the Jews to do that?'

The voice was cold, clipped, unpleasant. It belonged to the Minister for Information, William Joyce. He had a huge scar on his right cheek, running from his ear to his mouth, and his chin bore a pronounced dimple. He made up for his lack of height by being highly muscled, and his ability as a fierce and vitriolic speaker had gained him the position of Propaganda Director for the movement in 1933.

'Get them to do what exactly?' the Leader asked.

'Some real work, for a change! We should put them in camps where they can build machinery, houses – things the country needs.'

'I like it,' said the Leader, sitting back and grinning. 'It would certainly put them to good use.'

'Dr Goebbels tells me they're planning to do the same thing over there,' said Joyce. 'Get them out of their banks and shops, and make them actually contribute rather than just . . . steal.'

'So they're going to put *all* of them in camps?' asked Mosley.

'Precisely,' Joyce replied.

The Leader nodded to himself, chewing it over.

'I wonder how long it would take us to build such camps?' he asked, scribbling a note on some paper headed with both the royal coat of arms and the fascist lightning flash.

The Leader looked over to his Home Secretary for a response. A tubby man with a large moustache, Neil Francis Hawkins had been a surgical instruments salesman before he had taken over the running of the movement's enterprises as secretary, managing director and chairman of the Party's trust. A safe pair of hands, the Leader thought, an honourable man, and loyal, deeply loyal.

'I'd say a month, maybe two,' said Francis Hawkins. 'After all, we can get them to build the camps themselves!'

The five men laughed in unison.

'Excellent!' the Leader boomed. 'Excellent! These camps could of course be built near existing factories, so they can supplement the work forces.'

He scribbled down another note.

'All right,' he said. 'I'd like you, Thomson, to liaise with some of the more sympathetic industrialists about this.'

Alexander Raven Thomson, the Chancellor of the Exchequer, was the movement's 'philosopher'. He had studied philosophy and economics at universities in Germany, America and Scotland, and he saw in the Leader a man who could realise his dream of building a corporate state, a society modelled on the lines of an insect community, in which there was a 'communal spirit shared by every member of the hive'.

'I'm sure we'll have no problems there,' he said, sucking on his pipe. 'Incidentally, how many Jews do we have at the moment?'

'Our latest estimate puts them at around three hundred and fifty thousand,' said Francis Hawkins, 'with about two thirds of them in London, mostly in the East End, of course.'

'Christ!' the Leader exclaimed. 'It's worse than I thought! And no doubt these are only the ones we know about. There are probably *thousands* more entering the country illegally every month. Where do they all end up?'

'Major cities mostly – Leeds, Manchester, Cardiff, Bristol, Newcastle, Hull. There are areas in some cities where the Jews are actually in the majority.'

'Disgraceful!' the Leader snarled.

'Don't forget they're north of the border as well,' Raven Thomson chipped in, speaking slowly and authoritatively. 'They seem to be doing their best to infect the Clyde. I'm afraid not even we Scots are immune from their pernicious influence.'

'Soon, I hope,' said the Leader, tapping his pen violently on the table, 'soon we shall *all* be free from them. Let the camps be the first part of our solution, and then let's look at something more long-term, more permanent. I strongly believe, and I say it again, that immigration is the biggest problem we have to face.'

'PJ,' muttered William Joyce darkly. Perish Judah.

The others drummed on the table with their fists in response. Mosley paused before continuing.

'I'm going to Germany next week. I shall talk to Herr Hitler about it then, tell him that we no longer wish to be the dumping ground for these people. I'll keep you all informed, of course. In the meantime, let's get these camps underway and get some use out of these people. If they want to come here, then they can bloody well be made to work.'

The Leader paused once more and then clapped his hands.

'Right! Other business! Home Secretary, I believe you had something to say about the HMSSP building up some links with the Gestapo.'

The men relaxed as Francis Hawkins started to speak.

*　*　*

Henry Allen was a quiet man, an intelligent man, and a good husband to Louisa. His father had made a small fortune out of a printing business, which had enabled him to send young Henry to Eton, where the boy had prospered. Although not from the same stock as his contemporaries, his easy manner and his right-wing views meant that he fitted in comfortably. By the time Henry left Oxford in 1922, those views had hardened, and finding himself disenchanted with the Tory party, he went in search of something stronger. He found fascism, and later Oswald Mosley, a man he regarded as nothing less than a potential saviour.

In 1934, Allen published a book called *BUF, Oswald Mosley and British Fascism*, in which he hyperbolically lauded Mosley.

'In his greatest potentiality,' Allen wrote, 'he stands for new and revolutionary conceptions in politics, in economics, and in life itself.' Allen's loyalty to Mosley saw him rewarded with a seat in Parliament, the realisation of an ambition held for many years.

He should have been happy about his position, and for the most part he was, but as he swung his legs out of bed that morning, he was suffering under a barrage of doubt. For although Henry Allen was undoubtedly a fascist – a great believer in what he had described in his book as the 'movement towards national integration' – he was no hater of freedom. Yes, to his self-confessed discredit he had gone along with the brutality of the movement, but he had seen that as the price of realising his greater dream of a fascist Britain. But now that Britain had arrived, he found himself deeply disquieted. The treatment of the Jews, the censorship, the everyday scenes of Blackshirt violence – all these combined to form a nation whose people were at war with each other. Fascism was not bringing integration, thought Allen, but the very opposite – fragmentation.

Allen walked into the bathroom and urinated. After he had finished, he started to run himself a bath. As the water gushed in, he studied himself in the mirror. He needed to trim his moustache, he thought, and not only that, he needed to lose a little weight. His cheeks looked podgy and he had developed a slight paunch over the past six months. Perhaps he would take up running again.

He slipped into the bath and lay back, letting the hot water envelop him, appreciating its comfort with a long sigh.

'You all right in there?'

It was Louisa. He had obviously woken her up.

'Fine, dear,' he called back to the bedroom. 'Did you sleep well?'

'Loglike. That was quite a sigh, darling. Are you sure you're OK?'

Allen paused.

'Just a little groggy.'

He heard Louisa let out a slight chuckle.

'How much did you drink?' she asked.

'Must have had at least a couple of bottles,' he replied, which was true. But he didn't have a hangover.

'You're a disgrace,' said Louisa, her tone suggesting that the remark was only partly in jest.

Allen didn't respond.

'Still alive in there?'

'Sorry,' he said, sitting up. 'I was miles away.'

'Where?' Louisa asked.

'What?'

'You said you were miles away – where were you?'

'Oh – nowhere really.'

'Henryland, was it?'

'Henryland' was Louisa's condescending term for her husband's extended moments of deep thought. It was hard to reach him in Henryland.

'No,' Allen replied, his tone serious. 'I was somewhere else.'

'This is intriguing.'

He didn't reply for a while, unsure whether to confide in her. Would she understand?

'I'll tell you when I'm out of the bath.'

'Can't wait.'

Allen spent the next minute briskly soaping and rinsing himself. He *would* tell her, she *would* understand, even though she too was a Blackshirt, the daughter of Earl Hallowes, himself a leading member of the Party. He had met her a few years ago at a meeting of the January Club – a BUF offshoot for the aristocracy and captains of industry – and they had quickly fallen into a love that drew much strength from his money and her pedigree. As far as both parties in the marriage were concerned, the other was a committed fascist. But now Allen wanted to tell his wife that it was a mistake, a vast mistake. Fascism had attracted the wrong crowd – a crowd of dangerous idiots and fools who saw it as a route to wielding absolute power. It had become rotten, perhaps even evil.

He stepped out of the bath and wrapped himself in a towelling robe. As he walked into the bedroom, Louisa was sitting up.

'Well,' she said, 'what were you thinking?'

Allen looked intently at his wife.

'If you really want to know,' he said, 'I was thinking how funny it is that fascism seems to attract only beautiful women.'

She grinned back at him.

'You charmer you,' she said. 'Come here.'

Allen hadn't wanted to make love, feeling that it would be a sort of lie. He partially enjoyed it, but even as he was inside her he wanted to be as far away as possible. There was no way he could tell her what he was feeling, he realised, for the very simple reason that he couldn't trust her. He had become a stranger, a stranger to her, to the Leader, and to the movement. It felt different, but it was beginning to feel right.

* * *

The bedside telephone started ringing just after four o'clock in the morning. Armstrong was a light sleeper, especially during the last few weeks, his dreams dominated by images of running towards Philip and yet never getting any closer. His waking mind knew that Philip was safely in a hotel just outside St Malo with his grandmother, but the images flooded his brain with such force that he would regularly wake up in a cold panic.

He answered the telephone at the third ring, his heart already starting to race.

'James?'

The voice was familiar, but it sounded deeply strained.

'James, it's me, Anne. They've . . . they've . . .'

Armstrong sat up. It was Alec's wife.

'What, Anne? What is it?'

'They've taken him away.'

'When? When did they come?'

Armstrong had no need to ask who 'they' were – they would be the HMSSP.

'About . . . about ten minutes ago.'

'What happened?'

Anne couldn't reply, her voice heavy with tears.

'Anne!' Armstrong insisted, instantly regretting that he sounded so harsh. 'What did they say?'

'Not very much,' came the reply. 'They simply said that they . . . that they had a warrant for his arrest.'

'Arrest? What for?'

'Unpatriotic activities,' Anne managed to mumble through her tears.

Armstrong closed his eyes. How many others had been spirited away into the night and fog under that hateful term? There were many rumours now about the actions of the HMSSP, about beatings, disappearances, torture, some even said executions. God knew what the truth was, as the truth served up by *Action* and *The Blackshirt* was a distorted version of it. Armstrong disagreed even with that notion, that the truth could be 'distorted'. There were no gradations of truth, he said, because truth was an absolute. If something wasn't true, no matter how closely it approximated to the actuality, then it was time to start regarding it as a lie.

'Was that all they said?' Armstrong asked.

'Yes, just that, unpatriotic activities, that's all. What's he been up to, James? I know he's been seeing you a lot . . .'

'He's been doing nothing, Anne, not as far as I'm aware.'

How hateful, Armstrong thought, that husbands were being forced to lie to their wives, and yet how reassuring that Alec had been so discreet.

'He's also been away quite a bit,' she said. 'Said he's been seeing a few old friends—'

'Anne!' Armstrong interrupted. How could he explain to her that the telephone might well be tapped?

'Anne, please, just keep calm. I'll be right over, as soon as the curfew ends.'

'Would you do that?'

'Of course,' he replied. 'I'll come as soon as I can.'

'James?'

'Yes?'

'Are you sure he's not done anything? I mean . . .'

'*Anne* – don't worry. I'm sure it's just a mistake.'

'You . . . you think so?'

'Positive. Now, you hold on, and I'll see you in an hour or so.'

'All right – but you will definitely come?'

'Of course,' said Armstrong, and put the phone down.

It briefly crossed his mind that it was a trap, but he quickly dismissed the idea, knowing that the HMSSP would have no need to lure him over to Chelsea – they could just as easily arrest him here in Victoria.

'Dear God,' he said to himself as he got out of bed.

How much did they know? Everything? Had one of his Army contacts betrayed them? Or did the HMSSP in fact know very little, and so had decided to go to work on Alec? Would Alec hold out? Armstrong had to assume he wouldn't, in which case the entire nascent network was blown. The chances were that arrests were being made simultaneously up and down the country, and that a carload of secret policemen were already drawing up outside.

He knew they would come, there was no doubt about that. If not now, then soon. He had already seen the signs, subtle signs – that face under a grey snap-brim hat he had spotted too many times, the wrong numbers late at night, his neighbours' recently acquired wariness. Put together, they formed a picture of imminent danger, a picture that was forcing him to pack a small suitcase. He was tempted to leave now, to break the curfew, but that would be foolish, an unnecessary risk. The time for bribery had gone. Into the suitcase went a small washbag, some underwear, a few shirts and a pullover. Apart from a spare pair of trousers and some stout hiking boots, his packing was complete. He would wear a plain blue suit – it was suitably anonymous.

He left his bedroom, and walked down the long corridor to his book-lined study. The room was dominated by a large oak desk. He sat at it and unlocked a drawer before pulling it out fully. Attached to its back was a cream envelope, from which he extracted two sheets of foolscap writing paper. At the top of each sheet was engraved 'The Right Honourable Captain James Armstrong PC MP DSO MC', and covering all four sides was a hand-written list.

The Leader

He looked carefully down the list, refreshing his memory. These were the names of towns and counties, and of those he had met in them over the past few weeks, men who had agreed to help him. Armstrong was delighted with the reports made to him by Major-General Clifford and General Galwey, both of whom had sounded out and secured the assistance of army officers they knew to be anti-Mosley. It was an impressive list, thought Armstrong, but it was a fragile one nevertheless. All that was required was for a few whispers to reach the ears of the regime, and Mosley would instigate a purge, ridding the army of suspect elements. Although Mosley's grip on power was firm, it was not yet an iron one, and Armstrong knew that anything that challenged that grip might only serve to give Mosley the excuse to tighten it.

Every county had a name, the name of a man he hoped he could trust. Armstrong believed that trust, unlike truth, did have its gradations. These men could certainly be trusted, but whether any of them could withstand torture was a different matter. Each man knew only the identity of those in counties adjacent to his own. If one of them broke, then the network would not collapse, but would merely lose a limb, a limb that could possibly grow back. But Alec's arrest was a severe blow, one that could see all these men in custody by the end of the day.

He took the list to the fireplace in the drawing room. He was tempted not to burn it, but if it was found, he knew that would be the end of any chance of a return to democracy, a return to a country whose inhabitants did not live in fear of each other. The sheets burned quickly, and he broke their ashes up into minute fragments, remembering that even a burned piece of paper could still reveal some of its inked secrets.

He yawned and walked quickly back to the bedroom. He changed out of his pyjamas and into his suit, then opened the door of a large mahogany cupboard and reached up to the top shelf, his hands scrabbling around under a pile of blankets. It was there, his Smith & Wesson from the Great War – fully loaded. He slipped it into his jacket pocket.

It felt like the hours before a battle, his thoughts urgently flitting between what was to come and what had already happened. Part of him wanted to leave immediately, but he had to restrain himself. He hated to wait, it was not in his nature, but for the next few minutes he would have to. He had to hope that he was ahead of them, or that they were keeping him on ice.

Fortified by a hasty bowl of Shredded Wheat and a large cup of Camp coffee, Armstrong stepped out on to the street at five past five. A bright summer morning's sun forced him to squint as he walked up to his Daimler 'Light Twenty' saloon. Before he climbed in, he looked up and down the street, trying to establish whether he was being watched. It was hard to tell. All he could see was the slow progress of the milkman's horse and cart. If someone was keeping an eye on him, they were keeping themselves well hidden.

What Armstrong didn't notice was the movement of a curtain in a window below his flat. For the past two weeks, Mrs Catherine Hill, a light sleeper and eccentric widow in her late sixties, had been performing her patriotic duty by keeping an eye on her upstairs neighbour. Two *charming* young men had popped by for a cup of tea one afternoon, and had told her that they suspected Mr Armstrong might be up to no good – something to do with Communists, they said – and so would Mrs Hill let them know whether he had any visitors, and at what times he went in and out? They gave her a number she could call any time, day or night, in case she wanted to report something urgently. Mrs Hill closed the curtain and walked over to her telephone. It felt good to do her bit, she thought, not that she was a fascist – heaven forbid! – but if there was one thing her late husband had hated more than anything else it was Bolsheviks.

The car started easily, as it always did. Although the Daimler had cost him some £700, Armstrong maintained it was worth every penny. He turned into Victoria Street and headed towards the station. There, he turned left and accelerated sharply down Vauxhall Bridge Road, making his way towards the river. He allowed himself to breathe out a little, aware that his shoulders were abnormally tense. He would see Anne, albeit very briefly, and then get out of London.

The side of the black van read 'Steinberg & Son – Purveyors of Fine Groceries'. Saul Steinberg was proud of his business, although he was far more proud of Ben, his thirteen-year-old son, who had been acting as his delivery boy during the summer holidays. He had painted the '& Son' on himself, his chest swelling with paternal pride. One day Ben would inherit the business, and he would doubtless make a real go of it. He had a good head, Saul reckoned, had taken after his father.

But such moments of optimism were few. Saul knew that there might not be a business for Ben to inherit. The pages of the order book were filling far more slowly these days, and they had only a few remaining customers up West. No reasons had been given by those who would tell them abruptly one morning, 'I'm afraid we have a new supplier, Mr Steinberg – good day.' Some of the housekeepers were a little more kind, would apologise profusely and remind him conspiratorially how difficult it was to employ someone from the East End these days, how the lady of the house couldn't have it. Saul hated the euphemism, because 'East End' meant nothing more than 'Jewish'.

Saul knew from the smashed-up windows of his shop, from the Star of David repeatedly painted on his van, not to mention the graffiti – 'Filthy Jew', 'Back Home Shylock' – that times were bad, almost as bad as they were in Germany. He had cousins there, and they were telling him the most horrific stories, stories of Orthodox Jews having their beards shaved off in public, stories of beatings, even murders.

It was happening here as well. Only the other night, his wife Anja had come home in tears, her clothes dishevelled and torn. It had taken her twenty minutes to calm down enough to tell Saul how she had been surrounded by a gang of Blackshirts. They had threatened to cut her up, to rape her, to kill her. They had called her the most terrible names, and the more she pleaded, the more they laughed. The worst thing about it, she said, was that people had walked past, not wanting to get involved – even a policeman! What was going to happen to them if even policemen were ignoring their plight? She hadn't thought it would be like this in England. Were they to be hated wherever they went? It had taken a gang of Jewish boys to set her free, their presence giving her the opportunity to run away before a vicious fight broke out between the two gangs. It'll get better, said Saul, hugging his wife, knowing in his heart that his words of comfort were hollow words.

This morning found Steinberg & Son making their weekly deliveries in Victoria and Pimlico. Ben's job was to unload the boxes and take them to the tradesmen's entrances of the grand houses, while his father waited with the van, sorting out the next delivery. It had not been the best of mornings, as Ben had already returned to the van on two occasions to tell him that Mrs So-and-So had no further need of them, and that they should regard that as the last delivery.

Their next stop was a house just off Vauxhall Bridge Road, on Vincent Square. Just as Saul was about to turn left into the square, he found his way blocked by three men wearing uniforms that sent a chill through him. Blackshirts, and from their expressions – expressions he had seen many a time on the streets of Whitechapel – they were looking for trouble.

'Dad?'

'Don't worry, son,' said Saul. 'Just keep calm. Stay in the van, yes?'

He could hear Ben gulping. He wanted to gulp too, but he stopped himself. He wasn't going to let Ben – or *them*, for that matter – see that he was afraid.

'Hello, Yids.'

Saul looked over their heads, refusing to make eye contact. Experience had taught him that that was the best thing to do.

One of the Blackshirts made a great play of looking at his watch.

'We're a little late this morning, aren't we, Mr Steinberg?'

They had been waiting for him, Saul thought; somebody must have told them they were coming this way. Who could it have been? It had to be one of the staff at the house in Vincent Square. Slowly, Saul moved his hand towards the gear stick.

'Not so fast, Jewboy!' one of them shouted.

Saul ignored him – there was no way he was going to stay here. Gunning the engine hard, he slammed the gear stick into reverse and started to shoot backwards, not thinking what might be behind him.

The van's progress was abruptly halted – not by an obstacle to its rear, but by a large stone that had been hurled through the windscreen, hitting Saul in the face. The shock caused his foot to slip off the accelerator, bringing the van to a shuddering stall.

'Dad!'

Blood was streaming from Saul's nose. He could dimly hear his son's voice and the laughter of the Blackshirts. The pain was excruciating, but rather than paralysing him, it enraged him, causing him to open his door and get out of the van.

'Oooh,' mocked one of the Blackshirts. 'Coming to get us, are we?'

Saul could barely speak. Instead, he charged towards the nearest Blackshirt, fists raised. But he had never been much of a fighter, and his swing went wide, so wide that his assailants burst out laughing.

'Dad! Stop it! Leave them!'

Saul swung again, and for his efforts was rewarded with a well-aimed fist in the solar plexus, causing him to double over. He was fighting with men who had spent the best part of seven years in such brawls – there was no chance he was going to get the better of it. Nevertheless, instinct told him to protect his son, his flesh and blood, no matter how great the risk to himself.

The Blackshirt who had punched him nodded to his companions, jerking his head in the direction of the van. The gesture did not go unnoticed by Ben, who quickly resolved to run and get help. He knew there was nothing he could do on his own to help his father – he needed to find a passer-by, or even wave down a car.

He sprinted back on to Vauxhall Bridge Road, panic seizing him. Tears began to fill his eyes as the image of his father's bloodied face played repeatedly in his head. He ran hard, not daring to look round, knowing from the times he had run away from his classmates that turning round slowed you down.

'Help!' he shouted as he ran, waving his arms in the air. 'Help!'

The street was empty, with no sign of a passer-by. He prayed for a policeman, even though Mum and Dad had told him that the police were on the side of the Blackshirts. He ran out into the middle of the road, trying to stop a tradesman in his van, but the response was an angry sounding of the horn. He continued sprinting, receiving rebukes from two more cars. He allowed himself to look round, and saw that two of the Blackshirts were no more than ten yards behind him.

'Come here, you fucking Jew!'

He redoubled his pace, willing his legs to go faster than they had done before, faster than he had thought possible. Someone had to stop, please God; there had to be someone who could save him and Dad.

The last sort of car he expected to slow down was a dark blue Daimler. Normally people in cars like that took no interest, but the Daimler was definitely coming to a halt.

Ben ran up to the car, looking desperately into the driver's eyes. He had a strong face, a kind face, Ben thought; he looked as if he was going to stop.

'Please help!'

But the driver needed no encouragement. He had already opened the door, and to Ben's surprise as much as that of the two Blackshirts, he was holding a gun in his right hand.

There had been no indecision. As soon as Armstrong had seen the dark-haired young lad running from the two Black-shirts, he knew he had to stop. He couldn't drive past and leave the boy to whatever fate the thugs had in mind. The look in the boy's eyes was one of utmost terror, and he would never have forgiven himself if he had continued.

The revolver forced both the boy and the Blackshirts to a panting standstill.

'I bet you weren't expecting this, were you?' Armstrong shouted.

The Blackshirts didn't reply, their chests heaving from the exertion of the run. They slowly raised their hands to chest height, palms outwards, evidently accepting that the tables had been turned. Armstrong suddenly felt naked and exposed. Here he was, a senior politician, threatening a couple of thugs with a gun in the middle of a major London street. Such an occurrence would have been unthinkable six months ago. He needed to defuse the situation quickly. He waved the men away with the revolver. They needed no second prompting, and ran back down the street.

The boy looked up at him.

'You'll be all right now,' said Armstrong. 'They won't touch you again.'

'My dad!' the boy said. 'They've got my dad!'

'Where?'

'Back there with . . . with one of them. My dad . . . he's being . . .'

The boy's voice drifted off. Armstrong could guess what was happening.

'Come on! In the car!'

They overtook the two Blackshirts who were running along the pavement, and pulled up behind the van less than a minute later. The boy had got out before the car had stopped, and Armstrong followed him, once more taking his revolver with him.

What he saw sickened him. A bloodied shape on the ground was being savagely kicked by a Blackshirt, his mouth formed into a smirk that indicated grim satisfaction at a task being well done.

'Stop it!' the boy screamed.

The Blackshirt looked up and opened his mouth to speak, but the words were arrested when he saw Armstrong approach.

Armstrong walked up to the stunned Blackshirt and smashed the side of the revolver hard into the man's left cheekbone. The thug crumpled with a groan. Armstrong was tempted to do to him what the Blackshirt had done to the boy's father, but he resisted the urge and instead put the revolver into his jacket pocket and bent down to examine the victim.

He was joined by the boy, who was crying and shaking his father's unconscious form.

'Dad! Wake up! Dad?'

The man's breathing was shallow, but Armstrong was relieved to find that he was breathing at all. He was in a bad way, his face smashed into a featureless ball of puffy and bleeding skin. There was no doubt that the Blackshirt had broken a few of his ribs, and the kicking would probably have damaged the man's internal organs as well. Armstrong shot a glance at the assailant, who thankfully remained on the ground.

'Run and get help,' said Armstrong to the boy. 'Go to one of those houses. Tell them to ring for an ambulance.'

The boy seemed reluctant.

'He'll be safe here with me,' Armstrong said, gripping the boy's shoulder firmly. 'Go on – that house over there.'

The boy nodded through his tears and ran off, constantly looking back as he did so. Armstrong smiled back at him.

For the next few minutes he attended to the man, wiping his face with his handkerchief, talking to him, reassuring him. How many men had he seen like this? Hundreds. But that was twenty years ago, during the war. And now he was doing it again, but this time in the middle of London, a place that he and his men had regarded as the centre of civilisation, the centre of the Empire they were fighting for. But they had not fought for this.

Neither the sound of a car pulling up behind him nor the hurried footsteps of those who got out of it disturbed his thoughts. He turned round only when he heard his name being called.

'Captain Armstrong?'

He saw three men, all dressed in ill-fitting suits and all wearing snap-brim hats. Briefly he shut his eyes. He knew exactly who they were.

* * *

What interested them greatly was the presence of the revolver in his pocket. They cared neither for the delivery man and his son, nor for the Blackshirts. All they wanted to know was why a senior politician like Captain Armstrong was driving around the streets of London early in the morning armed with a Smith & Wesson. Did he not know that carrying a gun was a serious offence? What was he planning to do with it? Was he not aware that the streets were safe now, far safer than at the beginning of the year with the mayhem of the riots? It was a bit rich, wasn't it, that a politician from the old regime should be carrying a gun when it was his lot that had got them into the mess in the first place? There was no need to carry a gun these days, they told him, not now the Leader was in power.

The interrogation took place in a small basement room in a large nondescript office block at the bottom of Kensington High Street. Armstrong knew it to be the headquarters of the

HMSSP, although there was nothing to indicate it as such. A few clues lay in the hand-painted signs that were peppered along the corridors, showing the way to places such as the Department for the Investigation of Unpatriotic Activities, the Army Political Liaison Office, and the Centre for Co-ordinating Cultural Activities. These were indicators of a dictatorship, Armstrong thought as he was bundled down the dimly lit corridors, these were the secretariats that would ensure that people stayed in line, that they didn't break the rules. We're good at this, he thought; by the looks of things far too good. He had never suspected that there was anything in the British character that would embrace fascism in this way, but here it was, in the face of every individual he passed, all of whom were wearing Party armbands or lapel badges. These were the silent ones, the ones who had never dared express a dislike for democracy, and were now living out their dreams of a Britain in which the concept of liberty was being thrown out in the name of order and action. And who was to stop them? Armstrong thanked God that he had burned the list.

He had two interrogators, both of whom smoked the Party's own brand of cigarette, Black Cap. The tobacco smelt suitably cheap and acrid, Armstrong thought. His interrogators were short men, and both wore neatly trimmed moustaches that were clearly modelled on that of their idol, Mosley. They looked like twins, but were more like clones, who had been mass-produced by a huge metallic machine in one of those new science fiction pictures.

'We've been keeping an eye on you for a while now,' said clone number one.

So his suspicions had been right. Armstrong said nothing, but merely folded his arms. He was feeling bullish, his mood one of defiant impregnability. It was a good way to dispel fear, a method he had used until his breakdown all those years ago. He had used it then because he was trying to stop the horrors of the trenches catching up with him. He was using it now because to think himself into a funk would be counterproductive. His position might be hopeless, but there was no point in behaving as if it was. He shrugged, making it clear that he was uninterested in what the clones had to say.

'You've been keeping yourself very busy,' clone number one continued, 'especially as Parliament isn't sitting any more. Most MPs have been putting their feet up—'

'*Plus ça change*,' clone number two butted in, laughing at his own observation. Number one allowed himself a laugh before resuming.

'But you, Captain Armstrong, you on the other hand have been an eager little beaver, haven't you?'

'It's a free country,' said Armstrong provocatively.

Clone number one raised his eyebrows and coughed. He looked a little awkward. Clone number two, who was leaning against a wall in the gloom at the back of the room, shifted on his feet.

'Well, it is, isn't it?' Armstrong asked, attempting to press home for a small victory.

'No, Captain Armstrong, it most certainly is not a free country,' said number two.

'So you admit it then?'

'Most certainly – look where freedom got us.'

'What do you mean by that?'

'You saw it for yourself,' said number two. 'The country was out of control – it was anarchy. Surely you must remember that, Captain Armstrong? Or have you democratic types conveniently forgotten all about it? Remember Birmingham? Have we had anything like that since?'

Armstrong did remember Birmingham. Nearly seventy men had been killed in a four-way clash between striking factory workers, the police, Blackshirts and Communists. It had been a bloodbath, one that had marked the beginning of the end of Churchill's ill-starred King's Party, the collapse of which was to lead to Mosley taking power.

'Birmingham happened,' said Armstrong slowly, 'because you wanted it to. Birmingham happened because nasty little men like you were there to agitate, to make sure that there was violence. It was you who wanted the deaths—'

'That's enough!' shouted clone number one.

Armstrong grinned.

'What? Something I said?'

'It was not us who wanted the deaths,' said number two, his voice calm. 'It was the Jews and the Communists. Come, come, Captain Armstrong, the evidence is quite clear. Or are you like all those other ostriches that we see in here, digging their heads into the sand?'

Number two's voice sounded tired. He evidently regarded what he said as so obviously the truth that it seemed facile to have to repeat it.

'I would love to see your evidence,' said Armstrong.

He could make out number two's yellow smile in the gloom, smoke dribbling out from between his bared teeth.

'You shall, Captain Armstrong,' he said. 'You shall have no end of evidence to look at. And you shall have plenty of time as well. It is our intention to make sure you stop running around and sit still and listen.'

Armstrong was sick of this patronising lecture coming from a man just over half his age. He wanted to turn the table over, lay into the men the way that Blackshirt had done with Steinberg. Instead he took a deep breath through his nose and reflected on what he had just been told.

'So what are you going to do with me?' he asked. 'Charge me for having an illegal firearm? Go ahead, so long as you do something about the thugs who beat up the delivery man.'

His interrogators stayed silent. Number one started flicking through a thick file.

'We were talking about what you've been up to, Armstrong,' he said. 'About the fact that you've been keeping very busy lately.'

Armstrong leaned back, said nothing.

'You've been away for a while,' number one continued. 'Last time we saw you was when you jumped out of that tea room in Bristol. Bill too expensive for you, was it?'

Again Armstrong said nothing. The only answers he could think of were flippant ones.

'In fact, it might almost be thought that you were organising something, some sort of . . . I don't know . . . movement, perhaps? A resistance movement, even? In short, Captain Armstrong, we'd like to know where you've been, who you've been seeing.'

Number one was evidently trying to adopt the same tired tone as the more dominant number two.

'It's none of your business,' said Armstrong boldly. 'I'm entitled to go where I want and see who I damn well please.'

'Yes, Captain Armstrong, I can see that that is so. What we find a little curious is why you chose to run away from our men in Bristol. They were only following you for your own safety.'

'That's very kind of them,' said Armstrong. 'But you see I don't particularly like being followed around.'

Number two tutted slowly.

'There are other ways of getting through to you, Captain Armstrong,' he said, 'ways that are unfortunately somewhat more time-consuming and difficult. I'm sure none of us want to go down those paths.'

'If you mean to torture me,' said Armstrong, 'then why not just say it?'

'All right then, I will. Yes, I do mean to torture you.'

Number two ground his cigarette out on the stone floor, muttered briefly to his colleague, and then walked to the door. When he reached it, he turned round.

'I'll see you after dinner, Captain Armstrong,' he said, and went out into the corridor.

It was only when he reached his cell that the first pangs of dread started to appear. They were brought on by the appearance of his cellmate, whose face was badly cut and bruised.

'Hello,' said Armstrong gently, reaching out his hand. 'My name is Armstrong, James Armstrong.'

The man briefly lifted his head from his mattress and then let it fall back down. Armstrong paused, and then lay down on the other mattress. It reeked of sweat and urine, but his mind was elsewhere. Until he had seen this man, he had supposed that the threat of torture was merely a bluff. But the damage to this poor bugger's face had not been caused by falling down the stairs.

Armstrong lay in silence for a few minutes, debating whether he should talk to his cellmate. His thoughts were interrupted by the man's coughing, a death rattle of a fit that wouldn't stop. Armstrong looked around for some water, but there was none. He sat up on his mattress.

'Is there anything I can do?' he asked.

The man shook his head and continued to cough, albeit marginally less convulsively. After another half a minute it had dwindled to an occasional – but painful-sounding – hacking.

'How long have you had that?' Armstrong asked.

'Since I came in here,' the man replied. He sounded well-spoken.

'When was that?'

A pause, and then:

'Fuck knows.'

'Can I ask why?'

This time there was no pause.

'Fuck knows. And you?'

There was no other way to reply.

'Fuck knows,' said Armstrong.

This caused the man to laugh, which set off his cough again. After it had subsided, the man spoke once more.

'How do you do,' he said, stretching his hand across the gap between the mattresses. 'I'm Fergus Walker. What did you say your name was?'

It transpired that Walker had earned his place in the cell for the crime of booing at a cinema newsreel.

'I was down at my local fleapit with my girlfriend,' he said, 'and we were waiting for the main picture to come on – something with Jean Harlow I think it was – when they started showing one of those SBC broadcasts about how great everything is now. You know the type of thing . . .'

Armstrong nodded.

'This one was a particularly noxious example, all about Mosley touring some steelworks in Wales with the King. Did you see it?'

Armstrong shook his head while Walker erupted into another coughing fit.

'Anyway,' Walker resumed, 'both Mosley and the King are walking around in their fascist uniforms, radiating superficial bonhomie, with "Hail good fellow" and all that sort of crap. Then there's this appalling scene in which Mosley turns to the King and says something along the lines of . . .'

At this point Walker affected a passable imitation of the Leader, his tone drawling and patrician.

'. . . "Your Majesty, last November you visited these good people at their factory and said, 'Something must be done to see that they stay here – working.' And was something done? No. However, I hope you can see here today that something *has* at last been done, and that these people are not only still working here, but are here to stay!" '

As Walker started coughing again, Armstrong reflected that such a broadcast was typical. Mosley had hauled the King out at every opportunity – it gave him a legitimacy, if not an electoral one, then at least a legitimacy in people's hearts.

'So did the King reply?' Armstrong asked.

'You bet,' Walker replied. 'In that silly American accent of his. He thanked Mosley for all the good "wurk" he had been doing to get the country back on its feet, and all the time Mosley stood there sporting that grin of his, lapping it up. Then – and this is the point at which I started booing – some steelworker leads the others in a three cheers for "The King and Our Leader". You should have seen their faces – smug and just, I don't know, repellent. I suppose I'd had a bit to drink beforehand, so I made my feelings quite plain.'

'What happened next?'

'An usher came down and told me to shut up, that I was disturbing the rest of the audience. I told him where to get off, and said I was entitled to make my feelings clear. He warned me not to do it again, and I said I most certainly would start booing again if the management insisted on showing those two clowns on the screen. Then he walked off and the film began. My girlfriend was a little embarrassed by all this, especially as everybody else in the cinema was turning around and looking at us.'

'Did they say anything?'

'Who?'

'The audience.'

'Not a word. They just tutted – you know what people are like. Anyway, after the film has been running for about ten minutes, there's this commotion at the back, and the next thing I know three men in suits come and wrench me out of my seat.'

Walker paused for another cough.

'Did they take your girlfriend too?'

'No. They left her there and wouldn't even tell her where they were taking me. I kicked up a hell of a fuss and tried to break free, but they were big chaps. I demanded to know why they were taking me, who the hell they were, all that. But it was useless. The next thing I know – whack! – I get this terrific bash on the back of my head and wake up in this shit-hole.'

'And what happened after you woke up?'

Walker didn't reply, not because he was coughing, but because he didn't want to.

'Sorry,' said Armstrong, 'I didn't mean to . . .'

'No need to apologise. Um . . . after I woke up . . . well, that's when it started.'

'What started?'

'I . . . I don't think I want to talk about it. Not now, if you don't mind.'

Walker's voice had become subdued, croaky.

'Sorry, Walker.'

Walker waved his hand as if to tell Armstrong not to worry.

'It's Fergus,' he said. 'I think cellmates should be on first-name terms, don't you?'

Cellmates, thought Armstrong, the full reality of his new situation sinking in. They had taken his watch away, but he guessed it was late afternoon. It had already been a long day, and it was about to get longer. He was both hungry and thirsty, but he was not going to ask for anything, was not going to show any signs of weakness. He had prepared himself for this moment, albeit over twenty years ago, at the outbreak of the war. Then, he had wondered how he would cope if he was incarcerated by the Germans. It would never have occurred to the young Lieutenant Armstrong that one day he would be locked up by his own people.

He feared the torture because he feared the unknown. If that clone had told him that they were going to pull his nails out, then he could have prepared himself. But his mind raced, conceiving horrors that should have been inconceivable. What had they done to poor Fergus here? He had been just another drunk young man at the pictures with his girlfriend, expressing himself in the boisterous fashion common to all men at some time in their lives. And now he had been locked up for it, and worse, physically savaged. However, the difference between Fergus and Armstrong was that Fergus had nothing to tell. Armstrong, on the other hand, knew too much, too much that they would love to know.

He looked across at his cellmate, who was staring up at the ceiling. Something about Fergus's story didn't add up, thought Armstrong, something about it stank. Surely the HMSSP had bigger fish to trawl for than those who had committed minor misdemeanours, no matter how unpatriotic? No, Fergus was a stooge, a 'new best friend' sent to tempt him into telling him what he had been doing. Armstrong could see it now, could see how Fergus would like their relationship to grow. The gradual building-up of confidence after the abrasive start, which would lead to the mutual sharing of secrets. For all he knew, Fergus might even be a real prisoner attempting to atone for whatever crime he had committed by helping the HMSSP. People would do anything to get out of this hole, even help their tormentors in exchange for freedom.

They came at three in the morning. Armstrong had been drifting in and out of sleep, his throat parched and sore. He had come close to asking for some water, but had decided against it. The door slammed open, the light from the corridor making him squint as he sat up. Silhouetted in the opening was the figure of a man in a suit, whom he recognised as being clone number two. Behind him he could make out two more figures, both in the Blackshirt uniform of black fencing jackets, black breeches and knee-length black riding boots.

They remained silent as they took him away, as they dragged him down the corridor, as they tied him to a chair in yet another small room. He readied himself for the violence that was to come – the punches, the kicks, God knew what else. He was afraid, but he knew he could take it.

To his surprise, the men left the room. What was this? Were they making way for some expert? Armstrong took several deep breaths, steeling himself. He had seen and suffered enough violence in the war, had killed and seen friends killed, but had never had to endure drawn-out sadism. The violence he had experienced was sudden and explosive. One second you were alive, the next you were dead, or – perhaps worse –

savagely maimed. But torture was different, horrific in its slowness, in its anticipation.

The lights snapped out, causing a momentary surge of panic to overwhelm him. A few more deep breaths – in through the nose, out through the mouth, not too quickly – and he could feel himself approach what approximated to a relaxed state in a torture chamber.

A white square appeared on the wall in front of him. Armstrong recognised it as the light from a slide projector. What were they going to show him?

A clicking sound from over his head told him that he was right. It was a projector, and it was showing its first slide, which consisted solely of three crudely written words:

HE DIDN'T TALK

A click, and then:

SO WE DID THIS

Another click.

It was a black-and-white photograph. The image was slightly out of focus, but the noose was clear enough, as was the face. It was Alec's.

Behind him, hidden hands adjusted the focus.

*   *   *

One of the advantages of Otto's flat is that no one can see who comes in and out. The block, on Lawn Road in Hampstead, is of a radical design called 'deck access', which features external walkways along each floor. But while the front doors of most of the flats in his block can be seen from the road, Otto's – number 7 – is hidden by a staircase. Naturally, it is no accident that Otto has chosen this flat. It suits his purposes very well, especially today, as he is expecting a visit from Tony.

Otto knows Tony likes whisky, so he has bought him a bottle of the finest Scotch. Otto is sophisticated enough to know the difference between blended and malt, and he has procured a bottle of Glenfiddich from a pub on Haverstock Hill. He goes into the small and virtually unused kitchen, and takes two tumblers out of a light green cupboard. The tumblers are new, and still carry the maker's sticker just below their rims. Otto picks them off with a little difficulty.

The doorbell rings. Otto looks at the clock above the kitchen door. Six o'clock – Tony is on time. Otto hurries to the front door, not wishing to leave Tony exposed on the walkway. Yes, he knows the front door is hidden, but there could be others around, not least that nosy old woman from next door.

Otto looks through the keyhole, sees the bottom part of Tony's face and smiles. He unlocks the Yale and slides the chain across. Tony walks in without saying a word. No pleasantries are exchanged, no chitchat. It feels as if they are about to commit some crime, perhaps a sexual crime, thinks Otto, who knows a little about that. Otto leaves Tony standing while he fetches the tumblers.

He returns, brandishing one towards Tony, who nods back.

'I've got you some finest malt,' says Otto. 'I hope you approve.'

'I do,' says Tony, taking a glass into which Otto has poured a generous inch.

'Well, I thought we should congratulate ourselves on your new position.'

The two men clink their glasses together.

'And,' says Otto pointedly, 'our new recruit.'

This time no clink, but a slight raising of tumblers.

'What are you going to call him?' Tony asks.

Otto grins and walks over to a low white cupboard. He bends down, slides its door open, and takes out the Monopoly set that Tony gave him in March.

'My wife and I enjoy it,' says Otto. 'It's rather good . . .'

'For something so capitalist,' says Tony.

'Precisely,' Otto continues. 'Anyway, I was rather tickled by the idea of naming him after one of the counters.'

'Oh yes? Which one?'

'I thought "Dog".'

Tony takes a sip of his drink.

'Very appropriate.'

'I thought so,' says Otto. 'And I've got a new name for you.'

'What?'

'Top Hat.'

'I approve.'

'I doubt the game's makers would feel the same way!'

'I expect not,' says Tony. 'Anyway, Top Hat is better than Boot, at any rate.'

'Perhaps we'll find someone to fill that name, as it were.'

Top Hat chuckles slightly, hiding the fact that he is taken aback by Otto's verbal dexterity in what he knows cannot be his first language.

'Why don't we sit down?' says Otto.

Chapter Three

A Funny Place

August 1937

ARMSTRONG STAYED SILENT for three weeks. His reticence was brought about by a mixture of shock, stubbornness and disbelief. He spoke neither to his captors, nor to Fergus, who left the cell after a few days. They had actually *killed* him, Armstrong kept thinking, cold-bloodedly executed him within a few hours of arresting him. He was shown the picture repeatedly, and its impact never diminished. He had known Alec for decades, had known every expression that his face could bear, and yet here was a new one, one that told Armstrong there was no life behind this face, that it was merely a collection of protuberances. Here was a nose that would no longer have air rushing through its nostrils, here was a mouth that would no longer smile, here was a pair of eyes that would never again open. It seemed unreal, and Armstrong couldn't help but feel that perhaps it was. He thought that it might be a fake, but each time he looked at the picture there was no doubting its awful veracity.

The clones never touched him. They threatened torture, but none came. They questioned him endlessly, deprived him of sleep, starved him, but they never so much as slapped him. That surprised him – if they were capable of killing Alec, then they were capable of lesser horrors. Why did they leave him alone? Did they want him to remain unharmed so that he appeared presentable for some form of trial? At first he fancied that his position still gave him some protection, but he soon dismissed it. The rules, if there still were any, had changed, replaced by the thin laws of barbarism. And how quickly it had happened! In just a few months, society had mutated, had allowed itself to show a hidden face, one set in a permanent sneer of violent hatred. Armstrong knew the face was not that of the majority, but it was threatening that majority, forcing it apart.

How much did his captors know? As the days went by, Armstrong became increasingly convinced that the answer was very little. The clones, as well as the men in full Blackshirt uniforms, asked him plenty of questions, but it became apparent that whatever information they had was risibly incorrect. Armstrong had expected them to know more, had reckoned they would have mentioned at least some of the names on his list, but the names they did spit out meant nothing to him. Although he did not allow himself to assume that the network was intact, there was a good chance that it was. Still, without a leader, it was little more than a collection of decent men.

Eventually they had seemingly got bored of him, and he was sent under armed guard to his present home – Peveril Internment Camp in Peel on the west coast of the Isle of Man. For the next two months he received the occasional beating and constant verbal abuse – what one of the guards liked to euphemistically call 'thorough debriefings' – but the authorities had seemingly decided that Armstrong was less of a threat than they had supposed. The food was minimal in quantity and abysmal in quality, a near starvation ration that was designed to keep the inmates weak and listless.

Normally it was Churchill's snoring that kept him awake, but tonight Armstrong had no need of sleep. Even though Winston had lost nearly two stone since he had been interned in April, it hadn't made any difference to his nocturnal rumblings. The guards, perhaps out of a sense of mischief, had seen fit to place Armstrong's bed next to Churchill's, which meant that Armstrong had slept badly every night for the past several weeks. Winston was apologetic – after a fashion – but he growled that he couldn't help it, and that Armstrong was perfectly within his rights to hit him when he snored, something Armstrong could never bring himself to do.

But tonight it didn't matter, because this was going to be Armstrong's last night of captivity. By tomorrow he would be miles away, back on the mainland, away from this hellhole. No longer would he have to stare out at the blueness of Peel Bay, gazing at the fishing boats through fifteen feet of barbed wire. No longer would he feel the intense claustrophobia of being trapped in what had been a row of boarding houses, packed in with a couple of hundred of his parliamentary colleagues, all understandably bellyaching at the lack of creature comforts, let alone the deprivation of their liberty.

He looked at his watch. Half past eleven. Armstrong had wanted to go later, but Paddy had told him that earlier would suit them better, especially on a Saturday night, when the guards would be carousing with the local girls down at the Albert Hall on Shore Road. Armstrong could hear the sound of the band even now, carried in through the window by a slight breeze. The dance hall was only three hundred yards away, but that was further than he had been able to walk since he had been interned. Even if the escape failed, Armstrong thought, it would be good just to be able to stretch his legs.

Armstrong got out of bed, cursing the anguished creaking of the tired springs. Winston stirred in his sleep and stopped snoring. Armstrong paused, hoping not to rouse him. Churchill had wanted to come, of course, but he had reluctantly accepted that, at sixty-two, maybe his escaping days were over. Perhaps if he had lost some more weight, Armstrong had told him, he might have been able to squeeze through. Winston had glowered at this, not knowing whether Armstrong, his junior by nearly twenty years, was being serious.

After giving his roommate half a minute to resume his deep sleep, Armstrong slipped his jacket off the back of the room's only chair. It was the same jacket he had been wearing when he was arrested on Vauxhall Bridge Road. Even nearly three months on, Steinberg & Son occupied his thoughts almost as much as Alec did, but now was not the time for reflection. Now was the time for thanking God he had not been wearing a pinstripe suit that morning. The jacket was a plain dark blue, and after months of daily wear, and with some deliberate distressing, its former conspicuous Savile Row provenance was no longer apparent. He had even carried out some extra tailoring on it, by inserting around £20 in the lining. If the plan went well, this money, bought from the more amenable guards at usurious rates with the camp's own paper money, should get him to London.

Armstrong put the jacket on, over a scruffy shirt he had been given when he had volunteered for some gardening duties. A flat cap and a pair of workman's boots completed the picture of a labourer trying to look his best on a Sunday morning. A full beard was another part of the disguise, albeit a reluctant one. It was ironic, Armstrong had told Paddy, that he had never gone for longer than twenty-four hours without a shave in the trenches, and yet here he was, two decades later, having to grow a beard just to get around his own bloody country, the country he had fought for.

As quietly as the boots would allow, Armstrong tiptoed out the room. He took one last look at Winston, smiled at a particularly loud snore, and then slipped into the corridor. He crept down the stairs, and made his way into the small common room at the back of the house. A sash window, the bolt of which had been broken a week before and then made to look intact, slid open easily. Armstrong swung his legs out into the night air and then jumped the few feet into the back yard.

He remained still after he had landed. Once more he could hear the music wafting over from the Albert Hall. He could hear female laughter too, presumably coming from those who had been lured outside by lustful guards. Although the guards rarely patrolled inside the camp – just around it – and even though it was Saturday night, Armstrong was ready for the unexpected. Both politics and the army had taught him that lesson.

In front of him was a grass bank that rose a hundred feet within the same number of yards. At the top was a row of houses, which were also part of the camp. Armstrong's objective was a row of smaller houses beyond them, a row that bordered the top perimeter of the camp.

Just as he was about to start walking, something stopped him. It wasn't a sound or a figure – it was his legs. They were shaking violently, preventing him from moving. He knew what would happen if he didn't control himself – he would have an attack, a seizure. They had started in northern France, and had only stopped when the war was finally over. But they had returned in '23 with a vengeance, and had nearly been the end of him. It happened to a lot of them, but you didn't ever talk about it, you kept it quiet. Never mind that it nearly killed you, because you were a *hero*, and heroes weren't supposed to crack.

Armstrong took several deep breaths. God only knew why this hadn't happened before, and yet here it was, a repeat of something from within that he feared the most. Perhaps it had accumulated, built up as it had done throughout the war, and had now picked its moment to release itself. He felt like lying down and weeping. He felt tired, sick and faint. He could see, as if it was happening in front of him, the explosion at La Quinque Rue, the explosion that had torn six of his men to pieces, caking him in their entrails and sending a mass of mud and limbs into the air.

Don't give in to it, they had told him, don't surrender to it, whatever it was. Not that the doctors had believed him at first, but then there were so many of them, so many of them who had suddenly lost it, ended up in asylums or been shut away in a kindly relative's country house. You could be walking down the street years later and it would hit you, a massively delayed reaction from the years of shelling and death. It was like a shell in itself, shellshock, because it came out of nowhere and it was indiscriminate.

He was taking control of it now, concentrating on his legs, making himself stop them shaking. If he didn't, then his whole body would tremble and he would collapse in a gibbering heap right there in the yard, and would only be noticed when his screams woke someone up. But he was taking control, steadying himself, sorting it out. He used to need whisky to do this, a lot of whisky, but he was managing without, had no need of such medication. Good, he thought, it was going, just another minute and he'd be able to move. He just had to hope it didn't happen in the tunnel.

Perhaps he shouldn't go; perhaps it would endanger the others. But they had insisted, telling him that he was needed on the outside, that it was essential he get out. He started walking slowly, telling himself that this was nothing, that there would be worse to come.

The tunnel started in the small house – number 13 Peveril Road – inhabited by Paddy and two others, one a hard left Labour MP by the name of Jimmy Craven, the other a Liberal called Neil Wigan. It led out from the porch and across the road, running underneath the barbed-wire perimeter fence. After thirty feet, the tunnel surfaced in the middle of a small path that ran between a building that had been requisitioned as a guardhouse, and a small bungalow. It was hardly ideal, but they couldn't go any further.

It had taken nearly three months to dig it, three gruelling months of toiling, of lying in the filthy darkness hacking away with scavenged pieces of iron. To make matters worse, the tunnel passed over a sewer, making conditions inside nearly unbearable, as well as causing the house to stink of drains, something Paddy had jokingly explained away in public as being inevitable if you had a socialist like Craven living with you.

The tunnel had needed to be shored up, and so timbers had been appropriated from some bunk beds left in a store cupboard. The earth – and there was more than they had bargained for – had been deposited in the small garden behind the house. By the time the tunnel had been completed, the level of the garden had risen by about two feet. So far that had gone unnoticed, but it would only be a matter of time before some sharp-eyed little guard noticed how the garden at number 13 was significantly higher than those at numbers 11 and 15.

After a couple of minutes, Armstrong found himself tapping five times on the house's rear window. A pair of hands emerged from the gloom and opened it.

'Come on in, dear fellow.'

Armstrong did so with ease, the extra height of the garden enabling him to almost step into the small kitchen.

'Good evening, Chief Whip.'

Armstrong could make out Paddy's smile above a shielded candle.

'Evening, Paddy,' Armstrong replied. 'All ready?'

'Everything seems tip-top – good trip up here?'

'Fine,' said Armstrong. 'Seemed fine.'

'Excellent – guards on the sauce then?'

'It would seem so.'

It was impossible, thought Armstrong, for Paddy Evans to act seriously. In the House, this had made many regard him as a lightweight, but Armstrong knew better, insisting that Stanley Baldwin make him one of his junior whips. What he lacked in gravitas, Paddy made up for in loyalty and doggedness, and he made an excellent whip, using his charm to cajole those who were tempted to vote the wrong way.

'Craven and Wigan?' asked Armstrong.

'Wigan's on lookout upstairs. Hasn't seen a soul. Craven's all ready for you.'

'The guardhouse?'

'Empty. Seems nobody's been a bad boy recently.'

'Good.'

That was unusual. Along with the MPs, Peveril Internment Camp held another few hundred 'enemies of the state': trade unionists, journalists, artists, academics and peers, all out to give the guards as hard a time as possible. Many had found themselves locked up in one of the guardhouses for committing some unpatriotic misdemeanour. It was a blessing, then, that the guardhouse opposite lay temporarily vacant.

A form approached out of the darkness. It was Craven, who was to be Armstrong's escape partner that night. Powerfully built, and with seamlessly conjoined dark eyebrows, Craven was a real rabble-rouser, a militant, and certainly not someone for whom Armstrong had a great deal of political fondness. But he had a good war record, and hated the fascists – two attributes that Armstrong found admirable. However, it was Craven's links with the Freedom Council, an underground movement set up by Communists and Jews, that now made him a uniquely useful ally. Their plan was to get down to London, where they would make contact with the Council and persuade them to take part in Armstrong's coup. The Council was well placed to set up a network of opposition cells that could whip up public support for Galwey's temporary administration in the event of Mosley's removal.

'Have you got everything?' Armstrong asked.

Craven nodded, but Armstrong insisted they check they had what they needed: bread, some unattractively desiccated ham, cheese, water, a compass, money. They stepped into the front room of the house, Paddy shakily carrying the candle with him. Armstrong noticed the stench of drains was stronger than usual.

'The smell's got worse, hasn't it?' he asked.

'I know. There's even been a little more, er, seepage in the tunnel.'

'How bad?'

'Bad enough to use these,' said Paddy, producing a pair of canvas mail sacks from underneath a table. 'You can crawl along on them. I don't expect you fancy reeking of crap for your little sea voyage.'

'I'm sorry you've got to stay here,' said Armstrong.

Paddy shrugged.

'Hah! I'm getting used to it!'

As he and Wigan would make their attempt next Saturday, they only had to endure another week of the vile smell that had impregnated the very fabric of the house.

Paddy tapped five times on the ceiling. After a few seconds, five taps came back, giving them the all-clear.

'All right, let's get moving,' said Armstrong, taking a mail sack.

In truth, he had no wish to hang about, fearing another attack. If he kept going, he would be fine, he knew he would. Together, the three men went to the porch, and lifted up a piece of lino to reveal a rough handleless trapdoor, under which Paddy inserted a small piece of metal. Slowly he lifted the door, causing Armstrong and Craven to put their hands over their noses and mouths as the full stench of the sewer made itself known.

'Christ almighty!' Armstrong swore quietly to himself. It was worse than the trenches.

Paddy suppressed a cough and then extinguished the candle. Armstrong and Craven had no need of it, because they knew every inch of the tunnel.

'Best of luck, you two,' said Paddy. 'See you at White's for a whisky mac on Sunday week.'

'Not me you won't,' said Craven.

'All right then,' said Paddy. 'See you at the Stepney Working Men's Club for a London Pride.'

'That's more like it,' Craven replied, chuckling quietly.

Armstrong stepped down, finding the first rung of their

makeshift ladder with his right foot. He descended swiftly and confidently, and then turned to face down the tunnel. The smell was so bad he thought he might pass out, but he told himself to stop being a fool. He would crawl through miles of crap to get out of this place, he thought, let alone a mere thirty feet.

He bent down, and holding the top corners of the mail sack laid it down on the damp soil before kneeling on it. He would doubtless get somewhat dirty, but the sack would help. He started crawling, listening to the sound of his own breathing, as well as that of Craven behind him. After half a minute he felt for the large stone they had stuck in the left-hand side of the wall to indicate the halfway point, the point at which they crossed underneath the fence. As soon as he touched it, Armstrong started to feel a sense of freedom. It was exhilarating, despite his having toiled past this point on countless grimy occasions.

The sewage got bad here, and his hands were soon made damp by a festering mixture of reeking effluence. He could feel his knees getting wet, but he ignored it, knowing that in another few seconds he and Craven would be making their way up out of here and into the fresh air and freedom. It really did stink of the trenches though, especially like those at Le Plantin. There, the water was so deep that some of his Gurkhas, shorter than the average British soldier, had drowned as they had tried to seek cover from a bombardment.

They were approaching one of the riskiest moments of their attempt – the lifting of the sod of earth that lay in the middle of the path between the guardhouse and the bungalow. Paddy had made a small wooden frame to support the sod, and he claimed his creation could take the weight of a person. Armstrong knew that all he could do now was trust him.

Armstrong got to his feet, crouching just below the exit. He listened carefully, although his ears had never recovered from the shelling. Damn, he should have made Craven go first – he would have much better hearing. But it was too late for that, for there was no room for them to swap positions. He waited for another minute, sensing Craven's restlessness behind him. There was nothing, he was sure of it. Cautiously he lifted Paddy's frame.

The night air smelt sweet, and beckoned him upwards. He pushed the frame with its sod carefully to one side, and heaved himself up with the slightest of grunts. Craven helped him with a leg-up, and, heart pounding, he crawled out on to the path. For a moment he lay still, taking in his surroundings. He had spent three months looking at this patch of turf, and now he was actually on it.

Then he stood up, and reached down to take Craven's outstretched hands, the only part of him that was above ground. The image reminded Armstrong of the Lady in the Lake. He pulled silently, dragging Craven on to the turf. Together they replaced the sod and brushed away any telltale clods of earth from where it joined the rest of the path. Craven smiled at Armstrong but he didn't reciprocate. He didn't want Craven to feel relaxed, not even slightly. He knew that it was best to stay calm, firm and expressionless. Armstrong looked back at the house, detecting a slight twitch in the curtain of an upstairs window. He could only imagine how delighted Paddy and Wigan would be.

Walking briskly rather than running, Armstrong and Craven made their way down the Peveril Road, down into the town proper. They had gleaned much of the layout of Peel from the same guards who had sold them their money. They were tempted to turn right, to go down Jib Lane, but that would take them too near the Albert Hall, which overlooked the bay. Instead they would have to navigate as best they could through the warren of streets, and find their way to the long, narrow harbour that lay on the other side of town. It was there that they would steal a boat, some suitable craft that would take them off the island.

The streets were quiet, and Armstrong was grateful for the absence of street lighting. Occasionally the two men found themselves lit up by dim yellow lamps above front doors, but for the most part they moved in darkness. The noise from the Albert Hall retreated, but Armstrong was constantly on his guard for the sight of a uniform around a corner.

It came sooner than he had feared. They were walking down a narrow lane of stone two-up-two-downs that curved to the left. Armstrong was slightly ahead of Craven when he spotted the unmistakable domed silhouette of a policeman's helmet. Normally it was a sight that he would have found reassuring, but now it made him come to an abrupt halt, his senses dramatically alert, his left arm stretched behind him, signalling Craven to stop.

The policeman was walking up the street towards them. As the two escapers crouched in the shallow doorway of one of the cottages, they could see that the policeman's gait was relaxed, his arms behind his back, his pace slow and measured. Armstrong presumed that the man was looking forward to his bed, that this was his home stretch before he curled up with the missus. It suddenly occurred to him that perhaps they were even crouching in the doorway of the policeman's own cottage. That would be just their luck.

By now, the constable was twenty feet away. It was time for a decision. Should they rush him, knock him out? The thought didn't appeal to Armstrong, not just because he found the notion of assaulting a policeman anathema, but because when the man came to, the alarm would be raised. Neither could they talk their way out of it – after all, how could they explain what they were doing skulking like this? Where do you live, sir? Out and about this time of night, sir? It was hopeless. Armstrong decided all they could do was wait, motionless. The street might just be dark enough.

It looked as though their luck was in. As the policeman approached, he showed no sign that he had noticed the two men. Then he stopped.

'*Hello*, there.'

Armstrong could feel Craven tense behind him; he himself stayed rigidly still.

'Who have we got here?'

Craven made to move, but Armstrong didn't budge.

'You're out late tonight. Shouldn't someone have shut you up?'

Armstrong momentarily closed his eyes. All that tunnelling, only to end up being caught by a policeman on his way back home.

'I know what *you'd* like. A saucer of milk, wouldn't you? *Yes*.'

Armstrong felt a wave of relief that almost knocked him over. It was a cat! He was talking to a bloody cat. The policeman walked right past them, holding his hand out towards the ground.

'Come on, you, let's get you home.'

The constable was past them now, as was the sound of a slight and appreciative mewing. Armstrong didn't dare to breathe, waiting instead for the policeman to disappear up the lane with his no doubt tailless friend. The footsteps got fainter, and then he heard them stop, followed by the sound of a key in a lock and a door being quietly shut. Armstrong exhaled.

'Christ,' Craven whispered behind him. 'That was . . .'

'Close,' Armstrong finished for him, allowing himself a slight smile. 'Let's get going.'

They carried on down the lane and soon found themselves on the road in front of the harbour, an inlet about a hundred feet wide that ran into the bay. On the other side, Peel Hill loomed solidly in the moonlight, a silvery path snaking up to its peak. To Armstrong's right, guarding the harbour's entrance, was Peel Castle, its medieval battlements visible against the night sky.

The harbour was packed with every form of boat that Armstrong could imagine. Ropes occasionally slapped against masts, and there was something reassuring in the gentle creaking sound of craft rubbing against each other in the lightest of swells. The two men scuttled across the road and down some stone steps to the floating decking that ran alongside the harbour wall. As neither of them was in any way an accomplished sailor, they had agreed to steal the simplest boat possible, not wishing to complicate matters by attempting to hoist sails or fiddle with keels. A motorboat was what they were after, a vessel small enough to be rowed quietly out to sea before its engine could be started out of earshot.

'There!' hissed Craven, pointing at a gap between two smacks. 'That looks as if it might do.'

He was right. Bobbing gently up and down against the decking was a clinker-built wooden dinghy, about fourteen feet long, complete with a small outboard engine. It even boasted a pair of oars.

'Great,' said Armstrong. 'That should get us there. I'll get in, you cast us off.'

Within a couple of minutes Armstrong was rowing them out of the harbour towards the bay. The exercise, together with sharp inhalations of sea air, felt refreshing, and he permitted himself a further ounce of satisfaction that they had got this far. As they reached the bay, he looked to his left, along the line of dark houses and cottages that culminated in the camp. There was no more music emanating from the Albert Hall – just laughter sounding across the water.

'When should we start the engine?' Craven whispered.

'Not for another hour at least,' Armstrong grunted back.

'Shall I take over?'

'No, not yet.' Armstrong's pride stopped him from yielding to Craven. Just because he was in his mid forties it didn't make him an invalid. In fact, he was in much better shape than most of his colleagues, many of whom had lost their post-war leanness to a surplus of dinners. He liked to keep fit, although he had never found as much time as he would have liked, not until he was brought here, at least.

After ten minutes Armstrong had rowed them out into the bay. The coastline disappeared up to the north-east, which was to their starboard side.

'Have you got the compass?' Armstrong asked.

Craven fished it out of his pocket.

'We want to be heading north,' said Armstrong.

Craven held the compass right up to his face.

'Bang on target,' he whispered.

'Great – make sure we stay that way. I don't want to end up in Ireland.'

'Look, are you sure you don't want me to take over?'

Armstrong continued rowing, ignoring the question. He'd change positions in a few more minutes, and then allow himself a mouthful of bread and cheese as a reward. They had a good twenty-five miles to go, and he wasn't going to take the engine's capability for granted. So long as they got to Scotland before it was light, they could rest up all day. He didn't fancy being stuck in the middle of the Irish Sea in daylight, even if the alarm hadn't been raised.

Their objective was the Mull of Galloway, Scotland's most south-westerly point. Armstrong had two reasons for choosing it – first, it was the closest part of the mainland to Peel, and second, Richard Collyer, one of Armstrong's fellow Gurkha officers, lived nearby. The two men made contact once a year, when Collyer was on his annual visit to London, and on each occasion, as they sat in the Carlton Club, Collyer would insist that Armstrong should 'really come up one of these days'. Armstrong had never found an opportunity, but if all went well over the next several hours, he would soon be knocking on the door of Logan House.

'All right, your turn,' said Armstrong, and the men swapped places.

Initially, Craven's efforts were cack-handed, and Armstrong feared that he would have to resume rowing, but Craven soon established a competent rhythm. Looking back, Armstrong could see the harbour lights becoming more distant, but he still did not wish to start the engine. Another half an hour, he reckoned.

Armstrong first pulled the starter cord at half past one. By a quarter to two, both he and Craven had given up. The engine refused to start, not even allowing itself to turn over. They had unscrewed the cap and gazed into the fuel tank, seeing that there was indeed petrol in it. Could the boat be a dud? Of all the bloody hundreds in the harbour, it seemed as though they had picked the wrong one.

'If it's not even turning over,' said Craven, 'that can only mean one thing.' His tone was one of resignation.

'What?'

'There can't be any spark plugs. The buggers must have taken them out.'

Armstrong breathed out – it sounded plausible.

'Shit,' he swore softly.

Craven sat back in a deflated heap.

'My turn to row,' said Armstrong.

'What's the bleeding point? We'll never make it.'

But Armstrong ignored the dejection.

'Come on – let's unscrew the engine and dump it. We'll go a lot quicker without the damn thing.'

The dawn couldn't have been more beautiful, but Armstrong cursed it. As the pale yellow light got stronger, he felt increasingly exposed. They had been rowing, mainly in silence, for three hours, and the coast of Scotland appeared still to be several miles away. To their starboard side, the peaks of the Lake District were visible. It was only the second time in his life he had seen them – the first occasion was on the boat that had taken them from Liverpool to Douglas back in June. To port they could see Ireland, another place Armstrong had never visited. He remembered being told about it when he was growing up in India, but it had been a place that had been impossible to imagine.

'How's it looking ahead?' asked Craven, who was rowing.

'We've still got a way to go.'

'Any company?'

Armstrong looked around – nothing, but that surely would not last for long. At any moment, a naval patrol boat could appear on the horizon, routinely scanning the waters. Even a trawler posed a risk, its crew's suspicions doubtless raised by the appearance of two workmen rowing a dinghy miles from land.

'Not yet,' he replied.

'How much longer do you reckon we've got?'

Armstrong stood up cautiously to get a better view – with the sea being slightly choppy, he did not fancy a swim. Their destination looked further away than ever, but a quick glance over his shoulder towards the Isle of Man suggested they were well over halfway. He estimated they had a good seven or eight miles to go.

'About four hours,' he announced, much to Craven's obvious distaste.

'Great,' he groaned. 'Do you think there'll be any breakfast for us when we get there?'

Armstrong laughed a little – more out of relief that Craven still had his sense of humour.

'I'm sure my friend Richard will serve us up an excellent lunch.'

Craven paused before speaking.

'Roast chicken,' he said. 'I feel like chicken.'

'I can do better than that,' Armstrong replied.

'What?'

'Foie gras sandwiches.'

'Foie gras? What in God's name is that? Some sort of French thing?'

'It's delicious,' said Armstrong. 'It's a pâté made out of goose livers. Foie gras sandwiches go exceptionally well with single malt.'

'You're pulling my leg,' said Craven, taking a big heave on the oars.

'Not at all – always my favourite snack at the House.'

'Typical bloody Tory! I bet one of your fancy sandwiches costs more than a coal miner's weekly wage. Anyway, I didn't think you drank whisky any more.'

Armstrong gazed down at the water before replying. He missed his whisky; he had missed it every day since she had weaned him off it. In reality he hadn't eaten a foie gras sandwich since then either, because the thought of them without whisky was unbearable.

'Just because *I* don't go well with whisky,' said Armstrong, 'doesn't mean that foie gras sandwiches have stopped doing so.'

Craven grinned.

'I still think I'd prefer roast chicken,' he said.

'You'll be lucky,' said Armstrong, and then he stopped talking and scanned the sea for any other craft.

As they approached the coast, the sea got choppier, much choppier. By Armstrong's estimate, they had only an hour to go, but as he rowed, he was far from counting chickens, roast or otherwise. So far, barring the outboard motor, they had been lucky, far more so than he had dared hope.

'This isn't too pleasant,' said Craven, his smile doing a bad job of masking his unease.

'It's nothing to worry about,' Armstrong replied. 'Just keep a lookout.'

Armstrong was feeling exhausted, but his will kept him aflame, kept his muscles going, ensured that he was never going to stop. The last thing he wanted to show Craven was that he too was feeling uncomfortable with the dinghy's violent pitching and rolling. If he'd been on his own, he suspected he might have had an attack, seen that explosion all over again, found himself shutting down. But with Craven here, someone for whom he felt responsible, he found it easier to stay in control. It was the same as in France. With his men around him, he was more or less fine. But alone – that could be a different story.

'A lighthouse!' Craven shouted, interrupting his thoughts.

Armstrong turned round. Craven was right – there it was, on top of a headland, a thin white pillar that marked their objective.

'*Good*,' said Armstrong emphatically. 'That's our mull, bang on target.'

With those words, he pulled on the oars even harder. They would definitely get there now; nothing was going to stop them. A couple of curious seagulls circled overhead, reminding Armstrong for a moment of vultures. He dismissed the thought as crass.

'This is hopeless!'

They were only fifty yards from the shore, but the current and the waves were rudely dispatching them in the direction of Ireland. They had actually gone past the lighthouse, and were being forced to attempt to row northwards, parallel to the coast, which was to their starboard. They were both utterly spent, as well as being drenched through. At any moment the dinghy would either capsize or sink.

'Terrible! We're buggered!'

It was Craven doing the yelling.

'Stop that!' Armstrong barked. 'Keep rowing up the coast! We'll get in somewhere!'

Every few seconds a wave broke over the bow, mercilessly depositing another few inches of water in the dinghy. Armstrong attempted to bail out with a small bucket, but it was a gesture at best. He tried not to look at the grisly black rocks, unwelcoming in their steep jaggedness. They had to get to a cove, an inlet, a beach – anything to avoid being swept away or, perhaps worse, slammed and shattered against the rocks.

'I can't go on!'

'Of course you can!' Armstrong yelled back. 'Come on, twenty more and then I'll take over!'

Armstrong counted each of Craven's strokes.

'One! Come on! Two! That's it! Three!'

He had got to twelve when, as they had both known it surely would, a particularly savage wave smashed into them. It happened almost slowly, gracefully, but its effect was brutal. It hit the dinghy on the port side, turning it over, knocking both men into the water.

For what seemed like hours there was cold, unyielding blackness and a rush of water. Armstrong could only flail, grasping nothing, feeling himself being dragged in an unknown direction. Which way was up? he wondered. He didn't know – there was nothing to give him a clue. His lungs howled, longing to be refilled, but he forced himself to disobey his body's cruelly stupid demand that he open his mouth.

And then light. A huge gasp, mostly air and spray, but it was invigorating, life-giving. And then another wave, and the process repeated itself, but it was easier this time, because he knew which way round he was. Up again. He looked around for Craven, but couldn't see him. Another wave came towards him. He took a deep breath, and then ducked beneath it. He was getting the measure of this now, establishing a routine. But he was tired, so very, very tired.

'Craven!' he screamed. 'Craven!'

Nothing. He could see the upturned dinghy a few yards away, in the direction of the rocks, and he made for it, swimming as hard as a man who hadn't spent the night rowing several miles. He would look for Craven when he reached the dinghy – he had to get himself secured first, otherwise any attempt was hopeless.

He reached the upturned boat and clung on to the side of it, his hands being torn by a coating of ancient barnacles, blood streaming down his wrists and arms. He tried to clamber up, but it was impossible. He decided to save the little energy he had by remaining still.

'Craven! CRAVEN!'

His head turned from side to side, he kicked himself up, but he couldn't see anything but the water, the murderous water. He felt enraged, impotent. He *wouldn't* panic, he wouldn't lose it – he would stay calm, in control.

'Craven! Over here!'

As he searched, he realised that he was being sucked towards land, every wave taking him and the dinghy nearer to being wrecked. It was impossible to avoid it, but it also offered him his best chance. He would use the dinghy as a buffer when it hit the rocks, and then attempt to clamber up them. Perhaps Craven was being brought towards land as well, and hadn't been taken down. Perhaps.

With a sharp crack, the dinghy met its end. Armstrong felt his legs being swept upwards, bending his spine the wrong way, forcing him to release his grip before his back snapped. Another wave flung him forwards, and with a terrific jolt he felt his knees crunch on to the hardness of the rocks. Instinctively he reached in front of him, his arms flailing to get hold of something, no matter how sharp, how vicious. It was his right hand that was successful, gripping the point of a rock. He held tightly to it as another wave surged onwards, scraping his chest roughly against more rocks and, by now, shreds of dinghy. He wanted to yell out in pain, but his head kept submerging, and he needed his moments above water solely for oxygen.

His left hand grabbed some rock too, and he pulled, yanked

himself upwards, feeling his muscles almost tear themselves with the effort. His feet were touching something, and so he attempted a step, which was only half successful as a mass of water punched him over. Another step, this one more effective, and he simultaneously moved his hands up another few feet, both of them finding new holds.

Armstrong noticed the rocks were not that steep, just arranged haphazardly. He scrambled up them in a furious burst, feeling the anger of the sea behind him, the killer annoyed that it had failed to claim another victim. With a few more steps and scrabbles, he found a patch that was flat and relatively smooth, somewhere he could sit and look for Craven. He hauled himself up, and then sat, breathless, bleeding.

He stared down at the grey-blue foaming water beneath him. There was no Craven, just the battered, splintered dinghy. He looked further out, and saw what looked like a body. He screwed up his eyes, and realised that it was an oar. His gaze darted to and fro, settling on patches of darkness, scraps of seaweed, driftwood, all of which played tricks on him, all metamorphosing into Craven.

But there was no Craven. As Armstrong's breath subsided, he knew that it had been too long. Craven had gone, been taken from him not by the sea, but by that bastard Mosley, by the fucking Leader. He was too exhausted to weep, but the tears would come later. He had known so much death, far too much. Only very occasionally had death come at the right time, and this was certainly a wrong time, as wrong as every bloody time when one of his comrades had been killed.

And the forms death took . . . In his lifetime, it had liked being bullets and bombs best, but sometimes it was more insidious and liked to come as a creeping gas, or the sharp end of a twisting bayonet. Drowning was common enough too, not only in the trenches but in shell holes. But the sea was a new one for Armstrong; he had never seen death come as a wave. There was one other way he had seen it come, but for now he was only going to permit himself to mourn Craven, because that seemed fair, felt proper, felt *correct* for heaven's sake.

For the next two hours Armstrong walked in a stupor. He knew he had to head north, along the coastline, because that was the direction for Logan House. God knew where it was exactly, but as the southern point of Galloway was not much more than two or three miles across, he knew he would stumble across a clue at some point – a road sign, an estate wall, something, anything.

He stopped at a cove for a while, mesmerised by the immensity of a ship's boiler that had been washed up. It must have been twice his height and forty feet long. Watched by some sheep, he sat next to it, among the salt-stained beer bottles and drums of engine oil, trying to imagine what had happened to the ship that once held this giant metal cylinder. Had those on board been luckier than Craven? Or had they too been thrown below, never to resurface, except as dead men?

He didn't know how long he had paused there, because his watch was broken – smashed against the rocks. He guessed that it was late morning, and he felt faint and sick. He needed food, but he had none left. He debated whether he should risk knocking on the door of the next farmhouse he came across. Could Mosley's reach have extended even here? Surely there were some parts of the country that were untroubled by the secret police. It seemed incredible to imagine that there might be informers around, but he knew that word would travel quickly round here. The farmer whom he asked for food might be well-intentioned, but he would doubtless tell someone about this bedraggled, well-spoken Englishman who had stopped by for some bread. No, Armstrong resolved, he would have to keep going until he was about to collapse. There were plenty of streams, and he could drink from them. The hunger was unimportant – food would have to be regarded as a luxury, something that he would get at Richard's.

An hour later he was looking down at a row of cottages that lined a sandy bay. A few boats were moored near a small lighthouse. On the other side of the bay he could see some woodland, which he suspected might contain Logan House. He remembered Richard had been very proud of his garden, and had planted thousands of trees to act as windbreaks for his more fragile botanical specimens. So far this was the only woodland he had seen. It had to be worth exploring.

It took little more than twenty minutes to circumnavigate the village, a process that saw him stumble into a brook, once more soaking himself through. The woodland was surrounded by a stout fence – another good sign – which Armstrong climbed over with difficulty, his energy so low that every subsequent step was an ordeal. He stumbled and lurched forward, and soon found himself slithering down a slope and landing in the middle of a well-tended path.

He tried standing up, but he couldn't. This wasn't an attack, this was pure exhaustion. His body demanded sleep, insisting that he lay where he was. Armstrong fought hard, but he knew that this time he would have to surrender to his body. He had punished it ruthlessly, exerting it more than a man half his age would be capable of.

As he drifted off, he didn't notice the two young women in colourful bathing costumes rounding a bend in the path. They stopped, and then approached him cautiously, bending over his wet and bloodied body, exchanging confused, slightly frightened glances.

'Quick!' one of them said. 'Go and get Father! Tell him to bring a wheelbarrow or something!'

Perhaps Armstrong heard that, because the woman who stayed behind to cover him with their towels thought she detected a slight smile on the man's face.

* * *

Abram Aronovich Slutsky sits very still at his desk in the headquarters of the NKVD in Lubyanka Square in Moscow. As head of the INO, the Inostrannyi Otdel – the foreign intelligence department of the NKVD – Slutsky has a lot to think about. His superior and chairman of the NKVD, Nikolai Ivanovich Yezhov, has just had a meeting at the Kremlin with Stalin, who says that he wants to see the fascist regime in Britain torn down. Yezhov has told Slutsky that it is up to him, as head of the INO, to do it. In turn, Slutsky knows that it is Otto who will really have to make it happen.

Slutsky is a great believer in Otto, and knows him to be brilliant. Certainly, Otto is an eccentric, but then many brilliant men are. As a young man, Otto was a disciple of Wilhelm Reich, a German Communist and sexologist based in Vienna, and even published Reich's writings on the quest for the better orgasm and his views on Freud and Marx. The Party is aware that Otto has a healthy appetite for the joys of the flesh, but the Lubyanka knows that it needs its complement of men with unusual qualities.

Otto has been a great recruiter, Slutsky thinks as he gets up and walks slowly to the two small windows of his third-floor office. He looks out on to the square, gazing at the statue of

Feliks Dzerzhinsky, the founder of this great organisation. Otto has had a lot of success with men at Cambridge University, although he has recruited many more from outside that privileged institution. One of the most successful has been the man Moscow now calls Top Hat, a name chosen by Otto for no explicable reason. It is on the shoulders of Top Hat that the burden will fall, because he is the man best placed, the most high up.

There is a soft knocking on the door.

'Yes?' says Slutsky.

The door opens. It is Natalya, his assistant.

'A package from Denmark, Comrade Slutsky,' says Natalya.

Denmark. Denmark is the route Otto uses to send information back to Moscow. Slutsky likes packages from Denmark, because they are normally full of good news. Slutsky nods, whereupon Natalya deposits the parcel on his desk.

'Thank you, Comrade,' says Slutsky.

Slutsky waits for Natalya to leave the room, and then carefully opens the parcel. It is a game of some sort, a board game. What is this? *Monopoly*. He opens the box's lid, and finds a note written in Otto's large, looping hand.

Comrade, allow me to introduce you to Dog.

Perhaps Otto is a little more than eccentric; perhaps he is in some way cracked. However, after Slutsky has perused the contents of the box for little more than five minutes, he knows that Otto is even more brilliant than he could possibly have hoped. The Comrade Chairman will be very pleased with this, but in the meantime, Slutsky is going to keep Dog to himself.

Chapter Four

He Do the Police

ARMSTRONG AWOKE WITH a start. It was around four in the afternoon, and he had been asleep on a large faded sofa in the conservatory at Logan House. He had not slept well. Even two days on, the image of the boat capsizing kept playing through his mind, along with the look of horror on Craven's face as they were thrown into the water. The helplessness he had felt was stirred up in his dreams, transformed into guilt, a guilt he couldn't help feeling despite the fact he knew that Craven's death hadn't been his fault.

'James?'

He turned round to see the tall figure of Richard, accompanied by Molly, a grey-muzzled black Labrador, standing in the doorway to the garden.

'You all right, old chap? You were making a frightful din.'

Armstrong rubbed his eyes and looked at his new watch, a present from Richard.

'Sorry – I was . . . dreaming.'

Molly came over and licked his hand. The tenderness of the bitch's gesture put a slight smile on Armstrong's face.

'D'you need anything? Something to drink? A tablet?'

Armstrong shook his head.

'No thanks, Dick, I think I'll be okay. Perhaps a walk. Yes – a walk. Clear my head.'

'Now that's an excellent idea! I can bore you at great length all about my plants.'

Armstrong got up slowly and walked over to the door. He was limping slightly, and every limb felt stiff.

'Want a stick?' Richard asked.

Armstrong glowered back.

'What, to hit you with?' he replied.

For the next couple of hours the two men walked slowly around Richard's gardens. They were indeed impressive, featuring plants from all over the world, including South Africa, India, New Zealand, even Chile. Richard told Armstrong that the gardens had been started by his great-grandmother seventy years ago, and he felt it his duty to look after them. His wife Pamela was also a keen gardener, and he joked that he wouldn't have married her if she hadn't had green fingers. Sadly, their two daughters, Emma and Daphne, seemed to have little if any interest in things horticultural, and he feared that unless one of them married a gardener, then the gardens were surely doomed.

At the estate's highest point, Armstrong found they were strolling down a walkway flanked by trees whose foliage consisted of curving bristles with thick green points.

'Monkey puzzle trees?' Armstrong guessed.

'Correct! How did you know? I thought you were a duffer at this.'

'Mary liked them. She thought the branches looked like pipe cleaners.'

For a moment Richard felt awkward. His friend had been a widower for six years, and whenever Mary's name had come up he hadn't known what to say. He leaned down and scratched Molly's head.

'Er, you know, James, I'm still very sorry about Mary. Dreadful business that. Don't know how you cope.'

'Well, it was she who gave me the strength to cope in the first place,' said Armstrong. 'It was ironic really, as though she was preparing me for her own death. Not that she was, of course.'

'A fine woman, Mary. One of the best.'

'Thanks, Dick.'

They walked in silence for a few more yards.

'Christ!' Richard exclaimed, stopping in his tracks. 'Nearly forgot to ask! How's young Philip? Have you had any news since you were locked up?'

'He's with Mary's mother. They're staying—'

Armstrong checked himself. He knew he could trust Richard, or at least he was pretty certain he could, but surely there was no need for him to know?

'What's that, old boy?' asked Richard.

'I'm sorry, Dick,' said Armstrong, 'but I've decided not to tell anybody where he is. I'm sure you understand.'

Richard turned to him. Armstrong braced himself for an indignant comment as his old friend looked him in the eye.

'This is what it's come to, hasn't it?' said Richard.

Armstrong nodded.

'We can't trust each other any more, can we?'

'It's not that, Dick . . .'

Richard held up his hand.

'No need to say it,' he continued. 'If you can't keep your own secrets, then how can you expect me to keep them for you?'

'Thanks, Dick.'

'It's not just us, though, is it? It's the whole bloody country! It's happening even up here, even in little Drummore of all places.'

'What happened there?'

Richard breathed out.

'Well, we had a teacher – a Mrs Norris – at the school in the village. Nice lady she was, had lived and worked here for twenty years, give or take. She was a widow with no children of her own – her husband had died in the war – and the school and the children were her life. Well, one day she decides to teach a class of eleven-year-olds about the difference between fascism and democracy. She tells them – and this is only what I've heard, I can't promise it's deadly accurate – that "democracy is a form of government controlled by Parliament and the majority of the people and fascism is a form of government controlled by one man's will". She left the children in no doubt as to which system was preferable.'

'Good for her,' said Armstrong, although he was aware that Mrs Norris was being referred to in the past tense. 'So what happened?'

'Well, one of her charges was a girl called Iona Keith, whose father, Donald Keith, only happens to be a leading member of the Party up here. He lives a couple of miles up the road, makes his living repairing tractors and what have you. Anyway, take it from me, he's a really nasty piece of work. So, young Iona gets back home that afternoon and tells her parents what she's been learning in school, and, well, you can imagine what happens next.'

'I think I can.'

'At ten o'clock the next morning, two policemen arrest Mrs Norris in front of her class for "unpatriotic activities". She's taken to Stranraer Police Station, where she's held and questioned all day. Eventually she's released on bail, but told by the school that she cannot go back to her job until she's been cleared.'

'This is—'

'Wait a second. Two days later her body washes up over at Terally Point. They find a note in her cottage, on the kitchen table, saying that if she cannot teach any more, then she might as well not live.'

'Jesus Christ,' said Armstrong softly.

'Quite,' said Richard. 'The place is in an uproar about it. A few nights ago Donald Keith's workshop burned to the ground, so of course the whole village is under suspicion. We've had police and Blackshirts all over the place, and we've been told that if the offenders don't give themselves up they'll impound all the boats in the harbour, which would be a disaster for the fishermen. So now the fishermen are going around telling those who they think are guilty to hand themselves in or they'll get what's coming to them.'

'Divide and rule,' said Armstrong.

'Quite,' said Richard again. 'All because poor Mrs Norris wanted to do what she thought was right.'

Armstrong looked down the line of monkey puzzle trees. In the distance he could see the blueness of Luce Bay. His mind slipped back to a time before Mosley, before the crisis, back to a time of innocence. Alec, Craven, Mrs Norris – three people who would still be alive if the Blackshirts had never come to power. They were gangsters, thought Armstrong, nothing more than criminals in uniforms, mere costumes that gave them a veneer of military order and respectability.

Molly started nuzzling Armstrong's thigh, as if she was trying to coax him out of his reverie.

'Stop it, Molly!' Richard snapped. 'You greedy animal!'

Armstrong gave the bitch a pat and a rub.

'I think she deserves an early supper, Dick.'

Armstrong had a look in his eyes that meant Richard couldn't refuse. It wasn't a particularly pleading look, he thought, not even a very sad one. But it was distant, as though Armstrong had seen a ghost with whom he'd made an appointment. For you, dear, said Pamela later, that's really rather good.

Armstrong left at eight o'clock the next morning. Richard had given him the use of the girls' car – a two-seater Austin 7. Armstrong had refused at first, saying that he could take the train, but he knew that the modest little car would afford him more anonymity. He would drive the 130 miles or so to Carlisle, and from there take an express train south to London, where he intended to get in touch with Craven's wife. It would take too long to drive all the way; he just didn't have the time.

It was a beautiful morning. Ten minutes after leaving Logan House, he was driving along beside the still waters of Luce Bay, the brightness of the early sun reflecting off its surface. He drove through small villages, sensing faces watching from upstairs windows. He was glad that the car was modest – he could imagine what the reaction would have been had he been in his 'Light Twenty'. Because of its size, the Austin made for a pretty uncomfortable ride on the rough roads, but this was only a small discomfort.

He drove through the village of Sandhead, after which he took a right turn that brought him round the top of the bay. In another ten minutes he would be on the main road that would take him to Newton Stewart, Dumfries and then on to Carlisle. He estimated he would get there by mid-afternoon. If his luck was in, he might even be able to catch a sleeper, paid for out of the money sewn into his jacket. He also had an additional very healthy £50 given to him by Dick. What was even more potentially useful was the contents of his left jacket pocket – Richard's old service revolver, a Smith & Wesson, complete with six rounds of ammunition.

Had Armstrong left Logan House half an hour later, he would have changed his plans completely. Had the police phoned only ten minutes after he had left, Richard reckoned he would have been able to use his powerful Humber to catch up with him. As it was, they phoned just before half past eight. A body had been washed up at Drumbreddan Bay, they said, the body of an internee who had escaped from the Isle of Man. It was thought that the dead man had had an accomplice, and that if he too wasn't dead he would be on the loose. Had Captain Collyer or any of his workers seen any suspicious figures? Not at all, Superintendent, Richard lied with much aplomb. What does this fellow look like, what name does he answer to? The policeman said that he wasn't at liberty to divulge his name, but he could help with the former, which he proceeded to do, supplying Richard with an exact description of his friend. If you see him, he added, phone PC Stewart at Drummore first, and then ring us immediately up at Stranraer. Before he put the phone down, the policeman assured Richard that his family would be perfectly safe, as the escaper would doubtless be caught at one of the many roadblocks they had set up. Pamela noticed Richard's face visibly draining of its usual hearty colour as he clumsily replaced the receiver.

He was driving through heavy woodland now. According to the map, he would reach the main road in less than five minutes, come on to it just after a village called Whitecrook. This was an idyllic part of the country, he thought – he would come up here again, when all this was over. He would come back and remember Craven, he resolved, build a memorial to him.

Armstrong approached a T-junction, and slowed down gradually. This was the main road, the road that would see him through to Carlisle. He had many more hurdles to cross, but the fact that he had made it this far made him feel good, that he had achieved something.

As soon as he saw it, he swore out loud.

'Shit.'

A large police Wolseley and two Triumph motorcycles were straddling both carriageways, and there must have been at least half a dozen policemen on duty. Parked on the verge on the left was an unmarked black Vauxhall, the car that Armstrong knew to be favoured by the secret police. He thought he could make out the shadowy forms of two figures seated inside.

He was about a hundred yards away, and there was no chance of turning round – it would look too suspicious. Besides, those cars were far too powerful for the Austin 7 to be able to outrun them, not to mention the motorcycles. His car could only manage forty – perhaps fifty – miles per hour; they would catch up within two minutes. He would just have to act the innocent, bluff his way through. He knew that the roadblock was here because of him – they would have guessed that he and Craven might have made their way to this part of the mainland, and no doubt there would be similar obstacles placed around Ulster and the Lake District.

Armstrong slowed gradually, changing down through the gears smoothly. They would also have a description of him, and presumably a photograph. His English accent too would give him away. He automatically gripped the steering wheel tightly, his heart starting to race. He had come all this way, had lost Craven, and now he was driving helplessly straight into the enemy's arms. Now was not the time for a seizure, he told himself, stay calm, stay in control. Remember, you have the revolver, and with it the element of surprise.

He felt for the gun in his pocket. He still had some qualms about shooting a policeman, but if that policeman stood between Armstrong and freedom, then he would not hesitate. Although he knew that the police were merely lackeys, carrying out their orders, and that it was the secret police who were the out-and-out fascists, he still had to be ruthless.

However, there was not a chance of his killing all of them, as the occupants of the Vauxhall would certainly be armed. It was hopeless. And if he was caught, what would they do to him? Execute him as they had done Alec? It was unlikely that he would simply be sent back to Peel with a slap on the wrist. And if he killed a policeman too – well then, that would certainly mean the gallows, as it had done even before the days of the Leader.

One of the policemen signalled for Armstrong to stop and wind down his window. He did as he was told, but kept the car in gear, his left foot pressed down lightly on the clutch pedal.

'Good morning, sir,' said the constable, his Scottish accent broad.

'Good morning,' Armstrong replied, doing his best to appear calm. But his gut was churning, a feeling reminiscent of that terrible period before going over the top of the trenches. He feared an attack, dreaded seeing that explosion again, but so far it hadn't come.

'Can I see your identity papers, please, sir?'

Armstrong made a great play of searching for them.

'Sorry, officer,' he said, politely apologetic, 'but I must have left them behind.'

The constable sighed. No doubt he was used to such forget-fulness.

'And where is that?'

'Sorry?'

'Where have you left your papers? Where are you staying?'

'Oh, right – I see. Sorry. I'm staying at Damnaglaur House near Drummore.'

This was a punt. Armstrong had seen Damnaglaur House on a map at Richard's – it was the first name that came into his head.

'Aah! So how is old Mrs Collins?'

Armstrong couldn't help but pause slightly before replying. In for a penny, he thought.

'She's . . . she's very well. Much better, in fact.'

The constable smiled.

'I'm very glad to hear it. The poor wee dear's had a tough time.'

'Oh yes,' was all Armstrong could think of. 'Very tough, very tough indeed.'

'And what's your connection with Mrs Collins, Mr . . . ?'

'Mr Standing, David Standing. I'm her son-in-law.'

'Really? And where do you live, Mr Standing?'

'In the Lakes – near Keswick.'

The constable raised his eyebrows.

'Long drive, sir,' he said, to which Armstrong merely shrugged.

'Could you turn off your engine, please, sir?'

'Why? Is there a problem?'

'No, sir. Could you turn it off, please?'

Armstrong put the car into neutral and turned it off. For a moment it felt quiet and still, eerily still. He could feel several pairs of eyes scrutinising him as he pulled up the handbrake. He watched his interrogator walk over to the Vauxhall and start talking to the figure in the driving seat. Armstrong looked to his right, down the length of the bay, all the time aware of the Smith & Wesson in his pocket. It felt reassuring, but if they found it, its presence might do him more harm than good.

He glanced casually back to the Vauxhall. The driver was staring at him, and then referred to something on his lap – a photograph no doubt. The other occupant spoke excitedly, and then the doors opened. This was it. This was the moment of his arrest. As the two men got out, Armstrong noticed they were both wearing thick black double-breasted suits – far too hot for an August morning, he thought. He clutched the gun in his pocket. He had killed before; this time would be no different.

The driver of the Vauxhall leaned in through the open window. The other man stood in front of the car, smiling at him through the windscreen.

'Captain Armstrong?' said a voice in his right ear.

Armstrong ignored it.

'Captain James Armstrong?'

The voice was English – Armstrong guessed Yorkshire. Once more he ignored it, putting the finishing touches to his plan. It depended on the secret policemen having left the keys in the Vauxhall's ignition. If they had then he would be free – for the time being at least.

'Come on, Armstrong, the game's over. Time to go back to your holiday camp.'

Armstrong took a deep breath, steeling himself. He was all right, he thought, he could do this, he felt clear-headed.

*

The subsequent events took place within less than a minute. They started with Armstrong gently opening the door and then pushing at it hard with his right shoulder, knocking the secret policeman over. As he leaped out of the car, he produced the Smith & Wesson from his pocket, cocked it, and then fired a round into the man's heart, killing him instantly. So far the other secret policeman had not moved. What caused him to was the impact of a bullet in his chest, which punched him to the ground. He started screaming, and Armstrong thought about shooting him again, but his intention was escape, not slaughter.

By now, the six policemen had taken cover behind the Wolseley and the motorcycles. Thank God, thought Armstrong, thank God they were not armed. He ran to the Vauxhall and found that the keys were indeed in the ignition. He started it up, gunning the large engine, and then began to move off along the verge, gently manoeuvring the car back on to the road. Out of his right eye he could see a policeman running towards him, his truncheon raised high. Brave man, thought Armstrong, before shooting the constable in the leg. He could have gone for the chest, where it was far easier to ensure a hit, but he still couldn't let himself kill an ordinary member of the police. The man's screams joined those of the secret policeman, who was yelling as loudly as men had done in the trenches.

For a few moments the sound made Armstrong freeze. He could feel himself start to lose control, thinking of those poor bastards at La Quinque Rue, at Festubert, at Aubers Ridge. He wasn't on a road in Scotland in the middle of August, but back near Neuve Chapelle. Some of his Gurkhas had been killed by the gas which had just been released by the 3rd London

Regiment. A change of wind direction had blown it back towards their lines. The men had screamed like that, yelled as they drowned in the open air, gargling with blood and mucus. The sound had horrified him then, and it horrified him now.

But he had gone on to win the high ground that day, had led the only company that had got through. Whatever he had had in the September of 1915, he had to find it again. He had to move, otherwise he was dead. Come on, man, get going, get going.

The car edged forward and was now fully on the road. His presence of mind was returning, flooding back. He paused near the Wolseley and once more took aim with the revolver. The policemen hiding behind the car moved back, utter fear in their eyes, but Armstrong was not interested in them. Instead he shot out one of the rear tyres, causing the car to jolt violently down. He had two bullets left – one for each motorcycle. Each of their engines received a round – ammunition well spent. In a perfect world, the Austin could have taken a slug too, but he knew the police wouldn't waste their time trying to chase him in it.

Armstrong tossed the revolver on to the passenger seat, oblivious to how the heat from the muzzle was scorching the leather, and then accelerated sharply away. It was Mosley who had killed those men, he thought. They wouldn't be lying there bleeding if he hadn't come to power. And the King, Armstrong also blamed the silly little King, so desperate to keep his bloody throne.

* * *

A career policeman, and a clandestine member of the BUF since its inception in October 1932, Sir Roger Ousby was the natural choice to head His Majesty's Secret State Police. Six foot three, slim, and with a thin, sallow face, Ousby's physical presence was offset by his quiet nature. It was often said of him that he could enter a room unnoticed, and would remain silent until he deemed it absolutely necessary to speak. When he did so, people listened, because he spoke so softly that they had to strain their ears to hear him. His voice was hypnotic and carried with it an air of threatened menace that made listeners shudder slightly, as if they had heard fingernails on a blackboard. It was unsurprising, then, that Ousby had few – if any – friends. He had a wife called Peggy whom he was said to adore, but the only evidence of her existence was a slightly dog-eared snapshot kept in a cheap frame on his desk.

The telegram arrived at his office at around ten o'clock in the morning. It was from the police station at Stranraer and marked for his eyes only.

HMSSP AGENTS OGDEN AND MACKENZIE SHOT DEAD AT ROADBLOCK OUTSIDE STRANRAER AT APPROX 9.15 THIS MORNING STOP SUSPECT PRESUMED TO BE CAPTAIN JAMES ARMSTRONG STOP SEEN HEADING EAST IN AGENTS VAUXHALL ON MAIN ROAD TO NEWTON STEWART STOP ONE POLICEMAN WOUNDED ENDS

At first, Ousby could not believe his eyes. He read the telegram again and then put it down, exhaling gently. It was inconceivable – Captain Armstrong, Conservative chief whip, privy councillor, a war hero even, had killed two of his men. The bastard. The sodding murdering bastard.

Sir Roger picked up one of the two phones on his desk – the red one. The line was connected to the switchboard at

Downing Street, from where a female telephonist's precise voice was saying, 'Leader's office.'

'Sir Roger Ousby here – I need to speak to the Leader immediately.'

'Certainly, Sir Roger. Would you wait, please?'

Before he could answer, the line went dead. All switchboard operators were like that, Sir Roger thought, no matter how important you were. After a minute's wait, however, he was rewarded by the unmistakably patrician voice of the Leader.

'Hello, Sir Roger. How can I help?'

'It's Armstrong, sir.'

'Yes?'

Mosley drew the word out, his tone patiently inquisitive. Sir Roger imagined him sitting back in his chair.

'He's killed two of my men. This morning, up in Scotland, near Stranraer.'

The line went silent. For a moment Sir Roger thought he had been cut off.

'Carry on, Sir Roger.'

'It was at a roadblock. Apparently he stole the agents' car and drove east towards Newton Stewart.'

Another silence.

'You'll have to forgive me, Sir Roger, I'm afraid my knowledge of Scottish geography is a little, ah, sketchy. Where exactly are we talking about?'

Mosley's voice was still calmly measured, but a hint of menace was creeping in.

'The far south-west of Scotland, sir, one of the areas we suspected he would have made for from the Isle of Man.'

'And Craven?'

'His body was found this morning, sir, washed up on a beach round there.'

'Well at least there's *some* good news. Nice to have one fewer Communist around!'

'Yes, sir.'

'Sir Roger?'

'Yes, sir?'

Sir Roger expected the phone to explode in his ear, but the Leader's voice remained calm, though it was a strained calm.

'Fucking find him. Is that understood?'

'Yes . . . yes, sir.'

'And when you fucking find him, which you bloody well shall, I want you to keep him alive. Is that also understood?'

'Yes, sir.'

'I want a trial. Do you see? I want a great big trial that'll show them what happens if they try to escape. And then he's going to hang.'

'Yes, sir,' said Sir Roger, and the line went dead in his ear.

As soon as the Leader had slammed the phone down, he immediately picked it up again. A secretary in the outer office answered.

'Hello, Rebecca my dear,' he drawled. 'Would you get me the Home Secretary on the line?'

'Yes, my Leader.'

'And then tell the editors of *The Blackshirt* and *Action* to get round here immediately. Oh yes, and the Minister for Information, get him along.'

'Yes, my Leader.'

Just before he put the phone down, something occurred to him.

'Rebecca?'

'My Leader?'

'You're not . . . *Jewish*, are you, Rebecca?'

'Er . . . no, sir.'
'I'm so glad,' he replied, and hung up.

By midday, the editors of *The Blackshirt* and *Action* were under no doubt as to what would fill their newspapers tomorrow morning. The face of the 'foul murderer' would take up most of the front page, the Leader told them, and they would devote a large part of their issues to the story of how Captain James Armstrong had slaughtered two upstanding members of the police force. The victims were most certainly *not* agents of the HMSSP. A reward of £5,000 would be offered to whoever supplied the information that led to Armstrong's arrest. In addition, the SBC would broadcast a newsflash at one o'clock today, furnishing the public with a full description of Armstrong. The text of the newsflash would be repeated on the hour, every hour, along with the latest developments. This would be the country's biggest ever manhunt, Mosley told them, and the nation would pull together in its search for the MP-turned-assassin.

* * *

It took them an hour to make the petrol bombs. They made sixteen in all, enough to ensure that the police station would burn all night. The bottles were an assortment reflecting their respective tastes in drink – Tizer, Guinness, lemon barley water, Lucozade. They filled each bottle up with petrol, and then tightly twisted an oily scrap of old sheet into the neck.

'I don't think we'll be getting our pennies back with this lot,' said Danny.

The joke caused the other three members of the group to laugh, breaking the nervous silence.

'My father would kill me,' said Benny. 'Just think! Over half a crown down the drain!'

'Or rather up in smoke,' said David, raising another laugh.

The remaining member of the group was the most nervous of the lot – this was to be her first 'outing'. It had taken her three weeks to get this far, three weeks of persuading the Freedom Council's leaders that she was as capable as any man. Eventually they had relented, telling her that as Alan had done so much for the cause, it was only fitting that his girlfriend should be allowed to join. She had bristled at this, saying that she wanted to join up in her own right, that the fight was as personal for her as it was for any of them. Besides, she said, not all of them had fathers and boyfriends who were imprisoned. Point taken, they told her, but all their fellow Jews were suffering, she mustn't think she was anything special. She would need to prove herself as well as any male member of the Council. Just give me a chance, she said.

They had come for Alan just under a month ago. They had been making love in Alan's bedsit one Sunday morning when they heard the quick and heavy footfalls on the stairs. Before they had time to react, the door had been kicked open and three secret policemen had splintered in, all brandishing revolvers. She had screamed, and even now, as she recalled those few moments, she was ashamed that she had done so. Alan had been snatched off the top of her, leaving her naked white form quivering in front of them.

'What shall we do with this Jewish bitch?' one of them had asked.

'Leave her,' their leader had replied. 'We were told just to bring him. Anyway, she looks like just another Yid whore.'

'Well, we know we've got a Jewboy all right,' said the third policeman. 'Look at his cock!'

The three men laughed at Alan's rapidly wilting penis.

'Not too much foreskin there!'

'Where did you leave it then? Inside this bitch's cunt?'

They had laughed at that, laughed long and loud. Alan had redoubled his struggle, which had earned him a savage punch in his groin.

'There! Perhaps it'll grow back now!'

Lucy remembered that Alan was in so much pain that his scream had just come out as a strangled croak.

'Keep struggling and we'll have a rummage for your foreskin around your whore!'

'Now *there's* an idea – she looks well worth a rummage!'

'No!' barked their leader. 'No time for it! Anyway, you know Party members aren't allowed to play with Israelites.'

They had left after that, dragging Alan's crumpled and naked form down the stairs. She had screamed again, but even as she did so, Lucy knew that she had to get her revenge, that she was not going to let them win.

They finished assembling their arsenal just after midnight. Each of them would carry four bombs, stowed in the baskets of their bicycles. It felt so amateur, Lucy thought, but she kept her mouth shut. Bicycles were the Council's favoured means of transport. Not only could a bicycle outrun a policeman giving chase on foot, but it could also go where a police car could not. Many of the alleyways in the maze that was the East End were far too narrow for the police Wolseleys and Vauxhalls to negotiate.

They pedalled out of the lock-up ten minutes later, taking a carefully planned route of side streets to get to the target. All of them had made the journey at least half a dozen times, although never during the curfew. They had also ensured that the bottles were tightly packed, wrapped in cloth to stop them from chinking together as they rattled over the cobbles.

Lucy felt both exhilarated and terrified as she rode, her head buzzing with nervous energy. At last she was doing something for Dad, for Alan, for all of them. The occasional light came on in a house as they cycled past, but for the most part the streets were quiet. At times, with the absence of any form of lighting, they had to slow down to walking pace to negotiate the heaps of rotting fruit, splintered wooden packing crates, piles of hay mixed with manure, and all the other detritus that could be found on the reeking streets.

These were the streets the Leader had promised to tear down, to clear away. But here they were still, a testament to yet another broken promise, another lever he had pulled to enable him to get into power. Mosley needed the opposition that lay within these streets, was Machiavellian enough to know that to stay in power one needed an enemy. And the Jews, the filthy, slum-loving Jews, the parasites that crawled out of these stinking gutters, were his perfect enemy. Well, thought Lucy, they were going to clear the slums of one thing tonight, and that was one of Mosley's police stations. In the Council's eyes, the police were no better than the Blackshirts themselves, because they were enforcing Blackshirt laws, and as far as Lucy could tell, agreed with those laws. Policemen – and there was no discussion about this – were a legitimate target.

They were now only two minutes away. David, who led the group, came to a gentle halt underneath a dripping railway arch.

'Matches,' he whispered.

They all checked their pockets and nodded back.

'You all know your positions?'

Once again a collective nod. Lucy could see in David's eyes

that he was petrified, even though this was his fifth bombing mission.

'Lucy,' he whispered, 'are you sure about this?'

She glowered back at him in the darkness, her resolve now strengthened. They said that the HMSSP were raping female prisoners now, seeing it as a privilege, a reward for work well done. Lucy knew that would be her lot if she was captured, knew that the days before a noose went round her neck would consist of a non-stop procession of faceless men beating her, brutally slamming their groins into her. Rumours, only rumours some said. Lucy found that attitude at best hopeful, at worst cowardly in its willingness to pretend that bad things weren't happening.

She looked around the group one last time. They were all breathing heavily, and not just because of the cycling. She hadn't known these men – were they really *men*? They looked so young – for very long, and yet she felt closer to them than she ever had to Alan. The excitement of shared risk was a powerful thing, she thought, so powerful that she could barely control her shaking legs as they pedalled off. Within ten minutes she would know what was going to happen to her. What, she asked herself, would the Lucy from ten minutes in the future make of the Lucy of now?

They approached the brightly lit police station from the rear. A large red-brick Victorian edifice, it stood out from the slum housing that encroached on it. Its very cleanness and brightness suggested an ill-deserved moral superiority, an arrogance that would shortly be paid for. Normally this side of the building was unguarded, and tonight was no exception. They dismounted, and left their bicycles propped up in a nearby alley. The plan was to split into pairs, each pair taking one side of the building. It would be harder for them to put out two fires, David said, and the occupants would be under the impression that they were surrounded.

David beckoned Lucy to come with him. Clutching their bombs, they ran silently round to the right-hand side of the building. The lights from the station illuminated the narrow street with a yellow glow, making Lucy feel vulnerable. She could hear voices and gruff male laughter spilling out on to the street from an open window on the first floor, a window David was pointing at. In the winter they would have had no such luck, but tonight the air was warm, and the occupants were confident enough to let the night air cool them down.

They crouched down on the other side of the road, in the doorway of a vandalised grocers' shop. Although the window was smashed, Lucy could make out that the shop was called Steinberg & Son, or rather, used to be called Steinberg & Son, as it was clearly no longer a flourishing business. A Star of David had been daubed on the door, and beneath it the crudely painted words 'No more Yid fruit!' All this had happened right next to a police station, she thought – well, they had it coming for turning a blind eye.

With trembling hands, David and Lucy unwrapped their bottles and placed them gently on the ground. Lucy had thought that getting off all eight was ambitious, but David had reassured her by confidently stating that it would take the police at least two minutes to react, by which time they would already be pedalling away.

'Ready?' whispered David.

Lucy nodded back and retrieved the matches from her pocket. Her hands were shaking so hard, she could barely strike the first one, but on the third attempt it flared into life. As she brought the small flame towards the first bottle, she knew that as soon as she lit that cloth, there would be no going back – her life would be spent constantly on the run. She had wanted to follow in her father's footsteps, but as the cloth caught light, she knew that her political activity would have to be more direct and confrontational than she could possibly have imagined.

David picked up the flaming bottle and ran across the road to the police station. Lucy was mesmerised as she watched the arc of the petrol bomb's trajectory. It sailed through the air like a firework and then disappeared through the open window.

For a second, nothing.

Then came the strangely gentle whoosh of bright ignition, followed by a silence. The flames punched out the window, and in their glow she could see that David was running back towards her.

'Where's the next one?' he said urgently.

It was Lucy's job to keep them coming, but, distracted by the first bomb, she had neglected to light a second.

'Come on, come on, for fuck's sake!'

Lucy rapidly lit the second bottle, which David snatched from her. As he lobbed it through the window, she was lighting the third. By now she could hear shouts coming from the building, along with a loud scream, the sound of a man in agony. It was a horrific sound, one she wanted to blot out.

She watched as David sent the next two bottles through the window. He attempted to throw the fifth through a closed window on the first floor, but it only smashed against it in a cloud of oily flame. However, the sixth bottle successfully broke through, causing another bright whoosh. A bell started ringing within the station and the shouts were getting more intense. It would not take long for the police to emerge, she thought; surely it would only be a matter of seconds.

David took the seventh bottle.

'You do the last one!' he shouted.

Lucy paused. Could she? And then a voice from within stirred her up. Yes, you can, dammit, you bloody well can. She lit the final bottle and ran as if in a trance towards the building. With all her might, she threw the bottle towards the second window, and watched as it disappeared into the blazing room.

'Let's go!'

Lucy found herself starting to run. She stumbled over the cobbles, slipped on some effluence, but somehow managed to keep up with David. When they reached the back of the police station, they looked up the other side of the building to see Danny and Benny running towards them. It looked as if they too had been successful, for flames were licking out of a ground-floor window.

Benny was laughing. It was a hysterical laugh, a laugh that annoyed her. There was nothing funny about what they were doing. This wasn't a prank or some schoolboy lark – this was about showing the fascists that they were opposed, that they were hated. Lucy was not to know that Benny's laugh was born out of nervousness.

They heard the first whistles as they mounted their bicycles.

'Stop!' came a shout from somewhere behind them.

For one irrational moment Lucy was tempted to obey. It was the sound of authority that was tugging her back, appealing to the small part of her that revolted against what she was doing. How easy to stop and face your fate, how tempting just to do as you were told. But she had no choice, and she forced her legs to pedal harder and faster.

'Stop!' yelled another voice. 'Or we'll shoot!'

She didn't believe it until she felt a high-pitched whizzing puncturing the air above her head. What was that? It couldn't be a bullet, surely not, but then she heard the sound of a gun firing. How funny – she had heard the bullet before the shot . . . and then another whizzing, and still another. This wasn't real, this was just play-acting. Neither did it look real when David, who was cycling just ahead of her, was knocked off his bicycle by an invisible blow. She overtook him and glanced back, noticing that his face looked contorted, pained. Once again she nearly stopped, but she knew there was no point. He's dead, a voice told her, David is dead.

She didn't remember the rest of the ride. She was on automatic, her feet pedalling hard, her mind stuck on the image of David. In a way, she hoped that he *had* died, that he would be spared the inevitable torture that would ensue if he had been taken alive. She could just imagine the bastards allowing him to recover at the London Hospital before going to work on him. Presumably it wasn't so much fun torturing someone who was already in pain. No, she hoped he was dead. Her own ruthlessness surprised her, took her aback. What was doing that to her? Was it the regime, or was it something within her, something she knew to be a defence mechanism?

When the three of them arrived back at the lock-up, they hugged each other through their tears. There were a few 'if onlys', but Lucy didn't add to them and stayed silent. Her mind was crowded with those she had lost – Dad, Alan, and now David. She tried to stop herself thinking about what Alan was going through, and told herself that what she was imagining was far worse than the reality. And then another voice: Don't delude yourself, Lucy. This was the new voice, the voice that wanted David dead, the voice that also wanted Alan to have died. It was both strong and merciful, this voice, its strength lying in the cruel realisation that the only mercy to be found these days was in death. It was this voice that started speaking now.

'David knew the price. He knew that he might get himself killed. He wouldn't have thought it unfair that they'd shot him.'

'What are you saying?' asked an incredulous Benny.

'That's what you get if you throw petrol bombs into police stations.'

'Hang on!' said Danny, his voice high-pitched. 'Are you saying that we shouldn't have done it? That's what you're saying, isn't it? Come on – spit it out.'

Lucy was shaking her head.

'I'm not saying that at all, Danny.'

Danny snorted.

'Please!' said Lucy. 'Hear me out! I'm saying the very opposite. What David saw as being unfair is that we *have* to do it – that we haven't a choice. It's unfair that instead of getting on with our lives we've had to become . . . to become terrorists. That's what's unfair, Danny. It's not about a policeman shooting you for setting light to his petrol station; it's about why that situation has to exist.'

Danny and Benny stayed silent.

'I'm sorry if I sound callous,' said Lucy, 'but I promise you I'm not. David was fighting to win. It would be the easiest thing in the world for us to curl up now that he has gone, but where's the point in that? I say that we should go out tomorrow night and do another.'

The two men looked at her.

'What?' asked Benny.

'You heard me,' said Lucy.

'You're just like your father,' said Danny. 'A Craven through and through.'

Chapter Five

Washing Hands

AFTER HE HAD been driving for a couple of minutes, Armstrong realised he had left the roadmap in the Austin 7. He could remember the direct route, but he knew that would soon be blocked. He needed to find some back roads, and for those he would certainly need a map. Perhaps there was one in this car. Without lifting his foot from the accelerator, he looked round the interior of the Vauxhall. On the back seat he noticed a briefcase – he would investigate that later. Reaching down with his left hand, he opened the glove compartment and scrabbled around its contents. A tube of Rolos and a packet of Senior Service cigarettes fell out. He felt something smooth and cylindrical – a torch. After rounding a sharp bend, he once more rummaged inside and pulled out a pair of sturdy black handcuffs. Useful, but not as useful as a map. He would just have to follow his nose, and hug the coast.

He reached the outskirts of Carlisle just before lunchtime. He had successfully avoided Dumfries and Gretna, and had crossed the border into England just south of Milltown. Reckoning that there would certainly be more roadblocks, he abandoned the Vauxhall just off a wooded lane that ran down to the River Eden. He took the briefcase and handcuffs with him, although the Smith & Wesson was dispatched into the river's dark waters. Without ammunition the revolver was not only useless, but was also an unnecessary indicator of his guilt. God knew what was in the briefcase – he would break it open when he got on the train.

As he started walking briskly into the town, something was nagging him, something that his subconscious was insisting he should listen to, be aware of. And then his heart started thumping, as if he was waking from a nightmare. The Austin 7! The police would soon find out that it belonged to Richard. He felt almost sick with guilt, anger and helplessness. Fool, Armstrong, you fool! He should have carried on in the Austin instead of greedily taking the Vauxhall. What was going to happen to Richard and his family? What had already happened?

He had to call him, and call him immediately. He looked at his watch: it had just gone noon, over two and a half hours since the shooting at the roadblock. Would the police have had time to trace the owner of the Austin? Almost certainly, but that didn't mean that Richard had already been arrested.

Armstrong walked fast, and then broke into a half run. He knew that if someone spotted him it would look suspicious, but that was too bad. Half a mile ahead were some factories, and cutting through them he could see the raised railway line. He would follow the line into town, where he would surely find a phone box. He looked at his watch again – ten past twelve – and began to run even faster, the contents of the briefcase rattling and knocking against the leather interior.

He crossed the river by a small footbridge next to a pockmarked cricket pitch. He felt the eyes of a few dog-walkers boring into him, but better their gazes than those of policemen. Passing some tennis courts and a bowling green, Armstrong ran up a small road until he reached a busy street. He paused, catching his breath, his eyes desperately hunting for a bright red phone box.

The street was wide, the sandstone buildings tall and elegant. The pavements were bustling, and the passers-by scarcely gave him a look. Armstrong walked calmly, following his nose towards the centre of town. As he passed a chemist's shop, a display made his head turn, stopping him in his tracks.

Beauty products would never normally have held Armstrong's attention, but these were different. The display consisted of smart boxes of powders, lipsticks, creams and other such products whose functions Armstrong found largely mysterious. Each box bore a stylish black-and-white portrait of an attractive young woman, a face that Armstrong instantly recognised. It was that of Diana Mosley, the Leader's wife no less, and the brand was simply called 'Diana', with the legend, 'For Leading Ladies'. It was not just odious, thought Armstrong, but farcical. He had never imagined that the fascist cult of personality would make its way into the window of a high-street chemist.

But he had no time to ponder. He continued to walk briskly, and was soon rewarded with a phone box, one of the new concrete ones that people were calling 'vermilion giants'. Armstrong was surprised to find that it hadn't been painted black, but that would surely come. Just as he was about to wrench open the door, he realised that the box was occupied. Damn. Once more he looked at his watch – it was now twenty-five past. Come on, he urged the occupant, looking around to see if there were any other phone boxes. There weren't. He would have to wait.

Armstrong's luck was in. He could hear the caller saying goodbye and replacing the receiver, then the door was pushed violently open, and out stepped a man of about Armstrong's height dressed in a Blackshirt uniform. The two men's eyes met briefly, Armstrong doing his best not to look startled. The Blackshirt's eyes narrowed, causing a wave of dread to crash over Armstrong. Had he been recognised, or was the man only staring back because Armstrong was staring at him?

'Afternoon.' Armstrong nodded, and then pulled on the phone box's heavy door.

'Afternoon,' the Blackshirt replied, flicking his right forearm in the air in a fascist half-salute.

Armstrong returned the salute, but decided to go one better.

'The Leader,' he said, wondering whether he wasn't over-egging it.

The Blackshirt smiled, evidently believing he had met a fellow traveller.

'The Leader indeed,' he beamed back, and then turned on his heel with military briskness.

Armstrong stepped into the phone box and exhaled. He looked hard at himself in the small mirror, chastising himself for being so uneasy, so on edge. He had to be tough, had to listen to the inner voice that insisted he remain in control. It was the same voice that had carried him through the war, the same voice that had joined forces with Mary to help him recuperate.

He carefully placed the briefcase on the floor and turned to the phone. He lifted the receiver and pressed the button marked 'A'. After a few seconds a crisp female voice came on the line.

'Operator.'

'Hello, I'd like to place a call through to Port Logan 231.'

'Port Logan 231?'

'Please.'

'One moment.'

The line went dead and stayed that way for at least half a minute. For Armstrong it was an age.

'Caller?'

'Yes?'

'That'll be sixpence for the first minute.'

Armstrong rooted through some change in his pocket and inserted a sixpence into the slot.

'Hold on, please.'

After another age, he eventually heard a ringing tone. The phone was answered after about a dozen rings.

'Hello?'

The voice was Scottish, and therefore emphatically not Richard's.

'Is Captain Collyer there?' Armstrong asked.

'Who is this, please?'

'I'm an old friend of his.'

There was a hateful pause.

'I'm afraid Captain Collyer is not available right now. Who is this, please?'

'An old friend. How about his wife?'

'I cannot help you until you tell me who you are.'

Armstrong put the phone down gently, hearing one last 'Hello?' before the receiver was fully replaced. He'd heard all he needed to know. He just hoped Richard had had the wit to say the car had been stolen. He knew the Collyers would be loyal to him, because that was the type of people they were. If ever he needed another reason to succeed, then this was it. Temporarily lost in thought, Armstrong left the phone box, and started wandering down the street. He only regained his presence of mind when he saw the Blackshirt walking about twenty feet ahead of him. Here was an opportunity, thought Armstrong, an opportunity that was not to be dismissed. He found himself repeatedly flexing his free hand into a fist.

He followed the Blackshirt down the continuous thoroughfare that was Scottish Street and English Street, all the time taking in the changes that a few months of fascist rule had made. Not just the Diana Mosley beauty products, but the lightning flash rings in Carr's the jeweller, the posters of Mosley pinned up in many shop windows, the Party uniforms for sale in Howard & Sons bespoke tailors, the presence of only two newspapers – *Action* and *The Blackshirt* – in newsagents' shops. He even passed a poster advertising a Blackshirt Summer Camp, promising 'First Quality Food', an 'Ideal Site' and 'Free Transport'. The town's atmosphere felt strange – it was a typical British county town, and yet it wasn't. The architecture, the faces, the road signs, the cars – all were British through and through, and yet the atmosphere was dark, alien. *Le soleil noir.* Even the light felt black, Armstrong thought.

Armstrong's pursuit of his quarry was interrupted by the sound of rapidly approaching bells and klaxons. He turned to see a black police Wolseley and a black police van racing down the street towards him, sending pedestrians jumping out of their way. Armstrong froze, feeling his legs starting to shake. Not now, please not now. He took a series of deep breaths, attempting to steady himself as the procession came closer. The noise was unbearable, echoing inside his skull, pummelling his brain.

But the vehicles shot past, ignoring him along with every other pedestrian. As their noise receded, so did Armstrong's sense of panic. He felt his heart rate decrease, his legs become steadier. Thank God for that, he told himself, letting out a long sigh.

'I say – are you quite all right?'

Armstrong didn't hear the voice at first.

'Are you all right, young man?'

Armstrong looked down to his right to see that the voice belonged to a diminutive old woman. She must have been about seventy, and she was studying Armstrong with a kindly expression.

'You've gone terribly pale,' she said. 'You should sit down.'

Armstrong smiled weakly.

'Thank you, madam,' he said, shaking his head, 'I'm fine, just a little tired, that's all.'

'I haven't seen anybody look like that since the war.'

Armstrong looked at her quizzically.

'The . . . the war?'

'I was a nurse,' she replied with pride. 'I used to treat a lot of young men like you, for shellshock, y'know.'

Armstrong did know, but he wasn't going to let on. And then he saw the lightning flash armband on her right arm, which made him want to finish the conversation immediately. He looked up, his eyes desperately scanning for a glimpse of the Blackshirt. He *couldn't* have lost him, and if he had, it would be his own bloody fault for surrendering to an attack brought on by the mildest of triggers.

But his fear was not realised, because he spotted the Blackshirt just as he was being swallowed up by the revolving door of a hotel on the corner.

'Perhaps you're right,' he said to the old woman. 'Perhaps I should sit down. I was wondering – do you know the nearest place to eat?'

'The County Hotel does a nice lunch I'm told,' she said,

pointing to where the Blackshirt had disappeared. 'Although it's a bit expensive. Or of course there's the—'

'Thank you,' Armstrong replied. 'I'm sure it will be fine.'

He nodded his head slightly, doing his best to summon up a convincing smile. The woman, who had evidently been hoping for a longer exchange, appeared slightly peeved by Armstrong's abrupt dismissal of her. Thanking her once more, he turned and walked away. Get a grip, he told himself, sort yourself out. The Blackshirt looked tough, so if he was to carry out what he had in mind, then he would need to be tougher.

Armstrong declined the offer of a table next to a window as he soon realised that the restaurant overlooked the station, the area in front of which was swarming with policemen. He didn't fancy his chances that none of them would recognise the fugitive tucking into his lunch.

Instead, he opted for a corner table, and declining the wine list, made a show of studying the menu. He looked around the dining room, searching for his Blackshirt. His fellow diners were a mixture of commercial travellers, local grandees and businessmen, and well-heeled women of a certain age. Many of the men wore little metal lightning flash buttons in their lapels that indicated their political persuasion, a persuasion that Armstrong fancied to be the product of expediency rather than conviction. It was no doubt hard to secure a contract these days without the blessing of the Party, and it would be even more likely that the Party had its fingers in many a commercial pie. No doubt his Blackshirt, whom Armstrong had spotted laughing over a glass of whisky with a couple of rotund businessmen, was getting his entire hands covered in such pie. Keep drinking, thought Armstrong, keep drinking.

Even though he had little appetite, Armstrong knew he

should eat while he had the chance. Furthermore, it would be foolishly conspicuous not to eat something while he waited. He ordered leek and potato soup followed by roast beef, although he doubted whether he would have the chance to enjoy the second course.

The soup was lukewarm, but Armstrong barely noticed its temperature as he kept an eye on the Blackshirt. He and the businessmen were rapidly dispatching a bottle of claret, and it would surely not be much longer before the Blackshirt would have to excuse himself. Come on, man, Armstrong urged silently, you've got to go at some point.

His patience was rewarded a few minutes later. He waited for the Blackshirt to leave the room, and then summoned the waiter to ask for the whereabouts of the lavatory. Taking the briefcase with him, he walked down a softly carpeted corridor to the gents.

* * *

'Ruthless,' says Stalin, as he walks up and down his office.

'I quite agree,' Nikolai Ivanovich replies.

The head of the NKVD watches warily as Stalin grooms his large moustache, the contours of a smile forming beneath it. Ruthless. It is a word that Comrade Stalin is fond of using. Stalin continues walking, passing the death mask of Lenin.

'The Ukraine thinks, behaves and acts as though it is independent,' he says, pausing briefly to perch on the arm of a chair. 'So I want a Politburo Commission consisting of you, Molotov and Khrushchev to go there at once, along with a large force of NKVD.'

Nikolai Ivanovich nods. There is only one question that needs asking.

'How many?'

Another groom of the moustache, and then the hand turns up in the air, as if it is catching a number falling from the ceiling.

'Thirty thousand,' says Stalin. 'The local NKVD can select precisely who. If it ends up being more, then so much the better.'

Nikolai Ivanovich jots the number down.

'Some will need to be personally approved by me,' says Stalin. 'And you can tell everyone that as of next month there will be no more appeals or petitions for clemency.'

'That should make the job much . . . simpler.'

Stalin nods and then lifts himself off the chair's arm. There is a near silence for a minute or so. Nikolai Ivanovich can hear Stalin's heavy breathing through his nose.

'Now tell me about Slutsky,' says Stalin. 'Tell me about his progress in Britain. You must understand, Comrade Yezhov, that nothing is more important than ridding Britain of fascism. It will only be a matter of time before Mosley and Hitler join forces – not a day that I will allow to happen!'

Another near silence.

'Well?'

'Slutsky has been making excellent progress,' says Nikolai Ivanovich. 'Really very excellent indeed.'

'If it was not so then I would consider him a traitor.'

'Quite right, Comrade, and I would agree with you. However, we now have in position several agents who are capable of altering the fortunes of the Mosley regime. And not only that! They are also in a position to turn Britain into a Soviet state.'

Stalin raises an eyebrow.

'Who?' he asks. 'Tell me who.'

* * *

Armstrong entered the lavatory while the Blackshirt was washing his hands.

'Hello again,' said Armstrong, feigning surprise.

The Blackshirt ignored him, flicking the water off his hands.

'I said, *hello again.*'

He had the look of a thug, Armstrong thought, a typical Blackshirt thug.

'I heard you the first time,' the Blackshirt replied. 'I don't talk to fairies in toil—'

The Blackshirt was unable to finish the sentence because Armstrong's fist had connected with his stomach, winding him, bending him double. He gasped for air, clutching his front. Armstrong paused. In for a penny, he thought, and swiftly smashed his right knee into the Blackshirt's face, sending the man flying back across the floor.

For a moment the Blackshirt lay in near silence, moaning gently. Armstrong looked over at the door – this would be a bad time for someone to walk in. He rushed over and wedged the back of a wooden chair under the door handle, buying himself some peace. Now what? Kill him? He couldn't bring himself to do that, not in cold blood. Besides, this Blackshirt was not a secret policeman, just a thug who had found a cause. There were plenty of them around – there always had been. But if he let him live, the consequences could be disastrous.

The Blackshirt, blood streaming from his nose, was attempting to get up, but his movements were uncoordinated and clumsy. Armstrong grabbed him by the front of his tunic and bashed his head against the cold tiled floor. The impact knocked him out immediately. He would let the man live, but he would put him out of action for a few hours, by which time

Armstrong would be hundreds of miles south – if what he now had in mind came off.

Five minutes later, Armstrong walked out of the washroom dressed as a Blackshirt, complete with armband. His victim, still unconscious, was sitting naked on a lavatory, his wrists handcuffed together behind his back and around the pipe leading from the cistern down to the pan. A portion of Armstrong's shirt was stuffed in his mouth and his ankles were tied together with the rest of the garment. The remainder of Armstrong's clothes had been thrown on to the top of a tall cupboard, where they would remain out of sight, and hopefully undiscovered. Armstrong had locked himself and the Black-shirt into a cubicle, before climbing over the partition, picking up the briefcase and walking into the corridor, his pockets stuffed with cash and the Blackshirt's identity card.

Armstrong's pace was confident – neither too fast nor too slow. He made his way to the lobby, not looking through the large glass doors that led into the dining room. All it would require was eye contact with his waiter and his new-found cover would be blown. He passed the doors and entered the lobby, where a pair of rather overweight women were manning the reception desk and a well-groomed young man was looking nervously at his watch. A radio was quietly playing some light orchestral pieces. Armstrong was acutely aware that all three gave him a look that went beyond mere acknowledgement and entered into curiosity. He hadn't seen the young man before, but the two women he had. Would they remember his face, find it puzzling that he was now dressed as a Blackshirt? Or were they just grimacing at the uniform? He hoped for the latter and stepped out into the daylight just as the radio's music gave way to the news, the lead item of which gave a full description of the MP turned fugitive, the man who had just walked out without paying for his leek and potato soup.

The station was a mere fifty yards away, its grey Gothic appearance almost as forbidding as the sandstone citadel to Armstrong's right. He continued walking down the shallow hill towards the entrance, doing his best to ignore the fact that he could count at least a dozen policemen. Would the Blackshirt uniform be enough to stop the police from checking him over? He needed to find someone – anyone – whom he could engage in conversation in order to make himself less conspicuous.

A potential saviour came in the unlikely form of a Blackshirt who was walking ahead of him. Armstrong debated for a few seconds, and then bounded up to the man and tapped him on the shoulder. The Blackshirt turned round, an affronted look on his moustached face. He must have been a good ten years older than Armstrong, and he looked hard, as hard as the former pugilist Armstrong instantly supposed him to be.

Armstrong decided to play the fool.

'Oh, I'm so sorry – I thought you were someone else.'

For a second he expected the man to hit him, but his tough face broke into a craggy smile.

'You mean there's some other poor bugger who looks like me?' he asked, his accent broad Scots.

'Not really,' said Armstrong. 'But from behind you looked identical – please excuse me.'

'No problem at all,' the Blackshirt replied, taking in Armstrong's uniform. 'Anyway, which branch are you from?'

Branch. Armstrong said the first town that came into his head.

'High Wycombe. And you?'

'Dumfries – I'm goin' down to London for a meeting about immigration. You goin' as well?'

'I wish I was. No, I'm heading home – I've been up here to see my old mother.'

'Unwell, is she?'

By now Armstrong and the Blackshirt had resumed walking, Armstrong allowing the briefcase to swing casually in his hand.

'Well, she was, but I think she's going to be all right. The poor dear hasn't been the same since my pa died.'

'Aye, they never are.'

They were walking past the first of the policemen, who scarcely gave them a look. Armstrong did his best not to appear uneasy as they continued their conversation.

'What d'ye think all these coppers are up to?' the Blackshirt asked.

Armstrong shrugged his shoulders.

'Looking for someone I'd have thought,' he replied.

'I don't suppose it's for those bastards who escaped from the Isle o' Man the other day?'

'Well, you could be right there,' said Armstrong, willing the man to shut up.

'Let's ask,' said the Blackshirt.

Armstrong momentarily shut his eyes. Christ. This was not what he had had in mind.

'Hey youse!' shouted the Blackshirt as he and Armstrong walked towards a pair of policemen. 'What you boys up to? Them fellas from the Isle o' Man, is it?'

One of the policemen kept his eyes on the passers-by, while the other smiled and spoke.

'That's right, sir. Did you hear what happened this morning?'

'What?' asked the Blackshirt.

'One of them – Captain Armstrong it was – shot dead a couple of policemen outside Newton Stewart.'

The Blackshirt breathed out heavily. Armstrong did his best to act stunned.

'Jesus Christ,' the Blackshirt said, shaking his head. 'Dead you say?'

'That's right,' said the policeman. 'We're on the hunt for him. He won't get far, not with his face all over the papers tomorrow.'

'Jesus Christ,' said the Blackshirt again. 'The *bastard* should be hanged.'

'Oh, I'm sure he will.'

The Blackshirt walked off, Armstrong following, nodding slightly to the policeman in appreciation of his help. The policeman nodded back and turned to join his colleague.

'Did ye hear that?' asked the Blackshirt.

'I did indeed,' said Armstrong emphatically. 'I can't quite believe it.'

'If I got my hands on him, I'd . . . I'd . . .'

'I think I can guess,' said Armstrong. 'Do you need to buy a ticket as well?'

'Aye,' said the Blackshirt absent-mindedly. 'Let's do that.'

Armstrong didn't want to buy a first-class ticket, as it would have made him look suspiciously grand. Reluctantly, he knew he would have to join the Scotsman for the duration of the journey. Still, being with a Blackshirt afforded him some good cover, as the police appeared to leave them alone. They might have been looking out for him, thought Armstrong, but they seemed incapable of seeing any further than the Blackshirt uniform. The two men walked past at least half a dozen more constables, some of whom raised their arm in the fascist salute, which both Armstrong and his new friend returned with gusto. It was clear to Armstrong that since he had been interned, the Blackshirts had successfully established themselves not just as the dominant party, but also as a breed apart.

As they crossed the green and yellow iron bridge over to platform three, Armstrong discovered that his companion was called Duncan Fraser. Armstrong introduced himself as Andrew Carr, taking his name from the jeweller's shop back in town. With the train due at half past one, he had time to buy both *The Blackshirt* and *Action*, as well as a KitKat and a copy of *The Autocar* magazine.

The two men waited in what a casual observer and Fraser would have regarded as a companionable and gentlemanly silence, though for Armstrong it was anything but. At any moment a policeman could recognise him, or Fraser might trip him up on some matter of Blackshirt lore. He would have to pretend that he was a newcomer to the ranks of the Party, and he would certainly feign sleep for much of the journey. Armstrong scanned the platform, taking in the posters advertising Sunlight soap, holidays with Cook's to Baden and the Black Forest, as well as the omnipresent images of Mosley, striking heroic poses above captions that read 'Britain First!' and 'Mosley's Miles Better'.

The train drew in ten minutes late – so much for Mosley's promise to ape Mussolini and make the trains run on time. Armstrong had never seen a locomotive like it. Streamlined, with a nose like a fat bullet, it was painted in blue and silver, with two thick and two thin white lines running down its length. The front bore a fascist lightning flash, and Armstrong noticed – to well-concealed dismay – that he was about to be hauled down to London by a locomotive named *Queen Wallis*. The carriages bore the familiar maroon livery of the London Midland and Scottish railway, although on each door there was a small silver lightning flash, a device that Armstrong was beginning to realise was tirelessly ubiquitous. This was truly a fascist train, he thought, modern, absent of warmth, uncompromising.

'Quite a beast, eh?' said Fraser.

'Yes,' said Armstrong. 'As you say, quite a beast.'

'And bang on time too! Now that never happened before we came to power.'

Armstrong glanced at his watch. Was this how it worked? Was the Blackshirt self-delusion of greatness so complete that it even extended to lying about whether the trains ran on time? If I tell you that something is true, then I dare you to disagree. And if you do not disagree, then I can only assume that we are agreed, and therefore the thing is true. The only way to restore the truth, Armstrong thought, was to dare to disagree.

* * *

As the *Queen Wallis* drew into Carlisle station, the Leader was taking a phone call from Sir Roger Ousby.

'Hello, Sir Roger. What's the news?'

Once again, the Leader's voice was calm, not displaying the hectoring tone reserved for political rallies. It was a very upper-class drawl, thought Ousby, the type of voice more at home in the drawing room and the boudoir.

'We've tracked down the owner of the car Armstrong was driving.'

'Yes?'

'It belongs to a Captain Richard Collyer of Logan House.'

'And who, pray, is Captain Richard Collyer of Logan House?'

'We're establishing that at the moment, sir.'

'Where?'

'At Stranraer Police Station.'

'So who's working on him? Your people or the police?'

'Our people, sir.'

'Good. Keep it that way. Let's not be . . . too easy on this Collyer. He's bound to be some old army chum of Armstrong. Any family?'

'A wife and two daughters.'

'Lookers?'

'Er . . . I'm sorry, sir. I . . . I don't follow you.'

'Well, it's quite simple, are they good-looking?'

'Uh, I really don't know, sir.'

'All right, it doesn't matter. Anyway, if Collyer doesn't play ball, then sweat it out of the women. Let your men *enjoy* themselves, Ousby – understand?'

'Quite so, sir.'

'A sort of perk if you like.'

'Yes, sir – I am following you.'

'Good, good. And what of Armstrong?'

'No news, I'm afraid. The trail appears to have gone temporarily cold.'

'Cold, Sir Roger – I'm not so sure I like cold. Brrr!'

'We'll get him soon – every station, every road in the North-West is crawling both with my men and with the regular police. He won't get far.'

'I hope not, Sir Roger.'

The line went dead in Sir Roger's ear. He was getting used to it.

* * *

Armstrong had no need to feign sleep, for Fraser had nodded off as soon as they had sat down in their compartment. For a while, he read the papers, learning that seventy-five per cent of crime in urban areas was committed by immigrants – especially the Jews, apparently. He raised one eyebrow at the revelation that the Leader's wife had had a new rose named after her (*Rosa dianamosleyiana*) and both eyebrows when he saw that the Leader himself was shortly to visit Hitler in Germany. Armstrong also read of his own escape, finding it grimly amusing that apparently he had seriously assaulted a camp guard during his bid for freedom. Such a lie meant that the camp authorities had not discovered the tunnel, which gave Paddy and Wigan a chance. Tomorrow's newspapers would doubtless make even more entertaining reading.

Just as Armstrong was putting the papers to one side, a small news item at the bottom of the front page of *Action* caught his eye. He snatched up the paper and read it quickly, then read it again slowly. This was it, he thought, putting the paper back down on the seat, this was the trigger he needed. There was no doubt that it was a bold idea, but if it worked, it would work spectacularly. The more he turned the plan over in his head, the more it appealed. It would strike at the very core of the regime, deal it a knock-out blow. It would be risky, but then he had no choice. Anyway, why shouldn't it work? There was a chance that his framework was still in place, good men ready to spring into action as soon as Major-General Clifford broadcast the codeword from London. If it came off, then the conspirators could take control of the country within no more than three or four hours, perhaps less. It seemed fantastic, but the more he considered it, the better the idea became. He would attempt to contact General Galwey as soon as he was in London, as well as looking for Craven's wife.

He glanced over at the sleeping Fraser, and then up at the luggage rack above his head. There was the briefcase, its contents still a mystery. Now was the time to take it to the lavatory and open it. Armstrong stood up quietly, reached for the case, and slipped out into the corridor. Outside, a young couple were having an earnest conversation, a conversation that was clearly making the woman upset. As Armstrong squeezed past them, they fell silent, and Armstrong could have sworn that they both inhaled sharply when they saw his uniform. Did they fear it? Or respect it? It didn't matter. All he wanted to do was to eradicate its presence from the streets, make Britain British again.

Armstrong shut himself in the lavatory and closed the seat, laying the briefcase on top of it. With a small pocket-knife he had acquired from Richard, he forced open the catch with some difficulty, fearing at first that the blade would snap. But it held firm, and with a satisfying click the catch snapped back against the leather. Armstrong paused before opening the lid, taking time to disabuse himself of a slight sense of apprehension. It was *not* going to be a bomb, he told himself – just get on and open it.

The briefcase contained a large green file, along with a few odds and ends such as a lighter and a small pack of playing cards. The front of the file was marked: 'Supremely Confidential – for HMSSP station heads only'. Armstrong undid the small red bow on the side.

It took him no more than a few seconds to realise what he was flicking through. There was page after page of directives, orders, reports, studies, costings, graphs and maps, all of which were concerned with just one topic, 'The Reassignment of the Jewish Workforce'. Armstrong breathed out heavily. It looked as though Mosley meant to get every Jew in the country to live and work in what were described as 'resettlement camps'.

By concentrating the Jews in resettlement camps, we shall fulfil the following aims:

1. That the Jews become – finally – an economic unit that is of BENEFIT to the country.
2. That the deleterious effects of Jewish culture and commerce are removed from the cities and towns of our great land.
3. A welcome disenfranchisement of the Jews from the political process.
4. The destruction of the twin threats posed by International Finance and Bolshevism to this country.

The German people have shown us the lead. Now it is time to pursue an equally rigorous course of action as regards the question of the Jews.

Armstrong closed the file. It was madness, but yet here it was, written in a hybrid mixture of the language of the bigoted demagogue and that of the rational civil servant. He tied up the small red bow and placed the file back in the briefcase. In a way, he wished it had been a bomb.

* * *

In late August 1892, James Armstrong, only a few weeks old, set sail from Southampton for India with his mother. There, his mother married the man Armstrong was to regard as his father until his eighteenth birthday. Lieutenant-Colonel Hugh Armstrong of the 8th Gurkha Rifles was a good man, and although he brought up his adopted son strictly, he indulged him in a way that many men of his generation – he was already forty when Armstrong was born – would have thought abominable. James was allowed to join his parents at the dinner table, he was allowed to make friends with Indians, he was not sent back to England but schooled by an elderly tutor, a Mr John Dyson.

When his father sat him down that hot June evening in 1910, Armstrong was expecting a lecture about the dynamics of human reproduction, a subject in which he was well versed, as he – along with many others – had experienced the intimate company of a Miss Elizabeth Morgan, a friend of the CO's daughter. Armstrong remembered that his father's voice had been clear and measured – he had obviously spent the past eighteen years preparing what he was about to say.

'I have to tell you, James,' he began, 'that as you will become an adult in the next few years, it is best that you know I am not your real father.'

The light was fading, and the two men were sitting on the veranda drinking large glasses of cold beer. His father was in his full mess kit, which seemed to creak every time he adjusted his position. Armstrong looked over to the hills, watching the sun's glow turn their dusty slopes a deep orangey-red. He was too shocked to speak. His father continued, eyeing him intently.

'Your mother and I believe that it is only fair you should know the truth about who you are. There are some who would not tell their children such a thing, but we both think it right that an individual should know who he is.'

'So who . . . who *am* I?'

His father proceeded to tell him that his mother had had an 'accident' – something that was far more commonplace, he said, than many people supposed. James was not to think worse of his mother because of this; it only showed that she was human. His father told him that he had always loved his mother, even though she had once turned down an offer of marriage from him. The rejection had sent him out to India, where he immersed himself in soldiering. Over the next few years, he had had little time or opportunity for female company, and when he discovered from a mutual friend that Armstrong's mother had fallen pregnant, he wrote to her, asking her once again to marry him. James was not to think that his mother had made the approach; it had come purely from his father. He had wanted to save her the disgrace of bringing up a child out of wedlock, and yes, he admitted with the trace of a smile, if that was the only way in which to win her, then so be it. He loved James's mother very deeply, and he loved James as if he was his own true son. He would understand if James found the whole thing shocking, would understand if James rejected him, would quite appreciate it if James went to England to seek out his real father. But for him, James was his son, and nothing was going to change that.

Armstrong looked at his father, and noticed a tear roll down his left cheek. That tear told him all he wanted to know – that he was loved by a man who cared for him more than his real father, whoever he was.

He stood up, his father looking up at him expectantly. James smiled to reassure him.

'Just so I know,' said James, 'what is his name?'

His father told him. The name meant nothing, as he should have known it would. Armstrong resolved then and there that he did not want to know anything more about the man. He knew he would not find love there, so what was the point of searching?

'I'm sorry – I shouldn't have asked,' he said, seeing the pain his father was in. 'Please don't worry. You will *always* be my father. What you did for my mother and me was the most honourable thing imaginable.'

James bent down and softly placed a kiss on his father's forehead.

'Thank you, *Father*,' he whispered.

'Thank *you*,' his father whispered back.

Neither of them had noticed James's mother watching them from inside, her face set in an expression somewhere between joy and grief. It looked as though it had gone well, more than well. Such a good young man, she thought, so unlike his real father, so much more like his adopted one.

Armstrong's father was delighted when his son joined the regiment's second battalion as a second lieutenant in the August of 1911. Towards the end of that year, James was attached to the first battalion in a campaign against the Abors in north-eastern India. It was near the village of Kebang that he was to do his father proud. For years afterwards, Lieutenant-Colonel Armstrong would read a certain passage from the regimental history every night before going to sleep:

No sign of hostile Abors was seen until 7th November, and it was not until 19th November that any resistance was met with. 'J' Company had proceeded beyond the camp site as escort to the General Officer Commanding when they were fired on, and found they were under a hidden line of stockades which blocked the steep path. Fire was at once opened on the stockade, and reinforcements ordered up from camp by telephone. A small party under Lieutenants J. H. Armstrong and T. P. Smith and Subadur Parbir Rekhbahadur was sent to outflank the enemy's right. Under a hail of arrows, and the discharge of stone chutes, the party succeeded in reaching the top stockade. Charging with kukris drawn, they cleared the stockade, and, enfilading the lower stockade, forced the Abors to retire. In hand-to-hand fighting, Subadur Parbir, who had displayed great gallantry throughout, closed with one of the Abors, and they rolled down the cliff fighting hard until Lieutenant Armstrong was able to shoot the Abor. Lieutenant Armstrong was Mentioned in Dispatches. The Subadur received the IOM. The GOC received a graze on his hand from an arrow.

Not only did he have a son, but he had a hero for a son. It was as if God was confirming that James was really his, and not that other man's. But his son's real test was to come in the trenches in France, the horrors of which neither man was able to anticipate.

Promoted to captain, Armstrong said goodbye to his parents on 21 August 1914. Along with seven other British officers, seventeen Gurkha officers, and 735 other ranks, he marched from his base at Lansdowne to the port of Karachi, where he and the second battalion embarked on the BISS *Erinpura*. He was not to know it at the time, but he would never go back to India, and he would never again see the man he called his father.

fingers down his throat, forcing them as deep as they would go. He bent down and turned away from Fraser and the passengers behind him – hopefully no one would see that his suffering was self-inflicted.

As the first wave of bile spewed out, he felt a hand come to rest on his shoulder.

'Jeezus, man!' he heard Fraser exclaiming. 'Are ye all right?'

Armstrong expelled the remnants of lunch's leek and potato soup and the KitKat on to the platform. He continued coughing, then fell to the ground and writhed around, clutching his stomach, breathing in and out rapidly.

'Go and get help!' Fraser shouted. 'Get one of them policemen!'

Armstrong kept his watering eyes open just enough to detect that a crowd had gathered around him, all of whom had concerned looks on their faces.

'What's up with him?'

'Looks in a bad way.'

'What's the matter?'

'Would you like a glass of water?'

'Is someone getting help?'

After less than a minute, Armstrong became aware of the presence of two policemen. This was it.

'What's happened here?' one of the constables asked.

'This poor fellow is having some sort of fit,' said Fraser. 'He just started coughing and then he was sick . . .'

'What's 'is name?'

'He's called Carr, Andrew Carr. I only just met him.'

'Mr Carr!' the policeman shouted. 'Mr Carr! Can you hear me?'

Armstrong ignored the question and continued to writhe.

'Mr Carr!'

Still Armstrong didn't reply.

'Peter,' said the policeman to his colleague, 'get an ambulance here! This chap's in a bad way.'

The other policeman hared off as Armstrong did his best to mask any feelings of relief. So far, so good.

'All right, people,' the policeman announced. 'Move along! He'll be all right – come on, move it! Curfew's in half an hour! Let's go.'

'I should stay with him,' said Fraser.

'That won't be necessary, sir – everybody's got to go through the checkpoint, even Party members such as yourself. He'll be taken to University College Hospital – you can see him there.'

Fraser bent down to Armstrong.

'You hang in there, old man,' he said. 'I'll come and see ye tomorrow.'

Armstrong croaked out some indistinguishable words accompanied by a faint smile of gratitude. Fraser clicked his heels together and offered him an erect fascist salute. Armstrong lifted his hand weakly in reply.

Five minutes later, Armstrong found himself being eased on to a stretcher. Within that time another train had pulled up alongside the adjacent platform, disgorging a mass of passengers who found themselves being shepherded into the same queue. Great, thought Armstrong, that could only work to his advantage.

He was carried along the length of the queue, the policeman walking next to his head. He kept his eyes shut as they reached the checkpoint.

'What's wrong with him then?' came a gruff voice.

'He's had a fit of some sort,' said the policeman. 'He's being taken to University College Hospital.'

'Do we know his name?'

'He's called Andrew Carr.'

'And what's that?'

'His briefcase.'

A pause, that seemed to go on for hours.

'All right, get rid of him. I don't fancy his smell for much longer. See him into the ambulance, Rogers, and then get back here. There are far too many bloody people to deal with and only a few minutes before the curfew! They could have given me a bit more notice!'

Relief, sheer bloody relief. As he was carried across the concourse, he looked up to see a giant portrait of the King and the Leader, both dressed in their full fascist uniforms. Underneath ran the slogan 'Hail Britannia!' which caused Armstrong to grimace involuntarily.

'All right, Mr Carr,' said the policeman. 'You're nearly there. You'll be fixed up right as rain.'

As Armstrong was loaded into the back of the ambulance, along with his briefcase, the policeman gave him a fascist salute. Thank God he hadn't tried to bribe his way out, thought Armstrong. The man was even wearing a Party armband.

A somewhat perplexed doctor put it down to food poisoning and insisted that Mr Carr spend the night in hospital. Armstrong was nervous about that, worrying that if his deception was rumbled he would be trapped. However, it was now well after the curfew, and he didn't want to be caught tramping the streets. He would discharge himself first thing in the morning.

* * *

'How perfectly delightful of you to come!' said Lady Cunard, her voice ebullient, her vowels revealing the slightest hint of her American roots.

'We wouldn't have missed it for anything, Emerald,' the Leader replied, kissing his diminutive hostess on each cheek.

'And Golden Corn! You look as *glowing* as ever! Power suits you, my dear!'

The Leader's wife was not the blushing sort, but at this particular instant she came close to it. 'Golden Corn' was Lady Cunard's nickname for the strikingly blonde Diana, who had been an habituée of her salons for many years.

'You're very naughty to say that, Emerald,' she replied, miming a smacking motion with her hand.

Lady Cunard's eyes twinkled for a brief second before she replied.

'Well, I hope you don't have me locked up for it!'

The Leader and his wife forced out a laugh. The joke was a little close to the bone, but then Lady Cunard was renowned for her outrageous sense of humour. No one was immune, not even the Leader. She lived in a vast house on the corner of Grosvenor Square, and over much of the past two decades had established herself as London's leading hostess. The Leader had attended her salons as a young man, attracted less perhaps by their assembly of men of influence than by Lady Cunard's ability to procure the most beautiful young women in London.

Of these, Diana had been the most exquisite, and in 1932 the young baronet Sir Oswald 'Tom' Mosley had started a passionate affair with the then Mrs Bryan Guinness. By the time the Leader's first wife died of peritonitis in the spring of 1933, the affair was in full blossom, and the couple married in October 1936 at the lakeside villa of Dr Goebbels near Berlin.

Hitler had attended the luncheon after the ceremony – it was the second time the two men had met, and they found each other good company, Mosley delighting in the Führer's excellent mimicry of Mussolini. Mosley thought Hitler a 'cool customer', and later remarked to his wife that if, in a fit of canine rage, 'it be true that he bites the carpet, he knows to a millimetre how far his tooth is going in'.

'Now come on through,' said Lady Cunard. 'There are plenty of people who are *dying* to meet you.'

She led them into the elegant drawing room, where their fellow guests were assembled, cocktails in hand. The Leader and his wife steeled themselves for Lady Cunard's habit of announcing new arrivals, which she did with 'the clarity of a toastmaster at the Lord Mayor's banquet', as the Leader had once described it.

'Ladies and gentlemen!' she boomed. 'Our dear Leader and his wife – Sir Oswald and Lady Mosley!'

Glasses and fascist salutes were raised in unison as the Leader scanned the room. The guests were certainly familiar – the German ambassador Joachim von Ribbentrop and his somewhat dowdy wife, Annelies; the Duke of Westminster – known as 'Bendor' in reference to a device on his coat of arms; the famous aviator Lord Sempill; the landowner Lord Brocket; the popular historian Arthur Bryant; the newly reappointed head of naval intelligence Admiral Sir Barry Domville; Captain Archibald Ramsay, a former Conservative MP who was now a British Union MP; and one of the Leader's longest-serving and most loyal colleagues, Henry Allen. In addition to the men's wives were two other guests, who were standing arm-in-arm. They made a striking couple, not least because the male half was wearing the smart black dress uniform of an SS captain, while the female half was a podgier version of Diana. This was not surprising, given that she was in fact Diana's sister, the Honourable Unity Mitford.

For the next hour, the talk was dominated by three subjects – the Jews, Bolshevism, and relations with Germany. Although the Leader had no wish to talk about business, von Ribbentrop was able to trap him in a corner, where the German spoke at great length about Mosley's forthcoming visit to Berlin. The Führer was looking forward to it immensely, von Ribbentrop was able to report, and the Leader and his wife would have a most enjoyable trip. Although the Leader found von Ribbentrop a bore, he was nevertheless patient with him, all the time thinking about what he had been told a few weeks ago by Sir Roger Ousby – that the ambassador had a serious infatuation with the Queen, and would regularly send her seventeen carnations. Sir Roger had been unable to establish the significance of the quantity, although his spies in the Palace were working on it.

Dinner was a sumptuous affair, washed down with a conversation largely concerned with the Jewish menace and the threat of communism. Stressing that everything he was about to say was to go no further than the table, the Leader held forth, once in a while allowing a fellow guest to add his or her tuppenceworth. Without wishing to reveal too much about his recent Cabinet meeting, Mosley said that plans were afoot to allow the Government the opportunity to deal with the twin dangers of Jewry and Bolshevism. Looking pointedly at von Ribbentrop, he suggested that Britain would need to work together with Germany on these problems, rather than letting the good Führer do all the hard work on his own. After all, he said, both countries, along with Italy, were at the start of a great adventure, an adventure that would lead to nothing less than the whole world embracing the glory of fascism.

The historian Arthur Bryant told the company that even in Germany the Jewish problem had not been fully dealt with, although he commended the ambassador for the steps that had been taken so far. The Jews had, after all, 'an inherited instinct to skim the cream rather than to waste vain time and effort in making enduring things'. It was time that this lack of productive work was rectified, he said, a sentiment heartily endorsed by the table. Bryant went further, stating that the Jews were sexually amoral and were extremely promiscuous. He told the table that German Jews held private parties at which 'mattresses were strewn about and petting was only the beginning'.

The Duke of Westminster, who smoked a large cigar the whole way through dinner, readily agreed, saying that the Jews were foul, and that he was glad the recent Treaty of London had averted a 'Jewish war', because that was exactly what the Jews wanted. Lords Brocket and Sempill agreed, and both chipped in with enthusiastic tributes to the Führer and wished the Leader well in whatever solution he and his Cabinet came up with. Sir Barry Domville described the Jews as a 'beastly little race', a view echoed far more forcefully by Unity Mitford.

'The Jews in England,' she warned the group, 'are more clever with their propaganda than in other countries.' She added that British Jews worked 'behind the scenes', and that she wished her dear brother-in-law well in dealing with them. It would be difficult, she said, because they never came into the open and so it was hard for the public to see them 'in their true dreadfulness'. She then went on to recount, to much amusement, how she had heard that some Jews in Germany had been made to cut grass with their teeth, and how she herself, when in Germany, had deliberately misdirected a heavily laden Jewish woman away from the railway station.

This brought more laughter, as well as a proud wink from her SS boyfriend.

Henry Allen was a little more reserved, telling the table that although it was true to say that the Jews certainly had a destabilising effect on society, it would be wrong to go so far as to suggest that they were evil. This caused an uproar, with the rest of the table saying that that was *exactly* what they were, and that Allen had better wake to up the fact. Allen gave way gracefully, and said that he was willing to be proved wrong. This brought forth a litany of Jewish crimes, especially from Captain Ramsay, who knowledgeably informed the group that the Jews, in league with the Freemasons, were behind the Bolshevik revolution, and that eradicating the Jewish influence from these shores was the only way to save the country from the evil of communism.

As the evening wore on, the tone became more light-hearted and jokes circulated. The one that caused the greatest laugh was told by Lord Brocket, who said that a friend who had recently stayed at the Metropole in Brighton had told him that there 'wasn't enough foreskin there to cover a thruppeny-bit'. However, the star turn of the evening was provided by Captain Ramsay, who sat down at the Steinway and sang, to the tune of 'Land of Hope and Glory':

> Land of dope and Jewry,
> Land that once was free,
> All the Jew boys praise thee
> While they plunder thee.
>
> Land of Jewish finance,
> Fooled by Jewish lies,
> In press and books and movies

The Leader

While our birthright dies.

Longer still and longer
Is the rope they get
But, by the God of battles
T'will serve to hang them yet.

Ramsay was soon joined in the singing by the others, and as Lady Cunard's guests left at around two a.m., many were humming the tune. Ramsay promised to make some copies of the lyrics over the weekend, which he would post out on Monday morning. The only person who said that he did not require a copy was Henry Allen, who told Ramsay that the lyrics were so excellent that he would easily be able to remember them. A lie, of course, because Allen had resolved over dinner that he wanted no more of this. It was not the wine talking, but the conversation of his fellow guests that had convinced him that the most honourable thing he could do was to work against everything he had helped to build up.

*　　*　　*

Armstrong discharged himself from hospital at seven o'clock the following morning. The doctor strongly advised him to remain for another twenty-four hours, but 'Andrew Carr' insisted that he had important Party business to attend to, and that he would not allow a mere stomach bug to deter him from carrying out the orders of the Leader. Armstrong could see the hate in the doctor's eyes, and he was glad of it. It was that hate that would ensure the coup's success, a hate that was coursing through all those who desperately wanted to see a return to freedom and an end to an atmosphere in which nobody could be trusted.

He found a telephone box outside the hospital, and was grateful for the temporary shelter it afforded. He felt naked out on the streets, aware that it would take just one pair of eyes to spot him. The Blackshirt uniform would remain effective for only so long, and he needed to get off the streets as soon as possible.

Armstrong called the operator, asking to be connected to a number in south-west London.

'Chelsea 9261,' came a familiar and welcome voice.

'Ted?'

'Yes?'

'It's James Armstrong.'

Ted Frost paused, and then exclaimed: 'Good God! James! Christ almighty! Where in God's name are you?'

'Listen, I've got to be quick – I'm in London, I need to come over.'

This time there was a longer pause.

'I'll understand if you don't want me—' Armstrong started, although if he was honest with himself, he wouldn't understand at all.

'Of course you bloody can!'

'Thank you, Ted.'

'Not at all. Get here as soon as you can!'

'I'll get a taxi,' said Armstrong. 'Still at number thirty-seven?'

'Yes. We'll have some breakfast ready for you if you want.'

'Good – see you in a bit.'

Armstrong didn't find Ted quite as welcoming as he had hoped. There was nothing specific, just an underlying tone of wariness.

When Ted had opened the door, he had paused before ushering Armstrong in. The handshake was not warm, but slightly formal. The introduction to Bridget, who Armstrong knew well, was laboured and awkward. Bridget's smile was forced, and she displayed little of the affectionate warmth that Armstrong was used to. Both were smoking, and Armstrong thought that Ted's breath betrayed a hint of whisky. Rather than dwell on it, he put their state down to the misgivings they might reasonably have over harbouring a wanted man. After all, Ted and Bridget were *decent* people, and decent people did not welcome fugitives into their homes, even if they were on the same side.

'Are you all right, Ted?' Armstrong asked.

'Fine! Just slightly surprised to see you, that's all. And, er, I don't deny that I'm a little startled to see you dressed up like that!'

Armstrong briefly closed his eyes – that was why they seemed so off.

'I'm so sorry, Ted. It's a disguise. I haven't gone all Mosleyite on you, I promise.'

'So how did you end up wearing—'

'Can I explain this over breakfast?' Armstrong suggested. 'I haven't really had a thing to eat since lunch yesterday.'

'Good God, of course! Eggs, bacon – *whisky* – what do you want?'

'Everything,' said Armstrong. 'Although perhaps not the whisky.'

Armstrong sat at the kitchen table, looking at the clutter on the Welsh dresser. There were many framed snapshots of the family – Ted with Bridget, Ted with Bridget and their daughter Flora, who had to be – how old would she be now? Christ, she had been born just after the war, so she had to be almost twenty.

'How's Flora?' Armstrong asked.

'Sailing down in Dorset with her boyfriend,' said Ted. 'She's mad keen on it. Says they're going to buy a yacht and sail away from Britain now that Mosley's in charge.'

'Sounds like a sensible girl,' said Armstrong.

Ted laughed and lit another cigarette.

'Well, she is most of the time. Anyway, I can't stand boats myself. Can't remember about you – you a sailor?'

Armstrong found himself involuntarily cast back to the crossing from the Isle of Man. He could hear himself shouting out for Craven, see himself sitting on the rock and desperately scanning the grey-blue water, knowing that with every passing second the chances of him still being alive grew slimmer.

'I'm a very bad sailor,' said Armstrong. 'The sea cost my friend Jim Craven his life.'

Ted passed over a cup of steaming black coffee.

'I'm so sorry. They said on the radio earlier that they'd found his body up in Scotland. It was foolish of me to talk about sailing, I should have thought. Want anything stronger in that, by the way? No? All right – I might treat myself, though . . .'

Ted's shaking left hand poured out an inch of whisky into a tumbler.

Armstrong sat forward.

'On the radio?' he asked. 'What's been on the radio?'

'You have mostly,' he replied. 'Bridget heard an announcement on the SBC at six o'clock. They said you'd killed a couple of policemen yesterday morning.'

Armstrong looked down at his coffee.

'Is it true, James?'

Armstrong nodded, then let out a deep sigh, and took a large mouthful of coffee.

Ted was in a bad way – that much was clear. Armstrong knew that he was a good drinker – most journalists were – but whisky for breakfast? It reminded him of the days before his own breakdown, when the whisky bottle had been his best friend. He could see the concern in Bridget's face as her husband poured himself yet another drink. Ted wasn't getting drunk, he was just drinking to make things look better. With the closure of the *Sketch*, he was out of a job, and was presumably not being paid.

But Ted was a good man and a good friend. Armstrong needed his help, and if Ted was willing to help, then he would need to know. Ted was on the side of the angels, thought Armstrong, even if he hadn't always particularly cared for the editorial line taken by the *Sketch*. He would put him in the picture, from his arrest in Victoria to turning up here in Chelsea.

His account lasted through the whole of breakfast, and afterwards they sat down in the drawing room.

'People are scared stiff, James,' said Ted as he lit what must have been his tenth cigarette since Armstrong had arrived. 'There are informers everywhere. It seems impossible to trust anybody at the moment. Things have changed hugely while you've been away. It's difficult to explain – it's as if everybody thinks everybody else is one of "them".'

'When in fact they're probably not,' said Armstrong.

'Precisely. He's doing just what Hitler and Mussolini are doing.'

Their conversation was interrupted by the sound of the letterbox.

'That'll be the papers,' said Ted, looking at his watch. 'Or what passes for them these days, now that decent journalists like yours truly have been put out of fucking business.'

He came back with a copy of *Action*, holding it up to show his guest. Armstrong looked back at a picture of himself taken nearly five years ago. In it he was smiling, which had given rise to the predictable headline, 'THE SMILING KILLER'. Underneath ran the captions: 'Two policemen brutally murdered by fugitive MP.' '£5000 REWARD for information leading to the arrest of CAPTAIN JAMES ARMSTRONG, the country's most wanted man.'

'You've caused quite a stir,' said Ted, the trace of a grin on his face.

'I certainly have,' said Armstrong. 'Pass it here.'

He flicked through the pages, noticing a photograph of one of the dead secret policemen with his family. He ignored it, knowing that to dwell on it would do the very opposite of strengthening his resolve. Anyway, Armstrong thought, the man was a fully paid-up member of a regime that was trying to enslave its own people. In the absence of democracy, blood had to be shed.

He passed the paper back to Ted.

'It's a start,' he said.

'That's one way of putting it,' said Ted.

The men sat in a ruminative silence for a minute or so. Armstrong looked around the room, every surface of which seemed to be dedicated to Ted's journalistic career, in the form of printing plates, framed front pages, as well as photographs of Ted meeting politicians, sportsmen, and even the King. An empty whisky bottle stood stopperless on the mantelpiece. Armstrong also noticed a large collection of board games neatly piled up on a shelf to the left of the fireplace. One particular box caught his eye.

'What's Monopoly?' he asked.

'Oh,' said Ted, suddenly mildly flustered, '*Monopoly*. Er, it's a board game in which you have to bankrupt all the other players. It's actually pretty good.'

'Never heard of it.'

'Well, it is brand new, although I suspect it may not be sufficiently in the spirit of collectivism for the present incumbent at Number Ten.'

'Sounds fun,' said Armstrong.

'Anyway,' said Ted, 'let's not talk about silly games. What in God's name are you going to do now?'

Armstrong put down his cup and leaned forward.

'I'm planning to kill Oswald Mosley,' he said matter-of-factly.

Ted spluttered into his tumbler.

'You're . . .'

'I'm not joking,' said Armstrong.

'But . . . how? When?'

'At the Coronation.'

'The *Coronation*?'

'That's right, Ted. I intend to plant a bomb as close to Mosley's backside as possible.'

'Where exactly?'

'In Westminster Abbey.'

'The *Abbey*?'

'That's right – unless you can think of somewhere better.'

'But James, the Abbey . . .'

'The Abbey can be repaired, Ted. A well-placed bomb would wipe out most of the hierarchy in one go. Just think, an instant end to not only Mosley, but the rest of those goons – Joyce, Francis Hawkins, Raven Thomson and Fuller. Kill them and we're well on our way back to democracy. If we're lucky, we might even kill a few foreign fascists as well.'

Armstrong paused. They all knew the implications of what he was saying.

'But the place will be crawling with soldiers, police-men, *secret* policemen,' said Ted. 'It would be almost impossible . . .'

'*Almost*,' said Armstrong. 'I've got to strike hard, and strike at the very heart. With any luck, I've still got the men in place to help, but they can only do so when they know we've succeeded in London. My job is to ensure that they have the best possible start. If I cut off most of Medusa's heads, then her confusion will be all the greater.'

'But won't a bomb kill innocent people? Priests, for example?'

'I've thought of that,' said Armstrong.

'And?'

'First, the bomb will not need to be so massive that it obliterates the entire building. Remember, we need only to ensure that Mosley and a few others are killed, not the whole congregation. Second, as brutal as it sounds, we may have to consider the deaths of a few innocent people as a price worth paying. If we leave Mosley in power, then many more innocent people will die, many, many more.'

Ted breathed out.

'Good God, James, you've set yourself a tall order.'

'That's why I'm going to need you to help me.'

'Help you?'

'That's right, Ted.'

Ted shifted uneasily in his seat before getting up swiftly, as though the cushion had suddenly reached boiling point.

'But James, I have a family . . .'

'So do I, so do a lot of people.'

'But what can I do? I'm just a whisky-soaked hack with a slightly suspect ticker. I can't do the sort of running around that you'd like.'

Armstrong reached down to the side of his chair and picked up the briefcase. He opened it and removed the green file, which he slammed down on the low table in front of him.

'What's that?' asked Ted.

'Just read it,' said Armstrong.

Ted looked back at him quizzically.

'Well go on,' said Armstrong. 'It won't bite.'

Ted walked over to the table and picked up the file. As he read the cover, his eyes widened. He pulled open the red bow and started to leaf through the pages.

'Good God,' he said after half a minute, shaking his head slowly. 'This is . . . this is madness, just . . . it's just lunacy.'

'I quite agree,' said Armstrong.

'If I'm reading this right,' said Ted, 'it looks as though Mosley means to get *every* Jew in this country to live and work in what can only be described as concentration camps. This is what they have in fucking Germany, not over here!'

Armstrong nodded.

'Have you seen this one?' said Ted, passing a sheet back to Armstrong.

Armstrong looked at it. Under the heading 'Corporations Willing To Take On Forced Jewish Labour' was a list of around thirty to forty household names.

'I saw this one,' said Armstrong. 'You'll notice that Iremonger is on this list.'

'No,' said Ted. 'But I thought he was . . .'

'So did I,' said Armstrong.

Ted shook his head.

'This is bloody dynamite,' he said. 'How did you get it?'

'I found it in the back of the secret policemen's car up in Scotland.'

Ted sat down with the file and continued to peruse it.

'Ted,' said Armstrong pointedly, 'will you help me?'

Ted looked back at him. Armstrong thought that a moment's indecision crossed his face, but then his features set themselves into an expression of determination that Armstrong had never before seen in his friend.

'What do you want me to do?'

Armstrong smiled back gently. It was hardly surprising that Ted hadn't immediately agreed to help – as he had said, he had a family.

'For a start,' said Armstrong, 'I'd like you to take me over to the East End.'

'Of course . . . May I ask why?'

'I want to see Jim Craven's widow. One of the reasons why Craven was escaping with me was because he had links with the Freedom Council . . .'

'The Freedom Council?'

'You mean you haven't heard of them?'

'Look, James, all we get to read and hear about these days is what's put out by the fucking fascists. I don't have the same—'

Armstrong held up his hands.

'Sorry,' he said, 'sorry. The Freedom Council is a Communist – mainly Jewish – resistance group. They're based in the East End. It's vital that I speak to Craven's widow and ask her what she knows about them, how we can contact them. Not only do I need their help, but I also think they should know about the contents of this file.'

'You're quite happy making allegiances with . . . with Communists, are you?'

'I don't see that we've got any choice,' said Armstrong. 'My enemy's enemy is my friend. The Freedom Council will be invaluable in whipping up support nationwide in the event that we successfully remove Mosley.'

Ted raised an eyebrow.

'I'm being quite serious, Ted – this is not the time for being fussy. We need all the help we can get.'

Ted remained silent. Armstrong stood up and stretched, looking out of the window on to the narrow street. For a moment he felt unbearably claustrophobic, knowing that he couldn't leave the house, not even to indulge in a stroll along the Embankment. He had plenty of friends out there, but for the time being he had to assume that Ted was the only one. He turned round to see Ted pouring another measure of whisky.

'Ted,' he said softly.

'What?'

'No more whisky, Ted.'

Ted's eyes bulged furiously.

'No more. You can get as blotto as you like when all this is over – who knows, perhaps I'll join you – but for now I need you to stay sober.'

'Come on, man,' snapped Ted. 'I'm just having a fucking sharpener!'

'I'd have thought the contents of the file were enough of a fucking sharpener!'

Ted slumped forward, letting the tumbler fall an inch on to the table, sending a few droplets splashing over the rim. He held up his hands in surrender.

'*Mea culpa*,' he said. '*Mea* bloody *culpa*.'

Armstrong smiled.

'Don't beat yourself up – I'm not too sure I like playing nanny that much.'

'I thought that's what you politicians were good at.'

* * *

The call is taken by Otto's wife Josefine later that morning. Josefine is not only Otto's wife, she is also his radio operator, trained in Moscow to the very highest standards. She and Otto met when they were both working for the OMS, the Comintern International Liaison Department, and they married in 1929. Their partnership is an unusual one, because Otto believes in maintaining many sexual relationships, an arrangement that suits Otto more than it does Josefine. Nevertheless, she knows that Otto is loyal to her, and not simply because he needs her for his work.

'Hello?' says Josefine, her voice slightly groggy. She and Otto are still in bed – last night's party at the Austrian Club was a good one.

'Is Otto there?'

Josefine recognises the brusque voice. She has heard it many times before, although she has never seen the face it belongs to. It is Andrei from the Soviet Embassy.

'Wait,' she says, and hands the receiver over to her sleeping husband.

He does not move.

'*Otto*,' she hisses, nudging him in the side.

Still no movement.

'OTTO!'

'Hmm?'

'The telephone!'

A hirsute hand reaches out of the blankets and makes a grabbing motion. Josefine smacks the phone into the palm.

'Thank you, darling,' says Otto sarcastically.

'Otto,' says the voice down the line, 'I must see you immediately.'

Otto sits up. He knows that this must be serious.

'Why?'

'It's Krivitsky.'

Andrei is referring to Major-General Walter Krivitsky, the NKVD's man in the Netherlands.

'What about him?'

'He's gone over to the Americans.'

Any colour that Otto had in his pasty, hungover face immediately disappears.

'Krivitsky? He knows nearly everything . . .'

'I'll see you in the park at twelve,' says Andrei before the line goes dead.

For a minute, Otto just stares towards the window, his eyes focusing on a point in the air somewhere between the bed and the partially closed curtains. This could mean the end of Top Hat, the end of Dog, the end of everything he has worked so hard to achieve. It could even mean the end of Otto.

Chapter Seven

Fellow Travellers

'OUSBY!'

'Sir?'

Sir Roger's grip on the telephone tightened.

'One question for you – I'm sure you can guess what it is.'

He could, but opted to say nothing. When the Leader was in a mood such as this, it was far better to stay silent.

'Well, can you?'

Sir Roger hated to be treated like a child. Armstrong had been the only thing on his mind for the past few days – all his other work had been put to one side.

'Armstrong,' he said, 'I take it this is about Armstrong.'

'Well?'

'No firm news, sir. However, there is a strong likelihood that he may be down here in London, disguised as a Blackshirt.'

'As a *Blackshirt*?'

'That's right – yesterday afternoon a Blackshirt in Carlisle was brutally assaulted and stripped of his uniform. His assailant matches Armstrong's description. We have further evidence from another Party member, who says he believes the man with whom he shared a train compartment on the way from Carlisle to Euston may well have been Armstrong.'

'Who is this Party member?'

Sir Roger shuffled through some papers on his desk.

'He's called Fraser, Duncan Fraser. He's a regional co-ordinator in Dumfries, down here for the conference on immigration.'

'And you mean to tell me that this Fraser sat next to Armstrong for several hours on a train and did *nothing?*'

'Well, he was disgui—'

'Where is Fraser now?' Mosley snapped.

'He's staying on the King's Road,' said Sir Roger, referring to the location of the Black House, the Party's headquarters.

'Arrest him,' said Mosley. 'And see to it that he never gets back home. Understood? The man's an idiot, Ousby. I will not have idiots in the Blackshirts.'

Sir Roger calmly noted down the Leader's request.

'Very well, sir – it will be done immediately.'

'So you have no idea where Armstrong went after he arrived at Euston?'

'He told Fraser that he was called Andrew Carr and said that he was on his way back home to High Wycombe. However, it seems that he pulled some kind of stunt in order to get past the checkpoint.'

'Stunt?'

'Apparently he collapsed and had a fit. He was taken to University College Hospital, from where he discharged himself early this morning.'

'For Christ's sake, Ousby! How incompetent do your people get?'

Ousby didn't reply. There was no point in justifying what

had been a cock-up. He would personally deal with the officer in charge of last night's arrangements at Euston.

'We cannot hope to restore order to this country with rogue elements like Armstrong on the loose,' said Mosley.

'Yes, sir,' said Ousby. 'I quite understand your annoyance. He will be found, my Leader.'

A silence, and then: 'So what do you think he's up to?'

'We're not sure, sir.'

'He'll be busy, Ousby, busy doing something that could harm us all. Armstrong's no fool, and he's well connected with those who are not as . . . *sympathetic* to our adventure as I would wish. I cannot relax when I know the man's on the loose.'

'We *will* find him.'

'I sincerely hope so for your sake, Ousby. And where are you looking?'

'It's my suspicion that he's stayed in London.'

'I take it you have no idea where.'

'We are working our way through a list of his former colleagues, fellow officers, friends – anybody who knows him. There are hundreds of addresses to check.'

'How long will this take?'

'Hard to say, sir, perhaps three to four more days.'

'You've got two. I want this cleared up before I go to Germany.'

Judging by the sharp click that Ousby then heard, the Leader had violently slammed down the phone. Ousby could have done with a drink, but secret or not, he was still a policeman, and policemen did not drink on duty.

* * *

'Telegram for you, sir!'

The NCO offered Major-General Clifford a smart salute, which Clifford acknowledged with a gruff expectoration. He was not in the best of moods, especially since he had spent the past several weeks in a state of near lethal anxiety. His wife, Patricia, concerned for his health, had insisted that he have his blood pressure read. The result – 190 over 110 – confirmed her suspicions. She and the doctor had begged him to take some time off, but Clifford had insisted that he had too much to do, essential work that nobody else could do. What was it, Patricia had asked, what was it that was so important? Clifford had brushed her off with 'essential army business', and Patricia, knowing when she had pushed her husband too far, had reluctantly left it at that.

Clifford took the flimsy telegram from the NCO's outstretched hand. It disgusted him that the man's sleeve bore an embroidered lightning flash, a device that Clifford had refused to wear on his own uniform. He knew that such petty acts of rebellion would get him into hot water, but his current state of mind was more than a little bloody-minded. Clifford rudely brushed the man out of the room with the back of his hand, not noticing the man perform another rigid salute.

Of all things, it was a greetings telegram. With a thick tobacco-stained thumb, he ripped open the envelope and extracted a small piece of paper, the head of which was garlanded with a rather florid arrangement of roses and thistles. Nestling in them was the royal coat of arms, and yet again, another bloody lightning flash. It was almost enough to make Clifford tear up the telegram before he had even read it.

A few seconds later, Clifford's mood had been entirely changed by the telegram's handful of innocuous phrases.

AUNT MARY HAS MADE A FULL RECOVERY STOP SAYS SHE IS LOOKING FORWARD TO HER BIRTHDAY PARTY STOP WILL SEND DETAILS OF VENUE SOONEST STOP PLEASE TELL REST OF FAMILY STOP BEST WISHES STOP COUSIN JIM ENDS

Clifford smiled and lit a most gratifying cigarette. Armstrong was a genius, he thought, a bloody genius. He took a blank sheet of paper from his letter rack and proceeded to draft a signal, the top of which was headlined 'Most Urgent'.

* * *

Armstrong resolved to keep the Blackshirt uniform. Along with his beard, it gave him a semblance of protection, and he felt more confident wearing it than in one of Ted's suits. Ted suggested that they might be able to doctor the identity papers he had removed from the Blackshirt in Carlisle, but as Armstrong had been born in a different century to the papers' holder, it would make alteration difficult. On balance, Armstrong decided that it was better to have no papers than clumsily doctored ones – his Blackshirt uniform would just have to do.

The two men were driving east along the Embankment, Ted at the wheel, a cigarette gripped between his right middle and index fingers. With his face on the front of *The Blackshirt* and *Action*, Armstrong felt extremely uneasy being out, but it would be pointless for him to languish indoors. That was not why he had escaped, and that was not what Craven had died for. He had to continue taking risks, and he would carry on until his luck had expired.

London had changed. The most obvious difference was the ubiquitous presence of fascist banners and flags. They were like acne, Armstrong thought, for they had erupted over the face of every building of note. Even the great Battersea Power Station had a massive banner suspended between its two riverside chimneys. On it were painted two lightning flashes, between which ran the predictable slogan, 'Hail Mosley – The Power of the Land'. Along the pavements walked an endless stream of Blackshirts and people wearing the fascist armband. Armstrong watched as passers-by saluted each other. The gesture had replaced the lifting of a hat or the slight nod of acknowledgement.

As they drove around Parliament Square, Armstrong looked hard at the Palace of Westminster, his place of work for nearly twenty years. He remembered his maiden speech, how nerves had caused him to speak far too quickly, so that the few Members who were in the House had no idea of what he was saying. He had in fact been arguing for an increase in the size of compensation payments to war widows, although it was to be another three years before his voice fell on ears that weren't conveniently deaf.

Armstrong also recalled the new Member for Harrow making *his* maiden speech in February 1919. The then Mr Mosley was only twenty-three, the youngest MP in the House, and he started his speech by quoting Chatham's line concerning 'the atrocious crime of being a young man'. Armstrong remembered wincing when Mosley had the gall to attack the Secretary of State for War, Winston Churchill, accusing him of lacking imagination. He had been impressed by Mosley's confidence, but repelled by his obvious vanity and naked ambition.

As they continued down the Embankment, Armstrong turned back to look at Big Ben. Although it was four o'clock, the clock's hands were stuck at five past five. He mentioned it to Ted.

'Rumour has it,' said Ted, 'that Mosley got it to stick there because in that position the hands look most like the lightning flash.'

Armstrong let out a gentle laugh, more a wry expulsion of breath.

'It wouldn't surprise me,' he said.

'Although I had heard that he was hopping mad about it. You can just imagine him.'

And Ted proceeded to imitate the Leader, his voice snarling and patrician, his teeth exposed like those of a savage hound.

'Fascist states have clocks that WORK!' he bellowed. 'Does our friend Herr Hitler have even ONE non-functioning timepiece? NO, I say to you!'

Armstrong laughed more heartily this time. Ted was a good mimic, and he didn't doubt that Mosley would have had such a conversation.

'So how long has it been stopped for?' he asked.

'Oh, weeks – although there hasn't been a mention of it in either *Action* or *The Blackshit*.'

The Blackshit. It was a good name for it. How childish the nature of dictatorship that it should censor what was obvious and apparent. No doubt it reported that the entire country was bathed in sunshine every day and that nobody caught colds any more.

They reached Whitechapel Road at quarter past six. They had tried ringing Mrs Craven, but the phone was out of order – 'Another triumph for the efficiency of the fascist machine,' Armstrong had said – so they decided to visit unannounced. The streets got progressively grimmer. Mosley had promised a programme of slum clearance, but that pledge – like so many others he had made when he had come to power – looked undelivered.

What had been delivered were stones through every other shop window – the windows of those shops that were owned by Jews. Stars of David had been crudely painted on every surface of these premises, along with anti-Semitic graffiti such as 'Jews Go Home', 'Don't Shop with Shylock', 'Only Traitors Buy from Yids'. This was Mosley's heartland, the spiritual home of the Blackshirt, the place where fascism had first taken root.

Armstrong and Ted drove in silence, both shocked by what they saw. This was racism in the raw, prejudice far more deep-seated and menacing than conversational antipathy. This was systemic, controlled. Although it had been happening all over Europe, Armstrong had never thought he would see it in London. As they drove on, they saw a couple of Blackshirts painting a Star of David on the back of an elderly Orthodox Jew's coat. Armstrong wanted to get Ted to stop the car, jump out and pummel the two thugs to the ground, but he knew it would achieve nothing. The only way he could help that old man was by not getting caught, and by carrying out his mission.

They drove slowly past the large villas that made up Victoria Park Road, a more genteel part of the East End north of Whitechapel. As Armstrong started looking at house numbers, he noticed a large black Vauxhall parked about fifty feet up the road. Ted was starting to slow down, anticipating that he would soon need to park.

'Don't stop!' said Armstrong.

'But I thought you wanted–' said Ted.

'Just keep going! But not too fast!'

Ted shook his head and gently put his foot down. As they continued down the long straight road, Armstrong sank low in his seat.

'What are you up to?'

'The Vauxhall on the right – ten to one it's full of secret police.'

Armstrong looked up to see Ted glance in the direction of the car.

'You're not wrong,' said Ted after a few seconds. 'There were two men in the front seat, both wearing snap-brim hats. Gave me a foul look.'

'Can I sit up?'

Ted looked in the rear-view mirror and nodded.

'Now what?' he asked.

'We've got to get rid of them,' said Armstrong.

'Yes, but how?'

Armstrong smiled.

'I've got an idea. Turn right up here.'

'Into the park?'

'That's right.'

'But what are we going to do in the park? Sunbathe?'

'Not in this uniform! No – I want you to go and find two or three of the most troublesome-looking scamps you can get your hands on. I want them to create a little diversion for us.'

'Get them to do *what*?'

'I want them to pelt that Vauxhall with stones, bricks, metal, abuse – anything they can get their hands on.'

'But those men are bound to be armed!'

'I doubt even *they* would actually shoot a gang of children,' said Armstrong. 'Run after them, certainly, but shoot them, I don't think so.'

Ted stopped the car.

'And how are you going to convince these children that it'll be worth their while risking their necks? Offer them a packet of Players?'

'Better than that,' said Armstrong, reaching into his trouser pocket. 'They can have one of these each.'

He passed Ted three five-pound notes.

'For that,' said Ted, 'they'll probably set light to the car.'

'Suits me.'

Forty-five minutes later, Armstrong and Ted were sitting in Ted's car about thirty yards behind the black Vauxhall.

'Are you sure they're going to come?' asked Armstrong.

Ted threw his cigarette end out of the window.

'Positive,' he said. 'Absolutely positive.'

He produced the five-pound notes from his jacket pocket. All three had been torn in half.

'Used to do the same trick in my reporting days,' he said. 'Never fails. I told the three rascals that they'd get the other halves if they turned up at the lido at eight o'clock.'

'But we can't guarantee that,' said Armstrong.

'I know,' said Ted. 'But they weren't to know that.'

Ted's attitude offended Armstrong's sense of fair play, but he knew that if Ted had simply given the lads the money up front they would never have seen them again.

'Oh well,' said Armstrong. 'I suppose one day we might be able to let them know how important a job it really was.'

Ted didn't reply, because he was looking intently in his wing mirror.

'Here they come,' he said. 'Just as the editor ordered.'

Armstrong turned round.

'I don't know whether they frighten the French . . .' he began.

'. . . but by God they certainly frighten me,' said Ted, finishing Wellington's words.

The three lads walked past them. Ted had certainly found the toughest-looking ruffians in the whole of the East End. Armstrong noticed that their clothes were filthy – one of them was even in barefoot.

'Go on, boys,' he whispered as the boys sauntered up the road.

'Proper little gangsters, aren't they?' said Ted.

'You certainly picked some great specimens.'

'Here we go,' said Ted. 'Looks like they're getting ready.'

Armstrong watched the boys glance furtively up and down the street. They looked almost comically suspicious, but no matter. So long as they bought them just a couple of minutes, then they could appear as suspicious as their amateur criminality allowed.

The taller of the boys reached into his trouser pocket and produced what looked like a piece of masonry. He flung it at the back window of the Vauxhall with all his might, causing the glass to shatter with a satisfyingly loud smash.

'Good one!' said Armstrong.

Ted rubbed his hands. The other two boys followed suit, and proceeded to hurl all manner of indiscernible objects at the car. Within seconds, the two secret policemen had got out.

'Excellent,' said Armstrong. 'They're both out.'

'Piss off, coppers!' they heard one of the boys shout.

Armstrong immediately turned to Ted.

'You didn't tell them they were secret policemen, did you?'

'No, swear on my life – they must have worked it out for themselves.'

By now the policemen were starting to chase after the boys,

one of whom had the gumption to throw a missile back at his pursuers.

'Brave lad!' Ted exclaimed.

But Armstrong was no longer watching the pursuit.

'Come on! Let's go!'

Before Ted could react, Armstrong was already out of the car and walking swiftly up the road.

With one eye on the road, Armstrong rapped firmly on the door of Craven's house, desperately looking forward to the security of being indoors.

He could discern a shadow approaching through the glass.

'Who is it?'

The voice was firm and clear.

'We're old friends of Jimmy's,' said Armstrong.

'Old friends? Who exactly?'

Armstrong paused. He wasn't going to bellow his name out loud.

'Old parliamentary friends,' he said, hoping that would open the door.

It didn't.

'What're your names?'

Armstrong bent down and lifted the flap of the letterbox.

'Mrs Craven?' he whispered through it.

'What? Who are you?'

'I've just come from the Isle of Man,' he said. 'I was with Jimmy when he died.'

Silence.

'*Please*, Mrs Craven,' Armstrong implored. 'It's absolutely vital that we talk to you. I'll tell you who I am when you let us in.'

Silence, and then the noise of a bolt being slid back. Armstrong stood up and waited while the door slowly opened.

The Leader

A wide-eyed face looked them up and down.

'But you're . . . you're a *Blackshirt*,' said Mrs Craven.

Armstrong could take no more of this. He couldn't stay on the doorstep a second longer.

'Isn't everybody these days,' he said with a reassuring smile, and with it gently barged in, quickly followed by Ted. The first thing he noticed when they entered the hall was a huge poster of Lenin which took up the whole of one wall.

'Jimmy told me you were even more left-wing than he was,' said Armstrong. 'It appears he was right.'

Mrs Craven eyed him suspiciously.

'Who are you?' she said, her voice stern. 'What are you doing in my house?'

Armstrong guessed that she was in her early forties, but she looked tired, very tired, which gave the impression of far more advanced years. She had evidently been doing a great deal of crying.

'Mrs Craven, my name is James Armstrong. I was in the boat when Jimmy died.'

Mrs Craven raised a hand to her mouth. What she did next took Armstrong aback. She hugged him, gripping him tightly.

'You're a bloody hero,' she said, her voice starting to tremble. 'Anybody who kills fascists is all right in my book.'

'I'm so sorry about Jimmy,' said Armstrong. 'He was a good man, a very principled man.'

Mrs Craven didn't reply, but gripped Armstrong tighter and started to sob uncontrollably. Armstrong understood these tears, because he had wept them himself, when Mary had died. He felt like crying as well, but stopped himself. This was not the time to think about Mary and Philip. When all this was finished, then he would, but not now, not now.

*

She insisted on making them a pot of a tea, and ten minutes later Armstrong and Ted found themselves sitting in the living room being served strong black tea in chipped mugs. The room was festooned with paraphernalia that signified the Cravens' political loyalties.

'In a way, Jimmy was a traitor,' said Mrs Craven as she eased herself into a chair, which Armstrong noticed was surrounded by books and political pamphlets.

'I'm sorry, Mrs Craven,' said Armstrong. 'In what way?'

'He sold out when he joined the Labour Party, stopped being a true believer like yours truly here.'

Mrs Craven's gaze led her guests' eyes to the mantelpiece, upon which was a small bronze bust of Marx.

'He was much more practical than me,' she said. 'Knew that the only way to *really* influence things was to get into Parliament. I saw that as compromise, and told him that the dialectic would not allow for it. I think Jimmy loved Westminster really, despite his reputation.'

'I think you're right,' said Armstrong. 'It liked him too.'

'Sometimes he used to come back home, and Lucy would still be up, and, and . . .'

Her voice drifted off. Armstrong saw her eyes glistening.

'Mrs Craven?' he asked.

She took out a handkerchief and gave her nose a sharp blow.

'My daughter, Captain Armstrong. She disappeared three weeks ago.'

'Disappeared?'

'That's right. Not long after her boyfriend was taken away by those . . . those *fascists*.'

She spat the last word out with venom. It was clear that Mrs Craven regarded the word as a vulgarism in itself; there was no need for her to add a swear word.

'What happened to her?' asked Ted.

'She told me that she was going to join the Freedom Council.'

Armstrong and Ted looked at each other.

'You know it, do you?' asked Mrs Craven, noticing the men's glance.

'Not as much as we'd like,' said Armstrong. 'It's actually the reason why we came.'

'What? Are you trying to find Lucy?'

'No, not exactly – we're trying to find the group itself. I thought that you might have some sort of contact with them.'

'I pleaded with her,' said Mrs Craven, ignoring Armstrong's request. 'I told her that she couldn't go down the same route as Alan had gone . . .'

'Alan?'

'Her boyfriend, Captain Armstrong. He's called Alan Jacobs. He was part of it, you see, part of the Freedom Council, and I told Lucy that she couldn't go out there and fight like he had, because she would only get hurt. But then she told me that I would have joined them if I was her age. She was right, but I didn't let on. Anyway, the next morning I came down for breakfast, and there it was, her letter.'

'What did it say?'

'That she had gone off to fight for what she believed in, and nothing was going to stop her.'

'Can we read it?' asked Ted.

'I burned it,' said Mrs Craven. 'She asked me to.'

There was a brief silence.

'I'm sorry to be so persistent,' said Armstrong, 'but we really must find her. Has she made any contact with you at all?'

'None.'

Mrs Craven shook her head and looked into the empty fireplace.

'Can you think of anywhere that we might try?'

'If there was somewhere, I would have tried it myself.'

'How about her friends? Do you think any of them might know? A friend of Alan's perhaps?'

She shook her head again. This was infuriating, thought Armstrong. Lucy was probably no more than a mile or two away from where they were sitting.

'How about a restaurant?' he said. 'A pub maybe? Did she work somewhere? Perhaps there was a colleague she mentioned a lot?'

Mrs Craven lifted her head.

'A restaurant! Why didn't I think of it before?'

* * *

She took it badly, and what made it worse was that it was too risky for her to go home and comfort her mother. It was Benny who told her – he had brought back a copy of *The Blackshirt* that morning, and as soon as she saw his face she knew that something was seriously wrong. At first she thought it had to be about Alan, that he had 'committed suicide' in prison, as so many others had done.

Nothing could have prepared her for what she read. There, underneath the main headline concerning the escape of Captain Armstrong, were the words 'Bolshevik MP found dead'. She could barely read the story, a story that revealed how her 'cowardly' and 'treacherous' father had assaulted a prison guard and escaped from the Isle of Man with Armstrong in order to instigate a 'wave of Jewish-inspired terror'. When she reached the sentence that gleefully informed readers that they should be thankful the sea was such a cruel mistress, Lucy started tearing up the newspaper, and kept tearing it until the bare wooden floor was littered with hundreds of smudged scraps. Benny could only stand and watch, occasionally stretching out a tentative hand of comfort. The hand was neither rebuffed nor ignored, but merely not noticed.

* * *

'And I say he's a goddamn phoney,' barked Ambassador Bingham.

'But sir, shouldn't we just . . . ?'

'No we darn well should not! I do not like reading reports about Commie generals who come out of nowhere, who may not *even be* real generals, and who are about as believable as a horse with feathers.'

Bingham threw the bulky dossier on to the desk. The idea of a plot by Moscow to secretly overthrow the British Government was preposterous, absurd. Stalin may well be a crafty so-and-so, but not even he could mount something this ambitious. It was horsecrap, pure BS.

'With respect, sir,' said Carl Parsons, Bingham's second consul, 'much of this does look real, and there has been a whole lot of talk on the intelligence grapevine . . .'

'Talk! Grapevine my ass! It's always talk, Parsons! Do you know how damaging talk is? If we listened to everything that came out of DC, every loose word, every scrap of gossip, every bit of tittle-tattle, every cranky document, well, we'd get no real work done. Do you know, Parsons, only the other day I received a letter from the FBI saying that one of their informants had sworn *on oath* that good Queen Wallis was buying dope down in Limehouse. Our job is not to believe nonsense, Parsons, but only to trust the *facts*, pure and simple. Do I make myself absolutely plain?'

'You do indeed, sir.'

'At last. I'm so *happy*, Parsons. It's so good of you to finally see things your dear little ambassador's way.'

Parsons smiled dutifully at the ambassador's sarcasm.

'When you're our great country's representative in, I don't know, the *Congo*, then you can deal in as much crap as you care for, Parsons, but while you're here at the Court of St James you leave off this bullshit. Goddit?'

'Goddit, sir,' Parsons replied.

'Now then, I'm sure you've got work to do.'

Parsons rightly took that as an invitation to leave. He turned briskly on his heel and walked over the soft carpet towards the door.

'One more thing, Parsons.'

'Yes, sir?'

'If you tell *anybody* about this, even one of your fancy women, then you really will find yourself in the goddamn Congo.'

'Yes, sir.'

'Without a paddle, Parsons!'

'Yes, sir!'

Parsons left the room and closed the padded door behind him. Bingham grunted and pinched the bridge of his nose. He opened his eyes and disdainfully flicked through the dossier. Jesus wept – look at this shit. 'Top Hat', 'Dog': even the general's codenames looked phoney. This guy Krivitsky was having a ball. What did he want? A house in Florida?

* * *

At first she thought they were HMSSP and had tricked her mother. They were the right age, and somehow their faces and their height didn't fit with their workmen's clothes. It was two days since she had learned about her father's death, and Lucy was standing in the vastness of an empty warehouse down by the river at Wapping.

Armstrong's escape and killing of the two policemen had earned him heroic status in the eyes of the Freedom Council. Like the rest of the country, Lucy and her fellow members had been following the news with much interest, and had started to find the exasperation in the tone of reports in *The Blackshirt* and *Action* almost amusing. The size of the reward for apprehending Armstrong had trebled in the space of two days, and the Leader's apoplectic fury could easily be discerned between the lines of his radio announcements:

'This execrable piece of vermin must be hunted down and dealt with with the utmost severity! I say to you all now, if any man among you is hiding this traitor, then he and his family will be met with a punishment equal to the one that awaits the cowardly captain. Let there be no lair in which this man can skulk! For the good of the country, I say to you this: Be vigilant! Be wary! Be patriotic!'

There were three of them waiting in the warehouse. Alongside her were two senior members of the Council, men she knew only as Martin and Nick. Both were in their late thirties, and carried guns, guns she knew they had used only a fortnight ago in an unsuccessful attempt to assassinate a member of the HMSSP.

A blindfolded Armstrong and Ted were bundled by Danny and Benny into the warehouse, their hands roughly tied up behind their backs. Armstrong knew that they were taking an understandable precaution, but for a hateful moment he feared he had walked into some outlandish trap, a view reinforced by the cold press of a muzzle against his temple.

'Search them!' a voice ordered.

The two men were vigorously frisked. The only items their clothes yielded were some coins and Ted's keys.

'Get on the floor!' the voice barked.

Armstrong and Ted were pushed down, their heads forced against the rough concrete floor.

'Who are you?'

Armstrong replied for both of them.

'My name is Captain James Armstrong and this is Ted Frost, editor of the *Daily Sketch*.'

'Do you have any proof of that?'

'No,' said Armstrong.

'Get him up! Not both of them! Just him!'

Armstrong was pulled up and made to face the source of the voice. The man sounded tough, thought Armstrong, and he was glad of it.

'You've got a beard.'

Armstrong nodded. 'Disguise,' he replied.

'Profile.'

Armstrong's head was turned ninety degrees. He slightly resented that he wasn't allowed to do it on his own, but he stopped himself getting angry.

'You certainly look like him.'

At last, thought Armstrong.

'I've got a few questions for you,' the voice said.

'Go ahead.'

'Where and when did you receive your Military Cross?'

The question took him aback. They had obviously done their homework.

'At Festubert,' said Armstrong. 'On the night of the twenty-third to the twenty-fourth of November 1914.'

'Which regiment were you in?'

'The 8th Gurkha Rifles.'

'Battalion?'

'The second.'

'What did you do in the years running up to the war?'

Christ, thought Armstrong, how did they know about this?

'I spent two years escorting map-making expeditions throughout Nagaland.'

'Where specifically?'

'The Dihang river mainly.'

'Where did you meet your wife?'

'In hospital.'

'Name?'

'Mary Elizabeth Armstrong.'

'Maiden name?'

'Elliott.'

The questions were beginning to make Armstrong wince. They had made their point.

'All right,' he snapped, 'I know what you're going to ask next. You're going to want me to tell you how and when she died. Fine, if that's what you want to know, I'll tell you that as well. It was the—'

The questioner interrupted him.

'Captain Armstrong,' he said, his voice losing some of its menace, 'you don't have to tell us. I'm quite satisfied you're who you say you are.'

Armstrong felt the grip on him relax.

'Good,' he said, 'I'm grateful.'

'Take off their blindfolds,' said the voice.

Armstrong squinted slightly, even though the light was dim.

'Hello, Captain Armstrong,' the voice said. 'We're very honoured to have you here.'

'Thank you,' said Armstrong, rubbing the back of his head.

'I'm sorry about the rough treatment – you too, Mr Frost. I hope you understand.'

'That's quite all right,' said Armstrong. 'You certainly know all about me.'

'Let's just say that we like to do our research properly. By the way, my name is . . . well, it's not my real name. For the time being, just call me Nick.'

Armstrong looked at the faces of the small group as Nick introduced them. Nick and the man who had shoved the gun against his temple looked hard and weary, as though they had not slept or eaten for the past six months. The younger men were a little more wide-eyed, more naïve-looking, but they seemed tough and keen. And then of course there was Craven's daughter, who shared her father's dark looks and diminutive height. Her hair was scraped back tightly, and although her expression was bordering on the fierce, Armstrong fancied that he could detect that her face could have its softer moments. However, for the time being she resembled her firebrand father in full flow on the floor of the Commons.

'You look very much like your father,' said Armstrong.

Lucy raised her eyebrows. It had been said before.

'I'm very sorry,' added Armstrong.

'Thank you,' she said. 'How's my mother? How's she doing?'

'Bearing up.'

Lucy nodded and smiled sadly.

'Bearing up,' she said, letting the words roll around her mouth.

There was a brief silence before Nick spoke.

'What can we do for you, Captain Armstrong?'

freedoms. They also agreed to Armstrong's suggestion that the Council could use its network throughout the country to set up opposition cells. However, both Martin and Nick were more immediately concerned with the contents of the HMSSP file, as Nick told Armstrong one morning at the Council's safe-house in a dilapidated Georgian terrace in Wapping.

'We *have* to stop this,' he said. 'There's *no way* that we Jews are just going to be herded into these resettlement camps like sheep.'

'I agree,' said Armstrong. 'But I think it's more important that we concentrate on dealing with Mosley and the aftermath of his assassination. If he goes, then the whole apparatus will crumble. We'll all be safe then, the Jews included.'

'But we have to sort this out NOW!'

Nick smacked the back of his hand violently against the file. Armstrong didn't say a word – he would let Nick's temper run its course. Over the past few days he had come to realise that he needed to handle both Martin and Nick with the very softest of kid gloves. They were clearly strained and tired, the bags under their eyes and their unkempt appearance testament to many wakeful nights. Although they were clearly resourceful men, doubtless brave, they were both hotheads.

'Look at this,' said Nick, nearly shouting. 'It's evil, pure EVIL. And it's going to start in a couple of weeks! And you know what'll happen when they get all of us into these camps? They'll work us to death, that's what they'll do! And what of the old, what of the sick? All it says here is . . . where is it?'

Nick thumbed roughly through the file.

'Here – "Those who are too old, young or infirm to work will be quartered in special sub-camps where they will be provided for at a minimum level of subsistence." That means starvation! They'll be given a slice of bread and an aspirin and left to die. Godammit, man, we can't just sit here!'

'I'm aware of what the file says,' said Armstrong quietly. It was becoming hard for him to hold his tongue – a few months ago it would have been inconceivable for him to be lectured by some unshaven Communist ten years his junior. He knew those days had gone, but he found it hard to abandon his former role.

'And you don't want to do a thing about it?' said Nick. 'You lot have never cared about the Jews, have you? You just want to let three hundred and fifty thousand of your fellow British citizens be locked up in *concentration camps*? Because let's face it, that's what these camps are.'

Armstrong was about to speak but Lucy beat him to it.

'That's not fair, Nick,' she said, her voice firm, assertive. 'I don't think Captain Armstrong said that. He just wants to go straight to the heart of the problem and get rid of Mosley. If he didn't like the Jews then I doubt he'd be sitting here with us.'

Nick glowered at her. It looked for a moment as if he was about to explode, but Lucy held his gaze.

'Thank you, Lucy,' said Armstrong. 'Although I don't mind if you call me James, by the way.'

He turned to Nick.

'Look,' he said, 'I can see why you're so frustrated, I really can. But we can't stop these resettlement camps—'

'Concentration camps,' snapped Nick.

'*Concentration camps*,' said Armstrong. 'We can't stop these concentration camps without stopping Mosley himself. And the only way to do that – I suggest – is to kill him.'

Nick chewed it over.

'But by the time you mean to kill him,' he said, 'God knows how many will have already died.'

'It's not that long,' said Armstrong. 'Just eight or nine weeks.'

'Sounds long enough.'

Armstrong noticed that Lucy was looking through the file.

'What are you looking for?' he asked.

'A compromise,' she said, continuing to turn the pages. 'A way that will keep both of you happy.'

'I'm all ears,' said Armstrong.

'Go on,' said Nick, his tone suggesting deep pessimism.

Lucy didn't reply immediately.

'Well?' said Nick.

'This is thinking out loud,' said Lucy. 'I think Captain . . . sorry, *James*, is right. We can't actually stop all this. But I'm sure we could do something to delay it. It occurs to me that whoever is organising this must be doing it from somewhere, there must be an office or a building where it's all put together . . . Aha!'

'What?' asked Nick.

'Here we go,' said Lucy, a tone of triumph in her voice. 'This looks like it. "The Department of Labour Reassignment, 5 Smith Street, London SW1." '

'I think I can guess what you're thinking,' said Armstrong, grinning slightly. 'Get rid of the building, and you'd delay the camps.'

'Exactly,' said Lucy. 'We could petrol-bomb it.'

'We could do better than that,' said Armstrong. 'We could blow it up.'

'Blow it up?' asked Nick. 'How?'

'Let me take care of that,' said Armstrong. 'But first I'd like to suggest a deal. I'll help you destroy this building, and you get to work setting up these cells.'

Nick looked uncertain.

'I'll need to ask Martin,' he said.

'You do that,' said Armstrong.

*

As Armstrong had suspected, Martin readily agreed to the deal, though Nick was still doubtful about how Armstrong was going to destroy the building. However, Armstrong's solution had come to him when he recalled sitting on the terrace of the Palace of Westminster in happier days, watching the procession of traffic on the Thames, especially the large barges.

'A barge,' he said to Ted, Lucy and Nick one afternoon.

'What?' asked Ted.

'A barge,' he said. 'There are countless barges carrying explosives up and down the river. We could get our hands on one of those. All we need to do is pack a car with enough explosive, park it outside the Department and – *voilà!*'

'Do you think the barges are still running?' asked Lucy.

'I don't see why not – things haven't come to a complete standstill. There are plenty of industries up and down the country that need explosives. Barges are much safer than the railways, even if they are somewhat slow.'

'But how the hell do we get hold of a barge?'

* * *

Gordon pours out two large mugs of greasy tea from the samovar. The customers never complain that the tea always tastes slightly of yesterday's soup – perhaps they actually like it that way, Eve once suggested. Anyway, the two fellows he is bringing the tea over to now never seem to notice – they are usually so wrapped up in their conversation that he could serve them cold dishwater and still they wouldn't twig. They are a funny couple, Gordon thinks, the stocky little foreign-looking one and the tall English one. God knows what they are talking about, but they always look as though they have the weight of the world on their shoulders.

Of course, Gordon is not far wrong. This morning, Otto and Tony are talking about how the defection of one renegade Soviet major-general may result in the termination of their network, and with it any chance of being able to topple the fascists.

'So you have heard nothing?' asks Otto as soon as Gordon walks away.

'The Americans are saying nothing,' says Tony. 'I've spoken to Hoover, as well as Bingham – they deny that there's even been a defector.'

'Perhaps the Americans want our plan to succeed.'

'That's always possible – but I would have thought that if they were given the choice between Mosley and Moscow, they would go for Mosley any time.'

A pause.

'Or perhaps they know that the man asking them the questions,' says Otto, 'is the man who is really working for Moscow.'

'I've thought of that,' says Tony. 'But how could this general have known my identity?'

'Anything is possible,' Otto replies with a shrug. 'But I think we can assume that if the Americans have told someone else in the regime, then you would already be hanging from a gibbet.'

Tony's face pales slightly.

'So what do you suggest we do?' he asks.

'I think we should take Dog out of his kennel,' says Otto. 'Set him to work as planned. It's about time the brave captain was given a helping hand. There! Almost a rhyming couplet! Let's see if I can't make it scan better.'

* * *

A few nights later, Lucy found herself walking past the entrance to a wharf in Bermondsey. It was just under an hour before the curfew, but that was not the reason why she was feeling uncomfortable. She had taken on the role of bait reluctantly, but the others had insisted that she would come to no harm, because they would be looking out for her. She found that hard to believe, especially as she was about to enter a pub wearing little more than a tight black satin cocktail dress and a somewhat tatty fur stole. Her scarlet lipstick completed a picture of availability, albeit one that came at a price, a price well within reach of the barge captain Armstrong and the others had staked out for the past two nights. He was a fat sot, they told her, but a fat sot who had a deckful of dynamite.

At least Armstrong and Nick would be in the pub, she thought. They had reassured her that if matters got out of hand they would step in. All that was required of her, said Armstrong, was to get her man back to his barge, and then he, Nick and Martin would take over. Martin was presently hiding in a nearby alleyway, ready to follow Nick and Armstrong when they emerged from the pub.

Lucy could feel her heart thumping as she approached the pub. The sound of laughter from its smoky orange interior grew louder, and she steeled herself for the reaction of the drinkers. Just remember why you're doing this, she told herself: think of Dad, think of Alan, think of David, think of Mum; Mum who would be put in a camp soon, unless she, Lucy, went through with this. Think of all of them, she told herself, and think of your beliefs. Think of your people.

With a shaking hand, Lucy pushed open the pub door.

'*Hello* there.'

'Now how about that.'

'Oi! Dennis! What's your missus doing here?'

'Give us a kiss!'

She looked straight ahead at the bar, avoiding the fifty or so pairs of eyes that were scrutinising her body, ignoring the predictable pinch she received on her backside. Armstrong had told her to look relaxed and approachable and above all to smile. She was meant to be a tart, he said, and tarts smiled. She found it almost impossible, but she did her best when she caught sight of Nick and Armstrong sitting to one side of the bar, both baring their teeth at her like subjects who had posed too long for the camera. The sight of them made her giggle nervously, which in turn made her smile.

'Hello, hello, what can I get you then, madam?'

'Er . . . a gin and tonic?'

The barman started laughing.

'Hear that, boys? Lady thinks she's at the Savoy! Sorry, love, no gin and tonic here.'

She watched Armstrong briefly put a hand up to his face as the pub erupted into laughter. She felt herself starting to lose control, found herself wanting to turn and run straight out of the door and on to Jamaica Road. Come on, she urged herself, pull yourself together.

'That's a shame,' she said, coquettishly leaning on the bar. 'In that case I had better leave. Or can you offer me something other than beer?'

The barman leaned forward with a lecherous grin.

'How about a nice cherry brandy?'

'Or a nice cherry!' came a voice to her left, causing another peal of drunken laughter.

Lucy smiled and turned to the voice. It was owned by a fifty-year-old man wearing a blue woollen hat and a black oilskin coat. He held a pint of stout up to his mouth and gave her a wink.

'I'd watch your lip, young man,' said Lucy.

'I'd rather watch yours!' he replied.

Lucy smiled back, inwardly hoping that this wasn't the barge captain.

'Your cherry brandy, milady,' said the barman.

'Thank you,' said Lucy, taking the drink. As she did so, she caught sight of Armstrong giving her a subtle thumbs-up signal just above the level of the bar. His eyes were motioning towards the stout drinker. Oh God. Just her luck. He really was the sot they had described.

'Allow me,' said the barge captain, reaching into his pocket for some change.

Cheers and catcalls erupted from the few men standing nearby, and Lucy gathered that the captain's name was Harry. She held her glass up to him and took a swig. It was syrupy and disgustingly sweet, but she did her best to force it down. Perhaps it would be better if she was half cut anyway. Harry was no looker – a fat nose and blubbery lips complemented a round face that bore the ruddy signs of either a life outdoors or a surfeit of alcohol, or – likelier still – both.

'So tell me, Harry,' said Lucy, sidling up to him as provocatively as possible, 'do you like paying for ladies' . . . drinks?'

'Only ones as charming as you, my dear,' the captain replied. He was clearly five or six pints down.

Lucy smiled back. He stank, a vile mixture of stale sweat, tobacco and alcohol.

'And isn't there a Mrs Harry?' asked Lucy.

'Not tonight there ain't!' the captain replied, addressing his neighbouring drinkers.

Lucy finished her cherry brandy.

'Do you know what, Harry,' she said, 'I think I'd like a nice big . . . beer.'

Harry laughed into his stout, sending some flecks of foam flying over her.

'Harry!' she admonished him. 'Look what you've gone and done!'

Lucy took a handkerchief from her handbag and proceeded to slowly wipe the foam off her dress. It occurred to her that she might be overacting, but then she thought of the girls she had seen on the streets of the East End. They laid it on thicker than this, she thought, much thicker. Besides, with the curfew, girls were having to work a lot more quickly these days, which called for a corresponding diminution in subtlety.

Harry ordered her half a pint of mild, the taste of which Lucy found surprisingly agreeable.

'Thank you, Harry,' she said. 'You're a real gentleman, did you know that?'

'That's the first time anybody's told me!' followed by another laugh to the gallery.

'I bet you know a lot of ladies, don't you, Harry?'

'I can't deny I've known a few,' he said. 'I like to get around!'

More laughter, most of it from Harry, who clearly considered himself a comedian.

'And where do you get around?' Lucy asked.

'All over the place, my love, wherever my barge takes me!'

'Your *barge*, eh?'

'The MB *Blackwater*,' said Harry, 'the finest barge on the whole bloody Thames.'

'I'd love to look at your barge, Harry.'

'Now there are not many ladies who say that!'

'Well I would. Where is it?'

Harry smiled, and bent close to Lucy.

'Right outside, my love,' he whispered, spraying her ear with saliva. 'You can have a look round now if you fancy.'

Lucy was aware that Harry was excitedly rubbing his thigh as she whispered back.

'I'd like that, Harry, I'd like that very much. But don't you have a crew, or some men? I would like to keep things . . . *intimate*, if you know what I mean.'

'Don't worry, my love, it'll be just me and you and the starry sky. They've all got the night off.'

Lucy walked out of the bar on Harry's arm, accompanied by even more catcalls than when she had walked in. As soon as they stepped outside, Harry made a lunge, roughly forcing his face towards hers.

'Harry!' she hissed in mock anger. 'Let's wait till we get on your boat.'

They stumbled across the road, and on to the pavement. After a few yards they turned left on to a gangway that led down to a series of duckboards, around which at least thirty or forty boats were moored. She prayed that the others were following.

'This is very romantic, Harry.'

Harry made another lunge, this time even less subtle. Lucy slapped his hand away from her breast.

'Harry! All in good time!'

She turned round, hoping to see some sign of the others. There was none, which caused a sense of dread to seep through her. The thought that she might end up having to sleep with this man was too revolting to contemplate.

'What are you looking for, my love?' the captain asked.

'Nothing,' Lucy replied. 'Just thought I heard something.'

'A rat, most like. But you won't find any rats on my barge, oh no.'

They were now walking alongside a long black barge, which Lucy noticed was a lot dirtier than many of the other craft.

'Is this it?' she asked.

'It is indeed,' said Harry proudly. 'Won't you come aboard?'

He stepped on to the barge and held out his hand with an exaggerated flourish of gentlemanliness. Lucy took it, and found herself being roughly pulled on to the deck.

'So what do you keep on your barge, Harry?'

'All sorts – things that go bang mostly!'

'Things that go bang?'

'Now don't you worry your head about it – I want you to see what I keep in here!'

Harry pointed to his crotch. Lucy forced a smile that fully tested whatever abilities she might have had as an actress.

'So where's the captain's cabin?' she asked.

'Follow me. Careful down these steps! We wouldn't want you to trip over, would we?'

Lucy edged her way down a steep ladder that led into the stinking bowels of the barge. As she stepped down, she snatched an opportunity to look round. Thank God. Three figures that she recognised were walking down the gangway.

She followed the captain down into the hold. It reeked of sweat and fuel oil, an odour that had accumulated over many years and had engrained itself into the fabric of the barge. On either side of her were stacked case upon case of wooden boxes marked 'Danger! High Explosive! Handle with Care!'

The captain unlocked a small wooden door at the end of the hold. So this was it, the place where she would have to surrender herself to his odious clutches. Harry paused by the door and ushered Lucy in.

'In you go, my love,' he cackled.

Lucy nearly fell into the cabin, forgetting that the doorway was raised.

'Whoops-a-daisy!' said Harry. 'I can see you're a bit of a landlubber!'

The cabin was tiny and smelt worse than the rest of the barge. To her left was a small cot, which consisted of little more than a heavily stained brown and cream mattress. She could barely see the deck, as it was covered by nautical paraphernalia such as ropes, buoys and pieces of driftwood, as well as a heap of stinking clothes. There was a washbasin to the right, cracked and filthy, and clearly not a source of hygiene. Lucy was speechless.

'Make yourself at home then.'

Lucy took that to be an invitation to sit down on the mattress, which she did. Harry then shut the door and locked it.

'Why are you locking the door, Harry?' asked Lucy, trying to avoid sounding as panicky as she felt.

'I'm sure you wouldn't want us to be disturbed.'

'Disturbed by who?'

'The crew.'

'But I thought you said . . .'

'I know, I know, old Harry can be a bit of a fibber at times.'

'But . . .'

'Don't *worry*,' he insisted. 'We'll be quite alone. Just you and me.'

A belch, and then Harry started fumbling with his trouser buttons. He waddled over to her, sticking out his stomach.

'Here,' he said, thrusting his groin in her face, 'this is your job. Undo 'em!'

Oh God, not *that*, thought Lucy. His smell was

overpowering, almost causing her to retch. With a trembling hand she reached towards his groin.

'Come on, love!' said Harry. 'Are you new at this or something?'

Lucy looked up at him.

'Well?' he said. 'Are you? If you are, I want a cheap rate, 'cos I ain't paying top whack if you're no bloody good.'

Lucy could take no more. Something snapped inside her, something that told her she didn't have to put up with this. What this man was saying was repellent. Her outstretched hand rapidly curled itself into a fist, and with a savage jab she smashed it into the captain's groin.

Her victim bent double, his mouth opening but no sound coming out. She punched him again, harder this time, her fist connecting sharply with his testicles.

'You . . . you bitch!' he gasped.

She punched him again. A further attempt was blocked by his hands.

'You fucking whore! I'll kill—'

No you won't, Lucy thought, landing a well-aimed fist on the captain's nose. That caused a yelp of agony, at which point Lucy stood up and punched him hard in the stomach. Her fist sank into his rolls of flab, barely making an impression. The face, she had better go for the face. Another punch, this time in his left eye, and to Lucy's surprise he fell back, moaning. For good measure she took a well-aimed kick at his ribs. Bastard, she thought, you utter bastard. She kicked him again, unaware of the hammering on the door.

'Open up!'

She turned to the door. About time too, she thought.

'Come on! Let us in! Are you all right in there?'

The voice was Armstrong's.

'Yes! I'm . . . fine. Hold on!'

It was only now that the captain felt Lucy's hands near his groin, though they were not there to arouse him, but to remove the key from his pocket.

'Thank you, Captain.'

The captain merely groaned in response. Lucy got up and unlocked the door, pulling it open to reveal three startled faces.

'Lucy!' Armstrong exclaimed. 'What's going on?'

'I'm sorry, Ja—'

Armstrong firmly clamped his hand over Lucy's mouth and brought a finger to his lips. Lucy nodded – she knew what she had done wrong. He released his grip and stepped past her into the filthy little cabin. He removed a rubber cosh from his jacket pocket and struck the captain twice over the head, which had the instant effect of silencing his groans.

Lucy held up her hands.

'I'm so sorry . . .' she began.

'No need,' said Armstrong. 'Find his wallet and take it. I want this to look like a simple case of petty theft. After you've done that, lock the door and throw the key into the water.'

Lucy nodded and Armstrong turned round to speak to Ted and Nick.

'Right, let's see what we've got here. Have you got the knapsacks?'

Nick nodded.

'Good, well let's get on with it then.'

In silence, they broke open one of the wooden boxes. To Armstrong's delight it was packed with dozens of sticks of dynamite. Within a couple of minutes they had loaded four knapsacks with about twenty sticks each – enough to blow up half the street, Armstrong thought. Nick had also found a box of fuses and timers, which he stuffed into a knapsack.

'Right,' said Armstrong. 'Seal the box and swap it with one at the back. I don't want them to miss this little lot for a while.'

Nick replaced the lid. As it had splintered upon opening, it did not close securely. Nick looked up at Armstrong.

'No matter,' said Armstrong. 'Let's hide it up here.'

Together the three men hauled the box on top of another and then shoved it into the darkness. That would have to do, Armstrong thought.

The sound of approaching footsteps caused them to freeze.

'The crew,' Lucy whispered.

Armstrong stared at her in the darkness, flashing her a filthy look.

'You might have bloody told me.'

Lucy shrugged in apology.

'How many?' Armstrong said.

Lucy shrugged again.

'Christ,' Armstrong murmured.

Laughter rang out. It sounded as though there were just two of them. And now voices.

'I could have done with her meself!'

'Typical 'Arry – I don't know how he does it.'

'Tell you what – let's surprise him!'

'How?'

'Burst into his cabin, catch 'im doin' her.'

'Nice one!'

'Sssh! Not a squeak!'

Armstrong allowed himself a slight smile. The crewmen would be on the wrong end of an entirely different type of surprise. He gestured to the others to hide behind some boxes, then drew out his cosh and indicated to Nick, who was standing on the other side of the passageway formed by the cargo, that he should do the same.

The crewmen made a bad job of getting on to the barge quietly, barely managing to suppress their grunting laughter as they climbed down the steps.

' 'Arry's not making a lot of noise!'

'Sssh!'

Armstrong listened as the men crept noisily towards them. He estimated they must still be twenty feet away.

'Do yer think 'e's 'ere?'

'Sssh, I said!'

With ten feet to go, Armstrong flashed a look at Nick, who was raising his cosh in readiness. Some more laughter came from the crewmen.

'She must be good, this one!'

'For fuck's sake, Pete, shut it!'

After another few seconds the first crewman drew level. Sensing Armstrong's presence, he turned to his left, only to be rewarded with a cosh smacked directly to the side of his head. He crumpled to the floor.

'Phil!' shouted the other crewman, but Nick was upon him, his cosh connecting with the man's cranium. However, he only managed to strike a glancing blow, and the crewman lashed out wildly. Nick attempted to hit him again, but was repulsed by the man punching him on the side of his neck, knocking him painfully on to a box.

Armstrong stepped over the fallen man and laid into the second crewman violently. It was too bad that the chap was innocent – one day he would like to explain to him why it was that he was being attacked with such ferocity by, of all people, the Conservative chief whip. Until then, he could make no apology for the repeated blows of his cosh, blows that were dispatching the man into an unconscious sprawl on the deck.

'Let's go!' Armstrong hissed.

The others needed no further prompting. As they stepped out of the barge, Armstrong looked at his watch. Ten to eight. They should make it back to the safe-house just after the curfew began.

* * *

Henry Allen unlocked the front door of his large house in Belgravia. To his surprise, his wife Louisa was there to greet him, her fingers anxiously twiddling her necklace.

'Darling,' she said haughtily, 'there's an American here.'

Allen couldn't establish whether his wife was put out by the fact that they had a visitor, or that the visitor was an American.

'He was most insistent that he wait for you,' she continued, 'so I showed him to your study.'

'Does he have a name, your American?'

'He's not *my* American, Henry, he's *yours*,' Louisa replied, handing him a card.

'One Carl Parsons from the United States Embassy, no less,' said Allen. 'Never heard of him. Did he say what he wanted?'

She shook her head.

'Is he on his own?' he asked.

His wife nodded, her eyes bulging.

'And how long has he been here?' Allen asked, removing his coat.

'Just over an hour,' she said, taking the coat and hanging it on an elegant oak stand.

'An *hour*?'

'That's right. One hour.'

Allen started to walk along the long corridor towards the large sweeping staircase.

'Henry?'

He turned round – there was an edge to her voice.

'Yes?'

'What's he doing here?'

Allen lifted his shoulders and dropped them again, letting his hands gently slap against the sides of his thighs.

'You know as much as I do, my dear,' he said. 'I shall reveal all after I've seen him.'

She nodded, her eyes narrowing. She didn't believe him. Henry had not been the same since that dinner at Emerald Cunard's. He was agitated, nervous. He had even lost weight. Perhaps he had taken a leaf out of her book and was having an affair – it would be about time. But this *American* – well, it was very odd.

'You'd better,' she replied. 'I don't like strange Yanks in my house.'

So it was *her* house now, was it? Henry bowed towards her, the exaggeration of the gesture revealing its utter insincerity. Then he turned and walked up the stairs, knowing full well the type of face Louisa would be pulling behind his back.

That the visitor was not sitting in Henry's desk chair was a good sign. Instead, he was perched awkwardly on an old nursing chair that had somehow found a home in Allen's study because his wife said there was no room for it elsewhere. He stood up as soon as Allen entered.

'Good evening, Mr Allen,' he said, confidently extending his arm. 'My name is Carl Parsons. I'm the—'

'I remember you now,' said Allen, shaking Parsons' offered

hand. 'You're the one who was tickled by my remark about our Minister for Information.'

'The very same,' Parsons replied.

Allen sat behind his desk.

'What do you want, Mr Parsons? I must tell you that it's most irregular of you to have invited yourself in – you have caused my wife considerable distress.'

'Forgive me,' said Parsons. 'I am truly sorry.'

Allen nodded and opened a drawer, from which he removed a wooden box.

'Cigar, Mr Parsons?'

Parsons lifted his hand to refuse and Allen lit one for himself. He removed a loose scrap of tobacco from his lower lip and deposited it in the ashtray.

'Go on then.'

Parsons took a deep breath. He looked scared, Allen thought, even going so far as to look over his shoulder. He shifted uneasily in his seat before replying.

'You have to understand that this visit is . . . unofficial. My ambassador does not know I am here. I know it is a liberty, sir, but I would like to request that things stay that way.'

'I shall not tell Mr Bingham a thing,' said Allen, trying hard to mask his keenness to hear what it was that Parsons had to say.

'Thank you, Mr Allen, it is much appreciated.'

'Not at all.'

Another deep breath.

'I'll cut to the chase,' said Parsons. 'There's a Commie plot to overthrow your government.'

Allen said nothing. Parsons paused, somewhat taken aback by Allen's sang-froid.

'Two weeks ago,' he continued, 'a senior Soviet intelligence officer defected to the US. He was fully debriefed in

Washington, and during that debriefing – which I understand is still in progress – he revealed that there is a network of agents, here in Great Britain, who are plotting to topple Sir Oswald and install a Soviet leadership in his place.'

Allen puffed on his cigar and sat back. He wanted to lean forward, but refused to allow himself to do so.

'Carry on,' he said, as calmly as possible.

'It's not clear exactly how they mean to do it,' said Parsons, 'but what we do know is that some of these agents are very highly placed within the British – I mean the *fascist* establishment.'

'You mean to tell me that these agents are British nationals?'

'Quite so, sir. Absolutely.'

A small piece of ash fell from Allen's cigar on to his right lapel. Parsons was about to point it out, but then remembered a nugget of etiquette about the British upper classes – they never flicked the ash off their cigars, and let it fall where it might. There were others who would clean it up.

'Do we know who these people are?' Allen asked.

'No – but we do know their code names. There's one called "Top Hat", who's meant to be very close indeed to Sir Oswald – perhaps even in the Cabinet itself. Then there's "Dog", who the defector says is a new recruit. He says he knows very little about him, except that he's key to the whole plot. There are some other minor players, but those are the two main guys. And then of course there is their controller.'

'Controller?'

'Goes by the name of "Otto". He's an Austrian apparently, and a real NKVD pro.'

'And what do we know about him?'

'Again, not much, except that he's smart, very smart, and he's been here for a few years.'

Chapter Nine

Evening Out

September 1937

THE AIR ON the heath hung heavy with smoke and the acrid smell of explosives. It was a struggle to make out the troops through their field-glasses, but as far as the assembled bevy of staff officers could tell, the exercise was going well. General Sir Edward Galwey had insisted that live ammunition be used, and therefore he had seen fit to wear a helmet, a precaution aped by his fellow officers.

'Looks like Merriman's men are going to take the ridge,' said Galwey to the officer on his left, a brigadier-general by the name of Acheson. Galwey didn't care much for Acheson, thought him a dreadful fascist toady, but he knew better than to openly insult him. Men like Acheson were on the rise, a rise that Galwey hoped to check.

'It looks like it, sir,' Acheson replied. 'He's a good man, Merriman, although . . .'

· He paused.

'Although what, Acheson?' asked Galwey, scanning the ridge for any further signs of activity.

'Although he's a little suspect in some ways, sir, not very loyal to the Government.'

Galwey momentarily took the field-glasses away from his eyes, and then continued to study the field.

'You think he's a traitor, do you?' he said.

'Not exactly, sir . . .'

'Think he wouldn't fight if we were invaded?'

'I'm not saying that, sir, it's just that he's rather outspoken about the Leader, thinks he meddles too much in army business.'

'He's entitled to his opinions, Acheson.'

Acheson didn't reply.

'Well? He is, isn't he?'

'Yes, sir, of course, sir.'

'Well there we go, then. As far as I'm concerned, he's a damn fine soldier.'

'Yes, sir.'

Galwey looked up at the ridge.

'He certainly seems to be giving your man Landale a good hiding up there.'

Once more Acheson didn't reply, causing Galwey to smile gently to himself. Acheson was not to know it, but Lieutenant-Colonel Huw Merriman was a key figure in the plot against Mosley – one of 'Armstrong's Army Boys', as they secretly styled themselves. Galwey made a mental note to tell Merriman to go easy on airing his opinions about the regime. It wouldn't do any good for him to get himself into trouble, not at this stage of Armstrong and Galwey's well-laid plans.

'Sir?' came a voice from his right.

Galwey turned to face an old friend – Major-General Charles Clifford.

'*Charles*,' said Galwey. 'This is a pleasant surprise – didn't think you signals chaps liked it out here in the mud and filth.'

'Well,' said Clifford, 'even us radio men need a bit of fresh air from time to time.'

'By the way,' said Galwey, 'before I forget – how is that dear old aunt of yours? Last I'd heard, she was on the mend. Still in the pink, feeling bonny, that sort of thing?'

'It's kind of you to ask, sir,' Clifford replied. 'She's very well, blossoming in fact. I even received a telegram yesterday saying that she was going to make her own birthday party this year.'

'Plucky one, your aunt.'

'Very much so, sir.'

'Good, good – now take a look at this man Merriman over on the ridge. We're just waiting for him to send up a flare to say that he's taken it . . . Ah! Speak of the devil! Acheson – I'd say that's one-love to me.'

Acheson forced a smile. He was sick of men like Galwey and Clifford – in his eyes, they were all aristocratic bluff, the type of men who were holding Britain back. For heaven's sake, he thought, they even rabbited on about their fucking aunts.

* * *

'But what am I going to say to Bridget?'

'Just tell her that it was stolen,' Armstrong replied. 'After all, cars get stolen all the time.'

'But we'll never be able to afford a new one,' said Ted. 'There aren't all that many vacancies for former newspaper editors.'

Armstrong had little time for this.

'All right,' he said. 'Then I will just have to steal one, with all the attendant risk that involves. I thought you might be willing to make a sacrifice, but it seems as though I was wrong.'

Ted sighed and lit a cigarette.

'All right, all right – you win. But you'd better make *damn* certain that the number plates are removed, and the chassis number is filed off.'

'That's not a problem,' said Armstrong. 'Although when it goes off, I doubt there will be very much left.'

'Yes, but just in case . . .'

'Don't worry – I'll make sure.'

The next day, Ted brought his car round to the disused warehouse in which he and Armstrong had been questioned by Nick and Martin.

'That's a nice motor,' said Nick. 'What is it?'

'It's a Hillman Wizard,' said Ted ruefully. 'It cost me two hundred and eighty quid a few years back. It's never gone wrong once.'

'It had better not have a change of heart,' said Armstrong. 'I don't fancy breaking down halfway along the Embankment with a boot full of explosives.'

' "The Car of the Moderns",' said Martin out of nowhere.

'What?' asked Nick.

' "The Car of the Moderns",' Martin repeated, gliding his open hand in the air as if to indicate a name up in lights. 'I remember the ad campaign for it. Pretty stylish stuff, with a couple of posh folks standing next to it.'

'Since when did they not have posh folks in those ads?'

'Well, they didn't for the Austin 7 . . .'

'All right, all right,' said Armstrong. 'We've got work to do. Ted – do you want to help?'

'No way,' he said, shaking his head. 'It would break my heart.'

They packed the dynamite in every conceivable hiding place – inside the spare wheel, in a couple of suitcases in the boot, under the wheel arches, in the glove compartment, under the seats. Armstrong also decided to place a knapsack full of explosive on the back seat. This would contain the fuse, which he would set for three minutes – plenty of time to enable the driver to make good his escape.

'When this goes off,' said Armstrong, 'half the street will disappear. I have no doubt that the so-called Department of Labour Reassignment will be obliterated.'

Nick and Martin grinned broadly. The only person who didn't was Lucy.

'Isn't this taking a sledgehammer to crack a nut?' she asked. 'I mean, if this explosion is going to be that big, we could end up killing people.'

'Not if we do it at night,' said Armstrong, 'just before the curfew starts. Most of the buildings on Smith Street contain civil servants, who like to leave their desks just before half past five I seem to remember.'

'Anybody who works in that place deserves to die,' said Nick.

'You sound as barbaric as them,' said Lucy.

'Take that back!'

'No,' snapped Lucy. 'I'm not fighting to replace one type of barbarism with another.'

'Oh very fine words indeed,' said Nick. 'Aren't we the politician now?'

'*Please*,' said Armstrong, his voice raised, 'let's not argue. All that does is help *them*. But I do think Lucy is right. If we blow up a load of civil servants, that will give Mosley plenty of useful propaganda to use against us. He's a master at that, as you know from when he started marching his men through the East End. You Communists attacked him with such ferocity that it made *him* look like the victim and you like the aggressors. Please don't forget that I'd rather not go through with this bombing, but we made a deal, and I'm going to keep my side of it, unless you just want to spend your time blowing up buildings and killing policemen.'

Armstrong drew breath before continuing. He was lecturing Nick, he knew it, but the man needed it.

'Decapitation – that's what it's about, Nick. I don't want to get bogged down in street fighting and missile-throwing. That will only strengthen them, convince the public that Mosley really is right, that he is trying to protect the country from the enemy within. Why else do you think I spent all those weeks trying to put a network together? Why do you think that I've asked you to set up all those cells? After we've killed Mosley, I want order and democracy to be restored as soon as possible. But the longer democracy is absent, the harder it will be to put it back in place. Your way, Nick, will keep Mosley in power for years, decades. I'll blow up your building – and yes, I think it's probably the right thing to do – but I won't do any more. After that, it's Mosley or bust.'

Nick stuffed his hands in his pocket – the surly schoolboy, thought Armstrong.

'He's right, Nick,' said Lucy. 'For each person we kill, we ratchet up Mosley's strength another fraction.'

Martin said nothing, merely nodded. He and Nick were old friends, but it was clear that the pressure was getting to Nick, and his edginess was wearing them all down.

'One question,' said Nick, pointing to the Hillman. 'Who's going to drive this car over to Westminster?'

'I will,' said Armstrong.

'That's just as well,' said Nick, 'as neither Martin nor I can drive.'

Armstrong paused before opening his mouth. It didn't particularly surprise him that the two men couldn't drive – after all, most people didn't – but he had expected that they might have tried to learn.

'Perhaps I should give you some lessons,' he said with a smile.

'What, in that?' said Nick.

'Well, it would certainly encourage you to drive carefully.'

'The Hillman Wizard,' said Martin. 'It goes with a bang.'

Lucy insisted on coming with Armstrong. He had refused at first, but she had convinced him by pointing out that a man and a woman in a car looked less suspicious than a man on his own. What could be more natural, she said, than a couple parking a car in a smart Westminster street in time to get home before the curfew?

A couple. The phrase resonated strongly with Armstrong. How long was it since he had been part of a couple? He missed Mary very deeply, and had accordingly sublimated any desires he had started to feel for others. He had told himself that the love he felt for Philip was enough, but he knew that there was still a void, that paternal love was just one sort of love. Most men married again, his friends had told him, but he hadn't. He had never stopped to ask why that was so – it was just the way it had happened. And now he was going to pretend to be part of a couple, and it felt as alien to him as exploding a car bomb in the heart of London.

Armstrong did his best to dismiss such thoughts as he started the car. Still bearded, he was wearing a suit he had borrowed from Ted, the tightness of a tie round his neck feeling unusual after weeks spent without one. He looked down at his left lapel to study the metal lightning flash badge stuck through the buttonhole – a nice touch by Ted, as such badges were becoming the norm rather than the exception.

The passenger door opened and Lucy got in. She was wearing a lightweight woollen coat with a fur collar, and a hat with an elegantly sweeping brim. Armstrong turned to look at her. She was wearing make-up – not the heavy paint of the night in the pub, but a subtler application that made her appear far more sophisticated. Armstrong felt obliged to say something.

'You look . . .' he began, and then faltered.

'Yes?'

'You look good, look the part.'

'Thank you,' Lucy said, peering at him under the brim of her hat. 'I thought I should make an effort if I'm going to meet my maker this evening.'

Armstrong smiled and started the car.

At a quarter to eight, Armstrong turned right off Millbank and drove slowly along Smith Street.

'Where will number five be?' Lucy asked.

'This end,' said Armstrong.

'How do you know that?'

'Because all street numbering in London starts from the end of the road nearest the river.'

'I don't believe you!'

'It's absolutely true,' said Armstrong, as he concentrated on looking for their target.

With only a few minutes to go until the curfew, the street was nearly empty, save for a few Blackshirts.

'Here it is,' said Armstrong.

They drew up alongside a tall Georgian building, its bricks blackened by the London air. Armstrong squinted at a shining brass plaque next to the large green door – *The Department of Labour Reassignment*. So innocuous, so innocent – just another Whitehall department doing its job, the plaque and the architecture of the building exuding an atmosphere of governmental legitimacy. The light coming from two windows on the second floor betrayed the presence of those working late.

'There are people in there,' said Armstrong.

Lucy frowned.

'I thought you said there wouldn't be.'

'I did – but it would appear that reassigning labour is a task that requires long hours.'

'What are we going to do?'

'I don't see any reason why we should call it off.'

'But . . .'

'Nick is right – partly. Whoever is working there now is obviously a fanatic.'

'But surely we could wait?'

'No,' said Armstrong, 'we can't. Anyway, you yourself are willing to kill policemen, so why are you objecting to blowing up those who are persecuting your people?'

Lucy stared hard at him.

'I just feel uneasy . . .'

'So do I,' said Armstrong, casting his mind back to India, to the war, to that roadblock in Scotland – all the places where he had taken life. He had been given medals for killing and leading men to kill, and now he was about to kill again, but this time he would not receive any reward, at least not immediately. In a way, everybody he had killed had been innocent – they had all thought they were doing right, especially the Abor tribesmen. It was the tribesmen who bothered him the most.

Armstrong returned Lucy's stare.

'I've killed people I haven't wanted to kill,' he said. 'But the men in there are doing a terrible thing. It's not just those in fascist and policemen's uniforms who are the enemy; it's also those who are listening to them, obeying them. You heard what I said to Nick, about how I don't want to go round committing indiscriminate killings, how that would bolster Mosley's support. But I'm not going to call this off just because there are a handful of civil servants up there who are cold-bloodedly working out how to enslave hundreds of thousands of their fellow countrymen. I'd rather they were brought to justice, but with the absence of justice, there is no other way. And if this is the way that enables me to get closer to getting Mosley, then I'm not going to flinch because of whoever's up there.'

Armstrong waited, tapping the steering wheel, as Lucy looked over her shoulder at the back seat. He admired her principles, but there was not enough time to have this discussion. If necessary, he would force the issue by simply setting the fuse.

'Well?' he said.

Lucy looked through the windscreen. Armstrong's remark about not just fighting those in uniforms had touched a nerve – he was right, but she still felt uncomfortable killing civilians. Maybe the lights were on because there were innocent cleaning ladies in there, or maybe— She stopped herself. There were too many ifs. Alan would not have thought like this, and neither would her father. Armstrong was like them, she thought; he was one of those men who made things happen, who refused to be stopped. It was strange how circumstances had thrown them together – the Tory army officer and the East End

Communist. On paper, she hated him – he probably hated her too – but it was clear that there was a mutual respect.

She turned to face him.

'How long do we have to get away?' she asked.

'Three minutes,' said Armstrong.

'Let's do it,' she said.

Without another word, Armstrong turned and set the timed fuse which had been placed at the top of the knapsack. Lucy watched him, her left hand poised on the door handle.

'Right,' said Armstrong, 'it's set. Let's go, but let's not run.'

They opened their doors simultaneously and stepped out into the evening air. Lucy walked round to the pavement and slipped her right hand through Armstrong's left arm. She clutched it tightly, drawing herself close to him. They strolled down the street in silence, away from Millbank and towards Victoria Street.

'How long has it been?' asked Lucy after no more than half a minute.

'It doesn't matter,' said Armstrong firmly, his attention distracted by a green Bentley which was approaching them slowly. As it passed them, Armstrong noticed that the windscreen bore a triangular red permit next to its tax disc. The permit indicated that the car was allowed to be driven during the curfew, which could only mean that the driver was a senior Party member.

'Don't look at the car,' said Armstrong through clenched teeth.

He heard the Bentley come to a halt a few yards behind them.

'Keep walking,' said Armstrong. 'Don't turn round.'

Lucy did as he requested, although Armstrong could sense that she was desperately keen to see what was happening.

'But whoever it is may be going into the building,' she said.

'Too bad,' said Armstrong.

'We can't just let someone walk in . . .'

'We *have* to,' Armstrong hissed.

Before he had a chance to stop her, Lucy had wriggled free and headed back down the street. Furious, Armstrong watched her run up to the Bentley, out of which was stepping a smartly dressed, slightly portly man in his early forties. What the hell was she playing at? She was about to get herself killed. He wanted to shout, but there was no point – she was as stubborn as her father. She was a fool, he thought, an impetuous bloody fool.

Armstrong looked at his watch. There were two minutes to go. He knew he should keep walking, but he couldn't abandon Lucy. Try to defuse the bomb? It was certainly possible, but the driver of the Bentley would see him. There was only one thing to do.

He ran towards Lucy and the driver.

'Get back in the car!' he shouted.

The two of them turned to him in surprise. God knew what Lucy had been telling him, as the man already looked utterly bewildered.

'What's all this?' he was saying.

His face seemed familiar, but Armstrong had no time to attempt to recall his name.

'I've got a gun!' said Armstrong. 'Now get back in your bloody car!'

The man froze. He was evidently no Blackshirt thug, thought Armstrong; he looked too patrician, a little too well fed.

'Get in the fucking car and drive!'

Still no movement.

'Get back in your car!'

After what seemed an age, the man did as he was told. Armstrong grabbed Lucy's wrist and dragged her with him into the back seat of the Bentley. The man was sitting in the front, although he had not yet started the engine.

'Come on!' Armstrong shouted. 'Unless you want me to shoot you!'

The man started the engine and pulled away.

'Where . . . where shall I go?'

'Turn right on to Millbank, and then go over Vauxhall Bridge.'

'Are you . . . are you *kidnapping* me?'

Armstrong glared at Lucy. This was a complete cock-up, but he wasn't going to let on in front of their new captive.

'Yes,' he replied. 'Just do as I tell you, and you'll be all right.'

They drove in silence for half a minute.

'But . . . but . . .' the man started.

'Yes?'

'But . . . why didn't she want me to go into that building?'

'You'll hear soon enough,' said Armstrong. 'What's your name?'

'My n . . . name?'

'That's right.'

'You don't know?'

'No. I wouldn't be asking you otherwise.'

'It's . . . it's Allen, Henry Allen.'

Gerald Reid had always hated the Jews. They were thieving scum, and they deserved what was coming to them. For a long time Gerald had kept these views to himself, although he would happily extemporise to his wife Enid about how the

Jews liked to kill Christian children and drink their blood. He had read about this 'Jewish blood libel' in *The Protocols of the Elders of Zion*, a work that confirmed all he had ever suspected. Gerald knew that his views were rather unpopular, and, unwilling to lose his job in the Ministry of Works, he kept them to himself.

Mosley had changed all that, giving ordinary men like Gerald the chance to speak out, to tell the world what was really happening. The Leader gave him a voice, gave him the courage to speak up for himself, to tell those around him that the immigrants would ruin the British way of life and that the only way to deal with them was to lock them up in some sort of camp. Gerald wore his black shirt with pride, and soon he was spending every night down at the Black House, his dedication to the cause ensuring that he was soon able to wear the full 'Action Press' uniform.

There was a light in his eyes now and a fire in his not inconsiderable belly. He had a new job in a new department that was the apogee of both his career and his convictions – he was finally using his administrative talents to bring about what he knew to be right. No longer was he carrying out the wishes of flabby lovers of democracy; now he was the executor – or executer! – of a tough new policy that would ensure that the Jews knew their place, a place that would hopefully grow smaller over time.

Along with two colleagues, Gerald was working late that night. He had only been with this department for three weeks, but it felt like three months, so heavy was the workload. It was worth the effort though. They were achieving great things, really making a difference. This evening they were putting the finishing touches to the problem of actually *moving* these damn people. How many trains? How many buses? Would the army be involved? How many Jews could they fit into a single carriage? How about goods vans – how many could they get in those?

And just this afternoon, brought round by a courier, a memorandum from the Leader's office – signed by the Leader no less! – giving the department advance warning that they would soon need to add the following types to their list: homosexuals, Freemasons, Gypsies, habitual criminals, proven Communists. The memorandum estimated another 150,000 to 200,000 persons – *initially*. That meant a lot more work, but for the time being they were to concentrate on the Jews.

Gerald lit his pipe and got up from his desk. The light was fading, and with it, the temperature was dropping. It was time to shut the office window. He puffed his pipe vigorously as he walked across the room, his attention briefly held by the time displayed on the clock – just gone ten to eight. He had better telephone Enid – he would be here for another hour at least. Still, she knew how much he was enjoying his work. He shut the window and stood at it for a few seconds, gazing across the street at a building similar to the one he was in.

If he had stayed at his desk, Gerald Reid might have lived. He might also have lived if he had walked away from the window as soon as he had shut it. But his ruminative gaze cost him his life. His death was sudden, because the shards of glass from the window he had just shut removed the best part of his head, mangling the cherrywood of his pipe with fragments of his brain and skull. His chest also received a hail of glass, and at least two of the dagger-sharp pieces lanced into his heart. In addition, his abdomen, his genitals and the tops of his thighs were also severely lacerated. What remained of his body was thrown back towards his colleagues, one of whom received a long spear of glass straight through his right eye and into his brain. The other colleague, who had been standing just behind the metal filing cabinet, lived for twenty or thirty minutes, but the ensuing fire that was to gut the building produced enough smoke to suffocate him as he tried to crawl down the stairs.

Just as Gerald Reid was being blown across his office, Henry Allen's Bentley was heading east down Albert Embankment. The explosion, although on the other side of the river, could be clearly heard by the car's occupants. Lucy turned to Armstrong.

'Was that . . . ?'

'Yes, it was,' he said.

Armstrong saw Allen looking at them in his mirror.

'That was a bomb, wasn't it? It was! That was why you wanted me—'

'Just keep driving,' Armstrong snarled.

'What did you blow up?'

It was Lucy who answered.

'Since you ask,' she said, 'it was the Department of Labour Reassignment. We thought it best that it didn't continue with its work.'

Allen didn't reply immediately, although they could clearly hear him exhale.

'Who *are* you?' he asked.

'None of your business,' said Armstrong. 'Just shut up.'

The warehouse, thought Armstrong, that's where they'd go. They needed to get this car off the road immediately – a Bentley in the middle of the East End would be far too conspicuous. Not only that, they also needed to find a way to silence the man who was driving them. There was no way Armstrong was going to leave him to go free and provide the police with full descriptions of him and Lucy.

'You know the way to Tower Bridge?' he asked.

Allen nodded.

They arrived at the warehouse fifteen minutes later. Nick, Martin and Ted were there, all three of them drinking from a bottle of whisky around a small brazier. They were also smoking their way through a packet of Ted's Black Cap cigarettes, cigarettes that were hurriedly thrown to the floor as the Bentley roared in through the vast entrance gate.

'What the hell is this?' asked Nick. 'Did you . . . ?'

'Yes we did,' said a furious Armstrong, springing out of the car. 'Although we ran into a slight difficulty.'

He looked pointedly at Lucy before continuing.

'Miss Craven here insisted on saving the owner of this car.'

'Who is he?' asked Ted, peering through the windscreen.

'Out!' Armstrong barked.

A terrified Allen slowly opened his door, and Armstrong roughly pulled him out.

'This,' he said, 'is Henry Allen. He's a Blackshirt MP, as well as one of Mosley's confidants. His wife and his father-in-law are Blackshirts too. I also think I'm right in saying that you've even written a book about our dear Leader.'

Allen nodded. All eyes turned back to Armstrong.

'How do you know all this?' asked Lucy.

'Part of my job,' said Armstrong. 'It's now *your* job to work out what we are going to do with him.'

'I think you can guess what I'd like to do,' said Nick.

'That's not going to happen,' said Armstrong.

'Well, he would make a useful hostage,' said Ted. 'A good bargaining chip.'

'No,' said Armstrong. 'I don't want to go down that road – far too messy.'

'We could simply lock him up here,' said Martin.

'Keep him on ice?' said Armstrong. 'That will do for the time being.'

He turned to Lucy.

'And since you brought him here,' he said, 'you're going to change his nappies.'

Lucy tried to protest, but Armstrong would not have it.

'Not a word!'

For a moment the warehouse was filled with silence, its occupants cowering under Armstrong's anger. It was Allen who spoke first.

'Thank you.'

'For what?' asked Armstrong.

'For saving me.'

Armstrong dismissed the words with a brisk wave of his hand.

'My fucking pleasure,' he replied.

'I'm serious,' said Allen. 'I'm very grateful. I never thought I would have cause to thank a Communist.'

'What makes you think I'm a Communist?'

'It's obvious, isn't it?' said Allen. 'Anyway, I know all about your plot. You're intending to get rid of Mosley and turn us into a Soviet republic.'

'*What?*'

'That's what I've heard.'

Armstrong drew closer.

'From whom?'

'From the Americans.'

'The *Americans?*'

Allen found himself surrounded by five pairs of inquisitive eyes.

'That's right,' said Allen. 'The Americans. And to be honest, good luck to you – at least in removing Mosley.'

'Mr Allen,' said Armstrong, 'you have some explaining to do.'

So closely was Armstrong looking at Allen that he didn't notice that Ted's stare was more intent than the others'.

Allen told them about Carl Parsons and what little he knew. He told them about Krivitsky's defection, and how the Soviet general had revealed that the plot was being run by an NKVD officer called Otto, who had at least two agents – going by the names of Top Hat and Dog – working for him. Apparently, said Allen, Top Hat was very high up, and might even be one of Mosley's Emergency Cabinet members. Dog, on the other hand, was a more recent recruit, although usefully placed, and he reported to Top Hat.

'Why are you telling us this?' Armstrong asked.

'Because I want you to succeed,' Allen replied. 'Let's just say that I've had a Pauline conversion.'

'I don't believe you,' said Armstrong.

'It's the truth!'

'Crap,' said Nick. 'Come on – let's beat the truth out of him.'

Armstrong held out his hand.

'Give the man a chance,' he said. 'Go on then, Mr Allen, the floor is yours.'

'May I have a cigarette?'

'Certainly.'

Ted passed Allen a Black Cap and lit it for him.

'All right, Mr Allen,' said Armstrong, 'I want you to tell us why you want Mosley overthrown.'

'The short reason is this – he's insane. He's twisted fascism into a means of controlling people, rather than using it as it is meant to be used–'

'Which is how?' asked Lucy. 'To pack Jews into camps?'

'Fair point,' said Allen. 'But when people like me first turned to fascism, we saw it as a way of restoring Britain to its glorious past, of attempting to mimic the great achievements of Tudor society – that is *our* historical precedent for fascism. Each country looks back for its own. The Italians look at the Romans, the Germans look at Frederick the Great and Heinrich the First. Fascism was never intended to be a means of control; rather a way to enable the peoples of a nation to achieve great things. It was intended to unite, to bring us all together to form a highly productive unit. I always felt that democracy was too muddled, too inefficient, far too slow. One spent a lot of time electing people who were clearly incapable, and it struck me as common sense that you should allow a ruling class – based on meritocracy – to do just that, to get on and rule. Sacrifice some of the freedoms that slow you down, and in exchange you get progress, modernity, a real dynamism.'

'Except it doesn't work, does it?' said Armstrong.

'No,' said Allen, shaking his head. 'I'm sorry to say that it doesn't – it doesn't allow for any opposition or discussion, and therefore it breeds corruption. That's why, for the same reason, I don't hold out any great hope for communism either.'

Lucy, Nick and Martin all spoke at once, although it was Lucy's voice that carried.

'Rubbish!' she cried. 'You only have to look at Stalin's achievements. The five-year-plans are—'

'Are killing thousands of peasants,' said Allen.

'Is that right?' asked Lucy sarcastically. 'Somehow I expected you to say something like that.'

'This is not the time,' said Armstrong.

'It's never the time, is it?' said Nick.

'When Mosley's gone, *then* it will be the time,' said

Armstrong. 'For now we have to work together, put these differences to one side, and resolve them democratically – in Parliament. Carry on, Mr Allen. You were saying that fascism doesn't work, but that doesn't tell us why you have turned against your own Party.'

Allen ground his cigarette out with his heel.

'Well – it's because I don't like what they're doing to people like you.'

'Who?'

'The Jews. But it's also going to be Freemasons, convicted criminals, homosexuals . . .'

'What are they going to do?'

'Put them all into camps.'

Nobody spoke for a few seconds. The brazier was dying down, and the last smudges of daylight were slowly blending into the dark grey gloom of the warehouse.

'If you're so against all this,' said Lucy, 'what were you doing on Smith Street this evening?'

'I was going to see what they were up to in there – I wanted to find out more.'

'A likely story,' said Nick.

'I swear it's the truth!'

Armstrong narrowed his eyes.

'I want to meet your American,' he said. 'This Mr Parsons.'

'But that will be—'

'Perfectly possible, I'm sure,' said Armstrong. 'That way I'll be able to work out if your story is true, won't I?'

'But . . .'

'I won't accept any objections.'

* * *

According to the SBC, *Action* and *The Blackshirt*, the building that had been bombed was none other than the recently established Department for the Welfare of Children. The outrage had clearly been carried out by the Jews, said Mosley, who were desperate to cover up the department's investigation into the Jewish blood libel. The only accurate piece of information contained in the newspapers' pages was that three hard-working civil servants had died in the blast. All would receive full fascist burials, complete with Blackshirt pipes and drums.

In private, the Leader was apoplectic. Neil Francis Hawkins, the Home Secretary, told him that the programme to get the Jews into their resettlement camps had been set back by at least two months. Volumes of important paperwork had been lost, as well as the knowledge held by the three men who had died. Gerald Reid would be especially missed, he told the Leader, even though he had only worked in the department for a few weeks. Reid had been one of the most loyal and competent of Blackshirts, Francis Hawkins claimed. In that case, said the Leader, we shall build a memorial to him. The man was a hero, and heroes should always be remembered.

* * *

Sir Roger Ousby received the telephone call at midday on his private line.

'Yes?' he answered, expecting it to be his wife.

'Sir Roger?'

Although the voice was female, it was certainly not familiar.

'Yes? Who is this?'

'Never mind – just listen to me.'

Sir Roger calmly picked up a pen. Calls from lunatics were sporadic, but he made a point of noting them all down.

'A Mr Carl Parsons from the American Embassy has contacted Henry Allen MP. I repeat, *Henry Allen*. He has told Allen that there is a Soviet plot to overthrow the Leader.'

Sir Roger stopped writing. He didn't want any record of this conversation.

'And can you prove this?'

'You had better ask him, hadn't you?'

The line went dead.

'Hello?'

Sir Roger gently put the receiver back down. He tapped the end of his pen against his chin. This was it; this was what he had been waiting for.

* * *

Wearing a bowler hat and a pair of spectacles with plain lenses, Armstrong turned up at Claridge's hotel at half past three. He had ordered Allen to book a room under the name of 'Mr Nugent' and arrange to meet Parsons there at four o'clock. The only other person who knew the details was Ted, who had wanted to come along, but Armstrong had refused, saying that there was no point in both of them risking their necks.

Eschewing the front entrance, Armstrong entered via the kitchens, posing as an inspector from the Ministry of Health and carrying an official-looking clipboard. The staff were bemused, not least because they had had an inspection only two days earlier. When Armstrong was told this, he calmly pointed out that the whole efficacy of such inspections depended on their happening at the least likely time.

He spent twenty minutes in the kitchens, and then headed up to the magnificent art deco lobby. He strode purposefully across to the reception desk, not allowing himself to be distracted by the posse of upper-crust Blackshirts milling around near the entrance.

'Good afternoon,' he said politely to a female receptionist. 'I have a meeting with Mr Nugent.'

The woman looked down at a sheet of paper.

'Ah yes, Mr Nugent. He is in room 312, third floor.'

'Thank you,' said Armstrong, and turned to walk to the stairs. He took them two at a time, and within less than a minute was on the third floor, his heart beating rapidly. He walked slowly down the corridor, looking at the numbers on the doors: 308 . . . 309 . . . 310 . . . 311 . . . 312.

Armstrong was about to knock on the door when he noticed it was slightly ajar. He gently pushed it open, concerned by the lack of voices coming from within.

'Mr Nugent?' he asked.

Nothing.

'Mr Nugent?' he repeated, this time louder.

Still nothing.

Armstrong stepped into the room, only to come across a tableau that caused a hectic surge of bile to rise into his mouth. On the floor were two fully clothed bodies. Both had been decapitated. Clotted streams of brownish-red blood had oozed across the carpet from the stumps of their necks and collected in a sticky pool underneath a writing table.

The table. Armstrong stared at the table, at the large bowl of fruit in its middle. There, in amongst the apples, pears and grapes, were the heads that had belonged to the bodies. One was clearly that of Allen. An orange had been stuck into its mouth.

'And who might you be?'

Armstrong looked over to where the voice had come from. Standing in the doorway that led into the bathroom were two men, both dressed in chalk-stripe suits, wearing snap-brim hats, and pointing revolvers at him. HMSSP.

'We thought these two might have a friend. Pray, please don't be silent.'

Armstrong didn't reply.

One of the secret policemen walked over to the table and took a bunch of grapes that had been resting on top of Allen's head. He plucked one off its stalk and walked towards Armstrong.

'Grape?'

Armstrong stayed silent.

'Sure?'

The man stared at him closely, his nostrils flaring wildly. He then slowly put the grape into his mouth and started chewing it noisily. Then he grimaced and pulled out a short brown hair from between his teeth.

'Yuck,' he said coldly. 'I hate it when I get hair in my food. Especially someone else's. You would have thought better of Claridge's.'

A madman, Armstrong thought, a creature from a nightmare.

The man reached out and removed Armstrong's glasses, and tried them on.

'Ha! I didn't think they were real. What are we trying to hide, Mr . . . ?'

Armstrong still stayed silent. He wanted to bolt for it, but he saw that the other man had kept his revolver aimed straight at him.

'I think I know who you are.'

Armstrong felt the bowler hat being slowly lifted from his head. There was something graceful, feminine, in the way that the man moved. He was relishing his work – if that was the word – exuding an aura that suggested that he was aroused.

'I don't think you are a mister at all,' he said. 'In fact, I think you are a captain. Am I right?'

Armstrong remained expressionless.

'What a bonus! Sir Roger will be pleased!'

* * *

'ARMSTRONG CAPTURED!' yells the front page of *Action*, beneath which is printed a photograph of the fugitive taken at a police station. The few lines of text on the front page inform readers that the most wanted man in the kingdom has been successfully located and apprehended by the police working closely in conjunction with the newly formed security forces. Further pages do not specify where the 'cowardly captain' had run to ground, neither do they mention the bodies at Claridge's, but readers are left in no doubt as to the professionalism of the investigation. What the pages delight in mentioning is the fact that the Leader has deigned that only one prison will be secure enough for Armstrong, the one prison that has always been associated with 'only the foulest traitors in our history' – the Tower of London.

Otto puts the paper down on the small low table in his living room. Tony is sitting opposite him and he looks uncharacteristically worried.

'*Please*, Tony,' says Otto in a soothing voice. 'Things are looking up! We have managed to eradicate this man Allen and the American – this certainly buys us more time. I am a very happy man, Tony, very happy.'

'I know that, but this news here was most unexpected.'

'I'm sure it's within your power to get him out.'

Tony studies his fingernails.

'I'm not so sure.'

'Come on, Tony!'

Tony looks at the fingernails on his other hand.

'How about Dog?' Otto asks. 'Perhaps he can help you.'

Tony bites a thumbnail.

'It's possible, I suppose. I'll have to get him ready.'

'Well there you go! How about a nice early-morning whisky to celebrate, to stop you biting those nails?'

Chapter Ten

Days Dwindle Down

'HAVE YOU EVER been to the Far East, Captain Armstrong?'

Armstrong didn't hear the question, or at least he could barely discern its words. His ears picked up the vibrations, but his brain was too occupied with overarching agony. His wrists were lashed to two metal staples high above his head. The staples, which were driven into a vast stone pillar that supported the roof of the chamber, were at a height that meant that Armstrong had to stand permanently on tiptoe. He was stripped to the waist, wearing only a pair of trousers.

'I asked you a question, Captain Armstrong. Now please will you give me an answer?'

Armstrong spat out a mouthful of blood and bile.

'What . . , what was it?' he croaked.

'The Far East – have you ever been there?'

'India,' said Armstrong, 'I was brought up in India.'

The man looked impressed. This man was no clone, Armstrong thought. He wore an expensively tailored chalk-striped double-breasted suit, the jacket of which was hanging on the back of a chair. He was well spoken, well groomed, and he smelt faintly of good-quality cologne. He also wore a wedding ring, an item of jewellery that had already made repeated contact with Armstrong's face.

'Well,' said the man. 'I never knew that.'

Armstrong stayed silent.

'So you've not been to China?'

'No.'

'*I've* been to China.'

Now it was Armstrong's turn to look impressed, or at least that was the idea. Instead he merely nodded gently.

'China is a fascinating place, Captain Armstrong.'

'So I hear.'

'A very advanced people, the Chinese.'

'Right.'

'Did you know the Chinese invented gunpowder as long ago as 206 BC?'

'I did.'

'I thought you might. After all, it is something that even a schoolboy knows! But how many schoolboys have heard of acupuncture, I wonder. Have *you* heard of acupuncture, Captain Armstrong?'

Armstrong had, and its presence in their conversation caused him to breathe more quickly and heavily. He could feel a deep panic coming on, a dreadful panic that he was willing into becoming an attack, because he could use an attack to escape from what was about to happen.

The man walked over to the chair and fished out a small cardboard box from his jacket pocket. He held it up with the cheap flourish of an amateur magician and then shook its contents.

'Tacks, Captain Armstrong! Common household tacks. I'm

afraid I couldn't find any acupuncture needles, so we'll have to make do with these. Sorry!'

Maniac. That was the only word that ran through Armstrong's agonised brain. The man was a maniac. He had no real interest in getting the truth out of him; he just wanted to indulge his psychopathic desires.

The torturer drew close to Armstrong, close enough for him to get another whiff of cologne. Armstrong's arms ached unbearably – all he could feel was a swelling sensation in them and his hands, and he did his best to stand up a little higher, trying anything to relieve the pressure.

He could take this, thought Armstrong, he could take every single fucking tack in that box. Anything not to betray the others, not to betray those who were now relying on him. Every tack that this bastard drove into his body would represent another life that he would not betray. As before, all they could do was drive the truth further into him, make it harder for them to dig it out. They would *never* get it out. Never.

The man approached him with a single tack in his hand. It was at least two inches long, enough to cause the most extreme pain if inserted in the right place, and this was a man who clearly knew where those places were.

'Where shall the first one go, I wonder?'

Armstrong shut his eyes, and then opened them again. He would rather see where it was going so he could prepare himself, steel whichever part of his body the maniac fancied.

The man stood in front of him, looking him up and down, from armpit to navel to nipple and back to armpit, from cheek to eye – please God, not the eye – and then to neck.

Pain. Sheer, extreme pain. The man had violently pushed the tack into Armstrong's left armpit, causing him to scream as he had never done before. He continued yelling as the man went back to the box and fumbled in it for another tack. *Fucking bastard.* Had he screamed that out loud? He no longer knew. He was somewhere else, somewhere where the only thoughts were those connected with agony and a desire to hold out.

Some more theatrical dithering, some more drawn-out selection of a new target, and then in it went, slowly and firmly this time, straight into and across Armstrong's right nipple. This was getting to be too much. His brain was now readying his body to shut down, to escape into unconsciousness. He tried to faint, tried hyperventilating, but still he remained awake.

The other armpit was the third selection, rammed in violently. By now, the pain had reached a plateau, but it was a plateau of constant agony. Two more tacks went into Armstrong before he passed out. One into the left nipple, the other into his shoulder, after which Armstrong could see only darkness.

* * *

Once more, Major-General Clifford's wife had insisted that he see the doctor, who now informed him that he really should take a rest – perhaps a couple of weeks at their cottage in Norfolk. But Clifford was having none of it, saying that he would rather perish than sit and rot on the Broads. Patricia had been desperately upset, saying she thought he was being selfish, and besides, she'd thought he liked Norfolk. Too fucking flat, too fucking wet, too fucking full of dwarves and madmen, he snapped back, instantly ruing his words. He was sorry for that, and apologised fulsomely, saying that he hadn't meant to insult Patricia's family, but that he was under a lot of pressure, and one day Patricia would see what it was all about.

Armstrong's capture had also greatly rattled General Galwey, as evidenced by the cable that Clifford held in front of him.

VERY SORRY TO HEAR ABOUT YOUR AUNTS RELAPSE STOP WHAT CHANCE OF HER PARTY NOW STOP LET ME KNOW ANY NEWS AS SOON AS POSSIBLE STOP BEST GALWEY

In truth, Clifford was helpless and he knew it. Armstrong's trigger was essential for a successful outcome, and only Armstrong knew exactly what that trigger was going to be. It looked as though they had failed; although for the time being Clifford was loath to send out a signal ordering the plotters to stand down. The best he could do, at least for the next few minutes, was to light a cigarette.

* * *

After two days, many of the punctures caused by the tacks – which numbered nearly twenty – turned septic, and Armstrong found himself being treated in his cell by a doctor. The torture had come to an end – presumably a temporary one – and Armstrong was left wondering who his tormentor had been. Where did such a man come from? Who had discovered his unlikely talents?

Armstrong shut his eyes, thinking of Philip, praying that he was still safe. He felt like sobbing, weeping uncontrollably, giving in to the full horror of his situation, trying to shut out the torture of the past few days. He had not revealed a thing, but he had come close, had wanted to say something to stop the pain. The torturer had revived him each time he had passed out, and made sure that his victim was fully conscious before he continued his work.

'Why are you doing this?' Armstrong asked the doctor.

'Hmm?'

'Why are you cleaning me up?'

'I'm sorry, sir – I don't know. I'm afraid I really am just a doctor.'

Armstrong let his head fall back on his pillowless mattress. He thought of others who had been imprisoned here – Richard II, the young princes, John Wilkes, Walter Raleigh, Thomas More. He would surely go the same way as all of them, but that didn't concern him.

Instead, what had occupied his mind over the past few days – when it was not being overrun by pain – was an attempt to work out who had betrayed him. He found the idea unpalatable, but Armstrong reckoned that it surely had to be Ted, because Ted was the only one who knew he had gone to Claridge's. It had to be him – the same Ted who had always been so reluctant to help. He remembered Ted's face when he had first turned up at his house, his expression more than just one of surprise, but also one of guilt.

But why had Ted done it? He was always complaining about money, so was it simply for the lucre? Armstrong knew that everybody had a price, but surely newspaper editors were too independent of mind to be bought like that. Or maybe not, maybe they really were the lowdown creatures so many of his colleagues had accused them of being. The only alternatives that Armstrong could think of were either that Ted's daughter was being held hostage, or that Ted had turned fascist. In the end, thought Armstrong, the reason didn't matter. All that mattered was that Ted had actually done it. He knew he would never see the man again, but if he did, Armstrong knew he would kill him. He thought of the others – of Lucy, Nick and Martin. Presumably they too had been arrested, receiving the same torture in other cells, perhaps in this very building. He also thought about his network of army officers, decent men like General Galwey and Major-General Clifford, all of whom Ted had no doubt betrayed too.

The reason for the doctor's visit became clear at half past seven the following morning. Armstrong had been in a fitful sleep, a state in which his mind knew it was dreaming and yet refused to yield properly to the physical demand of sleep. The dreams – which involved Mary and Philip – were violently interrupted by the metallic clang of cell door against stone wall.

'Atten-shun!' a guard's voice screamed.

Armstrong just lay there. If he was going to be executed, he wouldn't go to the gallows having obeyed their orders.

'Atten-shun!'

The voice was absurdly high-pitched. Armstrong smiled. It reminded him of his drill sergeant when he was a subaltern. He lay there, still, feigning sleep. Steel-heeled footsteps rapidly approached him.

'Up!'

Armstrong opened an eye.

'Up!'

'All right, all right.'

Armstrong pushed himself up on his elbows.

'What?'

'UP!!'

Armstrong got up, but took his time about it.

'What is it?' he asked, his voice calmly irritated, as though he was addressing a demanding child.

'You have a visitor!' shouted the guard.

'Who?'

'The Leader, sir! The Leader himself!'

The guard's eyes shone with the zeal of a religious maniac. Armstrong's closed. He heard laughter coming down the corridor, and recognised one of the voices. It was Mosley's, there was no doubt about it. The other voice was much lower, almost a whisper. It was not a voice he had heard before, and it was not one he liked.

'Atten-shun!' shouted the guard as Mosley entered the room.

Armstrong refused. There was no way he was going to stand straight for the so-called Leader. Fuck that, he thought, as Mosley and the other man – a very tall, thin man – walked towards him. Mosley was wearing full Blackshirt uniform, the other man a suit with a lightning flash armband. Mosley looked ridiculous, Armstrong thought, like some puffed-up popinjay.

'Good morning, Captain Armstrong.'

That voice, that whining, sneering, overly patrician voice that had rattled and annoyed so many in the Commons, that had hectored and cajoled so many in the country, that had spouted so much nastiness and hate, that voice whose owner was nothing less than an embodiment of everything that was dark and wrong – this was the voice that was now addressing him from under that manicured moustache. Armstrong stayed silent. He was not going to dignify the man with a response, was not going to play a game of false courtesy with a murderer.

'How are you feeling today? I trust your stay here is to your satisfaction.'

Silence.

'In a way you are privileged, Captain Armstrong. You join a

long list of illustrious names who have also found themselves residing here in the Tower.'

Armstrong wanted to tell him what he thought of him, wanted to unleash a bile-filled torrent of abuse. After he had done that, he would like to kill him, smash the life out of him.

'You *are* allowed to speak, Captain Armstrong.'

Armstrong stared back at him blankly. Mosley's eyes were smiling.

'Allow me to introduce you to someone,' said Mosley. 'This is Sir Roger Ousby. Have you heard of him?'

Armstrong had, but he hadn't known what the man looked like. So this was Mosley's evil constable, another man who would do his bidding just to enjoy the feeling of power.

'The thing is, Armstrong,' said Mosley, 'I would quite like you to *talk*. So far, you have been disappointingly silent, and we think that there is plenty going on in that brave head of yours. We'd like to know about your friends.'

'Friends? I don't have any friends.'

Mosley let out a false-sounding guffaw.

'In ordinary circumstances,' he said, 'I might believe you, but I'm afraid even someone like you must have *some* friends.'

Armstrong stayed silent. Ted must have betrayed the others, so why was Mosley asking him about them?

'Who are they, Armstrong? Tories? Well, I've locked most of them up, so I doubt it's them. Perhaps it's Jews? Now how about that! What a thought, eh? You and a load of scum like that! But somehow I doubt it – surely a man as thoroughly decent as the good Captain Armstrong wouldn't consort with the Israelites. No – I think it's the army. I think you've got some rogue officers under your wing.' Mosley's eyes bulged wildly.

'I've got nothing to tell you, Mosley. Apart from, of course, that I'd like to see you dead and gone.'

Mosley let out an uneasy snigger.

'Obviously the feeling is mutual, Armstrong, although I fear I am in a better position than you to carry out my wishes.'

'Let's just make this clear – you are going to kill me, yes?'

'No, no, no, no,' Mosley drawled. 'Well, at least not yet. You will obviously have to go on trial for the murders of Henry Allen and the American diplomat.'

'You know perfectly well that I didn't kill them,' said Armstrong. 'That was clearly the work of your imaginative policeman here.'

Armstrong noticed Ousby shifting a little on his feet – a sure sign of guilt if ever there was one.

Mosley let out a deep sigh.

'Sir Roger is most insistent that you did do it – two of his men even caught you in the act! Come, come, there is no point in protesting your innocence. It would be far more helpful all round if you simply told us *why* you did it.'

'Why I did it? For God's sake, I did not do it! What's the point in asking me why I did something you know I didn't do?'

Mosley turned to Sir Roger and smiled.

'Just as you said, Sir Roger – he seems most plausible.'

Armstrong felt something stir deep inside him, something that told him Mosley really did believe that he was the killer.

'Ousby is lying to you,' he said. 'It was his men who killed Allen and Parsons, not me.'

Mosley raised his eyes skywards in resignation before stepping closer.

'Now why would my chief of secret police wish to behead an MP and an American diplomat?'

'Perhaps you could ask him yourself,' said Armstrong.

Ousby remained impassively still, his face inscrutable.

'This is tedious, Armstrong, *deeply* tedious. I will not be fed cock-and-bull stories by a man as vile as you. It's funny how things have worked out, isn't it? You are a symbol, Armstrong, a symbol of the weakness of a democracy that had become corrupt and stale. I remember you in the House, all decent and ambitious, climbing your way up to the giddy height of chief whip. And you used to be so *proud* of your constituency, such a good little MP, and no matter how high you rose, so loyal and charming to the people who had elected you.

'And yet, Armstrong, you were deceived, like so many other lazy minds in that decaying institution. Could you not see that you were letting this great country go to the dogs? Did none of you actually realise that the Jews were taking over? Was it not plain? Could you not see how the Empire, so long our lifeline, was beginning to be treacherously regarded as nothing more than a burden? It was *you* who was letting this land down, you and your pathetic ilk who were turning this society into a feeble and lazy mass of spongers and lepers, when instead we should be a race of men keen for action and keen for change, a race of *supermen* rather than craven cowards like you. For men like you are traitors, only too willing to sell off this proud land to the sweaty hands of the Jew and the Bolshevik. You *disgust* me, Armstrong, and so long as you represent a threat to what I have built, you shall receive no mercy.'

Mosley paused. His voice had got steadily louder until it had filled the cell with its shriekingly pompous tones. Armstrong spoke gently.

'I'd rather live in a land in which the government doesn't lock up its own people for being Jewish.'

Mosley stepped forward and slapped Armstrong across the face with the back of his hand. It didn't hurt – nothing could hurt him any more. Then the Leader turned on his heel and led Sir Roger out of the room. As soon as they had gone, their footsteps clacking down the corridor, the guard added his fist to where Mosley had just slapped. Armstrong fell on to the mattress, his face throbbing with a dull pain, a pain that seemed so very small compared with the confusion that was currently reigning in his head. Why had the others not been arrested? That could only mean one thing: that Sir Roger was allowing them to remain free. For what purpose? And why indeed had Sir Roger wanted to kill Allen and Parsons?

Top Hat and Dog. The code names came back to him, echoing around the cell. *Top Hat was very high up . . . Dog was a more recent recruit.* It couldn't be possible, but the more he thought about it, the more he realised that it had to be.

* * *

'We must rescue him,' said Lucy. 'We can't just sit back and let him hang.'

'I couldn't agree more,' said Ted. 'But how do you propose we do it? Knock on the door of the Tower? Bribe a Yeoman?'

Lucy stared hard at Ted. Why did he always have to react so negatively? He was constantly creating obstacles, almost as if he was unwilling to help, a seemingly reluctant participant in their efforts.

'You could be a little more constructive, Mr Frost.'

'All I'm saying, young lady, is that—'

'Don't you "young lady" me!'

'Lucy!'

It was Nick.

'Please,' he said, 'let's not bicker. You're both right – we should do something, but it's next to impossible. What I do know is that arguing isn't going to help him. We need to at least come up with some sort of plan, even if we think it may be hopeless.'

'You're right,' said Ted. 'It's tough for all of us.'

He smashed his fist into his palm.

'I should never have let him go to Claridge's on his own.'

'He did what he thought was right,' said Nick.

Lucy sat in an angry silence. She felt excluded, as if this was all some game for the boys. Well, she had an idea, an idea that would make them sit up and listen to her. It was something she had suddenly remembered from school.

'Have either of you ever heard of a man called John Gerard?'

'Who?' asked Ted.

'John Gerard – I'm sure that was his name. I think he was some sort of Catholic priest.'

'What of him?'

'Well, wasn't he the man who escaped from the Tower of London?'

Ted peered at Lucy.

'What exactly are you suggesting?' he asked.

'What I'm suggesting is that we find out how he did it.'

'What? And then copy it?'

'Perhaps. It's got to be worth a try.'

Ted smiled.

'I'm sorry I called you "young lady". It was wrong of me. I think that's a brilliant idea.'

Lucy allowed herself a smile, although it came out rather more sarcastically than she had intended.

* * *

The corridor echoed with the sound of heavy footsteps. Two weeks had passed, although Armstrong would not have been surprised if he'd been told that he had been incarcerated for a month. He was becoming accustomed to the noise of footsteps, which signalled the arrival of either yet more torture or a pathetic bowlful of kitchen scraps. But these sounded different – they were slower, and were accompanied by a dragging sound.

'You could at least fucking help us and walk!'

So they had a prisoner, thought Armstrong. Who was it? If it was one of the group, it would be either Nick or Martin. If Lucy had been captured, she would no doubt be receiving some 'special treatment' somewhere else. He tried standing up, but he felt so weak that he had to collapse back on to his mattress. Part of him desperately wanted some company, but not at the expense of someone else's freedom. But just to be able to talk to someone, and not have to lie here alone in the stinking dark, his thoughts infected by the pain of his injuries – that would feel like a great mercy.

The footsteps came to a halt outside his door. A key turned clumsily in the lock.

'Visitor for you!'

The heavy door was pushed open with such force that it smashed noisily against the cell wall. Armstrong squinted at the three silhouettes in the doorway. Two Blackshirt guards were supporting a limp figure dressed in rags. He could not see the face of the prisoner, only the outline. Who was it?

The guards threw the man violently forward, causing him to fall across the stone floor. He let out a small grunt of pain, an almost measured grunt that indicated that he was used to such treatment.

'An old friend of yours to see you!'

One of the guards stepped into the room and reached for

the door handle. As he closed the door, he took the opportunity to land a brutal kick in the man's ribs. The grunt was louder and longer now, the sound of it revealing to Armstrong the man's identity. The door closed with a force equal to that which had opened it, the noise filling the cell like a small explosion.

For a few seconds the man lay on the floor, panting heavily. With great difficulty, Armstrong pushed himself up from his mattress and crawled over to him.

'You're alive!' Armstrong croaked. 'You're alive!'

As they got used to the near darkness, Armstrong's eyes confirmed the findings of his ears. He started shaking the man, pawing at him, almost hugging him.

'Can you hear me? It's me – James!'

The man lifted his head up from the floor. His face was puffy with countless bruises and cuts. His mouth opened. It took a while for any sound to issue, but when it did, Armstrong was overjoyed.

'Hello, old chap,' the man whispered. 'Fancy meeting you here.'

It was Alec.

Chapter Eleven

Blacker Still

October 1937

IT WAS RAINING when they came. Until that morning, the weather had been fine, and Manchester and the whole of the North-West had been enjoying an unusually extended summer. The rain was so bad that it had even woken them up during the night, and David had had to get up and put a bucket on the landing, under where the roof leaked. Their neighbour had been promising to repair the hole for weeks now, but there were so many vandalised shops and homes to deal with that it was hard for him to find the time. David had said that he would go up there and repair it himself, but Betty implored him not to, saying that at his age he was far too old for such acrobatics.

They had just gone back to sleep when they were awoken by the noise of lorry engines, doors being loudly knocked on, and shouts, brutal, guttural shouts.

'Out! Come on, Jews! Out!'

Betty slowly eased her legs out of their small bed and

walked stiffly to the window. The grey morning light seeped into the room through their flimsy curtains, whose opening revealed a morning so dim and wet that the room scarcely brightened. Not that Betty noticed the weather, for in the middle of the road she could see a large army lorry, out of which soldiers wearing helmets and dark-green oilskin capes were pouring.

'You have TWO minutes to leave your homes,' said a voice somewhere down the street through a loud hailer. 'Do NOT stop to pack your belongings. You are being taken into custody for your own protection. Your homes will be protected in your absence. You have TWO minutes to leave . . .'

Betty put her hand over her mouth and gasped. She shook her head – this had to be a dream. There, across the street at number 46, Mr and Mrs Morris were being manhandled out of their home by a couple of venomous-looking soldiers. Mrs Morris was in tears, Mr Morris was wearing an expression of resignation that Betty had never seen before.

She rushed back to the bed where David was sitting up and rubbing his eyes.

'What the hell is that noise?' he asked.

She shook him.

'David, David – please get up! They've come!'

'Who have?'

'The army – they've come to take us away. Listen!'

Out in the street, the noises got louder. Women and children were screaming. A window was smashed. The voice with the loud hailer continued.

'Please leave your homes immediately! Do not attempt to resist. You are being taken into custody for your own protection. I repeat – this measure is being taken for your own safety.'

'David, get up! You heard, we've got to go!'

'I'm not going anywhere, Betty. I'm staying here in my own bloody home!'

'But . . .'

'No! That goes for you as well! We're not leaving, do you hear?'

Betty went back to the window, tears in her eyes. The Morrises' door had been left wide open. Two soldiers were urinating into their house, laughing to each other as they did so.

'David! This is terrible. They're . . .'

'What?'

'They're spending a penny in Doreen and Leonard's hall. The soldiers! All over their front door and their hallway!'

David got out of bed and joined Betty at the window. She clutched his nightshirt so tightly that her entire upper body shivered, her knuckles turning white. David's nostrils flared in anger.

'*Gottenyu*,' he murmured under his breath.

One of the soldiers finished urinating and turned round. David twitched the curtain shut, hoping that the soldier hadn't seen him.

'Quick,' he said. 'We must hide!'

'Where?' said Betty. 'There's nowhere.'

David looked round the room and pointed at the wardrobe.

'You go in there,' he said. 'I'll go under the bed.'

'But they'll find us,' said Betty.

'Ssh! They might not! The one thing I'm not doing is just walking out of here willingly, like a lamb to the slaughter.'

David bundled Betty into the wardrobe, giving her a kiss before shutting the door.

'We'll be all right, love,' he said. 'Just you see. No one's taking us anywhere. This is our home.'

'I love you,' Betty said.

'Love you too,' replied David, and then he gently closed the door.

Outside, the commotion was getting louder.

'Move it! Come on, you fucking Yid!'

The voice with the loud hailer droned on.

'This is for your own safety! All Jews are to leave their houses immediately. You will be taken to secure camps where all your needs will be provided for.'

David slid under the bed, his arthritic limbs not best suited for the purpose. It was dusty under there, and he sneezed a couple of times.

'David?' came Betty's muffled voice. 'David? All you all right?'

'Sssh!'

For a minute, David and Betty lay in their hiding places, listening to the chaos outside. Doors were being kicked in, cars and lorries drove past, and the screaming of women and children intensified. David knew that their door would soon be knocked on, that somewhere outside there would be a soldier with a list that told him that a Mr and Mrs David Duchinsky lived at 43 Sowerby Road.

The knocking came another minute later, causing their small house to shake.

* * *

'I can't believe you're alive either,' said Alec. 'I thought they would have done you in for sure.'

'Not yet,' Armstrong replied. 'I'm still hanging in.'

He and Alec were lying on the floor of the cell, Armstrong's hand gripping Alec's right shoulder. Within a few seconds of recognising each other, both had burst into a mixture of tears and laughter, an outbreak that had lasted for the best part of five minutes. With the exception of Philip, there was no one Armstrong would rather have seen than his oldest friend and comrade, good old, dear old, bloody old Alec.

'They showed me a picture of your head in a noose,' said Armstrong. 'I was sure that you were dead.'

'My head *was* in a noose,' said Alec. 'And damn tight it was too. They had a gun pointing at my head. They told me that if I didn't do as they ordered, I would get a bullet for my troubles.'

'They tried to break me with that,' said Armstrong, 'but it didn't work.'

'I would love to see the picture.'

'I wouldn't if I were you – it wasn't your best side.'

More laughter. Such gallows humour reminded Armstrong of the war.

'So what did they ask you?'

'Everything,' Alec replied. 'Bloody everything.'

'And . . .'

'I know what you're going to say. Nothing, *nothing* is the answer. I told them nothing.'

Armstrong rested his forehead on the cold stone. He had been confident that Alec could not have broken, but it was reassuring to hear it coming from the man himself.

'I came close, though,' Alec continued. 'I nearly told them about—'

'Alec!'

'What?'

Armstrong edged closer to his friend so that he could whisper in his ear.

'They're probably listening, got a microphone. That's

presumably why they've put us together, to find out what we've been up to.'

He felt Alec nod his head.

'Sorry, old man,' he whispered back. 'Good thinking. Should be all right if we whisper, though?'

'Only as quietly as possible,' said Armstrong. Having been on his own, he had not thought of looking for a microphone.

'I didn't tell them a thing, James,' said Alec. 'Not a thing. I'm proud of that, you know, very proud.'

Armstrong could tell that Alec was near to tears again. Whatever he had been through must have been horrific.

'What did they do to you?'

Alec didn't reply, just sobbed quietly.

'All right,' said Armstrong. 'All right. I can't say that I've had a lot of fun myself.'

Alec might not have told them anything, but that silence had clearly had a price. He was sobbing like a child who had lost his parents, sure that they were never going to return. Armstrong had seen this happen to even the bravest of men, seen them come back from an assault into no man's land like little boys. They said that war put years on you, turned you into an old man, but Armstrong had sometimes thought the opposite was true. Some of his men had regressed, become young again, almost infantile. It was the way that some of them had coped, as if reverting to childhood and all its innocence could in some way blot out the horrors they had witnessed. The only problem was that it didn't work. The images were still there, and nothing could remove the horror of seeing a comrade being clumsily butchered into his constituent parts by machine-gun fire.

For an hour, they lay in near silence, Armstrong comforting Alec as if he really was a little boy. He knew he should make

Alec snap out of it, but the man had been here for at least four months – he deserved an hour in which he could escape.

'So what happened to you?' Alec asked a little later.

Armstrong told him everything – from the telephone call from Anne through to his arrest at Claridge's.

'This is one hell of a lot to take in,' Alec whispered back. 'Are you sure it's this man Frost who's betrayed you?'

'I'm certain of it,' said Armstrong. 'I suspect that he and Ousby are in cahoots and are attempting to use our network to gain power.'

'But that's fantastic!'

'From the little I know, it's never a good idea to underestimate the Russians. They're trying to use us, Alec.'

'But why did Ousby arrest you?'

'I wish I knew. If they were using me as some sort of patsy, then you would have thought they'd have kept me on the loose. It might just have been a mistake.'

A pause.

'It's academic, though, isn't it?' said Alec.

Armstrong swallowed.

'You're right. It is academic. At least it is at the moment.'

'What do you mean?'

'We've *got* to try to escape.'

'Christ, man, there's no hope of that.'

'Well, I don't know about you, but I wouldn't mind seeing my son again.'

'That's not fair James, you know I'd love to see Anne and the boys, but we're screwed, man, absolutely screwed.'

'Perhaps we are, but we've got to try. I'm not going to sit here and wait to die. And if there's any chance of stopping Frost, then I'm going to take it.'

* * *

The letter was slipped under the cell door a few days later.

Armstrong and Alec were still locked up together, although both had been taken away for the occasional beating and interrogation. They were getting steadily weaker, far too weak to attempt anything as exhausting as assaulting a guard. Perhaps Alec was right, perhaps their situation was hopeless and they would just be left to rot here, slowly losing their strength and will in a cell that stank of their effluence and despair. They would get beaten for that, for keeping a filthy cell, but Armstrong knew there was no point in arguing, for that would only make the punishment more severe. The beatings were certainly brutal, but Armstrong reflected that they could have been worse. The guards left his face and genitals alone, although it was hellishly painful whenever one of their rubber truncheons struck him, especially on one of his tack wounds.

At first Armstrong assumed that the letter was a fake. It purported to come from Ted.

James,
We can get you out. Tomorrow night, after supper, your cell door will be unlocked. Wait five minutes, then leave your cell. Turn left and make your way down the corridor. At the end is a staircase – go up it right to the top. At the top there is a door which will be left unlocked. This will take you on to the battlements between the Cradle Tower and the Salt Tower. Wait there. You will be able to see the river and Tower Bridge. We shall be down at the wharf waiting for you to appear. When you do so, we shall fire a weight with a string attached to it up to the

Come on, Ted, for Christ's sake. If he was there, he must have seen them by now. Armstrong shivered in the breeze, doing his best once more not to cough. His wounds ached, and he looked down to see that he was bleeding from his chest. One of them must have burst open. He forced himself to ignore it. If he forgot about it, then it would not hurt. Mind over matter, Armstrong, something he had often told his men; mind over matter.

A whizzing sound and then a dull chink ten or twelve feet to their left. Armstrong instinctively ducked, a part of him saying that he was being shot at.

'What the hell was that?' Alec hissed.

Armstrong crouched and waited for a few seconds. Of course – the string and weight! He scuttled over to where the sound had come from, and there, draped over the battlements, was some thick twine. Armstrong pulled it up and curled it a few times around the barrel of a cannon, and then pulled it.

It was heavier than he had expected, but he was frantic now, and he pulled hard. Eventually, out of the near darkness came the rope, advancing towards him like a bouncing snake. He grabbed it and tied it around the base of the cannon, wrapping it securely, then looked round at Alec, who nodded back to him.

'Let's do it,' Alec whispered. 'Even if it is a bloody trap.'

'In that case, I'll go first,' said Armstrong.

'Good God, no,' said Alec. 'It's got to be me.'

'Forget it!'

Armstrong turned and tugged on the rope. He felt a tug come back. That had to mean the rope was secure. It felt tight and strong, more than capable of holding their weight. Now for the difficult part.

The last time he had crawled along a rope was in India, when he was a subaltern. That was well over twenty years ago, and even then it had been difficult. And now he was about to try it again, when it was nearly dark, with wounds on his chest, and in a state of near exhaustion. It was foolhardy, mad, stupid, but essential. There was fear, plenty of it, but it was outweighed by a determination, a fundamental yearning to break free, to avenge.

He knew the worst part would be when he started. Arms shaking, he hauled himself up the battlement and grabbed hold of the rope. He would crawl along it, his arms out in front, his right leg stretched out behind him with his right foot curled around the rope. His left knee would hang down slightly, providing him with the means to maintain his balance.

'Good luck!' Alec whispered.

Armstrong tried not to look down as he gently felt along the rope. His feet had still not left the edge of the wall, and he could go back if he wanted. Not a chance. He pulled himself away, and for one terrifying moment felt as if he was about to fall. He wrapped his legs tightly around the rope and paused, catching his breath.

He was now fully on the rope, suspended fifty feet up. One slip and he would be dead for sure. It was time to move on. He tried to relax, but it was hard. The rope savagely scraped and chafed the wounds on his chest as he edged along, causing him to release the odd stifled groan. With every tug he felt as if he might lose his balance, but he managed to maintain his position.

It was coming back to him now, the technique stored somewhere for all these years. It wasn't easy, but he knew he could do it, knew that he *would* do it. He had to - for Philip above all else. He edged along a further seven or eight feet, which put him right above the middle of the dried-up moat. He refused to allow himself to look down, and resolutely kept his gaze above his line to freedom. He thought he could make out figures at the end of it, but he wasn't sure. He was sweating, perspiration running down his forehead, saturating his eyebrows. He desperately wanted to wipe it away, but he knew that was a luxury he could not afford.

And then it happened. He didn't know what caused it – perhaps the sweat, or a movement in the rope, or just a tiny lack of concentration – but he lost his balance. His body twisted round, flipping to the right. He gripped tightly with his hands, but his legs gave way and dropped away beneath him, causing a massive jolt that nearly made him lose his hold. He was starting to hyperventilate, starting to panic, but he told himself to calm down, that he hadn't fallen, and he wasn't going to have an attack.

He tried swinging his legs up to get hold of the rope, but found it impossible. The movement made the wounds on his chest and stomach feel as if they had burst open. Those in his armpits were in agony, blood oozing down his sides. Or was it just sweat? Keep going. Don't fucking stop. He would just have to make his way down the hard way, hanging by his hands, swinging one in front of the other.

But there was one other problem. He was facing the wrong way, facing the walls of the Tower. He needed to turn; there was no way he could make his way down backwards. Gripping tightly with his right hand, he released his left and moved it round behind his head. So far so good. He paused, and took a deep breath before releasing his right hand in order to turn himself round.

He nearly fell. His left arm felt too weak, the pain under his armpit too excruciating. He wanted to scream out, to roar, but he allowed himself only a slight grunt as he twisted round, his wounds tearing as he did so. The fingertips of his right hand brushed against the rope but could not manage to grab hold. Another swing of the arm, and then success. He was now facing the right way, both hands gripping the rope. Time to move on.

Every movement was agony, sending a new pain shooting around his body. He knew that his wounds were bleeding badly now, that the warm liquid trickling down his torso was certainly not sweat. Every time one hand left the rope, the other wanted to give up, to let him fall and dispatch him to the ground, where he could join Mary. Not yet, he told himself, not yet. He would get down this bloody rope, whatever the pain, whatever the effort.

He was making good progress now, had established a rhythm. He could make out shapes, of humans, boats, boxes. The human shapes were beckoning him on, but were making no sound. Who were they? Secret policemen, or Ted and the others? Their presence gave him a new surge of energy, pushing him beyond pain, to a state in which adrenalin and willpower had negated all other sensations. He wanted to laugh, because he was so close, because he was about to bloody succeed.

He could see where the rope ended now. It was lashed over the top of a ten-foot wall that marked the outer perimeter of the Tower. The wall was his last obstacle, but if he fell before it, then he would be trapped. He wondered whether he would be able to haul himself over it, hoping that the others would be able to pull him up.

Within a minute he had reached the wall and could make out the faces and arms of his rescue party. He thought he could discern their anxious expressions in the faded light, but perhaps it was only his imagination. His body was now flat against the wall, his hands still on the rope. His bare feet scrabbled for the semblance of a hold, anything to take even the slightest pressure off his arms.

'Give us your right hand!'

Armstrong obeyed Ted's whispered command and felt two strong hands grab his wrist and forearm.

'Your left!'

Armstrong released his left hand, abandoning the rope. Two more hands clutched him, and now he was being clumsily but firmly pulled up, his bare feet scraping against the rough stone. With a huge heave that scraped his chest over the lip of the wall, Armstrong fell into their hands.

They tried placing him on his feet but he collapsed. Without a word, he felt himself being hauled up with a fireman's lift on to broad shoulders. And then a rocking motion as they stepped on to a rowing boat and he was deposited somewhat roughly into the bow.

And there he waited, for what could have been hours, until Alec landed in a hyperventilating heap next to him. He watched glassily as the outline of the Tower slipped into the darkness, and looked up in wonder as they rowed under the darkly menacing span of Tower Bridge. He thought he heard a siren in the distance, but before he could be sure, he passed out.

* * *

Armstrong and Alec's escape had sent the Leader into a fury that not even his wife could calm. Lady Mosley had confided in her sister Unity, telling her that she was worried about him, that she had never seen him so angry. Unity's somewhat useless advice was that all great leaders were men of passion, and Diana should allow her husband to give full vent to his anger.

The country needed him to be angry, she said; after all there was a lot to be angry about, especially those wretched Jews.

Mosley's first act on hearing of the escape was to have Ousby arrest the entire staff of the Tower of London. There had to be a traitor amongst them, he said, and Ousby's men were the ones to find him. Ousby was to use any methods that he saw fit, although it would be preferable if nobody actually died under interrogation, at least not yet.

The Leader summoned Ousby to an Emergency Cabinet meeting a few days later. As usual, Francis Hawkins, Raven Thomson, Fuller and Joyce were all wearing full Blackshirt uniform.

'So then, Sir Roger, what news?' Mosley asked, drumming his fingers upon the highly polished table.

Ousby looked calmly at his notes.

'We appear to have had a breakthrough,' he said. 'As we suspected, they did have help on the inside.'

The room erupted into hubbub as the four other members of the Cabinet began to speak as one.

'Who?'

'The senior prison warder no less. Man by the name of Michael Martin. It seems he is some sort of crypto-Communist and felt sympathy for Armstrong.'

'So what did he do?'

Ousby looked through his notes once more.

'I can read you some of his confession if you like,' he said.

'Go ahead.'

Ousby cleared his throat before beginning.

' "My name is Michael Charles Martin of 75 Stanley Grove, Battersea. I am the senior prison warder at the Tower of London. On the night of the seventeenth of September 1937 I assisted in the escape of the prisoners James Armstrong MP and Alec Scott from the Tower. I did this because I have much sympathy with Captain Armstrong and I am against the Government . . ." '

'Is he, by Jove?' said Mosley.

' ". . . and all that the fascist regime stands for. My uncle is Jewish . . ." '

'Name?' Mosley barked.

Ousby flicked through his notes.

'Yes, sir – a Mr Isaiah Willimsky of 97 Dalston Road, London.'

'Francis Hawkins,' said Mosley, 'make sure he's on your lists. I don't want any of these people wriggling out of the round-up.'

'Yes, Leader,' said Francis Hawkins, jotting down the man's name.

'I'm sorry, Sir Roger, please continue.'

' "My uncle is Jewish, and I think what the Government is doing to the good Jewish people . . ." '

Ousby was unable to continue as the room was suddenly filled with laughter.

'Good Jewish people!' William Joyce exclaimed. 'That's reason enough to hang him!'

'Who are these people, men like this Martin?' Mosley asked. 'Where do they come from? They've got no sense of reality *whatsoever*. I almost feel sorry for them. Carry on, Sir Roger.'

' ". . . to the good Jewish people is despicable and should be stopped. When Captain Armstrong arrived at the Tower I resolved that I would do all I could to help him. On the night of the escape I left his cell door unlocked along with some instructions that told him how to get out. I also left him a length of rope, which I indicated he should tie on to one of the cannons near the Cradle Tower in order to let himself down. After that, it was simply a matter of waiting for him to escape, which I take it he did, otherwise you would not have arrested us all. I would also like to add that I am proud of what I did and I hope Captain Armstrong succeeds in whatever it is he is trying to achieve." '

There was a silence as the Cabinet chewed over Martin's words.

'Is that it?' asked Mosley.

Ousby nodded.

'More or less,' he replied. 'He goes into detail, but that is the essential part of it.'

'And this confession is reliable, is it, Sir Roger? I mean he's not just saying all this because he wants one of your boys to stop hitting him.'

'I'm quite sure he's telling the truth.'

'Good, good,' said the Leader pensively. 'And this man Martin had no other help? No one on the outside whom Armstrong was to meet?'

Sir Roger shook his head.

'He would have told us if there was.'

'What makes you so sure?' asked General Fuller.

'The questioning was very . . . thorough,' Ousby replied.

'So this chap Martin did the whole thing off his own bat, did he?'

'It would appear so,' said Ousby, his tone a little exasperated.

'Pretty risky stuff, I'd say.'

'What are you trying to insinuate, General?'

'I'm not trying to *insinuate* anything – I'll say it straight: I don't buy it.'

Ousby tilted his head to one side.

'Well, I'm sorry you think like that. If you prefer, I could come back with a new story that might fit in with what you believe to be the truth—'

'Gentlemen!' Mosley interrupted. 'Enough of this! I'm quite satisfied with this man Martin's confession.'

The General looked crestfallen. Ousby remained impassive, inscrutable. The Leader turned to his Home Secretary.

'Francis Hawkins, I'd like to have this man executed as soon as possible.'

Francis Hawkins nodded and made a note.

'And another thing,' Mosley continued. 'How do you mean to do it?'

'Sorry, Leader?'

'How do you mean to execute him?'

'Well . . . I thought we'd hang him.'

The Leader shook his head playfully.

'No, no, no, *no*. Far too boring! I thought we should bring back the axe.'

'The *axe*, Leader?'

'That's right! Herr Hitler was telling me only the other day that he has brought it back over there. It's been quite a good deterrent apparently.'

Francis Hawkins made another note.

'Perhaps you could find an antique one,' said Mosley. 'There must be a few kicking around. Let's get them back into use – the people will love it! A sense of history!'

'Can we publicise this?' asked William Joyce.

Mosley paused.

'Well, we're keeping Armstrong's escape secret, so it'll be difficult to . . . No, just make something up. Say he's a rapist or he murdered someone – something suitably vile, enough to make people think he deserves it.'

'And the SBC?' asked Joyce. 'Can they film it?'

Mosley nodded.

'Yes,' he said. 'Although I think not for public broadcast, don't you?'

Joyce smiled.

Mosley clapped his hands together.

'Good! I'm glad I remembered that! Now, *Armstrong*. I want all policemen – of both varieties – on this. In this instance I don't give a stuff about the law, so they can do what they like to find him. I want every lead examined, no matter how small. I want more random searches, more roadblocks, more barriers, more everything! But what I don't want is a word in the press about it. We shall look like fools if people know that Armstrong has managed to escape twice. They'll end up thinking he's some latter-day Robin Hood, and that's *not* going to happen. If any policeman breathes a word about this, he can expect to be locked up for the best part of twenty years for sedition. Got that? Good. I also want security around us to be doubled – Armstrong is clearly a lunatic and God knows what he might try.'

Francis Hawkins made another note. Sir Roger sat quite still. It looked as though he had got away with it. If the General had caused him any more grief, he would have set him up with a boy. Not that the General liked boys, but then who cared about the truth these days?

*   *   *

There was no news of the escape, which came as little surprise. The SBC merely announced its quotidian digest of vastly improved production statistics and reports that the Jewish population would soon be relocated for its own safety. If any Jews did not wish to participate in the process, they would be imprisoned – the Leader regarded this an essential measure to ensure compliance. Both *Action* and *The Blackshirt* concentrated on the Jewish story, and there was no mention of any disturbances whatsoever at the Tower of London. Instead, both papers looked forward to the Coronation of King Edward and Queen Wallis, which would take place on 12 October. Both Hitler and Mussolini were due to attend, which, gushed *Action*, should make the event the largest gathering of the New European Order ever to take place.

Armstrong spent the best part of a week recovering. Lucy had procured the services of a trustworthy doctor, who visited the fugitives as they lay in an upstairs bedroom of a dilapidated Georgian terraced house in Shoreditch. Many of Armstrong's wounds were seeping pus and blood, and they had to be cleaned and dressed frequently. Ted was there constantly, although Armstrong had told Alec that he was not ready to confront him until he was fully fit. It was an awkward few days, and there was many an occasion on which Armstrong came near to venting his feelings. He and Alec had agreed not to reveal to the others their suspicions regarding Ted's letter. Far better, Armstrong maintained, not to risk a change in behaviour by someone like Nick that would alert Ted to their being on to him.

*

'So why did you do it, Ted?'

'Do what?'

'Betray us,' said Armstrong flatly.

Ted looked back at him, his eyes wide with consternation. 'What's all this, James? Is it April the first or something?'

Armstrong didn't respond. He was sitting in the safe-house alone with Ted – he had insisted that the others leave him to deal with Ted in his own way.

'James, is this some sort of joke?'

'No joke.'

Ted took a cigarette out of a packet of Black Cap and lit it with a shaking hand.

'I'm sorry, James, I'm really not with you.'

'An unfortunate way of putting it.'

'What?'

'I know you're not with us. You're with *them*, aren't you?'

'For fuck's sake! Could you please explain what you're talking about? I don't take very kindly to being accused of being a traitor, if that's what you're insinuating.'

'What have they got on you? Is it your daughter? Or Bridget? Or is it just for the money? You're always complaining about money, so perhaps it's that, just pounds, shillings and pence.'

Ted shook his head. His expression, thought Armstrong, was almost one of genuine disbelief.

'You're a good actor,' said Armstrong, 'I'll give you that.'

'Look, James,' Ted replied, 'whatever it is you're accusing me of, you're wrong. I don't know what happened to you in prison, but they've played with your mind, can't you see that?'

It was Armstrong's turn to shake his head.

'No one's been playing with my mind,' he said, 'except perhaps you. I know all about it, Ted, all about how you and Sir Roger Ousby are working for the Russians, using my network to take control. I even know that he's the one called Top Hat, and that you're Dog, which somehow seems apt. It was you who set me up at Claridge's – don't deny it! And you only managed to get Alec and me out of the Tower because Ousby organised the whole bloody thing.'

Ted inhaled deeply on the Black Cap. Armstrong felt in his coat pocket for the revolver Nick had given him earlier that day. It looked as though it was about to see some use. Ted took another long drag before speaking.

'So what now?' he asked. 'Are you going to kill me? Well if you do, you'll have killed an innocent man.'

'I would have thought the honourable thing would be to do it yourself.'

'*Honourable*. That's rich. You're only saying it because you don't have the balls to kill me yourself.'

Armstrong calmly took the revolver out of his pocket and placed it on the table.

'Don't bet on it,' he said quietly.

Ted took a final draw on his cigarette before stubbing it out.

'All I know, James, is that I'm not your traitor. I don't know why you're accusing me. I can see why you think Ousby might be Top Hat, but whoever Dog is, it certainly isn't me.'

Armstrong folded his arms.

'Who else would it be if it wasn't you?'

'Any number of people – Nick, Lucy, Martin, even Mrs bloody Craven for all I know.'

'You know, none of those names really convinces me.'

Silence. Ted reached for another cigarette.

'All I want to know,' said Armstrong, 'is why.'

Ted held the unlit cigarette between his fingers.

'For God's sake, James! There is no "why"! I've done nothing but help you, stick my neck out, risk my life and my family's, and this is what I get. False accusations. Guns pointed at me. It's madness that you think I'm some sort of Soviet spy; it's preposterous!'

Armstrong picked up the revolver. He wasn't prepared to listen to any more of Ted's protestations.

'James! *Please!* You must believe me. I'm not a traitor!'

Armstrong pulled back the hammer with his thumb. He didn't want to do this, but he knew that he had to. Ted had been willing to see him die, and the bullet he was about to receive would be the most fitting penalty.

'James!'

Ted was almost shrieking now.

'I can't believe you had the gall to call yourself my friend.'

'Wh . . . what?'

'You know full well,' said Armstrong. 'In your letter.'

'Letter?'

'That's right, Ted, your letter, the one you managed to get smuggled into the Tower.'

'I never wrote you any letter.'

'Yes you did – you can't deny that as well!'

'Honest to God, James! I never wrote you a letter! You were the one who wrote the letter!'

Armstrong raised the gun.

Afterwards, he put Ted in the back of Allen's Bentley and drove him over to the Royal Victoria Dock. He watched as the car disappeared gently into the oil-stained water, then turned and walked away.

Lucy, Alec and Nick returned a few hours later to find Armstrong sitting on his own.

'What happened?' asked Alec.

Armstrong looked at them coldly. His eyes told them what they needed to know. As if to reinforce their message, Armstrong nodded slowly.

'Really?' Alec asked.

Armstrong looked at his old friend.

'Yes, Alec – *really.*'

'Sorry,' said Alec, 'but did he – did he confess?'

'Of course not,' said Armstrong. 'Said he was innocent right to the end.'

'So where is he?' Lucy asked.

'In hell, I hope.'

'His body, I mean.'

'In the boot of Allen's Bentley, which is now at the bottom of a dock.'

The group stood silent for a while.

'Now what?' asked Nick.

'We carry on,' said Armstrong, clapping his hands. 'Now that Frost is out of the way, Ousby has no way of monitoring our movements. Nick and Martin, how are your opposition cells?'

Nick nodded.

'They're all in place,' he said, 'ready for the word.'

'Good,' said Armstrong. 'I'm going to contact Galwey and Clifford and try to establish if our network is still in place. And Alec, I'd like to talk to you about the Earl Marshal.'

At first they thought he was delirious.

'The Earl Marshal?' asked Alec.

'The Earl Marshal,' Armstrong repeated. 'He's the man who arranges all royal ceremonies . . .'

'All right,' said Alec.

'. . . including of course the Coronation. If we are to gain access to the Abbey then we'll need the help of the Earl Marshal.'

'But how?' said Lucy. 'We can't just give him a ring and ask for a couple of tickets.'

Armstrong allowed himself a faint smile.

'We don't really want to go to the Coronation itself,' he said. 'But it's vital that we get into the Abbey the night before.

For that, we'll need a pass indicating that we're officials of some sort, or perhaps workmen. Ideally, I'd like to be able to get inside the Abbey even sooner, in order to scout around. I haven't been there in a while.'

'How about as foreign dignitaries?' asked Alec.

'Explain,' said Armstrong.

'Well, there are going to be hundreds – thousands – of visitors from all over the world,' said Alec. 'Perhaps you could disguise yourself as one of them.'

'But that wouldn't get us into the Abbey itself. Besides, I'm not sure that I fancy dressing up as a mad crown prince from an obscure Balkan state,' said Armstrong. 'It just seems too absurd. Bit too Gilbert and Sullivan for me.'

'I thought you liked Gilbert and Sullivan,' said Alec.

'Whatever gave you that idea?' Armstrong replied. 'I can't stick them. Why those two got knighted God only knows.'

'Touched a nerve there,' said Nick.

'Well it's nice to see that not all Tories like bourgeois culture,' said Lucy.

'Aha, the voice of the true Bolshevik!' said Alec.

'All right, all right, back to business,' said Armstrong. 'Alec, I need you to find out who works in the Earl Marshal's office. There must be someone there who is sympathetic. Get me a list of names – we should be able to identify someone useful. This person will also need to supply us with a seating plan. I don't want our bomb to go off under a load of bishops. Lucy and Nick, I need you to scout around the Abbey. I want you to pose as tourists and see if you can just wander in. Normally you can, but I expect they've tightened things up. If you can't get in, tell me what sort of people are – it may give us an idea what identity we can adopt. Got that?'

The others nodded. They could see in Armstrong's eyes that he was being deadly serious, and were surprised at how quickly he had snapped away from banter and back into the role of leader.

'How do you suggest I go about finding these names?' asked Alec.

'Actually, Lucy's idea of simply ringing up is not a bad one,' said Armstrong. 'Say you're calling from *The Blackshirt* or *Action*, and that you're writing an article about how plans for the Coronation are going. That should do the trick.'

Alec came back with a list of names later that afternoon.

'Well, it seems that there are six people working for the Earl Marshal,' he said.

'Let's have a look,' said Armstrong.

Alec passed him a sheet of paper, down which Armstrong scanned. The names were as expected – carrying either titles or senior ranks in the armed forces, or both.

Air Marshal Sir Richard Taylor
Lord Wilson of Canworthy
General Sir Peter Jackson VC
Sir James Owen MP
Brigadier-General William Wynne
Lord Oliver Fowlston

'Pretty predictable bunch,' said Armstrong, 'and all fascists to boot – especially Owen. He's one of Mosley's court favourites, a really nasty piece of work.'

He tossed the paper down in resignation. He would have to think of something else.

'They're not all fascists, are they?' asked Alec.

'Looks like it to me – these are types who'd probably sell their own mothers before doing anything to hurt the Leader.'

'What about Wilson?'

'Wilson?'

'I don't think he's a fascist,' said Alec. 'I remember him from the Olympics – he was one of those who refused to salute.'

'The Olympics? He'd have been far too old.'

'No, he wasn't an athlete, but he was on the Committee. He was a nice chap, I remember, a good sort.'

'And now he's helping to arrange the Coronation of the man who got us into this mess,' said Armstrong. 'He hardly sounds reliable, Alec!'

Alec raised his hands.

'Sorry, James! It's not my fault.'

Armstrong sat back.

'No, I'm the one who should apologise. What else do you know about Wilson?'

'Tall,' said Alec, 'a magnificent moustache, straight back. I remember something about his first wife dying in the flu epidemic.'

Another widower, thought Armstrong. He sometimes felt that being deprived of a wife put you into some sort of club.

'Did he marry again?' he asked.

'Yes, he did. I remember some talk about it happening rather soon after.'

Armstrong raised an inquisitive eyebrow.

'Perhaps number two was waiting in the wings,' said Alec. 'Happens a lot.'

'Not with me it didn't,' said Armstrong.

'Come on, James,' said Alec. 'He wouldn't be the first man to have immediately hopped on to a new mount.'

'That's one way of putting it. Anyway, it's not important. Do you think we can trust him?'

Alec shrugged.

'I'd say it's worth a try.'

* * *

They arrived at the same time every week – Wednesday afternoon at three o'clock – delivered by a car from the German Embassy. Seventeen carnations, of every conceivable colour that could be found. The footman would take them up to Queen Wallis's apartments as soon as they arrived – she had once been apoplectic when they had not been delivered to her after two hours.

'Goddammit,' she had bawled. 'My flowers used to arrive quicker when I was living in Dolphin Square!'

She had wanted to dismiss the footman who had brought them on that occasion, but the King had told her meekly that maybe that wasn't fair, that it wasn't the poor chap's fault. Anyway, why did von Ribbentrop send these blasted carnations to her in the first place? Such cheap little things! The Queen told him that it was a private joke, nothing important. Her David had then got jealous, and told her that she shouldn't accept flowers from other men, that it was not the queenly thing to do. Wallis told her husband that whatever she did as Queen was by definition queenly – a *ridiculous* word anyway – and if that involved accepting a bunch of simple flowers once a week from the ambassador of Britain's closest ally, then so be it.

That Wednesday afternoon proved to be no exception. The carnations arrived at precisely three o'clock, delivered by the same flunkey in the same car, a large midnight-blue Mercedes.

They were whisked up to the Queen's apartments, where they were then handed over to her attractive lady-in-waiting, Lady Katherine Massey, who viewed them with some suspicion, knowing full well from whom they came.

Lady Katherine knocked on the door of the Queen's drawing room, which was immediately opened by the Queen herself. Lady Katherine suspected that the Queen had been standing right next to it, as though she had actually been lingering there for her weekly carnations.

'Thank you, Katherine,' said Queen Wallis, who waited for her lady-in-waiting to curtsey before shutting the door on her.

The Queen took a deep sniff. The carnations smelt *divine* as usual – Joachim had once told her he had them specially flown over once a week from the finest grower in Germany. She took them out of their wrapping paper, and placed them one by one into a crystal vase which she had already had filled with water. They looked fine, mighty fine, she thought. She'd give him a call later, perhaps even see if he was free to drop by. He was normally only too ready.

Chapter Twelve

Idiots

MICHAEL CHARLES MARTIN of 75 Stanley Grove, London SW protested his innocence all the way through his two-day trial at the Old Bailey. However, the evidence was incontrovertible, and the jury had no choice but to return a guilty verdict for the rape and murder of a Miss Eileen Denman of 176 Queenstown Road, London SW. The judge, Lord Justice Matthew Upton, donned his black cap and sentenced the accused to the maximum penalty the law allowed.

As Martin was led away, he screamed out, telling the court that the whole thing had been set up by 'dark powers', and that he was the innocent victim of some far greater conspiracy. That outburst was not reported in the pages of *Action* or *The Blackshirt*, although the SBC noted towards the end of a sensational report that Mr Martin had subjected the court to 'a lunatic raving that was the stuff of such nonsense that some members of the public gallery burst out into a hearty laughter'.

Martin was denied an appeal, and spent his last few days in Wandsworth Prison writing to every person he thought might be able to help, including the King. He had no idea, he wrote, why this was happening to him. Why had he, a simple groundsman at the Tower of London, been framed for a deed that he did not commit? Why had the court refused to believe his alibi? Martin suspected, he wrote, that poor Miss Denman had been killed by somebody the 'dark powers' were trying to protect, and that he was the 'scapegoat'.

Naturally, he received no replies. In fact, his letters were never even posted, but handed over to the HMSSP. His only visitor was a priest, who saw him on the morning of his execution. Until that point, Martin had always claimed he had no religion, but that morning he prayed as hard as the most devoted of believers. Those prayers were interrupted by the swift entrance of two prison warders, both of whom were wearing fascist armbands. Without any apology to the priest, they bound Martin's hands tightly behind his back and placed a blindfold over his head.

He was bundled out of his cell and led to the place of his execution. He stayed silent, too petrified to scream or shout. This wasn't happening, he told himself, this was some sort of mistake, a trick, something like that.

A blow to the back of his knees forced him to fall to the floor. He then found himself being lifted up into a kneeling position, and bent over a low wooden block. Was this how he was going to be hanged; was this how they put on the rope?

Martin only started screaming when he felt a sudden coldness on the back of his neck. It wasn't a rope, but something metallic, something sharp. And then he knew what it was, knew how he was going to die. What he had felt was the cold edge of an axe, an edge that the executioner had briefly touched upon the condemned man's neck as he lined up his swing.

'No!' screamed Martin. 'No!'

He heard a grunt coming from behind him and then heard nothing. His scream, along with his consciousness, continued after his head had left his body. For two seconds, while there was still oxygen in his brain, Michael Martin was aware of the fact that he had been beheaded.

* * *

Otto is beaming.

'Well done, Tony!' he says, and pats Tony on the back.

Tony is not used to being patted on the back – he finds the gesture condescending – so he flinches slightly.

'It worked brilliantly!' Otto continues. 'And just as we thought, not a word in the papers.'

'Well, the regime has never been keen to publicise its failures.'

The comment causes Otto's face to darken momentarily, but he is soon back to his irrepressible self.

'And our canine friend?' he asks. 'What news of him?'

Tony takes a sip of whisky.

'He's in place,' says Tony. 'Well and truly embedded. There are a few things he needs, so I'm helping him with those, but otherwise he tells me everything is on target.'

'What sort of things?'

'People, mostly.'

'All right,' says Otto, crossing his legs. 'But after these people have served their purpose . . .'

'I understand,' says Tony.

'Even Allen's wife?'

Tony looks at his watch.

'She'll be found dead in her bedroom tomorrow morning.'

'Suicide?'

'Naturally,' says Tony, and drains his glass. 'Although it was very kind of her to inform on her husband like that.'

* * *

Mosley had allowed the gentlemen's clubs of St James's to stay open, although much to their secretaries' chagrin, the HMSSP had procured the membership lists and filleted out any members the regime deemed 'unreliable' or likely to use the clubs to foment resistance. The same process had also been applied to working men's clubs, which the regime regarded as breeding grounds for the evils of Bolshevism and trade unionism. The predictable result of this purge was that many clubs found themselves facing financial ruin, and had either to close or to merge with others.

One club that had managed to survive was Pooter's, not least because it had taken on the last few members of the Carlton Club and the Reform. Many of the members of those two clubs were currently residing in internment camps – 'The best clubs for them,' the Leader had once joked. But Pooter's, being a relatively non-political place, was, in its secretary's words, 'in good shape', and was even prospering.

Armstrong and Alec found themselves sitting outside Pooter's one wet afternoon in a Morris Cowley borrowed from an obliging friend of Martin. The man they were waiting for was having lunch, and so far that lunch had gone on for two and a half hours. Despite the rain, and the fact that he was sitting in a car, Armstrong felt exposed and vulnerable. He had brought Nick's revolver with him, which he was cradling in his lap.

'Bloody hell,' said Alec, breaking the silence. 'It's already quarter to four. How long is our noble lord going to be?'

'He's probably having his afternoon nap in the library,' said Armstrong.

'And then he'll wake up at six, just in time for a drink.'

Armstrong smiled. Wilson - or more properly, Lord Canworthy - was evidently at that stage in life in which each day was little more than one long meal. Armstrong looked through the windscreen as the smile slowly left his face. He was glad it was wet - passing policemen were keeping their heads down, and there was little chance he would be spotted inside a fogged-up car. He could have stayed at the safe-house, as Alec had wanted him to, but he needed to come along, had to establish whether Wilson was a man he could trust. Lucy and Nick had attempted to get into the Abbey the day before, but they had reported back with the not unexpected information that nobody was allowed in without some form of pass. It was Lucy who suggested that their best bet was to pose as architectural restorers - an idea Armstrong had immediately warmed to.

Wilson eventually left the club at half past four. He was as tall as Alec had remembered, and his stiff bearing was distinctly military, as was his magnificent moustache.

'That's him!' said Alec.

'You sure?'

'Quite sure,' said Alec, opening his door. 'All right - wish me luck.'

'*Bonne chance*,' said Armstrong.

'*Merci.*'

Armstrong wiped the windscreen and watched Alec hurry across the road. He would have liked to be the one making the approach, but he knew it would be foolhardy to walk down a street where there was a strong chance somebody might recognise him. He held his breath as he saw Alec walk up behind his prey, and only let it out when he saw the two men starting to talk.

The rain and the failing light made it hard to discern Wilson's expression, but Alec was certainly holding his attention.

'Come on, Alec,' Armstrong found himself whispering.

Alec seemed to be talking for an age. What was he saying? Perhaps the lord really was drunk, and had no idea what was going on. Or maybe he was as confused as anybody would be in such a situation. After another minute had passed, Armstrong was desperate to get out of the car. Alec seemed to be making no progress, and Wilson's demeanour suggested that he wanted to walk away.

Whatever Alec said next, however, obviously worked, because the two men started to walk towards the car. They waited for a bus to pass, and then crossed the road, Alec's hand gently pressed against Wilson's back, as if to steer him in the right direction. Alec opened the rear passenger door, and Wilson stepped in, accompanied by a waft of cold damp air.

Armstrong was tempted to turn round to face him, but he had no wish for Wilson to catch a glimpse of his face.

'Good afternoon, my lord,' said Armstrong. 'I'm terribly sorry about this.'

Wilson merely shrugged. Alec got into the driver's seat.

'I was wondering,' said Armstrong, 'whether I could interest you in a proposition?'

Wilson shrugged again and gave a half-grunt.

'Very well,' he said, looking out of his window.

There was something reluctant in his manner, Armstrong thought, but at the same time he sounded weary – not postprandially weary, but slightly resigned, as if he had been expecting something like this to happen.

Fifteen minutes later, Alec started the engine and pulled away, driving north up St James's Street. The conversation with Wilson had gone well, and he had impressed both of them with his anti-fascist convictions, even calling Mosley an 'odious fucker'. Armstrong did not tell Wilson exactly what he was planning, but he had secured his agreement to supply them with a seating plan and an order of service, as well as credentials in the names of 'Philip Howard' and 'Elizabeth Ball', which would identify Armstrong and Lucy as architectural restorers. Before Wilson had stepped out of the car, Armstrong reminded him that he wished to pick up the documents tomorrow morning from the porter at the club, and that Wilson was not to tell anybody – not even his wife – about this conversation.

The traffic light changed to green and Alec turned left and made his way down Piccadilly towards Hyde Park Corner. They drove past the Ritz, which Armstrong noticed had put fascist symbols in its windows. A few Blackshirts – evidently patrician sorts, wearing the full Action Press uniform – were walking briskly towards the hotel's entrance, clearly on their way to a meeting. Even the doorman was wearing a fascist armband, and saluted as the men entered the hotel.

Alec accelerated, and soon the railings that marked the northern perimeter of Green Park were flickering past. Armstrong looked at his watch – it was five o'clock. Suddenly Alec spoke.

'Shit!'

Armstrong looked up. About fifty yards ahead, just before Hyde Park Corner, was a roadblock.

'Turn right!' he barked.

'But . . .'

'Turn right!'

Alec wrenched the wheel clockwise and veered violently into the path of an approaching double-decker bus. For a second, Armstrong thought they were going to be hit, but a combination of Alec's acceleration and the bus driver's quick application of the brakes meant that they narrowly missed a collision that would certainly have been fatal. They sped up the narrow Half Moon Street, the sound of the bus's horn in their ears.

'Slow down!' said Armstrong, who had no wish to attract any further attention.

Alec did so.

'Now what?' he said. 'We can't just drive around hoping not to run into any more roadblocks.'

'You're right,' said Armstrong. 'Let's get rid of the car. We can walk back through the park – it's getting dark enough.'

The sound of a rapidly approaching bell debunked that idea. Armstrong felt his heart start to thud once more. He turned round to see a police car bearing down on them.

'Idiots!' Alec hissed, putting his foot down.

'Do you think we can outrun them?'

'It's got to be worth a try,' said Alec, taking a sharp left on to Curzon Street. After a few yards he turned left again, down into Shepherd Market. However, the manoeuvre had not outwitted the police car, the front grille of which was almost touching their rear bumper.

Armstrong shut his eyes as Alec swung the car round to the right, sending pedestrians jumping for their lives. The Georgian streets of Shepherd Market were not built for cars, and certainly not for cars travelling at speeds such as this. Armstrong felt the back of the car swinging out to the left, and opened his eyes to see Alec struggling to stop the vehicle skidding and smashing side-on into the front of an antiquarian bookshop.

He only partially succeeded. The rear left wing clipped the front of the shop and smashed its window in a spectacular shower of glass shards.

'We've got to get out of here!' Armstrong shouted.

'I know!' Alec yelled back above the din.

A massive jolt from behind knocked them forward.

'Fuck!' Alec shouted.

The police car had rammed them, trying to force them to crash. Alec pressed hard on the accelerator, causing the car to lurch and weave over the wet cobbles. He turned left, out of the market and back on to Curzon Street, then swung right and sped up South Audley Street. Away from the cramped Shepherd Market, they managed to pull clear of the police car. They brushed past a delivery boy on his bicycle, sending him and his produce to the ground. Someone else he needed to apologise to one day, Armstrong thought, looking back to check that the lad was all right.

If Alec had braked any harder Armstrong would have been sent through the windscreen. Instead, his forehead connected with the glass with an almighty blow, almost knocking him out. Alec then swung the car out to the right, sending Armstrong's left shoulder smashing into the door. A lorry had pulled out of Mount Street, right in front of them, and Alec only just managed to overtake it before avoiding a head-on collision with a taxi.

'Jesus Christ!' Armstrong exclaimed.

'Sorry about that,' said Alec. 'No choice.'

Armstrong was still rubbing his head as they hurtled into Grosvenor Square. Alec changed gear and slung the car round to the right, the tyres squealing in protest.

'Any sign of them?'

Alec looked in the mirror.

' 'Fraid so, but I'm going to lead them a merry dance round here. Hold on!'

They screamed round Grosvenor Square a total of four times. At one point, Armstrong watched the needle on the speedometer hit sixty-five miles on hour, but the risk seemed to be paying off, as the police car was now behind by almost the length of the square.

'If we carry on at this rate we'll be chasing them!' Alec announced.

'Or we'll be joined by some of their colleagues,' said Armstrong. 'Come on – let's get out of here.'

'Park Lane?'

'More likely to be roadblocks. We've a better chance if we head east. Try losing them in Soho or somewhere.'

Alec shot off down Brook Street, only slowing slightly to cross New Bond Street, then went the wrong way round the south of Hanover Square, all the time weaving through a succession of cars, delivery vans, taxis, buses, even horses and carts.

'I can't see them in my mirror,' he said.

Armstrong turned round. He saw a trail of stopped cars and brandished fists, but no police car.

'I can't see them either,' he said, 'but let's not bank on it.'

Alec shot across Regent Street and raced along Great Marlborough Street. He had eased off a little, deeming it pointless to take any more risks for the time being.

'Any sign?' he asked.

Armstrong's heart plummeted when he looked back. There it was, its blue light flashing, its headlights coming straight towards them.

'It's—'

'I see it,' said Alec. 'Hold on tight.'

'What are you going to do?'

'Play chicken.'

'*Chicken?*'

There was no time for Armstrong to discuss his friend's choice, because Alec was speeding up, the needle hitting forty miles an hour. Armstrong looked ahead. They were approaching a junction and it seemed as though Alec had no intention of slowing down.

Within two seconds, before Armstrong could take in what had happened, they were facing the other way, Alec having performed a deft handbrake turn, and accelerating towards their pursuers, engine screaming. All Armstrong could do was wait and see if the driver of the police car was willing to kill them all.

With a mere three or four yards to go, the policeman decided that he wanted to live. The police car swerved to the left, but its speed meant that the driver could do nothing to stop it from mounting the high pavement, causing it to flip on to its right side and career along the road. Alec slammed on his brakes, and the police car came to a grinding, scratching halt next to them.

For a moment, silence. Passers-by looked on incredulously. Armstrong and Alec sat in a daze, taking in the simple fact that they were alive. It was Armstrong who snapped out of it first.

'Go! Just go!' he shouted.

Alec didn't move.

'GO!'

Alec put the car into gear and pulled away.

'Idiots,' he muttered again.

*

They left the car in a street just north of Oxford Street. They removed the number-plates, in order to protect Martin's friend, then set off towards the East End in companionable silence. They had a good hour-and-a-half's walk ahead of them, which meant that they should reach the safe-house before the curfew. However, Armstrong anticipated that there would be many more roadblocks that would need avoiding. The temptation to take a taxi was overwhelming, especially as the weather was now vile, but Armstrong knew that most taxi drivers were sympathetic to the regime. He had once read that there were more taxi drivers in the BUF than any other trade or profession. Hailing a taxi would be as sensible as flagging down a police car.

'By the way, Alec, what did you mean by calling the police "idiots"?'

'Hmm?'

'You called the police "idiots". Seemed an odd choice of word.'

'Did I?'

'Yes – you said it twice, I think.'

'Well they are, aren't they? I've always thought policemen were pretty thick. After all, aren't there more policemen in the BUF than any other profession? I thought I read that somewhere a while ago.'

Armstrong laughed.

'I read that too – it was actually cabbies. I was just thinking about that.'

'Well, policemen probably come second,' said Alec. 'They're *idiots*. There – I've said it again.'

*   *   *

The next morning Armstrong dispatched Lucy to the nearest post office, from where she picked up a coded telegram from Major-General Clifford that confirmed Armstrong's most optimistic hopes – the network was still in place, and Galwey and other army officers were ready to seize key fascist installations and figures around the country as soon as they received word of Mosley's death.

Alec's task was to go to Pooter's, from where he successfully retrieved a small parcel from the porter. As good as his word, Wilson had provided them with two passes and a seating plan of the Abbey, over which Armstrong, Alec, Lucy and Nick were now poring in excited silence. According to the plan, Westminster Abbey's interior was being transformed to cope with the eight thousand guests that had been invited. A theatre had been erected in the lantern area between the north and south transepts. At its centre was a dais, upon which the thrones for King Edward and Queen Wallis would be placed. Tier upon tier of seating was positioned around the dais, although the plan showed that Mosley and other senior members of the regime would sit in the choir stalls, along with dignitaries from the Empire and abroad. Mosley and his wife would be in the front row, and alongside them were the names 'Hitler, Adolf' and 'Mussolini, Benito'. The members of the Emergency Cabinet, accompanied by their wives, would sit immediately behind the Leader.

'I can't believe,' said Alec, 'that in a few days from now, we can not only take control of the country but also wipe out every fascist bigwig in Europe. It beggars belief.'

'It's called a coup, Alec,' said Armstrong.

'And you and Miss Craven here are simply going to walk in the night before, place a bomb under the choir stalls, and then wait for it to go off halfway through the Coronation?'

'We're not just going to walk in the night before,' said Armstrong, 'but we are going to walk in every day from now on. I want Lucy and myself to be part of the furniture, as it were.'

'But you'll be recognised,' said Nick. 'It won't take long for someone to twig.'

'I doubt that,' said Armstrong, 'because I'll be in disguise. My hair and beard are going to be dyed grey, and I'm going to be dressed as a restorer. I don't doubt that I'd be spotted immediately if I sauntered in wearing a suit and having had a shave. But with a legitimate pass, accompanied by Lucy, and carrying a bag of tools, I don't think I should have too many problems.'

Alec breathed in pensively through his nose.

'All right,' he said. 'Although it's bloody risky.'

'That,' said Armstrong, 'is an occupational hazard when you're planning a coup.'

* * *

At eight o'clock the next morning, Armstrong and Lucy found themselves walking towards the north door of Westminster Abbey carrying beaten canvas bags. Armstrong hoped that they presented a convincing picture of a pair of restorers going about their business. It was a cold, bright day, and to their left the grimy whiteness of St Margaret's church reminded Armstrong of a life that felt so distant it could have belonged to someone else. It was in St Margaret's that he and Mary had been married, and Philip baptised, two occasions on which he had felt truly anchored, secure from the effects of war and the unpredictability of politics.

'You all right there?' asked Lucy.

'Yes,' said Armstrong. 'Yes. Sorry, I was miles away.'

'You certainly looked it.'

Standing in the door were two policemen, both of whom were wearing lightning flash armbands. They were stamping their feet and occasionally blowing on their hands. As he and Lucy approached, Armstrong noticed that their helmets also bore lightning flash badges, another new addition to their uniforms. He wondered why the regime didn't go the whole hog and simply make the police wear Blackshirt uniforms.

Armstrong and Lucy waited in silence behind a few workmen who were presenting their passes. The policemen were giving little more than cursory glances at the documents, and appeared to be more preoccupied with talking to each other. Armstrong was tempted to allow himself to relax, to tell himself that all of his and Alec's misgivings were overblown, but he didn't. One of these men could have sharper eyes than he had bargained for.

'Morning, officer,' said Armstrong as casually as possible, producing his deliberately crumpled pass from a tattered donkey jacket.

The policeman looked him and Lucy up and down.

'You two look new,' he said, without any trace of warmth.

Armstrong just shrugged. That was a good sign – it meant that the policemen must have regular shifts.

'What are you here for, Mr Howard?'

'The finials in the choir,' he replied.

'Come again?'

'The finials – the carvings – in the choir stalls. The Dean says they are looking a little tatty. We're here to do a touch of regilding, smarten them up.'

'I'm not sure I understand a word of what you're saying,' the policeman replied. 'Fingles indeed. All right, in you go.'

Armstrong nodded, and along with Lucy started to walk past them, maintaining an expression that did not represent how nervous he felt.

'Hang on a minute!'

Armstrong froze. It was the other policeman.

'Your bags, what's in them?'

Both Armstrong and Lucy turned to face him.

'Tools mostly,' Armstrong replied.

'Open them!'

Armstrong could feel Lucy glancing at him, but he refused to acknowledge it, knowing that to do so would look suspicious.

'Certainly,' he said, unfastening the top of his bag.

He opened it up and let the policemen peer inside. They were rewarded with a medley of chisels, brushes, glues, paints and pads of gold leaf. One of the policemen reached inside and took out a small white tin.

'What's in here?' he asked Armstrong.

'Rabbit-skin glue.'

'You what?'

'Rabbit-skin glue – we use it in water gilding.'

The policeman unscrewed the top of the tin, peered at the sand-coloured powder and took a sniff, which caused an immediate reaction.

'Blimey! That smells worse than my wife's canary cage! Here, take a whiff of that.'

The other policeman stuck his nose into the tin.

'Actually, I don't mind it,' he said. 'Smells like a nice piece of offal.'

The policeman put the tin back into the bag and returned it to Armstrong.

'Little did I know, Mr Howard, what it is that goes into making things look so grand.'

As he spoke, he gestured towards the door with his thumb.

'Thank you,' said Armstrong, refastening the bag.

They stepped into the vastness of the north transept, their eyes taking a second or two to become accustomed to its relative dimness. They walked slowly past the statues of many of Armstrong's political heroes – Palmerston, Gladstone, Pitt and Peel. Although Armstrong was briefly lost in reverence, Lucy was shaking her head.

'What?' asked Armstrong.

'Capitalists,' she said. 'They're all capitalists. They should have Marx here.'

Armstrong smiled.

'Well, if you Communists win any future general election, then you're more than entitled to put him up wherever you want.'

'We'll win all right,' said Lucy, 'and only then will the workers truly be free.'

This was no time to start a political discussion, thought Armstrong. But before he had a chance to speak, he was checked by the sight of a large black cloth covering a statue.

'Who's under there?' asked Lucy, noticing the object of Armstrong's sudden distraction.

Armstrong didn't need to lift the bottom of the cloth to find out.

'Disraeli,' he said. 'And I don't need to tell you why.'

Lucy paused, her expression suddenly taking on the same fierceness that had been exhibited by her father when in full flow on the floor of the Commons. Without warning, she darted towards the statue.

'Lucy!' Armstrong hissed.

She spun round.

'Not now!' he said. 'In ten days, just ten short days, then you can take it off.'

Armstrong could see that every muscle in Lucy's body was forcing her towards the statue, goading her to give the cloth a sharp, symbolic tug. However, her desire was no match for the firmness and directness of Armstrong's gaze, a look that had caused even hardened politicians to crumble in Armstrong's chief whip's office.

'All right,' she said, 'all right. But . . .'

'I know,' said Armstrong, who was just as angry, 'I know.'

They walked slowly towards the lantern area, where they could see the partially constructed dais upon which would be placed the thrones. There were at least a dozen carpenters and joiners working on it, and several more working on the scaffolding that surrounded the tiers of seats being specially constructed for the ceremony. Armstrong and Lucy attracted no more than a couple of glances, and Armstrong was glad that he had insisted Lucy wear a cap that covered up her shoulder-length hair.

They walked purposefully round to the right of the dais and looked down the choir aisle. On either side of the black and white marble flagstones were three rows of oak choir stalls, behind which were resplendent rows of gilded finials. Along the stalls were perched small lamps with red shades, under each of which was an assortment of hymn books and psalters.

Armstrong took a deep breath and looked down to the row immediately in front of him and to his right. This was it, he thought, this was where Mosley was going to be sitting. Here, in ten days' time, Mosley would meet his end, along with – if their luck was in – Hitler and Mussolini. To kill all three would be too much to hope for, but Armstrong retained a degree of optimism. He certainly did not feel unstoppable, but he definitely felt confident, a mood brought about by his success in outwitting his pursuers and getting this far. He looked up at the vaulted ceiling a hundred feet above him and said a silent prayer. He found it surprising that he did so – the prayer had come into his head almost involuntarily.

'Let's look busy,' he said to Lucy.

For the next hour, 'Elizabeth Ball' and 'Philip Howard' made a good – but subtle – show of restoration. Armstrong's first task was to deliberately scrape away with a sharp chisel a few inches of gold from a number of the finials. It felt instinctively wrong, vandalising a cathedral, but it was surely for a cause that the entity to whom the building was dedicated was bound to approve. Armstrong then extracted a jade-tipped polishing tool, which he gently ran over the gilding on the other finials. Lucy was doing little more than applying beeswax to the choir stalls, but to an observer they looked as though they were professional restorers.

While they worked, Armstrong studied the stalls. Clearly, the best place for any explosive would be underneath them, but that would involve sawing a hole in the wood, inserting the explosives and a timer, and then covering it up. The stems of the lamps engaged his attention for a while, but they were too small and would not be able to hold sufficient explosive. Armstrong quickly dismissed taping the bomb underneath the seat, as even the briefest of security checks would reveal it. He was left with two options – a device could be inserted either inside the seat cushion, or, better still, inside the kneeler. Mosley would notice a device inside the cushion, but might not do so in the kneeler if the bomb was set to go off before the congregation was required to kneel.

Armstrong looked at his watch. It had just gone nine o'clock.

'Let's stay for another hour,' he said to Lucy.

Lucy nodded.

'By the look of things you've had an idea,' she replied.

'I have.'

'What?'

'I'll tell you later. Just carry on with what you're doing.'

'I'm getting a sore arm,' she said, albeit with a trace of humour.

'Little did you know, Miss Ball,' Armstrong said quietly, 'what it is that goes into making things look so grand.'

Ten minutes later, a figure dressed in bright red vestments approached them. A verger, thought Armstrong, and despite his smile, he looked a right busybody to boot.

'Good morning,' said the verger, his eyebrows locking together. 'I must say, it certainly is a surprise to see you here.'

Armstrong wiped his nose with the back of his hand. Lucy looked up at him, and Armstrong calmly gestured to her that she should carry on with her work.

'A surprise?' asked Armstrong. 'I'm not sure I follow you.'

'It's just that we've had all the gilding looked at last week,' said the verger, 'and we're very happy with it.'

'Really?' said Armstrong. 'Well I'm not.'

The verger looked a little taken aback.

'But . . .'

'Have a look over here,' said Armstrong, pointing to the finials he had scraped away at earlier. 'Now I wouldn't say they were in great shape, would you?'

'Well, no, but . . .'

'So it's got to be put right. I don't know which of your toffs are going to be sitting here, but I doubt they'll be very impressed when they see how shoddy some of these look.'

'Er, yes, quite, but I'm just a little confused,' said the verger. 'When the Dean and I looked at them only the other day, we were both satisfied that they were—'

'Happens to all of us,' said Armstrong. 'Even me. Which is why I have such a capable assistant here.'

Lucy flashed her most charming smile at the verger.

'It's true,' she said. 'Sometimes you just can't see for looking. Mr Howard is always missing things.'

'Not always, my love,' said Armstrong. 'I think you're being just a little harsh on your employer.'

'Sorry, Mr Howard.'

Armstrong grinned at the verger.

'A little cheeky,' said Armstrong, 'but very talented.'

'I don't doubt it,' said the verger. 'But Mr Skillion himself seemed positive that he had finished the job . . .'

'Mr Skillion just wanted me to patch up a few things. And to be honest, I can quite see why.'

'And where is—'

'His poor ma died the day before yesterday.'

'I see,' said the verger. 'I shall say a prayer for her soul – and for him, of course.'

'That's very good of you,' said Armstrong. 'To have a prayer said in the Abbey itself! The old dear will be delighted!'

The verger smiled wanly.

'Quite, quite,' he replied. 'Tell me, how much longer will this take? The clock is ticking, you know, Mr Howard.'

Armstrong, thinking of his bomb, almost laughed at the man's unintentional irony.

'Oh, I'd say another day or two. Perhaps three. You can never quite tell.'

'Very well, Mr Howard, but please remember there is a deadline.'

Armstrong nodded respectfully.

'I shan't forget,' he said.

'One other thing,' said the verger. 'How did you manage to gain access to the Abbey this morning?'

'We had passes,' said Armstrong nonchalantly. 'Mr Skillion got some for us a while ago, just in case the job was bigger than he thought.'

The verger seemed satisfied.

'Very well – I shan't detain you any longer. Good day to you, Mr Howard.'

Armstrong touched his hand to his cap.

'Good day to you, sir.'

Within a couple of minutes of the verger leaving, Armstrong had placed the kneeler in his canvas bag. As well as working out how to turn it into a bomb, he reflected, his other technical challenge was learning how to replace the gilding he had worn away.

*　*　*

The offices had lain empty since April. Gone was the chatter of typewriters and the frantic rush of messenger boys. The air was stale, the ghosts of so many cigarettes hanging in the tired atmosphere. Waste-paper baskets had not been emptied, and some desks still carried half-finished mugs of tea and coffee, the contents of which had transformed themselves into thick mats of lurid green fungus. Every so often one of the many large black telephones would ring, slightly shifting its layer of accumulated dust, but it would remain unanswered.

He walked slowly through the offices with his coat over his arm. It was like being in a coffin, he thought, with the sunlight struggling to pierce through the filthy windows. The hum of Fleet Street's traffic was barely audible, much quieter than the terrific clanking the printing presses used to make in the basement come the late afternoon.

This office represented freedom, he thought. From here, a group of two hundred men and women had written what they damn well pleased, offered opinions on subjects people cared about, reported the truth as best they could. It was a funny representation of freedom, this ink-stained warren of distressed tables and wood-wormed chairs, quite unlike the gleaming white marble dome that a lazy imagination might offer as a more fitting home for Freedom.

He gave the metal wheel a vigorous turn. For a second, the row of shelves didn't move, but the ratchet soon engaged and the shelves budged. The turns got easier and as they did so the shelves gathered momentum. In fact, he had to use all his strength to stop them bashing into the next row, something he remembered as being near the top of the librarian's list of sins.

As he looked along the shelves, he remembered that the list of sins also included the hoarding of cuttings, putting cuttings back in the wrong chronological order, keeping cuttings in one's desk, and, worst of all, taking cuttings home.

He walked along the shelves, hunting for the subjects that he needed. After ten minutes he had assembled a large pile of manila folders under his right arm. With a grunt he plonked them down on a large table, then removed his jacket, hung it over the back of the chair, rolled up his sleeves and sat down. He lit a cigarette, another librarian's no-no, and took out the cuttings from the first folder. Somewhere in here, he thought, he would find what he needed.

* * *

'Not again,' said Lucy.

It was the afternoon of the day after they had visited the Abbey, and Armstrong and Lucy were sitting round the brazier in the warehouse. Armstrong hated to ask her to use her body once more, but he had little choice.

'I don't deny that it's distasteful,' he said, 'but it's vitally important.'

'What's so special about this man?'

'He's the one who knows everything,' said Armstrong.

'Knows what exactly?'

'I'm afraid I cannot tell you – at least not yet. You'll just have to trust me, I'm afraid.'

Lucy narrowed her eyes.

'That's not good enough,' she said. 'If you want me to do this, I'd rather you had the decency to let me know *why*.'

Armstrong stoked the brazier with a long piece of timber. The action released a wild shower of orange sparks into the air. Lucy had a point – she always did – but it was hard to impress upon her what was so important about this man without revealing his deeper suspicions, suspicions that he was not willing to share, not even with her.

'The answer is no,' he said. 'I'm not going to tell you.'

Lucy folded her arms.

'In that case, I refuse.'

'That is your prerogative,' said Armstrong.

Lucy's ensuing sigh signalled a long silence. Armstrong knew that she was waiting for him to break, waiting for him to blurt it out, but he was not going to be drawn.

'Well,' she said, 'you could at least tell me *how* important it is.'

'As opposed to how it is important?'

Lucy almost grinned.

'Typical politician,' she said. 'Anyway, I thought you were a soldier, not a lawyer.'

'Soldiers have to be precise too.'

'All right, all right – yes! How important is it?'

Armstrong sent another shower of sparks into the air before looking directly at her.

'It couldn't be more important. I'd stake my life on it.'

'You seem to be staking mine on it.'

'You are quite right,' said Armstrong. 'I *am* staking your life on it. In fact, I am staking all our lives on it. After you have gone through with this, then I shall tell you, and I shall also tell the others.'

'You promise that?'

'I promise.'

Lucy stood up, her arms still folded.

'When?' she said. 'And how?'

*　*　*

Lieutenant-Colonel Huw Merriman had always been a light sleeper, but tonight he was dozing even more fitfully than usual. Although he had been waiting for the orders for months, nothing could have prepared him for how he would feel now that they were actually here. The signal from General Galwey, sent from Major-General Clifford's headquarters, had arrived just before six o'clock that afternoon, informing him that he was to assemble his battalion on Coronation Day exactly as he had already been ordered. Furthermore, the signal continued, his men were to be in a full state of readiness. Merriman knew exactly what that meant – they were to be armed, which was unusual for troops who were to perform mere ceremonial duties outside Westminster Abbey. But Merriman's battalion was to do more than shine in the sun; its real role was to assist Captain Armstrong and General Galwey in arresting leaders of the regime inside the Abbey after Mosley had been killed.

Merriman was not so much nervous for himself; rather for his men. He would be leading them down a path that some might regard as treacherous, and worse, that might get many – or all of them – killed. It was fair enough to risk his own life, but could he really play with others' in this way?

He turned over. The night was strangely warm, and he threw off his bedclothes. He had to do what he thought was right, not merely what he was ordered to do. This was no time for the time-stained soldier's excuse – 'I was only following orders.' He hated Mosley, hated what the fascists had done to the country, and yet there was something in him that rebelled against taking action like this.

Merriman turned on his bedside lamp and looked at his alarm clock. Twenty to three. He would be up in just under three hours. Come on, man, get some sleep. Of course what you're doing is right, no doubt about it. It was his bullish side doing the talking. Well, he thought as he turned off the lamp, it had never let him down yet. There was no point ignoring it now.

Chapter Thirteen

Nail Cutting

THE LEADER HAD no desire to be seen meddling with the arrangements for the Coronation, but on one matter he was absolutely insistent. The ceremony, he told the King and Queen, should not only be a showcase for Britain and her Empire, it should also mark the complete synthesis of fascism with the British state. Therefore fascist banners should hang alongside the Union flags within the Abbey, and all those present should wear Party armbands. The King and Queen agreed, although the King said there was little room for armbands amongst his Coronation robes, and therefore it would be better if he wore a decoration bearing the lightning flash. The Leader accepted this, and then went on to ask for just one more slight change, involving one of the oaths the King was to swear. At present, the oath in question read, 'Will you solemnly promise and swear to govern the Peoples of the United Kingdom of Great Britain and Northern Ireland, Canada, Australia, New Zealand, the Union of South Africa, and of your Possessions and other Territories to any of them belonging or pertaining, according to their respective laws and customs?'

It was the Leader's wish that the words 'their respective' be changed to 'fascist'. The King was not sure, and told the Leader that he would need to seek counsel. The Leader, mindful that there were still courtiers in the Palace whose political allegiances were suspect, strongly advised the King that it was for him alone to make up his mind on this important issue. Queen Wallis agreed, and with pressure coming from both his wife and Mosley, the King relented. He had always thought fascism was the future, he told them, and here was his chance to show his peoples that it was the creed by which he would govern. The Leader said he could not have put it better himself, although privately he wished for the word 'govern' to be taken out of the oath and replaced with 'serve'.

* * *

'It's so simple,' said Alec, 'that it should work a treat.'

'Lucy and Nick?' Armstrong asked. 'How about you?'

They both nodded.

'You're quite sure he's actually going to be kneel on it, are you?' said Lucy.

'This isn't Sunday service in some dozy village,' said Armstrong. 'Believe you me, people *kneel* at coronations, especially if they're in the front row and especially if they happen to be prime ministers, or in this case, Leaders.'

'And let's get this right,' said Lucy. 'As soon as he kneels on it, the bomb goes off. Yes?'

'Precisely,' Armstrong replied. 'The pressure of his weight will simply complete the fuse's electrical circuit, and *voilà*! The end of our dear Leader.'

'And do we know when Mosley will use it for the first time?' asked Nick.

'I think you mean the *only* time,' said Armstrong.

They all laughed.

'Judging by the order of service, I'd say about twenty minutes in,' said Armstrong. 'Maybe slightly less. That'll mean it should go off at about twenty past eleven.'

'Will the King be crowned by then?' Alec asked.

'No,' said Armstrong emphatically. 'Which as far as I'm concerned is another bonus. The congregation first kneels after the introit at the beginning of the communion service. The choir sings a few lines from Psalm Eighty-four and then the Archbishop—'

'What are the lines?' said Lucy.

Armstrong referred to the order of service supplied by Wilson.

'Here we go,' he said. ' "Behold, O God our defender, and look upon the face of thine Anointed. For one day in thy courts is better than a thousand." Well, I don't think Mosley is going to get even a minute in those courts.'

More laughter.

'And do you think you can actually make this bomb?' asked Nick.

'I'm pretty sure I can,' said Armstrong. 'It's a simple case of embedding the mechanism in the stuffing. The one thing I'll need help with is some sewing.'

At that point, Lucy found herself being looked at by three pairs of male eyes.

'As if it wasn't bad enough working with Tories,' she said.

* * *

Whenever possible, Lord Wilson would motor down to Hampshire to cast a fly into one of the finest stretches of the

River Test. Despite the proximity of the Coronation, this weekend was no exception, and Wilson had driven down with his wife and two daughters on Friday night, ready for an early start the following morning. They needed to return to London that evening for a function, and although Lady Wilson had protested that it hardly seemed worth it for herself and the two girls to come down, her husband had insisted, saying that it would do them good to get out of the stale air of the capital.

Lord Wilson got up just before dawn on Saturday morning, and strode the half-mile down to the banks of the river on his own. He enjoyed the early-morning solitude, and he would wade in to almost the fastest point of the river, from where he could cast straight on to the surface of a dark pool that sheltered beneath the branches of an elder bush. There were rich pickings to be had there, and he would often present the breakfast table with one or two large trout that would constitute that day's lunch.

This morning was proving to be less fruitful than usual. It was bright and there was a lack of drizzle, and Wilson suspected that the fish could see him. They had been getting a little wary of late – perhaps he should walk downstream to a pool he hadn't tried for several days. He reeled the fly back in and turned to make for the bank.

To his surprise, he saw two figures standing there. Both were tall men in their thirties, and were dressed as he was, in tweed jackets and waders. They carried rods and landing nets, although their equipment looked brand new. Wilson also noticed that they appeared lean and fit, and quickly supposed that they were fighting men of some sort.

'Good morning, my lord!'

'Who the hell are you?'

'We need to talk to you. It's very important.'

'I don't care what it is! This is private property. Now bugger off, the pair of you!'

The two men started wading in towards him.

'What the *hell* do you want?'

'I'm sorry, my lord, but we really do have to talk to you.'

'This is most irregular – remove yourselves immediately!'

Wilson tried lashing out when the two men got close to him, but as he had already noticed, they were in good shape. They were strong, very strong, and although Wilson struggled hard, there was nothing he could do to stop them holding him under the cool dark water.

He could never of course have seen them as he struggled, but there had indeed been some trout in the pool, which darted away when the commotion started. They came back a few minutes later, when the splashing had ceased, and there they remained for the next two hours, at which point they were disturbed once more, this time by a woman's scream.

*   *   *

It took Armstrong and Lucy the best part of a day to make the device that would rid the world of Oswald Mosley. Using a similar kneeler swiped from a nearby church, Armstrong first satisfied himself that his design would work. He made his trial bomb without dynamite, and the detonator went off – harmlessly – when he knelt on it.

The afternoon was a more nerve-racking affair. First Lucy unstitched the kneeler as carefully as possible, removing the side on which a person at prayer would rest his knees. Armstrong took out most of the horsehair and straw, leaving a bed on which the bomb would rest.

He then wrapped quarter of a pound of dynamite in some greaseproof paper, and inserted an electrical detonator stolen from the barge. Next he attached one of the two wires leading from the detonator to the positive terminal on a nine-volt battery. Another wire was attached to the negative terminal, but so far this led nowhere. Lucy wanted to watch, but Armstrong insisted she stay well away, that there was no point in two of them dying if he made a mistake.

He placed the dynamite, detonator and battery in the kneeler, and gently secured the elements in place with some horsehair and straw. As soon as he had done so, he had a thought, and asked Lucy and Nick to forage around the house for some old nails and tacks, in fact anything small and metallic. After ten minutes they returned with handfuls of what Armstrong intended to use as shrapnel. Taking thirty of the nastiest and sharpest pieces, he inserted them around the dynamite and battery.

Armstrong found his hands starting to shake as he proceeded to the next stage of manufacture. It wasn't an attack, merely the result of nervousness brought on by the delicacy of the task in hand. He got up and walked to the window, looking out on to the damp and foggy East End street. A boy was leading a tired-looking grey pony down the road. He must have been about Philip's age, Armstrong thought. The similarity caused him to wince, made him well up. He allowed himself to watch until the boy and his pony had reached the end of the road, then disappeared down another street, merging into the fog.

He went back to the bomb. He held out his hands and found they were satisfyingly steady. Good, he thought, because this was the hard part. Out of his shirt pocket he removed a large nail cutter, the type in which a small metal arm is rotated and then squeezed to apply pressure on two blades. With a small screwdriver he undid the screw that held the two blades together, then glued a piece of rubber where the screw had been. When the adhesive had dried, he squeezed the arm, but found that the blades connected far too easily. He bent one of the blades away from the other, and tried again. This time they required a decent amount of effort to connect them.

Armstrong covered the existing parts of the mechanism with more horsehair, straw and nails, leaving the second wire from the detonator exposed, as well as the wire attached to the positive terminal on the battery. He kept these wires as far apart as possible – if they touched, parts of him would be spread over the ceiling.

With a soldering iron, he affixed the wire leading from the battery to one of the blades on the nail cutters. Now came the part in which he was exposing himself to the most risk. With another deep breath, he soldered the wire from the detonator to the blade that had not been connected to the battery. Without the piece of rubber, the blades would be touching, thereby creating a complete electric circuit, which would set the detonator off. The nail cutters were in effect a switch – a switch that could be operated only by applying pressure to the small metal arm.

He gingerly placed the nail cutters on top of the layer of packing, keeping the metal arm uppermost, then gently pressed more horsehair and straw around and over the switch, until the mechanism was completely covered. Only then did he call Lucy in.

'You've done it?' she asked, wide-eyed.

Armstrong nodded. He wiped his brow, finding it to be soaking.

'I need you to sew the cover back on,' he said.

'Now?' she asked.

'If you're up to it.'

'Ready as I'll ever be.'

She came and knelt next to Armstrong.

'I'll stay here while you do it,' he said.

Lucy shook her head.

'No, that's not right,' she said. 'The same logic should apply to all of us. There's no point in both of us getting hurt.'

Her logic was right, thought Armstrong, of course it was, but it felt wrong to leave someone alone with a bomb that he had created. He was confident that it was stable, but even so, he didn't care to abandon her.

'I mean it,' said Lucy.

'All right,' said Armstrong. 'But please be bloody careful. For your information, the switch is here, about half an inch down.'

'Thanks,' said Lucy, and Armstrong could see the intensity in her expression.

He got up, wished her luck, and left the room.

For the next hour, Armstrong, Alec and Nick waited for an explosion to come from upstairs. Nick made them a cup of tea, but it was impossible to drink it, to do something so mundane when Lucy was risking her life.

Eventually her voice came through the floorboards. 'It's done!'

Armstrong ran upstairs and into the bedroom. Lucy was smiling triumphantly, and lying on the bed was an innocent-looking kneeler.

'Well done,' said Armstrong. 'Thank you, thank you very much.'

'Next time, you should learn how to sew.'

'Point taken,' he said.

'So what's that going to do to him?' she asked.

Armstrong paused before replying. He knew the effect of explosions only too well.

'It's going to remove enormous chunks of him,' he said. 'It'll certainly blow his legs clean off, and send pieces of shrapnel into his lower torso. I expect his face and upper torso might be protected by the shelf on the pew, but there's a good chance something will smack into his chest and head.'

'So there's no chance of him surviving?'

'None, absolutely none. Even if he does survive the blast – which he won't – all that shrapnel and straw and horsehair carries enough infection to ensure that his blood will be poisoned, and that'll kill him instead.'

Lucy felt a little light-headed. Armstrong was talking about it so clinically.

'You sound as though you're an . . .' she began.

'Let's just say I've seen it happen before,' Armstrong said.

Lucy nodded.

'And those around him?' she asked.

'There's a good chance they'll get hurt too.'

'Killed?'

'Quite likely. That's why I put in the shrapnel, in order to make the bomb more lethal. I couldn't put in too much, though, as the kneeler would have been too heavy.'

The two of them stood in silence, looking down at the kneeler. Armstrong hadn't realised it before, but it bore an embroidered image of Christ.

'Now we've just got to get it back where it belongs,' he said.

* * *

Otto loves coming here. He knows the NKVD would frown on it, because the Flash is a real fascist nightclub, but he cannot resist it. The women here are something else, the best in London. Who would have thought Englishwomen would be so attractive! Perhaps these are not Englishwomen; perhaps they are Italians and Germans, maybe even French, but who cares? They are all ripe young things, thinks Otto, ripe and available.

The cognoscenti say that the Leader sometimes comes here, but Otto has never seen him. It would be impossible for Mosley to go anywhere incognito, but he certainly has a reputation that would suggest that the Flash would be very much to his liking. The women are dressed in the latest styles, fashions that are mainly based on the Blackshirt uniform. Some are even wearing long black boots, which drives Otto wild. In this he is not alone.

Otto sits at the bar, drinking whisky. One girl on the dance floor catches his eye, a real *belle de nuit*, just the type of girl Otto likes. Her hair is dark, and she moves – oh, how she moves! She is on her own – a whore perhaps? Who cares! – and once again she looks over at him. Otto smiles back at her, all but licking his lips in anticipation. This is the type of club they should have had back in Vienna, the type of club he knows they would never have in Moscow. Anyway, all that is a long way away. Tonight Otto knows that he is going to make love to the dark-haired girl, because that is what he is good at, and that is what he deserves.

Within two hours, Otto is in the girl's hotel room, unpeeling her tight silk top. She is stunning, this girl, her breasts firm and ready for Otto's hungry mouth. He knows full well she is a whore, but after he has been with her, she will not want to charge. She will not regard Otto as a duty, as a chore, because Otto is more of an expert at sex than she is. Otto moves his way down the bed, and starts to kiss those breasts, gently at first, his tongue poised above each nipple, letting her feel his hot breath before his mouth closes around them.

What Otto is not expecting is the cold press of a muzzle against the back of his hot neck. Neither does he expect to find his head being violently yanked back by his hair, which causes him to yelp in pain. Otto is clever enough to know that he is a dead man, to know that he has been a fool to fall for this, the oldest method of entrapment in the book. He knows that he deserves to die, and he is ready for it, because he knows that men like him often die like this, with a bullet to the back of the neck. Normally it happens back in the Lubyanka, so perhaps he is lucky to die here, with the last thing he sees being this tender-titted whore rather than the wall of a shit-covered cell.

'One question,' says a voice. 'Just one question.'

'Fire away,' says Otto.

The voice is momentarily checked. Otto knows that the man will be impressed by the fact that he can make a pun in such circumstances – and not even in his own language!

'Who is Dog?' asks the voice. 'Tell me who Dog is.'

Otto pauses. Perhaps he has another forty years left in him. How would he spend them if he got out of this? There is only one way to find out.

* * *

Ribbentrop's Mercedes pulled up in Downing Street at ten o'clock on Monday morning. The German ambassador stepped out of the car, briefly exposing himself to the torrential rain, and then dashed into the dry warmth of the hall of Number

10. A distinguished-looking gentleman in full Blackshirt uniform approached him and raised his arm in a fascist salute, a gesture that Ribbentrop returned.

'Herr von Ribbentrop, would you follow me, please?'

Ribbentrop nodded and walked up the thickly carpeted stairs behind the functionary. He noticed that many of the portraits which lined the staircase had been changed – gone were the oils of many former prime ministers, replaced with paintings the Leader evidently felt more in keeping with the tenor of his regime. Ribbentrop climbed past Henry VIII, Elizabeth, Richard III, and, unsurprisingly, Oliver Cromwell, although he saw that Lloyd George had kept his place.

Mosley stood as Ribbentrop entered the room. They exchanged rigid fascist salutes, followed by a stiff handshake.

'Good morning, Ambassador,' said Mosley warmly. 'Won't you sit down?'

Ribbentrop did so, on a small chair in front of Mosley's desk. This was all part of the effect of making him feel like a schoolboy, Ribbentrop thought, and Mosley the headmaster.

'How can I help you, Herr Ribbentrop?'

Ribbentrop smarted at Mosley's refusal to use the 'von'. There were many who disputed his claim to the title, although Ribbentrop would be quick to say that he had inherited it – quite legally – from his aunt, Gertrud von Ribbentrop, who had adopted him when he was thirty-two. What the ambassador failed to mention was that he provided his aunt with an income of 450 marks per month in return for this favour.

'I have some important news for you concerning the Führer's visit this weekend,' said Ribbentrop.

Mosley leaned back in his chair. Ribbentrop could tell that

he had already worked out what the ambassador was going to say next.

'Carry on,' said Mosley.

'The Führer has informed me, with great regret, that he is no longer able to attend the Coronation of King Edward VIII and Queen Wallis.'

Ribbentrop paused, enjoying his moment, enjoying the spectacle of Mosley's attempt at maintaining sang-froid.

'Is the Führer good enough to let the British people know why he cannot attend this joyful occasion?'

'The Führer has indicated to me that he feels that attending the Coronation would present an unnecessary risk to his person,' said Ribbentrop.

Mosley made a scoffing sound.

'Herr Ribbentrop,' he said, 'I assure you that our security arrangements are as stringent as possible. It is quite unfounded for your Führer to feel that he would be at risk if he came here.'

'I'm sorry, Sir Oswald, but you do have a problem with terrorists here. There was the bombing in Westminster the other week, and there is talk that there was an escape from the Tower of London too. These are not safe times . . .'

'These times are perfectly safe!' Mosley shouted, thumping the table. 'And what's more, they are times in which we can show the people of Europe that fascism is a united force, and that it meshes well with the traditions of the past. This opportunity is too good for us to miss! I really do insist that you ask the Führer to reconsider his decision. His personal security will be taken very seriously indeed.'

Ribbentrop slowly shook his head.

'I am sorry, Sir Oswald, but you know what the Führer is like when he has made up his mind.'

He looked straight into Mosley's eyes, which were bulging furiously.

'In that case, Herr Ribbentrop, I bid you good day.'

* * *

Armstrong regretted taking the Underground at eight o'clock the following morning. He and Lucy were on the District Line from Tower Hill to Westminster, and the train was crammed with people on their way to work. Armstrong was standing, his canvas bag between his feet. If someone fell on him or knocked it, there was a chance that the kneeler inside might explode. He did his best to distract himself by studying the advertisements for products such as Brylcreem and Lifebuoy soap on the inside of the carriage. There was even a poster depicting a large wooden cabinet, into the top of which was built a small screen. 'Radio receives its sight!' read the poster. 'Here is the new "His Master's Voice" television instrument . . .' Armstrong's attention was not focused on the television itself, however, but on the image on the screen. It was Mosley. Was there no getting away from him?

He studied his fellow passengers. These were the people he was trying to save, ordinary people who just wanted to get on with their lives, and not live in fear of each other. What would happen if he succeeded? Would they get their revenge on Mr Perkins at number 29, quiet Mr Perkins who someone said – they could swear to it – was an informer for the secret police? And if they got their revenge, how would it be manifested? Would they beat him up, perhaps even kill him? As soon as they seized control, a new government would have to ensure that such reprisals did not take place, that the due process of the law was obeyed.

Further down the carriage, Armstrong could see a Black-shirt, his eyes scrutinising a copy of *Action*. Armstrong noticed that there was more space around him than there was around anybody else. It was clear many would rather endure more cramped conditions than have to stand next to a Party member. The Blackshirt seemed oblivious, unaware that he was the object of a silent and fearful derision.

The train started to slow for the next stop: Blackfriars. A few passengers would get off here, but it was likely that many more would get on, as Blackfriars was a mainline station. Armstrong looked down at the bag. Could it take any more jostling? It wasn't only the presence of the other passengers, but also the rocking of the train itself that was making him concerned. He turned to look at Lucy, whose face indicated that she was sharing his worry.

Armstrong looked through the windows to see that the platform was thankfully not too crowded. He sensed that many passengers were about to alight, so he stayed still. The train came to a stop, and people started to stream past him. He stood firm, holding on to an overhead rail, not allowing anybody to move him.

As Armstrong was watching the passengers get on the train, he didn't notice the pair of dirty hands gently grabbing the handles of his bag. He only realised that it was being stolen when he felt its sides brush against the insides of his calves. He glanced down, saw that the bag had disappeared, and then looked up to see a boy of about fifteen or sixteen darting out of the carriage.

For a moment, indecision. Chase him? Attempt to wrestle it from him? That might set it off, killing both of them. But he needed the contents of that bag desperately, and he was not going to let some chancer just run away with it.

'Stop him!' shouted Armstrong, pointing at the thief. 'Stop him!'

The thief was running through the passengers on the platform, the bag being waved wildly around as he weaved in and out of the bemused office workers. Armstrong jumped out of the carriage, not knowing whether Lucy was following him. He had to stop him; he had to get his bomb back. Not only that, he couldn't just let the thief blow himself up – that seemed wrong, an excessive punishment.

Armstrong knocked into countless passengers as he gave chase.

'Stop him!' he shouted. 'He's got my bag!'

The boy was getting away – not only was youth on his side, but his slightness and, presumably, his experience at such chases were also in his favour. With each second, Armstrong was expecting a sudden explosion, which would tear the boy to pieces and shower those on the platform with a savage hail of shrapnel.

The boy was nearing the end of the platform, and was about to run up a staircase. Armstrong cursed as people just gormlessly turned their heads rather than do as he requested. The boy was sprinting up the stairs now, sprinting far faster than Armstrong could ever hope to. He could feel the wounds on his chest straining as he panted, feel the scabs being torn off with the heaving exertion.

Armstrong reached the stairs and took them three at a time. The boy was nearly at the top – the stairs had not slowed him down at all. Armstrong urged himself to go faster, to find the same reserves of strength he had had in the boat with Craven. Come on, he said to himself, come on. Mosley was not going to stay in power just because of some random encounter with a thief.

At the top, Armstrong caught sight of the boy once more. He was making his way to the foot of a large wooden escalator. Shit, thought Armstrong, just what he needed.

'Stop that boy!' he shouted at the passengers on the escalator. 'Stop him!'

The boy ran up the escalator, the bag knocking into people. Surely it would go off – any second now there would be carnage. Part of Armstrong wanted to keep his distance, but the other part knew that he had to stop innocent people being ripped to pieces.

'Stop him!' he shouted once more.

Someone had to do something, because the boy was already halfway up and would soon disappear from view. Armstrong started up the escalator, following the thief's route through the maze of indignant passengers.

At that moment, a large man wearing a heavy brown overcoat turned round to face the boy, his bulk blocking the escalator. The boy tried to shove past him, but the man was too strong and held the thief by his biceps.

'Get off!' the boy was shouting. 'Fuck you!'

The man was shaking his head, and Armstrong thought he heard him say, 'You're going nowhere, chum.'

But Armstrong was not listening any longer, because the boy had dropped the bag. For a second, Armstrong watched as it fell on to the reservation between the up escalator and the down escalator. He had to be quick – if it slid all the way to the bottom and hit the ground, there was a good chance that it would explode. In fact, it was unlikely that it wouldn't.

There were two people between Armstrong and the reservation, two people whom Armstrong was now shoving brutally out of the way, ignoring their pleas that he be more mindful. The bag was gaining momentum, and Armstrong doubted that he would be able to reach out and stop it.

He leaned over, stuck his left arm out and stretched, but he was too late and the bag careered past the end of his fingertips. He shut his eyes. There was about to be an explosion that would kill maybe half a dozen people, perhaps more. Instinctively, Armstrong ducked, readying himself for the pieces of shrapnel.

'Down!' he shouted, grabbing the woman next to him and shoving her on to the slatted wooden step.

Nothing. Surely it must have reached the bottom by now? Another second, and still nothing. Tentatively he stood up and looked down. What he saw made him almost collapse with relief, because there, near the bottom of the down escalator, was the diminishing figure of Lucy, who was clutching the bag by its handles.

'Thank God,' he said out loud.

Armstrong stumbled as the escalator reached the top. He was met by the struggling figure of the thief and the man who had stopped him.

'Shall we take this blighter to the police then?' the man was asking.

Armstrong, who was still breathless, shook his head. He looked the boy in the eye.

'Today,' he said, 'is your lucky day.'

The boy tried breaking free, but the man's grip was so powerful that he could barely move.

'You really don't want to hand him over?' the man asked.

'No,' said Armstrong, 'I'm just happy I've got my bag back. If you want to take him, then fine, but I've got a busy day ahead of me.'

The Leader

The man looked back at him quizzically, but before he could speak, Armstrong had turned away and was heading towards the down escalator.

* * *

Ousby had never seen the Leader in such a foul mood. He had already heard on the Blackshirt grapevine that Hitler was not attending the Coronation, and now there were rumours that not even Mussolini was coming. Of course, no announcements had been made in public, although with the ceremony only a few days away, Ousby knew that the Leader would have to tell the people why the leaders of Britain's closest allies were not joining in the festivities. That morning, just as Armstrong and Lucy were emerging from Westminster Underground station, the head of His Majesty's Secret State Police was sitting a few hundred yards away in 10 Downing Street. He was being left in no doubt as to who was to blame for the two great men cancelling their visits.

'Perhaps,' Mosley snarled, 'I should have taken up Hitler's offer and allowed this man Heydrich to come over and hold your hand!'

Ousby did not reply. He was not going to be drawn into a discussion he knew he could not – or rather, would not – be allowed to win.

'Armstrong has made a mockery of us!' Mosley continued. 'I'm told that people know that he has escaped, and that he has eluded us at every turn. The Germans and the Italians have got wind of it, and they quite understandably fear the risk of assassination. I cannot say I blame them! Why else do you think that my good friends the Chancellor and the Duce are not coming? Eh?'

Ousby sat impassively. He knew the Leader was lying, knew that he was looking to blame anyone but himself.

'Ousby,' said Mosley, getting up from his desk, 'do you have any idea where Armstrong is? What he is doing? Who he is with? Anything at all?'

'I'm sorry, we don't,' Ousby replied in a monotone. 'He's just disappeared.'

'Disappeared? Despite all the new powers and resources I have given you, all you can simply say is that he has disappeared?'

'I'm afraid so, sir, yes. That is the short of it.'

'Well it's not good enough! Even the King has been asking me about him. He and the Queen are concerned that Armstrong poses some sort of risk to them, maybe even to the Coronation itself. I have of course assured them that matters are being taken care of, and that they are not to worry, but the Queen seemed most anxious.'

'You can assure the Queen that the security arrangements for Saturday are completely watertight,' said Ousby.

'I hope so, Ousby, I do hope so.'

Silence. Ousby looked at the flames of the fire gently lapping away at the glowing nuggets of coal. The Leader was right, of course, the HMSSP had fouled up, or at least they had appeared to.

* * *

It was a morning for thanking God, and Armstrong had the opportunity to do so again when he saw the familiar faces of the two policemen on duty at the Abbey's west door.

'A little late this morning, aren't we?' said the policeman, examining their passes.

'The Underground,' Armstrong replied.

'Hasn't got any better, has it?' said the policeman with a smile.

Was this a trap? Was this what policemen did now – tricked you into making an unpatriotic comment and then arrested you for it?

'I wouldn't know,' said Armstrong.

The policeman winked.

'All right,' he said, handing back their passes, 'in you go, with your rabbit glue or whatever it was.'

Armstrong was tempted to correct him, but thought better of it. As they walked past the shrouded figure of Disraeli, he mused that 'I wouldn't know' summed up the way in which so many people dealt with the regime. Did you see what happened to our Jewish neighbours the other night? I wouldn't know. Do you know where so-and-so went? I wouldn't know. There's not as much food in the shops as there used to be, is there? I wouldn't know. Do you know that the police took away that nice young chap the other day? I wouldn't know. How do you think the Leader is doing? I wouldn't know. Feigned ignorance, thought Armstrong, that was one of the true friends of the regime.

The finials were just as they had left them – scratched. Although neither he nor Lucy had the first idea how to regild them, Lucy had bought a tin of gold paint from a toyshop, which Armstrong said would just have to do. They placed their bags on the pew, and after casually looking around, Armstrong removed the kneeler. It occurred to him that perhaps the device was not working, but then he assured himself that it had to be. It certainly would have exploded back in the Underground station had he not enlarged the gap between the two blades. He had only moved them a quarter of an inch further apart, but it was enough.

He hung the kneeler on its hook and then turned away. There was no point in looking at it – mere observation would not guarantee its success.

'Where's this paint then?' Armstrong asked.

'Here,' said Lucy, and threw the pot over to him.

* * *

'Here it is,' said General Galwey, thrusting the telegram at Major-General Clifford.

The two men were sitting alone in Clifford's operations room in Chelsea late that night, both nursing large undiluted whiskies, their medal-festooned tunics hanging over the backs of their chairs. An orderly had just left the room, having presented the telegram to the generals with a shaking hand. Clifford scanned its contents.

'Everything looks ready at his end,' said Clifford. 'But hang on – I don't like this here: "Suspect some of the partygoers are in on the surprise, start party an hour earlier." What does that mean?'

'It means Armstrong believes that some of those we're rounding up might be waiting for us. He wants us to go into action before Mosley is removed.'

Clifford looked down as he swilled the whisky around his glass.

'But if Ousby's men know the score,' said Clifford, looking up, 'then we're done for.'

Galwey shook his head, a relaxed smile on his lips.

'I doubt that,' he replied. 'If that was the case then I'm sure our good captain would have called it off. No, he just wants us to be careful, exercise some caution, and of course he's quite right. With only a few hours to go, I suspect rumours will be gathering pace. So, in order to scotch any nonsense, he simply wants us to *carpe diem* a little earlier, that's all. We'd better signal our units.'

Clifford drained his whisky glass.

'But if we're taking control *before* the assassination,' he said, 'then Armstrong might not need to kill Mosley.'

'Oh good God,' said Galwey. 'I don't fancy trying to hold on to power with that bugger still around, do you? There'd be civil war! No, killing Mosley is very much part of it. When he's gone, our control is absolute. Like all good soldiers, Armstrong is simply keeping his plan adaptable.'

'He's a clever man,' said Clifford.

'Wasted as a politician!' said Galwey, causing them both to laugh.

'If he'd stayed in the army he might have done one of us out of a job,' said Clifford.

'You're probably right,' said Galwey, draining his glass. He looked at his watch. It was two o'clock.

'Bedtime I think,' he said. 'Big day tomorrow and all that. You'd better get that signal out now. Tell them they'll be expected, but that H-hour is one hour earlier. All right?'

Clifford nodded and smiled. It was typical of the general to be so unflappable. He would make a good interim leader of the country, he thought, a steady pair of hands. Who else could remain so calm the night before he was to assume full martial control of his country?

Chapter Fourteen

Temporal Kingdom

SHE WAS ACTUALLY going to be *crowned* tomorrow. The thought made her feel giddy, intoxicated her. To think! All the way from Baltimore to becoming the Queen of England! Yes, yes, she was already Queen, but to actually wear the crown – that would secure it. Poor David – he was so nervous that she'd insisted he take a sedative. He said he wasn't feeling that bad, just a whisky would do, but she had snapped at him, told him that if he knew what was good for him he would do as he was damn well told. So David had obediently taken the sedative, and now he was asleep in his bedroom, no doubt sharing his bed with one of those darn pugs. Ugly little creatures.

The Queen examined herself in the mirror – an elegant eighteenth-century girandole bearing two slim white candles. It was late, around half past one, but she was not tired. She smiled at herself. She had won. They had lost. Those who told her that she was a plain little thing, those who said that she was merely a two-bit twice-divorced Yank without a cat's chance in hell. Those were the people who claimed that the British would never accept her as their Queen, and yet here she was! The British adored her! She was in the papers, in the newsreels, even on fine bone china – they loved her, for God's sake!

She was satisfied with her reflection. The only light in the room came from the candles, which gave her face a healthy, warm glow. Around her was darkness and silence, barring the occasional creak of an expanding palatial timber. It was as though she was floating in a nether world, a special place that only she could inhabit. She held a glass of vodka up to her lips, winked, and then drained its contents. Vodka was all she drank these days. Lettuce was nearly all she ate. She stayed slim that way, never to become the fat little Wallis she had always feared.

Licking her lips, she set the glass down next to a vase with seventeen red carnations in it – one for every time they had done it. He had been imploring her to allow him to add another carnation, but she enjoyed stringing him along. Poor Joachim, he was so devoted, such a puppy. Perhaps she would let it happen again – maybe she would even wear her crown for him. Now *there* was a thought. She took the stopper out of the vodka bottle. Just one more glass, and then bedtime for the Queen. Tomorrow was, after all, going to be a big day.

'Are we all clear?' asked Armstrong.

Everybody in the room nodded. Armstrong could tell they were nervous, but that was understandable. By this time tomorrow night, they would either all be dead, or presiding over a newly freed Britain. He tried not to dwell on the sheer weight of history invested in them and their plan. The stakes were so high, it was almost impossible to play the game. Better just to pretend it didn't matter, play it for the mechanics and not for the stake. Forget the fact that an entire fortune depended on rolling a double six; just go ahead and roll it.

'Lucy,' said Armstrong, 'tell me what you're going to do.'

Lucy stared at him.

'We've been over this . . .'

'Just tell me, Lucy.'

Armstrong's voice had an air of impregnable authority. Lucy sighed.

'All right – I'm going to be with you throughout the day. We're going to leave here at nine o'clock tomorrow morning and walk over to Westminster, mingling with the crowds. When the bomb goes off I'm going to accompany you with General Galwey and members of Colonel Merriman's battalion into the Abbey, where we're going to arrest senior members of the regime.'

'Good,' said Armstrong. 'What about you, Nick?'

'I shall be in Clifford's operations room on Chelsea Bridge Road,' he replied. 'At precisely ten thirty – about fifty minutes before the bomb goes off, I shall go with a company of the London Regiment along with thirty members of the Freedom Council to the main studios of the SBC in Portland Place. We shall storm the building at exactly eleven fifteen.'

'Excellent,' said Armstrong. 'And what will you do when you've got there?'

'As soon as we hear the code word for the assassination on the army frequencies, we shall broadcast your proclamation to the entire nation.'

'And your opposition cells? Are they ready to help?'

'Martin tells me they are just waiting for the word.'

Armstrong gave Nick a thumbs-up before turning to Alec.

'And finally Alec – you're all clear?'

'Certainly, James. I'll also be with Clifford, co-ordinating things from there. I'm going to help to ensure that all our units up and down the country act as swiftly and as firmly as possible.'

'All right, good,' said Armstrong. 'And just to recap, my movements will be these: I shall leave here with Lucy at nine o'clock. We shall get as close to the Abbey as possible. As soon as the bomb goes off, General Galwey and I will lead in a detachment of Merriman's battalion and take control of everybody inside. Once I am satisfied that Mosley has been killed, I shall have the code word broadcast to the operations room. I will announce to the congregation that there has been a change of government, and that forces loyal to democracy and freedom have taken control of key installations around the country. My role is to pacify the congregation, and if any resistance materialises to order Merriman's men to meet force with force. We can be thankful that the many thousands of other soldiers who are involved in the ceremonies will not be armed.

'After I have made any necessary arrests, I shall then make my way to Downing Street, where I will make arrangements for a meeting to be held as soon as possible between myself, General Galwey, the head of the civil service, the head of the Metropolitan Police, the Chief of the Imperial General Staff, and the head of the prison service. I shall tell them that parliamentary democracy will be restored after a period of martial law under General Galwey and that political prisoners are to be immediately released. And then, well, I think I shall have a very large whisky.'

'I think we all will,' said Alec.

'One thing,' said Lucy. 'What about the King and Queen?'

'I hadn't forgotten about them,' said Armstrong. 'I shall

respectfully suggest that they go back to Buckingham Palace and stay there.'

'But how about in the future? In a few weeks, I mean.'

'Hopefully,' said Armstrong, 'he will have the good sense to abdicate, which he should have bloody done in the first place.'

'And if he doesn't?' asked Nick.

'Then it will be explained to him that the first Act of Parliament after the restoration of parliamentary democracy will be to strip him of his crown and place it on the Duke of York's head. Whatever the constituency of the House, I see no problem in getting such an act passed.'

'If the House is going to be filled by those *I* would wish to be there,' said Lucy, 'then there will be no more monarchy full stop.'

'Too right,' said Nick.

Armstrong smiled.

'If you Communists win a general election fair and square, then you're entitled to do what you like,' he said. 'That, after all, is democracy. I don't agree with your politics at all, as you well know, but I'm fighting – we're all fighting – for a Britain in which we allow others to speak their minds, no matter how misguided we feel they are.'

'Misguided?' said Lucy, incredulous.

'All right then,' said Armstrong. 'Let's just say idealistic.'

'You're on thin ice.'

'I'm getting used to it,' said Armstrong. 'All right then, let's get some sleep.'

The call from the Leader came at two o'clock in the morning. Ousby was in his office, attending to some last-minute details with his deputy and a handful of commissioners.

'Ousby?'

'Yes, sir?'

'How are your arrangements for tomorrow? Or today rather?'

'Just going over them now, my Leader.'

'And I assume you don't have any good news to give me about Armstrong?'

'No, sir, I'm afraid not.'

The Leader paused.

'Well, Ousby, there is something you *can* do that will make me slightly happier with you.'

'Anything.'

'You can get the fucking French to arrest Armstrong's brat and throw him in the Channel.'

Ousby didn't flinch. He had been expecting this conversation.

'And when would you like this to happen, sir?'

'When do you bloody think? In a month? Twenty years? Goddammit, I want it done now!'

'Very well, sir. I shall issue the order immediately.'

The line went dead. Ousby held the receiver away from his ear, looked at it, then placed it gently back on the cradle.

'Excuse me,' he said to those in the room, 'would you mind leaving for a moment? I need to make a confidential phone call. You can leave your things in here – I'm not going to be more than a minute.'

The men stood up and left. Ousby dialled the number as soon as the last one out had closed the door.

*   *   *

London had known more enthusiastic Coronation mornings. For George V's Coronation, thousands had camped out along the procession route the night before, but this time there were no more than a few hundred. As with the parade following the signing of the Treaty of London back in June, there was a vastly complex ticketing system in place, which ensured that there would be a minimum attendance of at least 200,000.

For the past week, *The Blackshirt* and *Action* had carried photographs of the royal couple on their front pages, which readers were cordially invited to stick in their downstairs windows. Anybody doing so would be eligible to win one of the one hundred signed photographs of the King and the Leader – 'An heirloom of the future too good to miss!' said *The Blackshirt*. However, the bait was not taken, and soon Blackshirts could be found knocking on doors to 'encourage' people to put the pages up. One wag put the picture up all right, but in a window that faced his back yard. News of that spread quickly, and soon hundreds of thousands of houses in Britain had the picture up in the kitchen, or the privy – any window, so long as it did not face the street.

That morning's papers were bumper issues, and in amongst the articles concerning the happy event – complete with a full biography of the Queen in which it was revealed how the alcoholic Mr Simpson had beaten poor Wallis – more observant readers noticed a short paragraph that told of 'severe and inclement' weather that had unfortunately prevented both Herr Hitler and Signor Mussolini from flying over for the occasion. The sarcastic among them observed that the blue sky this morning was obviously a mistake, although such a comment was not to be heard expressed in public.

However, there were many who genuinely wanted to see the procession. Some wished to witness the pomp; others were simply curious. The keenest were of course the Party members, those who agreed wholeheartedly with the Leader's recent broadcast on the SBC declaring that the Coronation was not just the crowning of King Edward VIII, but the crowning of fascism – its coming of age.

It was in the ranks of these people that Armstrong and Lucy found themselves as they walked briskly along the Victoria Embankment on their way to the Abbey. Both were sporting fascist armbands, as well as flags that showed a picture of Edward and Wallis set in a Union Jack combined with the ubiquitous lightning flash. Such flags were hanging from every flagpole they passed, Armstrong noticed. The Union Jack had been violated, he thought. Indeed, was it even possible now to get hold of a Union Jack without the lightning flash?

Armstrong and Lucy reached Parliament Square just before ten o'clock. As they had got closer, the streets had become increasingly congested, and they had to jostle their way through to a position in which they could see the west door of the Abbey. The square was filled with the chatter of spectators, as well as the noise of the military bands that were parading along Whitehall. Armstrong occasionally caught glimpses of soldiers from every part of the Empire, men of different races and creeds, all of whom were now being dragooned into fighting not just for the Empire, but also for fascism.

For a few minutes, he and Lucy stood in silence, taking in the atmosphere. The air was clear and fine, making him wonder how many would have ventured out if it had been raining – no doubt the regime had made a contingency plan in such an event. One thing that became slowly apparent was the general lack of excitement amongst the crowd. Despite the hubbub and the flags and the smell of roasting chestnuts, there was something missing. Of all the crowds Armstrong had known, this one was different. What was it? It was soulless, he thought

– it had no core, no kernel. People were here because they had to be here, not because they wanted to be. It was a duty, a chore, an order. The crowd lacked any senses of unity or purpose, and as a result it was not cohesive. There were no exchanges, no connections being made between strangers. It was symptomatic, thought Armstrong. This was what Britain had become under Mosley – no longer a society, but an assemblage of hundreds of thousands of little groups, none of whom trusted any of the others. If there was any commonality, it was that mutual feeling of mistrust. Armstrong looked at the clock on the Abbey – five past ten. In just over an hour, the British people would be heading back towards a society in which they could talk openly to each other.

At first he thought it was a jostle, just the crowd surging forward, but within a second he knew exactly what was happening. His wrists were being firmly held, and then he felt the unmistakable cold, tight metal grip of handcuffs, something he hadn't experienced since his arrest on Vauxhall Bridge Road. A voice spoke in his ear.

'You're coming with us, Captain Armstrong.'

He turned to face Lucy, only to see that she was being similarly treated.

'Get off me!' she was yelling. 'Get off!'

'Shut up, bitch!' barked a man in an overcoat and snap-brim hat. Secret Police, thought Armstrong, Ousby's men.

Armstrong didn't speak as he was bundled and kicked through the curious crowd into the back of a windowless van. Things, he thought, were going according to plan.

The ride was shorter than expected – Armstrong estimated that it took about five minutes. As the van came to a halt, he spoke.

'Don't worry,' he said to Lucy.

'Don't worry!' she screamed in the darkness. '*Don't worry!* How can you say that?'

'Be patient,' said Armstrong. 'This is just what I expected.'

'What . . . what did you expect?'

'This,' said Armstrong. 'Just this.'

Their conversation was interrupted by the van door being opened.

'Out.'

The voice was neither threatening nor severe, but bland, emotionless. Armstrong and Lucy got awkwardly to their feet and stepped out of the van. They were in a small underground car park. Armstrong noticed about a dozen black Wolseleys and Vauxhalls – the favoured cars of the secret police.

'This way.'

With two secret policemen ahead of them, and at least six behind, Armstrong and Lucy were frogmarched over to a small wooden door in the corner of the car park.

'Downstairs.'

Armstrong didn't know why, but he had expected they would be going up, to an office, perhaps to meet Ousby himself. The staircase was made from rough concrete and it descended about the depth of two storeys. Where were they going? To some torture chamber?

They reached a long concrete corridor. It was almost dark and Armstrong could only see about twenty feet ahead. The air was stale and dank – it reeked of cigarette smoke and diesel fumes.

'In here.'

They were shoved through an open door to their right, into a small room in which there was a wooden table. A figure sat on a basic chair behind the table, but Armstrong could not see his face because a low-hanging light-bulb obscured it. There was nothing else in the room, apart from a door to the left.

'Good morning, Captain Armstrong, and to you too, Miss Craven.'

The door slammed behind them. Armstrong recognised the voice. He had heard it back in the Tower of London – it was that of Sir Roger Ousby. Neither Armstrong nor Lucy replied. Ousby stood up, walked round the table, and stopped in front of Armstrong, looking down at him from his vast height.

'I'm sorry to have brought you in so late in the day,' he said. 'I must have got your hopes up. I thought it best that the resistance beavered away merrily while I sat and watched.'

Armstrong couldn't resist a question.

'And how were you watching us?'

Ousby's eyes crinkled in what passed for a smile.

'I'll show you,' he said.

He turned on his heel and walked over to the door to the left. He opened it wide and said, 'I think he wants to see you now.'

'At last!' came a voice.

A few seconds later, a figure entered the room.

'Hello, old chap!'

'Hello, Alec,' Armstrong replied, his tone resolutely phlegmatic. 'Or should I call you Dog?'

* * *

It was quarter past ten, and the Leader and his wife would leave Downing Street in precisely thirty-five minutes, arriving at the Abbey at five minutes before eleven. The Leader was looking at himself in a full-length mirror in the dressing room whilst a valet brushed down the back of his immaculate uniform, complete with ceremonial sword.

'You know, my darling,' said the Leader, addressing the reflection of Diana on the other side of the room, 'today is going to be a triumph.'

'I know, dear,' his wife replied. 'I suspect it will be a day to remember.'

Diana looked a vision, the Leader thought. She was wearing a long eau-de-Nil dress in raw silk, a material that tightly hugged her figure, although not so tightly as to be indecent. Over it she wore a short jacket in the same material, on to which her personal dressmaker was fastening a brooch studded with jewels that formed the shape of the Party's lightning flash.

'That's new,' said the Leader. 'Where did you get that not so little bauble?'

'His Majesty gave it me.'

The Leader walked over to examine it.

'I like it very much,' he said. 'I always knew His Majesty to be a man of taste, but he has excelled himself here. I confess that I am a little jealous.'

Diana smiled coquettishly.

'You're not the only one with admirers,' she said.

For a second his face darkened, and then his mouth formed into a brilliantly white smile that elongated his pencil-thin moustache.

* * *

'I wish I could say this was a surprise,' said Armstrong, 'but I'm afraid I've known for quite some time what you've been up to.'

Armstrong had never seen an expression change so quickly,

from that of smug dealer of shock to one of utter astonishment. Alec did his best to maintain an air of togetherness, but it was apparent to both Armstrong and Lucy that it was a struggle. For his part, Sir Roger Ousby's normally blank features were registering what for him constituted a severe display of bewilderment.

'Is that so?' asked Alec eventually. 'May I ask how you came to know?'

Armstrong shrugged as if it was a trifle.

'Well, it was the letter, the letter that Ted was supposed to have sent us when we were in the Tower of London. He didn't write it – you did.'

Alec folded his arms.

'Carry on,' he said.

'I knew that our escape was too easy,' said Armstrong, 'and I knew that it required help on the inside. Of course we both knew that, although you encouraged me to think that it was Ted in cahoots with good Sir Roger here rather than yourself, and it nearly worked – I nearly killed the wrong man. Ted told me that he had written no such letter, and that's when I knew that it had to be you, Alec.'

'You mean Frost is alive?'

'Quite so,' said Armstrong. 'Prospering, in fact.'

'Where is he?' snapped Ousby.

'I'll come to that, Sir Roger,' said Armstrong. 'In the meantime I think it's best that you listen.'

Ousby stepped up to Armstrong and looked him in the eye. Armstrong could detect some uncertainty in that gaze, an uncertainty that he had to take advantage of.

'Especially,' he continued, 'as your friend Otto – sorry, I believe you call him Stefan – is being held by my friend General Galwey.'

Armstrong watched as Ousby's eyes scanned his face, desperately seeking some kind of uncertainty in his captive.

'That's right, Top Hat,' said Armstrong. 'It all went wrong for you when Krivitsky defected, didn't it? But what made matters even worse was your bad luck that Lucy ran into Henry Allen, who told us what was going on. And not only that, it must have been a real pain to discover that one of your men had mistakenly arrested me at Claridge's. In fact, it was something that nearly happened again, after Alec and I met your stooge Lord Wilson. Alec kept referring to the police as idiots, which I initially found surprising considering that chasing fugitives is their job. Of course, he was quite right, the police were being idiotic in chasing those you were allowing to run free. Alec was calling them idiots because they were about to repeat the same mistake – that of arresting me.

'Still, you certainly took advantage of my arrest. Locking me up in the Tower was an ideal opportunity to reinsert Alec. I must say, Alec, did you really allow them to beat you up in order to convince me? That was very impressive – I might even say brave.'

'Shut up!' Alec shouted. 'Just shut up!'

'No, Alec, I won't shut up. I don't think you've met this Otto creature, but the other night Lucy and I found him most communicative, especially with his trousers down and my gun pointing at his head. It was the good Mr Frost and his journalist's nose that sniffed him out. Otto told us all about your recruitment in the twenties, how you turned Communist after the war. Apparently there are lots more like you from Cambridge, though I think Otto was boasting a little bit. And of course you, Sir Roger – well, you're his real star pupil, aren't you? You've been biding your time all these years, and now look where you are! The chief of the secret police and an agent for the Russians no less! Quite an achievement – I expect Stalin has given you a medal, ready for you to pick up from the Kremlin. The bad news, of course, is that it's over for the both of you.'

'Really?' said Ousby. 'There are two small details that you're overlooking. One, you're the man in handcuffs, not me, and two, your brave army officers will soon be arrested by members of my police force. Your bomb will go off all right, and Mosley will be killed, but I'm afraid that it's me who will seize power, not you and the worthy General Galwey.'

Armstrong smiled.

'Goddammit!' shouted Alec. 'I don't see what's so bloody funny!'

'What's the time?' Armstrong asked. 'I'm afraid my hands are . . .'

Alec snatched a look at his watch.

'Half past ten – why?'

'Well, right about now, Galwey's men are seizing nearly every police station – including all your secret police HQs, Sir Roger – as well as every Blackshirt office and radio station in the country.'

'That's not possible!' yelled Alec. 'I was there when you wrote those final orders. Don't believe him, Sir Roger, it's all a bluff.'

'I'm afraid you weren't there,' said Armstrong. 'The orders I wrote out in front of you were merely for your benefit. As soon as you left, I simply brought everything forward.'

Before either Alec or Ousby could reply, there was a loud knocking on the door.

'Yes!' Ousby shouted.

A breathless secret policeman burst into the room.

'Sir! There are soldiers everywhere outside! They're demanding that we give ourselves up! They say that if we don't they'll storm the building in two minutes. What shall we do, sir?'

Ousby managed a weak smile before waving the man away. 'Sir?'

'Get out!' Ousby yelled.

There was a brief silence, which Armstrong was tempted to break. But there was no point – he knew that Ousby could work things out for himself. Alec had turned pale, his face reflecting the realisation that he had lost, and had done so comprehensively.

'So it's all true,' Ousby said quietly. 'Well done, very well done.'

Armstrong didn't reply.

'You . . . you bastard,' said Alec.

Once more, Armstrong held his tongue.

More knocking on the door.

'Sir! They're saying that we've only got one more minute!'

Ousby ignored the knocking, and instead pulled open a drawer and extracted a large revolver.

'Killing us won't achieve anything,' Armstrong said.

'I know that,' said Ousby.

He calmly checked the chamber and snapped it back into place, then cocked the revolver with a series of clicks that filled the room.

'Captain Scott?' said Ousby.

'Yes?'

'I'm much obliged to you. At least we can say that we did our best.'

'But Sir Roger, we can still—'

Alec's words were cut short by the fact that Ousby was aiming the revolver straight at his chest. Without another word, he fired. The bullet went through Alec's heart, out through his back and buried itself in the wall behind him. The look of surprise remained on his face as he fell to the floor.

Before Armstrong and Lucy had fully appreciated what had happened, Ousby had placed the smoking muzzle of the revolver in his own mouth and pulled the trigger.

* * *

The King had required two large whiskies to steady his nerves. The Queen had chastised him for being so weak, although naturally she would not admit to her own imbibing of copious amounts of vodka just after ten o'clock.

'*David*,' she said, 'you shouldn't drink so much. Can't you just get through *one* day without your darn Scotch?'

'I'm sorry, dear,' the King replied, 'but it's not exactly a normal day, is it?'

'Huh!'

It was quarter to eleven, and the royal couple were about to depart. The golden state carriage was waiting for them in the courtyard of Buckingham Palace. Valets and footmen were fussing around, adjusting their dress, ensuring that they looked perfect. Their route to the Abbey would take them down the Mall, right on to Horse Guards Parade, and then left on to Birdcage Walk, which led into Parliament Square.

An official approached them and bowed deeply.

'If your Royal Highnesses are ready, it is now time to depart.'

The King and Queen stepped out into the courtyard, and walked slowly to the carriage. The Queen got into the carriage first, and the King, having ensured that his wife was safely on board, walked round to the other side and climbed into it a little unsteadily. As soon as the door had shut behind him, he received another rebuke from his wife.

'David! Sort yourself out!'

The coach pulled away jerkily.

'This thing is so damn uncomfortable,' said the Queen. 'Why couldn't we have used a car?'

'But darling, cars are for—'

'For treaties,' the Queen snapped. 'Yes, yes, I know. Come on, David, it's time to wave.'

* * *

The cell door slammed open. They had heard much commotion and arguing outside, as well as the occasional sound of a pistol shot, and Armstrong had expected secret policemen to walk in. Instead it was the welcome figure of Ted.

'Ted!' Armstrong shouted. 'Get us out of here!'

Ted was accompanied by three army officers, all of whom looked down at the corpses on the floor.

'Go and find some keys,' Ted ordered them. 'Christ almighty, what happened here?'

'Ousby shot Alec before shooting himself,' Lucy replied.

'Never mind that,' said Armstrong. 'How's it going out there?'

'Clifford tells me he's heard of some resistance, but so far our men are making a clean sweep of it. But there is a big problem, James.'

'What?'

'The seating plan,' said Ted. 'It's been changed.'

'*Changed?* Changed how?'

'They've swapped round the congregation in the choir. Lady Mosley wanted a better view, apparently.'

'You're joking,' said Armstrong. 'You've *got* to be.'

He could tell by Ted's expression that he was not.

'This is a *fucking* disaster,' said Armstrong. 'So who's got the bomb now?'

Ted paused.

'*Who?*' Armstrong shouted.

'Roosevelt,' said Ted.

Silence. The occupants of the room looked at each other, appalled. They all knew that killing the American president would have an even worse outcome than leaving the Blackshirts in place.

One of the officers brought in a large bunch of keys. It took what felt like hours for him to find the right key.

'Come on, man, come on!' Armstrong barked.

'Nearly there, sir,' said the officer. 'Ah, this is it!'

Armstrong felt the pressure around his wrists suddenly diminish as the cuffs were removed.

'Jesus Christ,' he said, putting his head in his hands.

'What can we do?' asked Ted.

'We've got to stop Mosley,' said Armstrong, looking up. 'It's the only way.'

'Stop Mosley?' asked Ted.

'That's right – if we manage to kill him before he gets into the Abbey, then we'll fulfil our original goal as well as averting a catastrophe.'

Armstrong looked at his watch. It was nearly quarter to eleven.

'We should be able to get there in five minutes,' he said. 'Which might mean that we can get Mosley before he goes inside. We've *got* to try.'

They drove in the same van that had taken Armstrong and Lucy away. Armstrong took the wheel, and negotiated the crowds and the narrow streets as deftly as possible.

'This is impossible!' Ted cried above the sound of the engine.

'We'll do it,' said Armstrong. 'Don't worry.'

'This should help,' said Lucy, pushing a small button in the centre of the dashboard.

Armstrong and Ted started as the deafening noise of a police siren came from the roof.

'Thank you,' Armstrong shouted above the din.

'I don't know how you would manage without me,' said Lucy.

They pulled up a hundred yards or so from the west door of the Abbey. The crowds made any further progress in the van impossible.

'Let's get out!' shouted Armstrong.

The three of them jostled and barged their way through the crowd. Soon they could hear chanting. The words were indistinct at first, but within a few seconds they became apparent.

'Mosley! *Mosley!* MOSLEY!'

The chant was loud, but it didn't sound as though it had any conviction. Sullen, thought Armstrong, it sounded sullen.

'He's not yet in the Abbey!' Armstrong shouted.

He turned to look at the others, but they were not with him, had been trapped by the crowd. Never mind that, he told himself, keep going.

Armstrong could hear his own breath as he ran. It was like wearing a gas mask, it was like being back in France. Charging across no man's land, dealing with the panic, with the terror, the horror of watching death exploding all around you. All you ever wanted to do was stop, but you had to keep going, otherwise you would be killed for sure.

And then he saw the explosion at Le Quinque Rue. It was there, right there in front of him, showering the crowds in limbs and blood. Dizziness. Terrible dizziness. Then it would be the legs, and when they went, he would be on the ground. And when he was on the ground, then the screaming would start.

Except he wasn't on the ground. His legs were weak, but he was still stumbling forward, heading towards the barriers that separated the crowd from the road,

'MOSLEY!'

His quarry couldn't have been more than fifty feet away. All he needed to do was push through, but he lacked the strength. Terrible dizziness, terrible weariness. Keep going, he urged himself, keep going, don't give in to it. If you are moving, you are doing well. You are not going to collapse. You are going to win through, beat the shellshock, do as Mary told you. Deep breath, pause, deep breath, pause, deep breath. Take in the world around you, not the world inside your head. The explosion is not there, the limbs are not there. This is two decades later, you are not back there any more, because you have beaten that and it is gone. Never again will you be back there.

'Out of my way!' he screamed. 'Out of my way!'

He charged onwards, and the crowd opened up for him. Nobody was going to stop him. He was like that thief on the Underground, taking advantage of surprise and collective inaction. There was a barrier in front of him, a barrier that he vaulted.

Any second now he expected a bullet, but none came. In front of him was an open-top horse-drawn carriage, inside which were the unmistakable figures of the Leader and his wife. And then his view was blocked, obscured by a figure wearing a Blackshirt uniform. Armstrong smashed a well-aimed fist into the man's face and kept advancing, his view of his target restored.

He didn't know it, but the crowd had gone silent. What was this they were watching? Was it a joke? A stunt? It was a man charging towards the Leader. The one person who reacted faster than any of them was the Leader himself, who had leaped out of the carriage, rightly fearing that he was the target of a crazed attack.

'Stop that man!' Armstrong could hear him shouting. 'Stop that man!'

But no one came to stop him. This was theatre, you couldn't stop it. And more importantly, there was no one willing to do so.

Armstrong kept going. There was no way Mosley was going to outrun him; the man had a limp. But the Leader had a head start, and he was making towards a mounted guardsman. Armstrong saw him draw his ceremonial sword and hack at the booted leg of the soldier, causing him to fall off the horse in agony. Within seconds, Mosley was astride the animal and geeing it to go.

'Captain Armstrong!'

Who was that?

'Captain Armstrong! Here! Take my mount!'

The man was wearing the uniform of a lieutenant-colonel. This had to be Huw Merriman, the leader of the arrest party.

Armstrong put his left foot in the stirrup and swung himself up on to the horse.

'Whatever you do,' he shouted down to Merriman, 'do not allow the Coronation to go ahead! And get Roosevelt out of there!'

Merriman looked puzzled.

'Just do as I bloody say!'

'Yes, sir!' Merriman replied. 'And have this, sir!'

The officer passed Armstrong his sword. He would have preferred a gun, but this was the best he could hope for.

A horse. How do you ride a horse? He hadn't ridden one in ages. He kicked his heels into the animal's flanks and shot forward. He saw Mosley heading up to the north side of the Abbey, going east along Parliament Square, weaving between ranks of mounted troops. Armstrong was aware of a silent crowd watching from behind the barriers – even the policemen were just staring. His horse was following now, taking the same course as Mosley's.

Armstrong was not aware of it, but one of Ousby's secret policemen was levelling a pistol at his back. The man squeezed the trigger, but before he could depress it completely, a round passed straight through his neck, fired by a soldier from the London Regiment. It was only at this point that several members of the crowd started to scream, a scream that soon escalated into panic.

*   *   *

Armstrong was gaining on Mosley's horse. The Leader was bearing left, heading north towards Whitehall. Number 10, thought Armstrong, he was aiming for Number 10. Armstrong couldn't see the panic that was developing behind him, but the infection was spreading rapidly, causing the crowd to burst free of its barriers, overwhelming the policemen.

They were cantering up Whitehall now, and then Mosley turned left into King Charles Street, sending the crowds fleeing as his horse leaped the barriers. Armstrong didn't fancy his chances at taking a jump, but he knew that he had no choice.

He couldn't help but briefly shut his eyes as he sped towards the barrier.

'Come on!' he shouted at the horse, and then he was airborne for what seemed like far too long. He was about to fall off, there was no doubt about it, but then they landed, the horse sliding as it did so, but retaining its footing and its rider.

The street was nearly empty, and Mosley was cantering down its centre. Armstrong knew that it ended in some steps, so why had Mosley chosen this route? As soon as the thought had crossed his mind, he saw Mosley pull hard on his horse's reins and then dismount. Armstrong surged forward, watching as Mosley half limped, half ran down the steps.

Armstrong pulled up and dismounted. In the few seconds it took to do so, he lost sight of Mosley. He ran down the steps and looked around. Where had he gone? Ahead of him was some dead ground, and beyond that the back of the crowd that was lining the east side of Horse Guards. The panic had not infected that part of the crowd yet, because their attention was focused on the imminent arrival of the state carriage. From his viewpoint, Armstrong could see the carriage approaching from the north. It would not get much further, he thought. The Coronation would certainly be stopped, but where was Mosley?

That door. He had never noticed it before. A low wooden door set into the base of the Foreign Office. It was ajar; he had to have gone in there. Armstrong ran forward and kicked open the door, sending it crashing back into the wall. Inside it was dark, so Armstrong entered slowly, allowing his eyes to grow accustomed to the change in light.

A long, dim corridor extended in front of him. Where was Mosley? Holding the sword in front of him, Armstrong edged slowly forward, priming himself for a sudden assault. None came. He strained his ears for a sound, but there was only silence. Had he come the wrong way? Had Mosley in fact disappeared into the crowd? No – that was not possible, there would have been a commotion.

A distant clanging, a metallic reverberation. A door being slammed? Up ahead, the corridor turned left. Slowly, almost ridiculously so, Armstrong continued. He sprang round the corner, sword at the ready, only to be greeted by another corridor. He walked a little quicker now, only allowing himself brief glances at the signs on the doors he passed. *Signals. Laundry. Air Conditioning.*

Of course. He was in the war rooms, the bunker that was to be used by the Cabinet in the event of London being bombed. Shit. This place was a bloody maze – he would never be able to find Mosley in here. There was an alternative: he could simply go back to the entrance and seal it off, but that would assume there wasn't another exit. No, he would have to find him.

For the next five minutes, Armstrong made his way along the corridors with a mounting sense of fear. He expected a repeat of his shellshock, but none came. Perhaps it had gone for good; perhaps he had finally beaten it.

More rooms passed. *BBC Broadcast Room. Generator. Chief of Imperial General Staff.* It was good to see that the BBC still existed somewhere, thought Armstrong.

'Good morning, Captain Armstrong.'

Armstrong froze. The voice had come from behind him. It was that voice, that hectoring voice whose cadences had dominated the airwaves and newsreels for so long. Mosley.

Armstrong turned to see the Leader. He was standing side on, the tip of his sword resting on the floor. His face was dimly illuminated by a single yellow bulb above his head.

'I could have killed you just now,' said Mosley, 'but I wanted to allow you to have a decent crack.'

I'd love to have a crack at him. The conversation in the steam room with Alec – it suddenly came back to him, sending a chill down his spine. Mosley was a good swordsman, a very good swordsman. Runner-up in the British championships, no less.

Armstrong didn't reply, but readied himself for an onslaught. He lifted his sword and held it at forty-five degrees. Mosley did likewise, and then they paused, the tips of their blades hovering around each other with expectation. Armstrong had no wish for this sword fight, not only because he feared for his own safety, but also because he wanted to keep Mosley alive.

Mosley lunged first, but it was a dummy, merely a twitch to test his opponent's reactions. Armstrong attempted to knock the blade away, but met only with thin air. Mosely grabbed his opportunity and thrust forward, but Armstrong managed to recover from his error and twisted his torso away from the incoming point. This was going to be tough, he thought, perhaps too tough.

Once more, Armstrong tried to strike Mosley's blade, but it had already disappeared, pulled back rapidly only to come forward again in a swiping motion aimed at Armstrong's crown. He ducked, and heard the swish of steel pass inches above his head. He attempted to spear Mosley's left foot in response, but the foot moved back almost balletically,

Quick, back up, away from the crouch. Mosley was forcing him back now, towards the end of the corridor. Their blades were striking together, the force from the blows vibrating all the way down the steel shaft and into the handle. This was going badly, thought Armstrong, there was no way he was going to be able to beat him.

'Mosley!' he shouted. 'One thing you should know!'

'Oh yes?' the Leader snarled as he thrust forward.

'You've already lost!'

Not a long pause, but a pause nevertheless, enough to give Armstrong the opportunity to force Mosley back down what was now a piste.

'Ridiculous!' Mosley shouted.

'My troops have already taken control of much of your apparatus,' said Armstrong. 'Sir Roger Ousby is dead, and even now the army is ensuring that the Coronation does not go ahead.'

'Rubbish!'

'It's not . . . I assure you.'

'You're lying!'

'I'm not,' Armstrong shouted, forcing himself forward ever harder. He noticed that Mosley's eyes were beginning to bulge out of his head, a mannerism that Armstrong had seen often both in Parliament and on the newsreels. It meant that the man was losing his temper, making him charge furiously as he was doing now.

'That is not possible!' Mosley screamed, punctuating each word with a thrust or a swipe.

Armstrong held his cool, waiting for a chink. It would come soon, he knew it. Mosley was so angry that he had lost his swordsman's discipline.

'You . . . are a liar!'

And then it came, a split second in which Mosley's chest was exposed. He had lunged forward angrily, terrifyingly, but Armstrong had sidestepped and brought the tip of his blade up to Mosley's heart.

'Drop your sword,' Armstrong said coolly.

'Never,' said Mosley. 'You'll have to kill me before I'd do that!'

'Drop it!'

'No!'

'In that case, I've got another surprise for you,' said Armstrong.

Mosley flashed his familiar smile. In the dim light, it looked demonic.

'You're full of them!' he quipped.

Armstrong pushed his sword into Mosley's chest, stopping short of drawing blood.

'Sir Roger Ousby was a Communist agent,' he said. 'He was using the secret police to seize control in order to allow Moscow to take over.'

Mosley was speechless.

'That's right, *Moscow*. Ousby was in league with the Russians who want you dead. I, on the other hand, want to keep you alive. I want you tried in the courts, want you to face decent British justice, not the joke that you've turned it into.'

'What? This is—'

'How else do you think I have managed to stay on the run for so long? How else do you think I managed to escape from the Tower? Ousby! He was using me too, using my resistance movement as a cover!'

'This is—'

'That's what I thought, but it's true. Now put down your sword.'

Mosley did not move.

'Down!'

'Kill me!'

'No.'

'Why not?'

'Because,' said Armstrong, 'unlike you, I don't believe in summary executions.'

Mosley paused. Armstrong thought that he might have to kill him, find himself forced into obeying Mosley's will, even if that resulted in the Leader's own death.

Finally, the corridor rang with the sound of dropped cold steel.

'Thank you,' said Armstrong. 'And now I want you to make a broadcast, Mosley – your final broadcast.'

Epilogue

Higher Forms

THE LEADER MADE his final broadcast from the BBC studio in the bunker. At Armstrong's behest, Mosley ordered all remaining members of the HMSSP to give themselves up at their nearest police station. Any member of the secret police who did not do so, or who showed any resistance to members of the armed forces, could expect a summary reprisal. The Leader's only other order was to request that all members of the Imperial General Staff report to Downing Street, where they would be issued with further instructions. He then announced his immediate resignation.

For the next few weeks, the country was ruled under a martial law imposed by Armstrong and General Galwey. It was a difficult time, very difficult, but the troops managed to hunt down the more hard-line followers of the man they would always refer to as 'the Leader'. The army, as well as the civilian police, were also occupied in ensuring that the population did not carry out reprisals against suspected informers or known Party members. Armstrong told the country that Mosleyite fascism was not to be replaced by tyranny on the streets. If democracy was to make an effective return, then citizens who required punishment should receive it from the courts and not from lynch mobs. In the main, his wish was respected, although there were hundreds of violent incidents that suggested there would be divisions in many communities for years, if not decades, to come.

Sir Oswald Mosley was tried in November, and was found to be guilty of countless crimes. It was clear that many wanted him to hang, but the courts saw sense. They knew that executing Mosley would create a martyr and stir up those who remained loyal to him, so he was sentenced instead to life imprisonment, along with his wife, Lady Diana, and the four members of his Emergency Cabinet.

King Edward and Queen Wallis abdicated a week after their abortive coronation. The Queen had insisted they should remain, but a delegation led by Armstrong, and including the newly released Stanley Baldwin and Winston Churchill, insisted that the King should not listen to his wife in this instance, unless he wanted to suffer the indignity of an Act of Parliament designed to strip him of his crown. Renamed the Duke and Duchess of Windsor, the couple chose a life of exile rather than remain in a country whose citizens despised them. They were succeeded by the Duke and Duchess of York, who became King George VI and Queen Elizabeth. Although the new King was not a natural in his new role, he had the full support of his people.

A general election was held at the end of February. Some Communists did indeed win seats, among them Lucy Craven, who stood in her late father's constituency. However, much to the surprise of the electorate, Captain Armstrong revealed in an interview with the editor of the *Daily Sketch*, Ted Frost, that he would not be standing. He said that he had had enough of politics, and that there were plenty of capable men in Parliament who could run the country and see to it that Germany did not dominate the continent; men like Neville Chamberlain, for example.

Besides, said Armstrong, politics was not really compatible with bringing up a young boy. He was never to know that the late Sir Roger Ousby had possessed at least one drop of human kindness.

Select Bibliography

Readers who wish to delve into the subject matter of *The Leader* might consider the following. At the time of writing, most are in print. Further information concerning these titles – and the background to *The Leader* – can be found at www.guywalters.com.

Oswald Mosley and Fascism in Britain
Oswald Mosley, Robert Skidelsky
Fascism in Britain, Richard Thurlow
The Fascist Movement in Britain, Robert Benewick
Rules of the Game, Nicholas Mosley
Beyond the Pale, Nicholas Mosley
My Life, Oswald Mosley
A Life of Contrasts, Diana Mosley
Patriotism Perverted, Richard Griffiths
Fellow Travellers of the Right, Richard Griffiths
Hitler's Diplomat, John Weitz

The 1930s
The Dark Valley, Piers Brendon
The Long Weekend, Robert Graves and Alan Hodge
The Diaries of Sir Henry Channon, Robert Rhodes James (ed.)
Eminent Churchillians, Andrew Roberts
The Mitford Girls, Mary S. Lovell
The 1930s Scrapbook, Robert Opie

The Windsors
King Edward VIII, Philip Ziegler
The Duchess of Windsor, Diana Mosley

The Russians
The Mitrokhin Archive, Vassili Mitrokhin and Christopher Andrew

The Traitor

Guy Walters

There was something powerful about it, something magnetic. He had witnessed the effect of such uniforms in the newsreels; now he was about to wear one. But this SS uniform – the uniform proudly worn by so many maniacs and murderers – bore a Union Jack and the three lions. It was an insult to King and Country.

In November 1943 British SOE agent Captain John Lockhart is in Crete, fighting with the partisans. Captured by the Germans, Lockhart faces a stark choice: betray his country, or die.

Lockhart strikes a bargain with his captors. In return for the life of his imprisoned wife, he will change sides. But he is stunned to learn of his mission: to lead the British Free Corps, a clandestine unit of the Waffen SS made up of British fascists and renegades culled from POW camps. Aware that he, like them, will be branded a traitor, Lockhart seeks to redeem himself by destroying a terrifying secret weapon that threatens to change the course of the war . . .

0 7553 0056 4

headline

ROBERT RYAN

Early One Morning

In the flamboyant twenties, Englishman William Grover-Williams and Frenchman Robert Benoist are fierce rivals, racing their elegant Bugattis on the glittering European race circuits. Not only is the World Championship in their sights, but they have both fallen for the sensuous charms of the extravagantly beautiful Eve Aubicq.

But when war breaks out everything changes. Paris is in the iron-grip of German occupation and Robert and William join the Special Operations Executive to help the French Resistance undermine the brutal occupying regime. Their missions involve utmost courage and daring in the face of the horrors of war . . .

Based on a true story of British covert activity and the French Resistance during the Second World War, this is a gripping novel of heroism, self-sacrifice, love and betrayal.

'Robert Ryan writes elegantly and his prose is illuminated by provocative insights and descriptions. Comparisons may be drawn between *Early One Morning* and *Charlotte Gray*. Ryan's story is much the stronger' *Daily Telegraph*

'Ryan is terrific' *The Times*

'Essential reading' *GQ*

0 7472 6873 8

review

Now you can buy any of these other bestselling
Headline titles from your bookshop or
direct from the publisher.

FREE P&P AND UK DELIVERY
(Overseas and Ireland £3.50 per book)

Something Wild	Linda Davies	£6.99
Mandrake	Paul Eddy	£6.99
American Gods	Neil Gaiman	£6.99
Stone Kiss	Faye Kellerman	£5.99
Flesh and Blood	Jonathan Kellerman	£6.99
One Door Away from Heaven	Dean Koontz	£6.99
The Oath	John Lescroart	£6.99
The Jury	Steve Martini	£6.99
Long Lost	David Morrell	£6.99
2nd Chance	James Patterson	£6.99
Violets are Blue	James Patterson	£6.99
The Runner	Christopher Reich	£5.99
No Good Deed	Manda Scott	£5.99

TO ORDER SIMPLY CALL THIS NUMBER

01235 400 414

or visit our website: www.madaboutbooks.com

Prices and availability subject to change without notice.